THE NIGHTINGALE MURDER

ALSO BY LEENA LEHTOLAINEN

My First Murder

Her Enemy

Copper Heart

Snow Woman

Death Spiral

Fatal Headwind

Before I Go

Below the Surface

THE NIGHTINGALE MURDER

A MARIA KALLIO MYSTERY

LEENA LEHTOLAINEN

Translated by Owen F. Witesman

This is a work of fiction. Names, characters, organizations, places, events, and incidents are either products of the author's imagination or are used fictitiously. Any resemblance to actual persons, living or dead, or actual events is purely coincidental.

Previously published as *Rivo satakieli* by Tammi in Finland in 2005. Translated from Finnish by Owen F. Witesman. First published in English by AmazonCrossing in 2018.

Published by AmazonCrossing, Seattle

www.apub.com

ISBN-13: 9781503901117
ISBN-10: 1503901114

Cover design by Ray Lundgren

Printed in the United States of America

For Laura. Thanks for the name.

CAST OF CHARACTERS

Aaltonen: Commander, Espoo Narcotics Division
Aarnivuori, Jaakko: A friend of Arto Saarnio
Airaksinen, Jukka: Patrol officer, Espoo PD
Akkila: Patrol officer, Espoo PD
Asikkala, Mari: Nurse, Jorvi Hospital
Autio, Gideon: Detective, Espoo Violent Crime Unit
Eija: Secretary, Espoo VCU
Erkko-Salonen, Iiris: Riitta Saarnio's psychiatrist
Grotenfelt, Kirsti: Forensic pathologist
Haapio: IT specialist, Espoo PD
Haikala: Patrol officer, Espoo PD
Hakkarainen: Forensic technician
Helin, Mirja: Nurse, Jorvi Hospital
Hietamäki, Miasofia: Surgeon, Jorvi Hospital
Himanen: Patrol officer, Espoo PD
Honkanen, Ursula: Detective, Espoo VCU
Hytönen, Mauri: Small businessman, customer of prostitutes
Iivonen, Iines: Stripper
Kaartamo: Assistant chief of police, Espoo PD
Kallio, Maria: Commander, Espoo VCU
Kerminen: Forensic photographer
Klimkin, Johanna: Russian interpreter
Koivu, Pekka: Detective, Espoo VCU, Wang's husband
Konkola: Patrol officer, Helsinki PD
Koskela, Nuppu: Makeup artist
Koskinen: Patrol officer, jailor, Espoo PD
Lähde: Detective, retired
Lahtela, Pamela: Teenage prostitute
Länsimies, Ilari: Talk show host

Länsimies, Kaarina:.. Wife of Ilari, shoe shop owner
Leena:... Maria's friend
Liskomäki:... Patrol officer, Espoo PD
Mäkinen, Paavo and Anita:................................ Lulu Nightingale's parents
Marita:.. Antti's sister
Mikkola:... Forensic technician
Minttu:.. Receptionist, Hytönen HVAC
Mishin, Igor:... Pimp
Montonen:.. Patrol officer, Helsinki PD
Mustajärvi, Pate:.. A friend of Tero Sulonen
Mustajoki, Anna-Maija:................. Author, former Ministry of Social Affairs and Health official
Nightingale, Lulu (Lilli Mäkinen):............................ A high-class prostitute
Nordström, Lasse:................ Special agent, National Bureau of Investigation
Petrenko, Oksana:... Ukrainian prostitute
Pihlaja, Terhi:... Lutheran pastor
Puupponen, Ville:.. Detective, Espoo VCU
Puustjärvi, Petri:... Detective, Espoo VCU
Raila:.. Riitta Saarnio's friend
Raivionpää:.. Industrialist
Räsänen, Niina:.. Childhood friend of Lulu
Rasilainen, Liisa:.. Patrol officer, Espoo PD
Reponen, Katri:.. District prosecutor
Saarnio, Arto "Hatchetman":.......................... Corporate restructuring expert
Saarnio, Riitta:... TV producer
Saastamoinen, Mira:.. Patrol officer, Espoo PD
Sarkela, Antti:.. Maria's husband
Sarkela, Iida:.. Maria's daughter
Sarkela, Marjatta:.. Antti's mother
Sarkela, Taneli:.. Maria's son
Sarkela, Tauno:.. Antti's father, deceased
Söderholm, Kaide:.. Ballistics expert

Ström, Pertti: Detective, Espoo VCU, deceased

Sulonen, Tero: Lulu Nightingale's bodyguard

Taskinen, Jyrki: Director, Espoo Criminal Division

Urmanov, Yevgeni: Mishin's enforcer

Vesterinen, Eeva: Maria's sister

Vesterinen, Jarmo: Maria's brother-in-law

Vesterinen: Evidence technician, Espoo PD

Viitanen, Aila "Allu": Leena's aunt and godmother, entrepreneur

Virve: Antti's colleague at the University of Vaasa

Wang-Koivu, Anu: VCU detective, Koivu's wife

1

A woman stood on a sidewalk. High-heeled vinyl boots extended up to her thighs, leaving ample space between them and the hem of her miniskirt. Breasts burst from her skimpy top. Her smile was at once alluring and uncertain: What would her next customer be like? When a car finally pulled up, Richard Gere was in the driver's seat.

I changed the channel. I couldn't stand watching *Pretty Woman* for the third time. But the other options were lousy too: Formula 1 time trials, reality TV, and a meat market masquerading as a game show. I finished my tea and turned off the television set.

The kids were asleep, and I checked to make sure they were breathing. Our three-month-old kitten, Venjamin, lay curled up at Iida's feet. He purred when I scratched behind his ear. I felt lonely. I tried to reach my husband, Antti, but his phone was off even though it was only nine thirty. I didn't feel like bothering any of my friends. Everyone either had small children or an early morning.

When I couldn't come up with anything else to do, I called Koivu, who was the officer on call for our unit that night. Beyond being a colleague, Koivu was also my friend. He was only a year younger than me, and before coming to Espoo we'd also worked together in Helsinki and Northern Karelia.

"Hey, it's Maria. Anything going on?"

"One house call—the Janatuinens on Aapeli Lane. We hadn't heard a peep from them for a whole month. They were both drunk, so we tossed them in the tank and placed the kids in a foster home. Any chance we can get them removed permanently this time?"

"If the parents both regret it in the morning and neither wants to press charges, then . . ."

Koivu groaned. "Yeah, yeah. But should the parents' right to bring up their children really be so absolute?"

I didn't answer. Koivu and I had debated this many times over the years. He and his wife, Anu Wang-Koivu, who was also a police officer, had had three children in quick succession, and the youngest was barely two months old. Fatherhood had made Koivu so sensitive to anything having to do with children that sometimes I had to rein him in.

"Also, an ambulance brought in a woman who's all slashed up. She has cuts all over her body, including her face and genital area. She doesn't have any papers and doesn't seem to understand Finnish. The hospital staff thinks she's from Russia or somewhere thereabouts. She was yelling something in a Slavic language before the sedatives kicked in. They've been sewing her up for more than an hour."

"Where was she found?"

"In a vacant lot near downtown Espoo. A dog out for his walk smelled the blood. I have a team looking for footprints."

I thought of the scene from the movie I'd just seen, and even though I was ashamed of my assumption, I asked, "What kind of clothes was she wearing?"

"Winter boots and a fur coat," Koivu replied. "But nothing underneath, not even underwear."

Strange. If this was a prostitute beaten up by her pimp, why would she be dressed in a coat and boots instead of being left naked out in the cold March air? Had he—or they—just wanted to give her a warning, but the beating got out of hand?

Koivu's voice interrupted my thoughts. "Are you still there? The hospital said we could come in to interview her tomorrow. Cuts like that don't happen by accident."

"Book an interpreter. Will you be working in the morning too?"

"Yes. Speaking of which, when can I take my comp days?"

"You know the answer to that," I said and then hung up with a silent curse. Despite the recent reduction in the alcohol tax, the number of violent crimes wasn't growing nearly as fast as the number of drug crimes and white-collar crimes, which increasingly received more investigative resources. To the decision makers, crimes involving money were more important than the physical safety of citizens. This meant less funding for dealing with the violent crimes that did occur—my unit currently had two unfilled positions. Lähde, who had been in the department since long before my time, had taken early retirement at the beginning of the year for health reasons, and the other position had been open for going on two years. Plus Anu Wang-Koivu was out on maternity leave, and I'd hired Ursula Honkanen for successive three-month contracts to fill in.

I curled up on the edge of the window side of our double bed. Antti's side was empty. His research job in Vaasa meant two nights away from home each week, but since Christmas he'd started staying there for longer stretches. He told me that his current project at the University of Vaasa was in its most interesting phase, and he had a lot of conference presentations to give since the pilot study was garnering international attention. The department of economics was attempting to model the effects of globalization on the Finnish and world economies over a fifty-year time horizon by comparing different taxation and customs regimes. Even though Antti's specialty was category theory, he'd told me that digging into more practical mathematics was a pleasant change of pace. He felt like he was doing important work because the results could be used to direct the world's money flows more fairly. But the meaningfulness of the work didn't alleviate the loneliness.

When sleep finally took me, my dreams tangled Julia Roberts with this woman found bloodied in the snow. At some point in the night Venjamin nipped at my toes.

At seven o'clock the alarm clock forced me out of bed. After our regular morning routine, I took Taneli, who was four now, to day care, and escorted Iida and her friend Saara to their second-grade classroom. There were two dangerous intersections along the way. The half-mile walk was pleasant and gave my brain some oxygen. Though March was halfway over, it was still full winter. The sun didn't push the temperature above freezing even in the afternoon, and there was still enough snow on the ground for skiing.

In the conference room at the police station, everything was as usual. Ursula's makeup was perfect. Puustjärvi didn't arrive until the last minute because of the same traffic at the same intersection he always got held up at on the way from Kirkkonummi. For the umpteenth time, I wondered why he didn't just leave home five minutes earlier. Koivu yawned and said he'd only caught a few hours of sleep in the lounge. Puupponen ate a donut. Every day he consumed an absurd amount of fat and sugar, but somehow he stayed slim. Autio had a new tie. Its blue stripes went well with his brown suit.

"Ursula, you take the Janatuinen family and talk with DCFS about having the children removed from the home once and for all. Koivu, did you manage to get an interpreter for the woman at the hospital? For the time being let's call her Lady X."

"It doesn't look good. One of our Russian interpreters is on sick leave, and the other one is on loan to the Vantaa department. What about trying English or asking the hospital for assistance? And were you hoping I would head up the investigation?"

I smiled. Languages weren't the strongest weapon in Koivu's policing arsenal.

"Here's a few pictures." Koivu turned his computer around. Immediately Puupponen's second donut fell from his mouth. The very first shot depicted the woman's genitals, which had a knife cut all the way from the vagina to the anus. Both breasts bore deep wounds, and on her face a slash ran from her right eye to her mouth. The woman was slender, and I estimated that she was barely twenty. I tried to maintain my composure as I looked, but I felt sick to my stomach.

"Left-handed. The attacker," Puupponen said instantly, but I wasn't so sure. Perhaps the perpetrator had stood behind the victim. Puupponen had a habit of jumping to conclusions, and there were other aspects of his behavior that resembled those of a little boy's. But lately his compulsion to make everything a joke had subsided, and sometimes I even found myself missing his attempts to lighten the mood.

"This is where she was found," Koivu continued, moving to the next screen. The pictures showed a level field covered in a thin blanket of snow next to a road. Pushing someone out of a car there would be simple.

"Yesterday was pretty cold, and the snow was stomped flat, so finding footprints was difficult. According to the responding patrol, she couldn't have been cut there, because there was no blood spatter."

"But why dump her right there? Did they leave her to die? Or to be found?" Puupponen asked.

"It was revenge. They stole the tools of her trade," Ursula said coldly. "Strange that they left her alive, and that they let her go free. Usually pimps keep their whores locked up for the time it takes to recover after punishment."

"Let's remember that so far we don't have any evidence that this girl is a sex worker. Let's question her first," I said. I'd learned a lot from Anu Wang-Koivu, who was originally from Vietnam, about Finns' attitudes toward Asian and Slavic immigrants. She'd pointed out that usually we assumed they were either hookers or mail-order brides.

"I can handle it," Koivu said, and I also thought he'd be a good choice for the job. His gentle nature usually made people want to talk, but he wouldn't get anywhere without an interpreter. "There has to be someone who speaks Russian at Jorvi Hospital. Don't they bring in their cleaning staff from across the border since no Finns are willing to get their hands dirty anymore?"

"You sound like a politician. I'll come with you," I said suddenly. "How about right after this meeting?"

Puupponen whistled. "Do you know Russian, boss?"

"I studied it in high school, and lately I've been practicing a bit since we get Russian channels on our satellite." What I didn't tell my subordinates was that I thought knowing Russian would be helpful for getting a new job. I'd been with the Espoo Police Department for ten years now, although because of maternity leave I'd only done seven years of actual work. I also didn't let on that I'd chosen Russian back in high school because my first love, Johnny, had studied it too. How funny that a moment of schoolgirl fancy might help with a criminal investigation nearly twenty-five years later.

Koivu drove while I tried to remember relevant vocabulary and phrases. I'd practiced Russian with the assistant coach of Iida's figure-skating group, but terms for jumps and spins probably wouldn't be much use in an assault interview.

The last time I'd visited Jorvi Hospital was in the fall, when we'd said good-bye to Antti's father. That memory still brought a lump to my throat, even though Tauno Sarkela's passing after a long illness had been a relief. To me, Jorvi meant pain and death—both of my children had been born at a birthing center away from the big city in Tammisaari.

Koivu walked briskly from the parking lot, as if he wanted to get this job over with as quickly as possible. I suddenly felt as though I couldn't remember a single word of Russian.

The desk nurse directed us to the correct room. Our victim lay in a bed near the window. In the middle bed slept an elderly lady, and nearer the door was a woman about my age with curly hair, her leg elevated in a cast. She greeted us happily.

"So they finally found the window girl's friends?"

Of course, we couldn't interview Lady X with other people present. I asked the nurse whether they had any empty rooms on the floor. She looked at me like I was crazy.

"Even this room is designed for only two patients."

"What about a washroom or a linen closet? Any enclosed space will work."

The nurse left to fetch the charge nurse, and Koivu and I tried to dodge the curly-haired woman's questions.

"She's Russian. I've heard enough Russian in Tallinn to recognize it."

"Did she talk to you?"

"No, but during the night she was screaming in her sleep and we had to call one of the nurses. I've been in line for varicose vein surgery for four years, and I guess I just have to put up with this in order to finally get the procedure. Who knows what drug gang she's mixed up with. Is it safe to be near her right now? Anyone could just stroll in here."

I walked toward the window and found that the girl's eyes were open. One half of her face was covered in bandages. Her blond hair reached her shoulders, and the covers were pulled up to her neck as if she wanted to conceal as much of herself as possible.

"Zdravstvujtye. Vy govorite po-russki?" I asked. The girl's eyelids fluttered a little, but she didn't reply. I decided to wait to continue until we were alone.

The charge nurse bustled into the room and apologized for the cramped conditions. We would be able to use her office if the patient's bed would fit. An orderly rolled the bed down the hallway, and Koivu and I followed. Once we moved the chairs out of the way, the bed fit in between the desk and the doorway with just enough space to get the door closed.

Lady X's face bore a withdrawn expression. I introduced myself and Koivu, and then asked her her name. She gave no reply. The who, why, and where questions yielded similar results. I began to doubt whether this young woman understood Russian after all. Maybe she was from Poland or Slovenia. I tried Finnish, Swedish, English, and German without any luck. Her brown eyes stared at the blanket, and her attractively shaped lips remained closed. After fifteen minutes of trying to get her to say something, I asked Koivu to leave the room. Maybe she was afraid of men. But one-on-one didn't help either. Frustrated, I went to talk to the doctor.

I found the attending physician scribbling on a chart just down the hallway. He believed the girl's wounds had been caused by an abnormally sharp, small knife.

"She might be in shock and that's why she won't talk. I'm used to seeing the kind of cuts she has on her cheek and torso," he said. "But the mutilation of the genital area indicates that there was either an intimate relationship between the perpetrator and the victim or that this was part of an attempted rape. However, there were no traces of semen in her vagina. The cutting happened an hour or two before she was found, indicated by the fact that the blood had already begun to coagulate."

"How severe was her blood loss?"

According to the doctor, they'd only had to give her one bag.

"Does she have any identifying marks, like a birthmark or tattoos that might help us identify her?" A living, conscious person couldn't be examined like a corpse, which lost all rights to privacy in the pathologist's lab, so we had to rely on what the medical staff might have noticed as they treated her.

The doctor riffled through his papers. "An old, poorly stitched cut under her left shoulder blade. No other scars, no tattoos. One large birthmark on her left buttock. At least one poorly performed abortion, which supports our theory of her origin. Russian abortion hospitals are still practically torture chambers."

"Did any drugs turn up in her system?"

"We don't have the funding to perform expensive tests like that as a matter of routine. Do you want me to order one? We did run an HIV panel. Other than these injuries, she seems healthy. All vitals are good, her nutrition is fine, and she has good muscle tone."

"Where are the clothes she was brought in with?"

"In that closet."

"Wallet? Phone? Keys?"

"None of those, but her jewelry is in the box by her bed."

"Jewelry?"

"A couple of rings and a necklace with a cross. An orthodox cross." To do a legal search I'd have to get the girl's permission first. I left the doctor and returned to the charge nurse's office, then asked the orderly to roll the girl's bed back to her room. Her eyes now were closed, and they stayed that way as we went. In the room, the woman with the curly hair watched us closely. The patient in the middle bed still slept. I asked the girl if I could look at her jewelry, first in Finnish and then in Russian. When she didn't say anything, I opened the box sitting on the bedside table. That's when her eyes snapped open, and I thought I could see fear in them.

"It's OK," I said. "I'm just going to take a quick look and then put everything back where I found it."

The cross was small, about an inch long, and the gold didn't appear to be very high quality. The chain was thin. It really was an orthodox cross with a second, slanting crossbeam below the main one. I looked in vain for an inscription. One of the rings had an enormous ruby with diamonds set around it like the petals of a flower. This one looked valuable. No inscription on it either. The other ring was simpler, a thin double band with small stones set here and there. They looked like garnets. I held the ring up to the light. This one had an inscription: *Nad Oksanu. A.*

"*Nad Oksanu* . . . Oksana? Is that your name?" I asked in Russian, and I saw the girl swallow. Still she remained silent. Just then my phone began to ring. Apparently, I'd neglected to turn it off when I entered the hospital. I recognized District Prosecutor Katri Reponen's number before powering down the phone. I'd have plenty of time to call her later.

"Oksana, we're here to help you. Whoever did this has to be brought to . . ." When I couldn't remember the Russian word for justice, I let the sentence trail off. "Here's my phone number," I said and left my card on the bedside table, next to the box. Then I opened the standing closet next to Oksana's bed. The fur coat cascaded out. Its fur was long and thick, stained with blood on the front. I didn't recognize the blue-gray pelt, but Koivu thought it might be dyed chinchilla. In the pockets, I found a two-euro coin and a tissue. The boots were black lace-ups, with very high heels and narrow tips. They reminded me of the movie from the previous night. The side of the right boot had a small rip that someone had tried to patch with glue.

The old lady in the middle bed had woken up and was now complaining loudly that she needed to go to the bathroom. Her spirited roommate called the nurse. I tucked the fur coat back in the closet and then shut the door. As we were leaving, I exchanged a few more words with the nurse at the desk. She promised that they would alert us to any changes in the girl's condition.

"We'll have to get a Russian-speaking psychologist to talk to her," I said to Koivu as we walked from the elevator back to our car.

Koivu had arranged an interview for that afternoon with the woman who had found Lady X. He'd already checked the list of missing persons, but no one fit Lady X's description. We'd need to get a crime report posted online as soon as possible. Koivu and the department press officer could handle that. Maybe mentioning the jewelry would help us get some leads.

"There is a risk that the attacker will come at her again if he sees the crime report," Koivu said, stating the obvious. Of course, we wouldn't reveal that Lady X was at Jorvi Hospital. If a customer had attacked her, the pimp would probably go after him. But if the pimp had wanted her to get to the hospital, wouldn't he have brought her in?

"Just to be sure, check all women named Oksana living in Finland. There can't be that many. Call all of those who are between the ages of fifteen and thirty. How carefully has the place she was found been searched? Could we have missed a phone or a purse somewhere?"

"Rasilainen and Airaksinen did the search, and they didn't mention anything."

"There isn't a whole lot we can do if she refuses to tell us where the cuts came from. We can't arrest her for withholding that information, but we do have to find out who she is before we can do anything else. Contact the Pro Centre, even though they don't like giving out information about their clientele. Emphasize that Oksana is a victim, not a suspect. We'll need to contact the Immigration Police too."

Koivu yawned again, and I felt sorry for the poor guy. Juuso wasn't quite three yet, and Sennu was only eighteen months. The Koivu family certainly had their hands full. Fortunately, tracking down the identity of this girl, whom I now thought of as Oksana, wouldn't demand much thought.

Back at the station, I left Koivu to correct his botched parking job and headed to my office. A brief e-mail from my direct superior, Jyrki Taskinen, was waiting in my inbox.

> Everything's fine here in Quebec. Silja's doing well, even though she's uncomfortable, and Terttu seems to enjoy fussing over her. The big day is next week. Is there still snow on the ground in Finland? The skiing here in the mountains is fantastic. How are things at work? Say hi to everyone from me. Jyrki.

Taskinen was on a six-month leave of absence, which he and his wife were spending visiting their daughter, Silja, in Canada. Silja was expecting her first child, so Taskinen would soon be a grandfather. I missed him every day, even though the weekly lunches we used to schedule often didn't actually happen. Several years earlier, Taskinen's wife had been gravely ill, but two surgeries and a hysterectomy had beaten back the cancer. When it had become clear that Terttu would survive, Jyrki promised to take a break from work. Arranging that had taken more than a year. No one had been hired to fill in for him while he was gone, so in the meantime I was reporting directly to Assistant Chief of Police Kaartamo, which didn't please either of us. Kaartamo was retiring at the end of the year, and I wasn't the only one in the department counting down the days. Even the chief of police seemed to share the sentiment.

Kaartamo was a holdover from the Urho Kekkonen years, and he was used to operating through the good old boys' club. He'd never bothered to conceal the fact that he hadn't wanted me to head up the Violent Crime Unit. In Kaartamo's mind, it was fine for women to be cops, just so long as we weren't given too much power. Otherwise we might mess things up for the men. Our most recent conflict had been over participating in an exchange program with the Nordic-Baltic Network of Policewomen. The themes of the program were violence against women and children, and prostitution. Kaartamo thought that it was nothing but a waste of resources. After that conversation, I'd concluded that Kaartamo was an honest-to-god misogynist, and that those days weren't behind us after all, even though we thought we were living in an age of equality. Still, working as a female police officer now was much easier than it had been twenty years ago when I'd graduated from the academy.

I decided to wait to reply to Jyrki's e-mail. There were more important things to deal with. I dialed Liisa Rasilainen's number in Patrol. She and I had become friends over the years, and I'd tried in vain to lure Liisa out of the field and into my unit. But she liked the variety of patrol work. From our last conversation, I knew that we were both looking forward to the beginning of the soccer season so we could play in the department women's league again.

"Hi, Maria!" Her voice was oddly muffled. "Sorry, hold on, my mouth is full. I'm just grabbing some pizza with Jukka at the Big Apple." Jukka Airaksinen was Liisa's partner, a quiet man who didn't seem to have any issues working with a lesbian. That wouldn't have been the case for everyone in the department.

"Were you two the ones who dealt with the knife attack downtown last night?"

Liisa swallowed, then said that they were. "We showed up at the same time as the paramedics. We did a routine sweep of the area, but we didn't get a chance to question the victim because they whisked her off to the hospital right away. I sent the photos we took of the scene and the paperwork over to Koivu. It didn't seem like a job for Forensics, although it also didn't seem like the standard domestic violence incident. Who's the girl?"

"We don't know yet."

I heard Airaksinen's phone ring, and soon Liisa said that they had to go after a shoplifter in the mall. My next order of business should have been turning in the monthly time sheet report, but my mind kept drifting to my rusty Russian skills. All the states that had recently gained independence from the former Soviet Union needed modern police training, and there might be demand for a female trainer who spoke Russian. In the fall, I'd spent a week in Cologne training Afghan police, and the work had felt productive despite the enormous cultural differences. Our class discussions had renewed my faith in my own work, and my belief that an independent legal system and an incorruptible police force were cornerstones of democracy. I'd begun yearning for new challenges, but going abroad for long stretches while my family waited at home seemed impossible. Our childcare situation was difficult enough as it was.

While I'd been thinking, the department press officer had e-mailed me the press release to review.

> The Espoo Police are seeking information regarding the identity of a woman found yesterday with knife wounds in downtown Espoo. The woman in question is about 170 centimeters tall and slender, with blond hair and brown eyes. At the time she was found, the woman was wearing a dark blue-gray full-length chinchilla fur coat and black high-heeled boots. Anyone with information concerning the identity of this person is asked to contact the Espoo Police.

A telephone number was listed at the end. After giving my approval, I left for lunch.

The fur coat and boots aroused such a powerful mental image that the media were sure to take an interest. Maybe someone would pay Oksana to tell her story—cash often succeeded where the police failed. That might allow Oksana to buy herself protection and maybe even a new life.

After lunch I went to my Helsinki-Espoo-Vantaa Interdepartmental Coordination Meeting, the memory of which had entirely left my mind by the time I was in the car, driving to the day-care center to pick up the kids. I called Koivu to ask how the interview had gone with the woman who'd found Oksana, but his line was busy. Hopefully the press release would yield results.

First I picked up Taneli, then Iida, who was in after-school care at the house of one of her classmates. We'd really lucked out with that, since otherwise we would have been forced to leave our eight-year-old home alone for hours every day. Even though there was a law that was supposed to guarantee access to after-school care, the system was faltering. On top of that, there were some who were calling for an end to the entire public childcare system and scaling back of maternity leave benefits. From my perspective, it was better for a kid to spend her days in an overcrowded day care than with her inebriated parents. Our regular customers, the Janatuinens, were a good example of that. In day care, at least their kids would receive breakfast and lunch, which those two drunks couldn't be relied on to fix.

At home, we ate a quick dinner before it was time to leave for Iida's figure-skating practice, which was held at the Matinkylä Ice Arena twice a week. Venjamin meowed his complaint—I felt bad leaving our poor kitten home alone again.

During Iida's lesson Taneli and I killed time at the public library attached to the Big Apple Mall. The whole area had changed immensely in the nine years since I'd investigated the murder of the figure skater Noora Nieminen. The city of Espoo was like a jigsaw puzzle that could never be finished because new pieces kept appearing, pieces that didn't quite fit into what was already there. A few months back Antti had suggested that we reverse the national migration trend and move north to Vaasa. Sometimes I wondered what it would be like to work as a local cop in some tiny village up there. The Swedish-speaking population along the coast weren't in the habit of killing each other, but I'd probably end up investigating eco-terror attacks on fur farms. That wasn't particularly appealing.

Despite my chilling memories of Noora's murder, it had seemed like a good idea to enroll Iida in skating lessons. To my surprise, Taneli had also wanted to get on the ice, and he seemed to learn everything much faster than his sister. I knew how much time and money serious figure skating required in the long term, but for now I didn't want to quash my children's enthusiasm. Fortunately, children this young didn't have to compete.

As Taneli and I were making our way back to the ice arena, my phone rang. I didn't recognize the number.

"Hello, this is Mirja Helin. I'm a nurse in the surgical ward of Jorvi Hospital. You asked us to inform you if there were any changes in the condition of the Jane Doe who was brought in last night with knife wounds."

"Yes," I said, although I'd asked for any new information to be passed to the duty officer at the station, not directly to me. "What's changed?"

"She disappeared."

"What?"

"When we went to make our evening rounds, we found her bed empty. She must have ripped out her IV and put on her fur coat and shoes over her hospital gown. We don't have a clue where she's gone."

2

I had to devote the rest of the evening to updating the press release with the public relations officer. Oksana's description was sent to all patrol units. According to her hospital roommate, Oksana had walked out into the hall with her IV still attached. Then she suddenly returned in a rush, grabbed her clothes out of the closet, and left. The IV turned up in the elevator. Hundreds of people were constantly going in and out of that hospital, so hopefully someone would remember seeing a woman with a bandaged face in a full-length fur coat covered in blood. Interviewing all the witnesses who came forward would be a big job, so we'd have to ask Patrol to help.

Our notice was printed in the Thursday morning papers, and the local radio stations were talking about it as I drove to work. Less than two weeks remained until the vernal equinox, and it was already easier to get up in the morning because it was no longer so dark.

So far, we'd received a few tips, but none of them had led anywhere. An elderly woman from Kirkkonummi had been sure the missing girl was her neighbor, but we found the neighbor safe and sound at her job. A drunk had called to tell us he'd had a whore named Oksana in Estonia. The other tips had been even more absurd. The Pro Centre staff didn't know any Oksanas, but they promised to ask the sex workers they provided services to.

"We've had people questioning all the taxi and bus drivers, but so far no one has reported seeing her," Koivu said in our morning meeting. "She probably left the hospital in a private car."

"I guess all we can do is wait," Puustjärvi said.

"Maybe the press release will bring us something."

Puustjärvi was the most patient person in our unit, a skill he cultivated by playing the Chinese game Go and tying flies. He also did yoga with his wife. He had recommended it to the rest of us, but I hadn't tried it yet. The thought of blond, heavyset Puustjärvi bending himself into strange positions seemed silly, but then again there might be a side to Petri he didn't show at work. And I knew Autio even less, despite having worked together for nearly three years. The suits he wore were a costume he hid behind, and though he got along with everyone, he was no one's friend. He ignored Ursula's occasional attempts at flirtation, which obviously annoyed her. She was one of those women who had to take a shot at every man she met just for the hell of it. At first, that had irritated me, but now I just thought that it was a little pathetic.

According to the hospital staff, Oksana wasn't in mortal danger, but if her wounds weren't cleaned regularly she could suffer some serious inflammation and possible infections. I'd ordered Koivu to continue working through all the Oksanas listed in the official records and to check the immigration logs from the past few weeks. A lot of sex workers used three-month tourist visas. Koivu knew what to look for.

After the morning meeting, I conferred with Katri Reponen about a rape case that was going to trial, and then it was time for lunch. Since Katri was in a rush, we had to settle for going to the cafeteria. It was nice to trade news after having not seen each other for a while. Katri mentioned an open position in the criminal prosecution office and tried to convince me to apply.

"You seem exhausted lately. A change of scenery would do you good. Leena and I were talking about going to a spa for the weekend sometime soon. Maybe Haikko Manor or Caribia. You should come with!"

I promised to think about it. A moment later the thought of changing jobs crossed my mind again when I ran into Assistant Chief Kaartamo in the hall.

"We need your womanly sweetness at our morning leadership coffees," he said. "Don't you want to come anymore now that Taskinen isn't around?"

"I have to be at my unit's morning meetings. We've got some complicated cases right now," I said evasively.

"Oh, you mean the broad who disappeared from Jorvi? What's one more Russian whore, anyway?" Kaartamo scoffed. "The world's full of them. What's the point wasting time on her?"

"We don't know that the woman is Russian any more than we know that she's a prostitute. And usually people don't just disappear from the hospital like that."

"Didn't she leave voluntarily? Got her twat stitched up and walked out. Good riddance."

"How do you know about her wounds? As far as I'm aware the preliminary report isn't finished yet."

"You think word wouldn't spread when there are actual pictures of them in evidence? Boys will be boys, Kallio. I'd think you would have learned that by now." Kaartamo continued on his way, apparently not interested in hearing my response. That was well enough, since no appropriate quip came to mind.

Koivu was in the hospital all afternoon, interviewing members of the staff and Oksana's roommates, but he called in to report midway through. They'd made some progress: according to the roommate with the cast, the phone in the room had rung half an hour before Oksana disappeared. Oksana was the one who answered. She'd communicated in grunts and looked frightened, claimed the roommate.

"A phone call? Strange. How could anyone have known what room she was in? Talk to the hospital switchboard. I'll get access to the phone records," I said.

People downstairs in the hospital had seen Oksana leave, but where she'd gone no one could say, and no one knew anything more about who she was. An anonymous girl from nowhere, whom no one but the Espoo Police Violent Crime Unit missed.

I stopped by the grocery store on the way home, since Antti had picked up the kids. I was going to have the whole weekend off with my family, and it felt like a holiday. At the house, Iida showed us the plaster cup she'd made in school, and Antti asked her if he could take it to Vaasa to make his guest room at the university feel more like home. All winter we'd planned to go visit him there, but Antti's father's illness and funeral had messed up more than just those plans. And besides, it felt silly going on a trip to visit my own husband.

After dinner, we played cards. Taneli already knew his numbers and held his own at Last Trick and Black Maria. Antti opened a beer, and I poured myself a glass of red wine. Around eight Taneli nodded off, and I carried him to bed. When I returned, Antti was watching the news. Iida shouldn't have been there, since at any moment they might show starving children or mutilated bodies from the conflict zones in Africa. I was relieved to find that the broadcast was only about corporate restructuring.

"Copperwood Limited, a manufacturer of heavy forestry equipment, has announced impending layoffs at its factory in Arpikylä. At the moment, the company employs thirty-six people. Copperwood belongs to the Finnsteel Group, which has seen increases in revenue, particularly in Asian markets, in recent years. Arto Saarnio, Finnsteel CEO, joins us now. Mr. Saarnio, what's the cause of these layoffs?"

Thirty-six people didn't seem like much, but in my hometown of Arpikylä, that was a lot. My sister Eeva's husband, Jarmo, was the chief information officer for Copperwood, so this might mean he would be out of a job too. Prior to its purchase by Finnsteel a few years earlier, Copperwood had been a family business. Contrary to many people's expectations, no downsizing had followed the buyout, and I'd only heard good things from Jarmo about the new owners. But last fall Finnsteel had brought a new CEO onboard: Arto Saarnio, who had earned the nickname "Hatchetman" after his work reorganizing a couple of electronics companies. He was so effective that each company's stock price had doubled, but the number of personnel had also been cut by half.

I tried to call Eeva, but all I got was a busy signal. My mother must have beat me to her. I turned off the television and took Iida into the shower with me. Jarmo and Eeva probably still owed more on their house in Joensuu along the Pielisjoki River than we did on our White Cube in Espoo. If he lost his job, would Jarmo be able to find work in his field in Northern Karelia? As I pulled on my nightshirt, I thought with envy about my parents' generation. For them an academic degree had ensured lifelong employment.

It was Antti's turn to read to Iida, so after she and I had dried off and put on our pajamas, they headed into the bedroom. I returned to the living room couch and turned the TV back on. Now it was for work, in a way, since tonight's theme on Ilari Länsimies's talk show, *Surprise Guests*, was prostitution. "Should it be legal?" read the promo in the newspaper. "Should buying sex or selling sex be illegal? Or should brothels be an acceptable place of employment?" I wasn't interested in the topic just because of Oksana. Prostitution and its effects were constantly present in violent crime and drug policing. In fact, late last fall the Helsinki Patrol Division had completely given up on monitoring street prostitution, because the charges were usually thrown out of court for lack of evidence. And the same men who demanded harsher punishment for thieves and violent criminals were unwittingly supporting the world of organized crime whenever they bought sex. I'd just watch the show until Iida fell asleep, I thought to myself, and then Antti and I could enjoy some time together. Venjamin climbed into my lap and started to purr.

I muted the sound when the jaunty theme song began to play. Then the host, Ilari Länsimies, came on. He was about fifty, with a long and varied résumé that included stints in politics, business, and various media concerns. He seemed very comfortable in front of the camera. He had charisma, and he always did well in the women's magazines' "sexiest man" polls.

Surprise Guests had been on the air for about six months. The concept of the program was that the participants never knew ahead of time whom the other guests would be. According to Länsimies, this sparked more spontaneous conversation. The guests were marched out one at a time, and the cameras filmed the reactions of the others already seated. Of course, the more appalled the reaction, the better. Länsimies enjoyed it when the discussion devolved into a screaming match. Once, early on, Länsimies had lined up the foreign minister, a general, a peace activist, and an official from the Finnish Red Cross and made them argue about land mines. The woman from the Red Cross had ended up calling the foreign minister and the president "naive idiots." The media had had a field day with that one.

"So today we're discussing a topic that everyone's interested in: sex. However, we'll be focusing specifically on sex in exchange for money. Many of us would argue that the church tends to take a negative view of sexuality, and the recent scandal surrounding the divorce of the bishop of Turku has only reinforced that impression. But what does the church think about prostitution? Let's welcome Pastor Terhi Pihlaja from the parish of Tapiola."

The pastor was a woman in her thirties. Her black bob and pale face fit well with her clerical collar, but her bright-red lipstick and large earrings were incongruous with the costume.

"Good evening. First, I should say that my opinions don't represent the Finnish Evangelical Lutheran Church or the Tapiola Parish. Everything I say is mine alone."

"What about God's opinion?" Länsimies quipped, and Pastor Pihlaja looked irritated. There was no studio audience on *Surprise Guests*, since it would have detracted from the intimate mood. Länsimies was the only one laughing.

Pastor Pihlaja stated that she wanted to outlaw the selling and purchasing of sex. She said that people weren't commodities.

"But you support marrying gays and lesbians in the church? Isn't there a logical contradiction there?"

From the pastor's expression it seemed as though that this wasn't the first time someone had asked her this. "I don't approve of the selling of human beings. I do approve of people voluntarily pledging themselves to each other. Where's the contradiction?"

"Are you married?" Länsimies asked. Guests on the program understood from the start that they could be asked about anything, no matter how personal. Once Länsimies had pressed the prime minister's father about what he would have done if his son had married a black woman.

"I was married once, but now I'm divorced," Pastor Pihlaja replied, but Länsimies had already moved on. "What do we think the law has to say about this? For that perspective, we've invited Special Agent Lasse Nordström from the National Bureau of Investigation. He specializes in crimes related to prostitution."

Every now and then I crossed paths with Lasse Nordström. He used to play squash with my college boyfriend Kristian, and a few years ago we'd served together in a working group focused on domestic violence. I'd always thought there was more to Lasse than met the eye, that his joviality was partially an act. He had broad shoulders and a buzz cut, and today he'd worn a brown corduroy jacket and jeans to create an intentionally relaxed look. I couldn't help but think, *This man does not want to look like a cop.*

"Agent Nordström, as we all know selling sex in public is against the law, but the trade seems to be flourishing on the streets, in bars, and on the Internet. The Helsinki Police have made it clear they believe that the current laws are ineffective, that convictions for street prostitution are so difficult to get. What are your thoughts on this?"

"We have a duty to uphold whatever laws Parliament passes, even if we feel like our own list of priorities might be different than those of the government. We try to follow a zero-tolerance policy in all criminal activity."

"Isn't that unrealistic?" Länsimies asked.

Nordström looked uncomfortable, and he seemed too big for the plush brown armchair he was sitting in.

"That's all a matter of resources. Everyone knows the police force is already stretched thin as it is. And this summer's Track and Field World Championships are only going to make that worse."

"What's your personal opinion? Should buying and selling sex be illegal, or should we let people do what they want?"

Nordström declined to give his opinion. In an attempt to steer the conversation in another direction, he began citing statistics. I would have also found it awkward to express my own opinions on TV. A public servant was supposed to be loyal to the state no matter how we felt personally.

Eventually Länsimies took back the reins and invited the next guest, Anna-Maija Mustajoki, to come out. She had caused a stir the previous fall when her memoirs had been published. She'd devoted five whole pages to a description of a visit to a male prostitute in the late 1960s, in California. Since the author was a well-known feminist who had just retired from the Ministry of Social Affairs and Health, this revelation was guaranteed to cause a scandal. The reporters weren't interested in Mustajoki's analysis of the evolution of gender roles in Finnish society or her experiences working for UNICEF in Africa; they were interested in only those five pages. And Anna-Maija Mustajoki herself became a cottage industry for columnists and cartoonists alike. It was easy to portray her as a standard feminist caricature, with her shoulder-length gray hair, round glasses framing a face without makeup, and pointedly masculine clothing.

"Anna-Maija Mustajoki, you think that buying sex and pimping should be illegal, but that selling sex should not. Why?"

"Most women who work as prostitutes in Finland are human trafficking victims who end up in the industry because they have no other options. They need help, so placing them outside the law makes no sense. If they're afraid of retribution, they won't come to the police when someone mistreats them. Instead of focusing on punishing them, we should be chasing the pimps and human traffickers."

"According to your interpretation of the law, you committed a crime yourself forty years ago . . ."

Anna-Maija nodded, and her expression was reserved.

"Wasn't the exchange helpful to that young male prostitute, Jimmy? Why shouldn't the same thing be possible in Finland? These girls are earning money instead of starving."

"What I gave Jimmy probably bought him his next hit. But what he really needed was a stint in rehab."

"I have to admire Anna-Maija's honesty in her writing about her adventures in California. It's hard to find someone who is willing to go public as a customer of sexual services." Ilari Länsimies grinned. "Most of us assume that johns are losers who can't get it any other way. But according to the studies, men who buy sex are no different from anyone else. And here we have one of these gentlemen to talk about this issue. Come on out, Mauri Hytönen!" Länsimies clapped. No one else joined in.

The man who stepped onto the stage looked to be in his midforties, was of average height and was well dressed. His black hair and mustache looked dyed and stood in stark contrast to his pale complexion.

"Mauri Hytönen, you were one of the few men brave enough to volunteer, through the *Surprise Guests* website, to come on live television to tell us why you pay for sex. The floor is yours."

Hytönen straightened his tie. "I like to live life at my own pace. I've been married twice, but steady relationships just don't suit me. It's hard to find women who can have sex without then demanding commitment. With a professional, the rules are clear, and I can get what I want." Hytönen's voice had a note of Savo dialect, even though he tried to hew to standard Finnish.

"How do you choose your women?"

"I have girls I visit regularly. Some of them are here in the Helsinki area, and some are in Tallinn. I'm happy to pay for quality, and I prefer women who aren't junkies or under the thumb of some pimp. I think it's crazy that brothels aren't legal. That would be a lot safer for both the girls and us customers. No one would have to be afraid of getting ripped off. In my mind it is an honest transaction."

"Not as long as it's illegal," Lasse Nordström said.

"Aren't human relationships always about some sort of exchange, for good or ill?" Anna-Maija Mustajoki added, but Länsimies talked over her:

"But how many women's magazine articles suggest that men should clean the house to get their wives in the mood? Isn't that a transaction? The man is paying for sex, just in a different form."

"It's not always *the man* paying for it!" Pastor Pihlaja exclaimed. "Is sex something that only men want, and for women it's just a chore they sometimes submit to? That's just another way to say that a woman who wants sex is somehow sinful." Anna-Maija Mustajoki nodded so hard that her large breasts swayed and a lock of hair fell into her face. Länsimies raised his hands to interrupt the discussion. There was a dramatic pause.

"We've already heard several perspectives, but we're still missing the perspective of a woman on the other side of the transaction. Now

I'd like to . . ." Ilari Länsimies trailed off, and he stared into space. Apparently, his producer was relaying instructions through his earpiece. "In just a moment I'd like to introduce you to a person who is . . ."

The woman who rushed onto the stage was clearly out of her mind. She was wearing a suit skirt and seemed to be shouting, though she wasn't wearing a microphone. Reading her lips, I thought she might be saying the word "dead." Lasse Nordström jumped up.

"What are you talking about?" he asked, grabbing the woman by the shoulders. She was shaking. "Who's dead?"

"Is it Lulu Nightingale?" Ilari Länsimies had also stood up from his chair and was now standing next to the woman in the suit, and I saw her nodding and trying to explain something through her tears. Then Länsimies seemed to remember that the show was live.

"Shut off those cameras!" he bellowed. First the sound went dead, and then the screen showed people rushing about and waving their arms, and then a test pattern appeared. I turned on my cell phone. The studio of West Man Productions, where *Surprise Guests* was taped, was located in Espoo. A death there would fall under my unit's jurisdiction. I sprang off the couch, and Venjamin sank his claws into my thigh before leaping to the floor. Puupponen was on duty, so I grabbed my phone and started to dial his number. But then I paused. Was I jumping the gun here? Just because someone had died didn't mean a crime had been committed.

Antti came out to let me know that he and Iida had finished reading. I put my phone in my back pocket and then walked to the kids' room to oversee Iida's toothbrushing and tuck her in. The phone rang just as I closed the door behind me. The display read "Puupponen."

"Hi, I'm on my way to the TV studio in Tontunmäki. Something strange just happened. A death. The last guest on the program didn't come on stage, and they found her dead on the floor of her dressing room. There's a guy from the NBI already there. He called an ambulance and us. He thinks the death is suspicious."

"I know, I happened to be watching the program. Is a patrol car there yet?"

"Saastamoinen and Akkila are there, and I alerted Forensics. Apparently, the victim is a celebrity prostitute. Jesus."

I pulled my nightshirt over my head and started to dress while continuing to talk on the phone. I promised Puupponen I'd be at the studio in ten minutes, then hung up. I felt adrenaline surge through my veins, and in an instant I was fully alert.

"What now?" Antti asked when he saw me pulling on my jeans.

"Work." I grabbed a blazer from a hanger. It was a little wrinkled but would have to do. There was no time for makeup, so I just quickly ran a brush through my hair.

"Do you really have to go?"

"I'm just going to take a quick look. I won't be long." I gave Antti a peck on the cheek and grabbed my bag, then closed the front door softly behind me so as not to wake the kids. Outside the car windows were covered in frost, so after buckling my seatbelt I turned the heater on full blast.

Once I arrived at the studio, I confirmed that the deceased was Lulu Nightingale. I didn't know much about her, just that she was one of the more well-known sex workers in the country. She'd chosen her name because she thought she was doing the same kind of service for men that Florence Nightingale had done during the Crimean War.

Lulu's "office" in downtown Helsinki was named the Blue Nightingale. She'd waged a one-woman war against the prostitution laws, her activities constantly pushing the boundaries of legality. I knew she'd been under heightened surveillance by the Helsinki Police for years. If I remembered correctly, she was on probation for procurement, because a few years ago she'd hired some assistants and the courts saw that as equivalent to pimping. There were people who thought Lulu Nightingale was a hero and paragon of sexual freedom, and others who thought she represented the worst kind of moral decay. In their eyes, prostitutes weren't supposed to be proud about their profession.

The streets were quiet and most of the traffic lights just flashed yellow, so my drive took less than fifteen minutes. The television studio was on the first floor of a white industrial building, below a textile wholesaler and a software company. In the parking lot were two patrol cruisers and an ambulance. I tried the front door and found it locked, then rang the buzzer a couple times to no avail. My breath was visible in the clear March air, and there was only the barest hint of the moon in the sky. Just as I was looking for Mira Saastamoinen's number in my phone, the door opened.

"Kallio, hi. How did you get here so fast?" Akkila asked.

"I was watching TV. Puupponen's on his way too. How's it look in there?"

"Come have a gander," Akkila said. I followed him inside. "This place is a mess right now. One woman is completely hysterical, and Nordström from the NBI seems to think he's going to be leading the investigation. Mira's having it out with him right now. Rasilainen and Airaksinen are with the others. We've ordered everyone to gather on the studio floor."

It was all happening too fast: half an hour ago I'd been looking at this set from my couch at home, and now I was stepping onto it. The cameras weren't on anymore, but the lights still burned hot. The people who had been talking heads just a few moments ago were now suddenly standing in front of me. But instead of Ilari Länsimies, I was the one who would have to lead the discussion, which was unlikely to be convivial.

"Good evening. I'm Detective Lieutenant Maria Kallio from the Espoo Police. For the moment, we'd like to ask that everyone remain in the studio. Please be prepared to provide your contact information for further questioning."

Ilari Länsimies stood up from where he'd been sitting on the armrest of Mauri Hytönen's chair and approached me. My first reaction was astonishment: in person he was so short, barely five foot six. His dark-blue suit was well tailored, and he'd loosened his tie and undone his top button, revealing a dark shock of chest hair.

Länsimies shook my hand without introducing himself, assuming that I would recognize him. The handshake was firm, and his clear blue eyes gazed straight into mine. "Detective Lieutenant Maria Kallio," Länsimies repeated before releasing my hand.

Mustajoki, Pihlaja, and Hytönen sat in the same spots they'd been in during the show. In addition to them there were three men, apparently the camera and sound technicians. I wondered who the hysterical woman was, the one who'd rushed out onto the stage to report Lulu Nightingale's death. Where was she now?

"Hey, Kallio!" Lasse Nordström yelled from the studio door. "You've got yourselves some pretty damn bureaucratic patrol officers here in Espoo. Some hardheaded chick just shooed me away from the body even though I told her I was a colleague."

I went over to Nordström and pulled him into the hallway. He pumped my hand as if we were good friends, although in truth our acquaintance was limited to a few drinks during college and a few seminar sessions sitting in the same room.

"What's the situation?" I asked. "Are you sure this wasn't just a sudden illness?"

"I know this woman, and I think it's best to take every possibility into account. And besides—well, you should see the body."

"Are there signs of violence?"

"No, but the convulsion of the body suggests poisoning," Nordström whispered.

"Who found the body?"

"Riitta," Ilari Länsimies said before Nordström could reply. Apparently Länsimies had followed me into the hallway, and now he started to jabber. "Our program tonight was a little unorthodox. Usually our makeup artist, Nuppu, gets the guests, but she had a child-care snafu and left early because Lulu said she could do her makeup herself." Länsimies loosened his tie even more. "We work with a small team, just two cameras and a floor mixer, and Riitta said she could bring the final guest in because the cameramen know the routine." Nordström shot Länsimies a glance that was an obvious warning to shut his trap. The show belonged to Länsimies, but Nordström was a cop. Their jockeying for position was pointless, however, because from here on out, I was in charge.

"Riitta?"

"The producer."

"Where is Riitta now?"

"In my dressing room, resting. One of your lady officers is there."

Just then Puupponen and Saastamoinen appeared. I asked Saastamoinen to start collecting contact information and told her that I'd want to interview everyone after I talked to the person who'd discovered the body. When my phone rang, I was unsurprised to see the number of a crime reporter from one of the newspapers. I didn't have anything to pass on yet, so I set my phone on silent and tucked it in my jacket pocket, where it continued to buzz. I asked Länsimies to show Puupponen and me the way. It would be easier to get information from him without the others listening.

"I understand that the concept of this show is that the guests don't know anything about each other. How does that work in practice?"

"Well, everyone has their own dressing room, and they're only supposed to come out when accompanied by our makeup artist or me. Nuppu is something of a master of ceremonies, but today was different. We stagger the guests' arrival times, and Nuppu or Riitta meets them at the entrance and delivers them to their rooms, then fetches each one for their turn in the makeup chair." Länsimies fished in his pocket for a handkerchief and then dabbed his brow. The handkerchief came back with makeup stains.

"How do you prevent the guests from wandering the halls? Are their doors locked from the outside?"

"No, from the inside. Everyone understands the spirit of the game. People want to be on TV, and we've never had any trouble finding guests. Riitta's resting in Anna-Maija Mustajoki's dressing room—here we are."

"Thank you," I said, indicating to Länsimies that he could return to the studio. I subtly tried to copy Länsimies's on-camera style of speech to place us on the same level. "We'll pick up this discussion again in a moment." Just then two paramedics came out of a room farther down the hall and walked toward us.

"There was nothing we could do," one of them said. "We just need to take some pictures, and then we'll haul her off if we don't get another call before then. Is there any coffee here?"

Perhaps the ambulance crew was no longer in a hurry, but I was. Liisa Rasilainen must have recognized my voice, and she poked her head out of the dressing room to call me in. Puupponen followed me into the small room, which just had space for a couch, a chair, and a narrow dressing table screwed into the wall in front of a large mirror. On the couch lay the thin woman in a skirt and suit jacket whom I'd seen briefly on television half an hour before. Her face was gray, and her eyes, red from crying, stared at the ceiling. She had the smudged remains of mascara on her cheeks. I introduced myself and Puupponen, but she didn't seem to hear and didn't react to my questions at first. Then she began to cry again.

"I don't want to talk about it. It was too horrible!"

"She's in shock," Liisa whispered. "Here name is Riitta Saarnio. Age fifty-six. Should we take her to Jorvi?"

"Let's get in touch with her family and then decide what to do with her. Where's the body?"

"In the dressing room, next door. Here's the key." Liisa handed me a perforated plastic card with the number two printed on it. "Nordström and the paramedics have been in there, but everyone says she's in exactly the same position as when she was found."

I retraced my steps back into the hallway, but before I could open Lulu Nightingale's dressing room door, someone tapped me on the shoulder. I hadn't heard any footsteps, so I jumped. When I turned around, I saw a mountain of a man with black stubble and sad eyes.

"It wasn't my fault!" he shouted. "I was in the control room the whole time, I swear. Can I see Lulu now?"

"Who are you?"

"Tero Sulonen. Lulu's bodyguard. And her friend . . ."

"I'll speak to you later. Please move aside," I said. Then Puupponen grabbed the man by the shoulders and steered him away.

When I opened the door, the first thing I saw was a red vinyl boot with a nearly six-inch heel. Puupponen and I carefully slipped in and closed the door after us. The body of Lulu Nightingale lay on its side between the couch and a toppled chair. Blond hair covered the face, and a red-and-black leather skirt clung tightly to the hips and rump. Her fishnet stockings had a rose pattern. There was no sign of blood, but the table was askew and a long, black leather jacket with red fur collar and cuffs was lying on the floor. On the table was a bottle of Fernet Branca and an almost-empty glass with a small drop of dark-brown liquid at the bottom. On the rim of the glass was a thick lipstick print. The contents of a cigarette case were strewn around the body.

"Do you have gloves?" I asked Puupponen, who nodded and pulled two pairs of white exam gloves out of his pocket. After gloving my hands, I bent over Lulu. As I moved the hair from her face, I could feel the warmth of her skin through my glove. I shivered. Lulu's makeup was so thick that I couldn't discern the actual color of the underlying skin of her face, which was contorted in an expression of eternal torment. However Lulu Nightingale had died, it had been gruesome.

3

"Lulu!" The bodyguard, who had been waiting in the hallway, opened the door and pushed Puupponen in an attempt to force his way into the room, but the two of us managed to keep him at bay.

"Are you sure she's dead? Can't you do anything?"

"The paramedics examined her. I'm sorry."

At this he burst into tears. Puupponen and I dragged him back into the hall, where we found the forensics team marching up with Hakkarainen in the lead.

"Hi there! So we've got a lieutenant on the case, do we? Where's the body?" Hakkarainen asked, and I stepped aside so that he could enter.

Freed to move on, I decided to start the interviews with the bodyguard. The door to dressing room number four was open, and so I led Sulonen inside. There I found a pair of men's overshoes tucked under a chair and a thick, dark-blue overcoat hung neatly on the wall. I guessed this room had been Lasse Nordström's.

I gestured for Sulonen to sit on the small couch, and I turned the chair around and took a seat. Pupponen stood next to the doorway. "How long have you been working for Lulu Nightingale? And what's her real name?"

Sulonen wiped the tears from his cheeks and took a deep breath. "I don't want to tell . . ." he said, like a stubborn child. "She hated it. She changed her first name from Lilli to Lulu, but the government wouldn't approve Nightingale as a surname. So she was Lulu Mäkinen. I told her that she could take my last name, but . . ."

I interrupted his torrent of words and repeated my first question.

"She hired me after a client attacked her. That was two years ago last January."

"Where did Lulu find you?"

"I was a bouncer at the Mikado, and she came there sometimes to pick up guys. We happened to talk once, and she said I seemed like a man she could trust. But I wasn't! Look what I let happen!" Sulonen pounded his fist on the couch, which gave a muffled thud. His hands were as large as heavyweight wrestler's.

"What were your terms of employment? Were you Lulu's only bodyguard?"

"I was. I lived with her. I slept in the room next to hers and was always supposed to be on guard whenever clients were around."

"Did Lulu have any specific reason to fear for her safety? Did anything unusual happen recently?"

"I don't know! She chose her clients carefully. Sometimes religious people would come around and preach at her about the fires of hell, but she just laughed at them and said they were pathetic."

Just then there was a commotion in the hallway, and I heard Mira Saastamoinen shout that under no circumstances would the media be allowed into a crime scene, and then Ilari Länsimies begging to be allowed to give a brief statement. Puupponen closed the door, even though the dressing room already felt cramped and stuffy. Sulonen blew his nose on his sleeve. I fished in my pockets, but I couldn't find a handkerchief. Fortunately, I spotted a box of tissues on the dressing table. I tossed it to him and gave him a moment to collect himself before continuing the interview. "You said you were sitting in the control room the entire time. What control room do you mean?"

"The access control room. It's next to the sound booth. There's only one way in to the studio, and I wanted to make sure no one who didn't belong tried to get in."

"From the access control room can you also see who's moving around inside the studio?"

"There's a camera on the main door and another one at the beginning of the hall."

"Could that camera see Lulu's dressing room door?"

"No, but it fucking should have. Are you absolutely sure there's nothing that can be done? In the emergency room they can bring people back after all kinds of horrible accidents. Maybe if they could intubate or something . . ."

"So your address is the same as Lulu Mäkinen's?"

"Yes, in Helsinki. Where will they take her?"

"To the forensic pathology institute. Do you have a friend you can stay with?" I'd have to ask Mira Saastamoinen to arrange a hotel for him for the night and for a patrol from Helsinki to go seal Lulu's apartment and the Blue Nightingale, which was adjacent. We would need to search both premises as soon as possible. Maybe our perpetrator would turn up in Lulu's customer files.

"Why can't I go home?" Sulonen asked.

Instead of answering his question, I said, "How did you and Lulu get here?"

"In Lulu's car. I drove like always."

"Could I please have the keys? We'll need to search the car as well."

"But how will I get around?"

Rather than respond, I simply held out my hand, and after staring at me for a moment, Sulonen pulled the keys out of his pocket and gave them to me. Then I left and, in the hallway, asked Saastamoinen to write him a receipt. Back in dressing room two, the forensic photographer was trying to get as many angles as he could in the narrow space. Lulu looked like a model in an avant-garde fashion magazine as she lay on the floor with her limbs spread wide and her face hidden under her hair. I noticed that her red thigh-high boots were embroidered with black leather.

"Of course there's a whole battalion of fingerprints in here," Hakkarainen from Forensics said sourly. "Can we keep everyone in the building long enough to get their prints? Mikkola, you're young and you have lots of energy, you go do it. Get moving, kid, and no screwups this time!" I grinned at Hakkarainen. He was a precise and reliable colleague. Once or twice, over coffee, I'd listened to his appalled harangues about the portrayals of crime scene investigation on TV. "They've got Joe Blow CSI pulling off DNA analysis with a microscope. I shit you not!" he'd yelled in exasperation. Hakkarainen and Puupponen spoke the same ungodly eastern Savo dialect, to the point that sometimes no one in the department could keep up, not even me, though I'd grown up in the neighboring district of Northern Karelia.

Another cop from Forensics was logging Lulu's purse into evidence. I stepped back out into the narrow dressing room hallway. There were six rooms, each with a number except the one that said "Ilari." I tried that door, which was locked. The restrooms were at the end of the hall. I wondered how the guests would remain separate from each other if they had to use the same bathrooms. Luckily there would be security camera tapes, so we could review those. But first I wanted to figure out who had been the last to see Lulu Nightingale alive.

I returned to the studio, where Mikkola was currently busy taking fingerprints. Ilari Länsimies was pacing and swearing into his phone. Probably all the lines to the television station were jammed. Five messages were waiting on my cell too. I motioned to Länsimies, indicating that I wanted him to get off the phone so that I could talk to him. One of the cameramen was chain-smoking, and Pastor Pihlaja sat in her chair with her eyes closed. Anna-Maija Mustajoki appeared the calmest of anyone in the group, but when I looked closer, I saw beads of sweat along her hairline. No one had had the sense to turn off the studio lights yet.

"All of you will be contacted first thing in the morning to schedule interviews," I announced.

"I'm supposed to be at home in Vesanto tomorrow," Mauri Hytönen said. I glanced at Puupponen. It would be best to conduct Hytönen's initial questioning immediately, and then we could ask the police in Kuopio to assist with any follow-up.

"I don't know who did it!" Länsimies yelled into his phone and then wiped his brow with a red checked handkerchief. I touched him on the arm and gave him another look.

"I have to talk to the police now," he said, obviously relieved that he had an excuse to hang up. Again he patted his forehead and neck with the handkerchief. "I'm sorry. That was the network president. This appears to be a first for Finnish television."

"Just a few questions, and then we can continue tomorrow. Can you tell me who met with Lulu Nightingale here at the studio?"

"That's easy: me and Riitta. We asked Lulu to come to the studio at eight thirty, and Riitta met her at the door. Then I popped in to say hello just before we began taping. I always visit each guest to get them warmed up to the topic."

"Who chooses the guests for the show?"

"Same answer: me and Riitta. We are West Man Productions. My wife owns a quarter of the shares of the company, but she isn't involved in the practical side of program planning. That's been one of the nice things about doing this, that I can mostly determine the content myself."

"How many people knew Lulu Nightingale would be the final guest tonight?"

"Once again: me and Riitta. Plus our makeup artist, Nuppu. I also may have mentioned it to the camera and sound crew, since Lulu is . . . Well, she's the kind of woman men tend to be interested in."

"That bottle of Fernet Branca on the table in her dressing room . . . Was that provided by the show or did she bring it with her?"

"What bottle of Fernet Branca?" Länsimies asked. "Maybe Lulu needed some extra courage. How should I know? We aren't in the habit of liquoring up our guests."

"So you didn't notice the bottle when you visited Lulu in her dressing room?"

Länsimies shook his head. When his phone rang again, I let him answer. We'd have to go over all of this again in his formal interview anyway.

Before getting tied up in another interview, I established that the camera and sound crew had been in the studio itself or the break room at the back of the building since four o'clock. They hardly could have snuck back to the dressing rooms during a live broadcast, and the same went for Ilari Länsimies.

Mauri Hytönen had stayed put the entire time. "How about we go back to your dressing room?" I suggested. We walked back down the now-familiar hallway. His dressing room was the same as the others: small and cramped. Once settled in, Puupponen pulled a laptop out of his bag and opened an interview record template.

"Hytönen, Mauri Sulevi, born the sixteenth of April, 1959," Puupponen repeated after Hytönen.

"So you volunteered for the program through the *Secret Guests* website? Why?" I asked.

"To get my opinion out to the hypocritical masses. I wanted to make them look the truth in the eyes: there have always been prostitutes and there always will be."

"Was Lulu Nightingale one of the prostitutes whose services you employed?"

Hytönen gave me a quick glare and then turned back to Puupponen.

"No, I never had the pleasure. A while back I saw her show at the Sexhibition Fair, and it wasn't really my style."

"But you knew who she was?"

"Of course. I keep up on the industry."

According to him, Hytönen had arrived at the studio at six and sat down with the makeup artist immediately. Länsimies had visited him to buoy his courage, saying that it wasn't just any man who would dare to talk about his dealings in the world of sex for hire. Hytönen still seemed pleased with himself.

"I've already had calls from *Look* and *Oho*. I can give them interviews, right?"

"Preferably not while the investigation is going on," I said. Why did this case have to be so damn public? At least Lulu hadn't died on camera. Maybe Mauri Hytönen was determined to get his full fifteen minutes of fame. But for now he'd have to wait until we were done.

He reported that he owned an HVAC company, which also operated in Estonia. That was where his hooker hobby had started. Because Hytönen kept directing his answers to Puupponen, I let my colleague lead the questioning. And Puupponen was good at it. His hometown, Kuopio, was only fifty miles from Vesanto, and the two men quickly fell into their common dialect. Hytönen clearly hadn't had the opportunity to say everything he'd wanted to on the show, so he began lecturing Puupponen on the joys of commercial sex. "Every man wants more than one woman. It's in our nature. And every man will cheat if he has the opportunity. No healthy man can survive without sex, and why should he? We should admit that fact instead of moralizing," Hytönen said. Meanwhile Puupponen continued to try to steer the conversation back to the crime, asking him whether he knew any of the guests before the show. The answer was no. He glanced at his phone.

"I need to get going. I have a meeting at the Holiday Inn downtown at eleven," he said, grinning to remove any ambiguity as to the nature of the meeting. I paused for a moment after we let him go, feeling empty inside. Something in what Hytönen had said bothered me, something that didn't necessarily have to do with the case.

I went outside for a moment to breathe some fresh air. That was a mistake. Lulu's body was just being lifted into the ambulance, and beyond the police tape lurked a pack of reporters and photographers. A blond lock of hair had escaped the white sheet, and it was impossible not to notice the shape of her breasts protruding above the strap across her torso as only silicone implants can. The ambulance took off without lights or sirens.

I yelled to the reporters that I would give a statement about the case later and then went back inside. Things were going according to routine despite everyone being tired and in shock and wanting to go home. These people had experienced a death, and it was my job to refer them to the proper crisis assistance resources, but I also had to remind them that they needed to do their best to help the police.

"Are we suspects?" Anna-Maija Mustajoki asked. Pastor Terhi Pihlaja spun toward her, and from her expression it was obvious that this idea was new to her.

"That may be too strong a word," I replied, even though they were all suspects, every single person who had been in the building. They would all be under suspicion at least until we knew the cause of Lulu Nightingale's death. Fortunately, no one had plans to go abroad immediately.

Ilari Länsimies was still speaking in a steady stream into his phone. Liisa Rasilainen came to tell us that Riitta Saarnio's husband had arrived to pick her up and arranged for a doctor to visit them at home. Liisa gave us the doctor's contact information so we could find out when Saarnio would be ready for questioning.

We'd have to interview as many of the crew and the guests as possible tomorrow. It was getting late, and everyone seemed to be too tired to be of any use, so I decided it was time to let them leave. Puupponen's face looked gray once the studio lights were finally shut off. He would have to go back to the station to assemble everything he could find on Lulu Nightingale before our morning meeting.

When I finally got away, the gaggle of reporters had thinned. Flashes still fired as I walked to my car. As I passed, I answered their questions, although I didn't have much information to offer.

"I'll have more to tell once we have an initial theory about the cause of death."

"And when can we expect that?" asked the crime reporter from MTV3, whom I'd always liked.

"Depends on the line at the morgue. Maybe as early as tomorrow. I'll let you know. Now, good night, everyone!" I yelled as I got into my car.

The car felt like a refuge, as if for a moment within its sheet-metal skin I was out of reach of the rest of the world. I didn't need to listen to anyone else's phone conversations or the babbling of drunks on the bus. Was that why everyone in Espoo had to drive everywhere, to protect their privacy? You could always find people on the bus or the train who wanted to shout their business for everyone to hear. If you couldn't get into the tabloids as some celebrity's secret lover, at least you could force people to hear about your drama until their bus stop.

I scanned the radio channels and finally found one playing the Boys doing a cover of "Pet Sematary." That reminded me of Venjamin, whose adoption had been the best decision I'd made in a long time. It was nearly midnight, and the city was already asleep. I passed the last bus in our neighborhood and a couple of taxis headed east. A dog walker on the sidewalk probably wouldn't encounter any others of his kind. The moon and stars shone bright despite the city lights.

In our building, almost all the windows were dark. Venjamin padded up at the door and mewed hungrily, even though I knew for a fact that Antti had already fed him his evening meal. Still, I tossed the kitten a couple of treats, which he began batting around the kitchen floor. I drank a glass of buttermilk, washed up, and headed to bed. Antti sniffed beside me, not quite snoring but still making noise. I'd noticed that I slept better when I was alone. Venjamin, done with his snack, jumped onto the bed and sat on my stomach. He quickly purred himself to sleep, but none of my usual relaxation techniques seemed to help me.

I couldn't stop thinking about my unit, about how we were going to manage the workload of this new investigation. At two o'clock I was still awake, but gradually sleep began mixing images from the day's events into an absurd half dream about Oksana turning up in Mauri Hytönen's hotel room.

I woke up at six and decided that the best survival strategy would be to head out for a run. Antti opened his eyes just enough for me to know he was semiawake, so I told him I'd be home in half an hour. For an energy boost, I swigged some juice straight from the carton.

Outside it was still dim. I tried to stick to paths with fresh gravel, but sometimes that was impossible. The snows hadn't come until late January this year, and I'd enjoyed the cross-country skiing this winter, but now I didn't have time to get to the well-maintained tracks in Central Park.

After ten minutes of running, I finally felt myself waking up. Two cups of coffee and the morning headlines at home handled the rest. I was out the door by seven fifteen, leaving Antti to manage the kids' morning routine. He didn't bother to ask when I'd be home.

In the car, I plugged in my hands-free and called Assistant Chief Kaartamo.

"Hi, it's Kallio. You've probably heard about what happened last night at the TV studio. I'd like permission to borrow some people from Narcotics and Patrol. Our unit can't handle this case without backup."

I heard a yawn on the other end of the line. Apparently I'd woken him up.

"Damn it. Can't you just use your own people?"

"I can, but not without breaking the overtime rules. I need someone to review all the TV studio surveillance tapes and someone for interviews so we can run three teams at once."

"There's that nuclear power research conference in Otaniemi, so everyone from Patrol is tied up there. I'll talk to Aaltonen, but I'm pretty sure Narcotics is up to their eyeballs too. I wish the goddamn budget bastards would come out in the field every once in a while! And then there's our very own deserter, Taskinen, who should have known we wouldn't be allowed to hire a temporary replacement for him. So, yes, I'll see what I can do, but try to handle this with your own people!"

I grimaced into the phone because I'd forgotten the nuclear power conference being held at the Helsinki University of Technology. The meeting was being held in Finland precisely because it was considered to be a safe country. The antinuke activists were planning a demonstration for Saturday, and Antti was planning to go. We'd have to figure some things out, since I was likely to be stuck at work all weekend. Usually these sort of event-related security operations went to our colleagues in Helsinki, but now it was our turn to share the wealth.

Because of that, I had to assume I wouldn't be receiving any reinforcements, not even to review the security tape. Puustjärvi and Autio would have to start with that and then move on to investigating Lulu Nightingale's connections with other prostitutes. Ursula and Puupponen could conduct as many interviews as possible today, and Koivu could handle the searches. If we couldn't get any help from Narcotics and Patrol, I'd have to go with him. For some reason, the idea of going to a sex studio revolted me. But why? I'd never balked at people's sexual quirks before. My circle of friends included all different kinds of folks, and they'd introduced me to everything from gay bars to fetish clubs, and work had taken me to strip joints. I wasn't usually the type to recoil from something like this.

The parking garage at the police station was empty, so I cut across the other spots to my own. Inside the office I found a note from Puupponen on my door, which told me to look in my e-mail for Lulu Nightingale's personal information. As my computer booted up, I grabbed my work shoes from the closet and applied some mascara. In a drawer, I found a couple of leftover car-shaped *salmiakki* candies, which I munched as I read.

> Lilli Julia Mäkinen, now Lulu Julia Mäkinen, born November 15, 1973, in Inkoo. Her parents still live in Inkoo, and I arranged for the local police to deliver the news. Her brother lives here in Espoo, her sister in Salo. Both are older than Lulu. Lulu's current residence is listed as 6 Punavuori Street, Helsinki. Graduated high school 1992, au pair in Zurich 1993–95, restaurant worker also in Zurich 1995–97. (Maria, Zurich is chock-full of girly bars. I was there two summers ago, and I know!) Returned to Finland in 1997, worked at the Mermaid Restaurant in Helsinki, founded the Blue Nightingale in 1999. Charged for procurement in 1999, thrown out for lack of evidence, conviction for accessory to assault in 2003, fined €500. The perpetrator in the assault was Lulu's bodyguard, Tero Sulonen, who was fined €1000. Both claimed the victim attacked them first. This happened at the Mikado. Apparently, the plaintiff was one of Lulu's old johns. I'll look into that more tomorrow. No children or marriages. Who would know about her friends? No known drug connections, likewise with white-collar crime. Now this little boy's headed for bed. I'll come in tomorrow before the meeting to answer questions. Ville P.

The timestamp on Puupponen's e-mail was 2:00 a.m. He lived in Kilo, a five-minute bike ride from the station. I wondered about the comment about girly bars. Puupponen didn't talk much about his private life. A few years earlier I'd read his mystery novel manuscript, which played with the chauvinistic imagery of hard-boiled detective novels. From it I'd gotten the impression that in his private life Puupponen was completely bewildered when it came to women. At work, he got along with everyone.

Only our bad-tempered former colleague Pertti Ström, who'd killed himself a few years ago, had been too much for him. But Puupponen didn't speak ill of Ström after his death. I guess we were all still dealing with the guilt of having failed to interrupt our colleague's downward spiral.

I'd sent a request for a record of all calls into Jorvi Hospital on Wednesday night and was halfway through reworking our unit schedule when there was a knock on the door.

"Morning. I noticed that my note was gone and concluded that you must be here already. I'll get you some coffee. Do you want it with milk or without?" Puupponen said.

"Black, thank you. I imagine you're more in need of it than I am. Did you get a chance to sleep?"

"About three hours. That's all a real Finnish man needs. I'm going to go do some more research into Lulu's background," Puupponen said and then yawned. I smiled after him. I didn't like demanding that my subordinates work such insanely long hours, but there was nothing I could do about it at the moment. It was the same everywhere. The Working Hours Act only protected certain groups, mostly the male members of big unions who enjoyed levels of pay incommensurate to their education. Everyone else did part-time or freelance work, or simply weren't protected by the law. At worst, they'd have to put in fifteen-hour days. If they couldn't, the boss would just find someone else who could. No wonder many mothers with small children opted to stay home if they could afford it. But not everyone had that choice.

All five of my subordinates were in by eight. Aaltonen from Narcotics had hysterically screamed at me when I asked him about borrowing some manpower. They were in the middle of an important case that involved multiple simultaneous sting operations, and if they pulled it off the metro area drug underground would have one fewer big fish. Once he'd calmed down, he did promise to ask his people if the name Lulu Nightingale had ever come up in any of their investigations. I'd have to settle for that.

Per usual, I started the meeting with our easiest and most complete cases, since I knew that this made us feel like we were succeeding at something.

"OK, the Räsänen case can go to the prosecutor. Good. What about Oksana? Koivu, what did the folks on the hospital switchboard say?"

"It's hard for them to remember individual calls, since they get thousands every day. Finding the right operator took me a while. When I really pushed her, she remembered that the caller just asked to be connected to Oksana's room. Usually they only have two patients sharing a phone, but there was an extra person in Oksana's room."

"Was the caller a man or a woman? Did he speak Finnish?"

"It was a Finnish-speaking woman. Do we have a warrant to open the phone records?"

"It's in process. Autio, have we received any new tips about Oksana's movements?"

"Yes, and I've checked them." Autio picked a hair off his suit. He was the only one I didn't feel comfortable calling by his first name, perhaps because the name—Gideon—was so unique. "Nothing yet. My guess is Sergei and Ivan picked up their meat and now she's swimming with the fishes."

I looked at Autio in confusion since he wasn't usually one to break with decorum. "Trust me, Kallio. The sea might still be frozen, but professionals have their ways when it comes to getting rid of bodies. The only tip we received about a potential address took us to a house in Leppävaara, which ended up being the home of a Russian radiology professor and his family. This Oksana doesn't exist in any record or database, and she isn't going to. We don't even know if that's her real name."

"Keep accepting tips. Maybe something will click."

"Like the Lake Bodom murders?" Autio replied, referring to one of the most famous unsolved murders in Finnish history.

What stick did he have up his ass?

"OK, let's move on to Lulu Mäkinen. Puupponen has more information about her background."

Puupponen began with what he'd e-mailed me, then added new details.

"The Blue Nightingale is registered as an escort service and erotic dance parlor."

Koivu gave a long whistle. "So it's all aboveboard, is it?"

"Based on the charges for procurement, it seems like they walk a fine line with the law. Lulu hired another woman as an erotic dancer, and the boys in Helsinki suspected it was something more than that. So Lulu arranged a full-on strip show for them, but they weren't convinced. All in all, she seems to have made dupes of the cops and the taxman, and pushed the limits of just about every law she could find. On last year's tax forms, she reported an income of one hundred and twenty thousand euros."

"I'm switching jobs," Ursula said. "Who inherits all that now? She must have a lawyer we could talk to."

"Good call. Puupponen, will you find out?"

"Sure, and one more thing: that bodyguard had another assault conviction from when he was a bouncer. He got off with probation, but it had run out before the second case," Puupponen said. "Lulu paid him a salary and charged him rent for his room, so everything looked legal and aboveboard. But based on his behavior yesterday, we can assume Lulu was more than his boss."

"No surprise there. OK, let's get out there. I'm waiting for the search warrant. Koivu, once it's approved you can execute it with Forensics. I'll try to come along. Autio and Puustjärvi, start reviewing the security tapes. Let me know the instant you find anything. Once you're done with that, go interview Ms. Mäkinen's parents."

"Will you want me to come back afterward?" asked Puustjärvi, who lived in Kirkkonummi, which was on the way to Lulu Mäkinen's parents' house in Inkoo.

"Call me once you're done. Ursula, contact the lab and the pathologist, and attend the autopsy if necessary. Koivu and I will work up an interview schedule before going on the search. Ville and Ursula, also check if anyone who was at the studio last night has a criminal record and take a look at all the attacks and murders involving prostitutes in the last ten years for the whole country. And find this girl Lulu was accused of pimping. The stripper. I'll issue more instructions as we go. If you end up having some time, come back here to help with interviews."

Just then the unit secretary poked her head in and tossed the day's tabloids on the table. Naturally the murder of Lulu Nightingale was in the headlines in both papers, and one of them put forth a theory about Lulu being connected to the mysterious woman who had disappeared from Jorvi Hospital. I'd wondered the same thing. Even though the activities of the Blue Nightingale were ostensibly legal, Lulu could have easily hired more assistants, thus making herself guilty of pimping.

The tabloids had found out even more about Lulu than Puupponen had. One had interviewed her during the latest erotica convention and now republished excerpts from that story. The pictures were devastating. Under Lulu's thick layer of makeup there appeared to be a beautiful thirty-year-old woman. What did it say about her that she hadn't allowed the West Man Productions professional makeup artist to touch her face? Had that been a desire for control, to decide for herself what she looked like at any given moment?

"'I'm a sex industry entrepreneur, and I'm proud of my profession. I deal in the most basic human needs. If I ran a restaurant or cleaned people's homes, people would admire me. It's silly. Fulfilling people's sexual needs is a basic service!'" Ursula read Lulu's quotations. "'If I were president, there would be state-run brothels in every county, where everyone's needs would be met equally whether they were rich or poor. Sexuality doesn't discriminate by wealth.' Well, wasn't she a regular Robin Hood! Why didn't she run for city council on that platform?"

"I would have voted for her," Puupponen said. I snorted, even though I didn't really find it funny. I had something more important to think about: Who might have wanted Lulu Nightingale killed?

4

"Can we construct a comprehensive timeline of who arrived when at the studio last night?" I asked Koivu once the morning meeting was over and we were sitting alone in my office. The makeup artist had sent her schedule via e-mail, and Länsimies had sent the guests' arrival times. We could probably verify those from the security footage.

"The broadcast began at 9:30. Terhi Pihlaja was asked to arrive at 7:30 and went straight to makeup. Nordström, Mustajoki, and Hytönen arrived at fifteen-minute intervals, and Lulu Nightingale came last, at 8:30. Hytönen's makeup time was 8:00, Mustajoki's 8:15, and Nordström's 8:45. The makeup artist, Nuppu Koskela, arrived at the studio at seven, and the cameramen and sound technician came at around four. Länsimies said he was at the studio from five on with Riitta Saarnio, ironing out the final structure for the show."

"That's an awful lot of back-and-forth. Today we need to talk to at least Länsimies, Nordström, and Sulonen. Hopefully Nordström's position doesn't complicate the investigation."

Koivu snorted. "You think they'll give it to SIS instead of us?" Relations between the Security Intelligence Service and the National Bureau of Investigation weren't particularly good, and the Sonera Telecom phone-snooping scandal had only made that worse.

My door buzzer sounded, and outside I found Vesterinen from the evidence locker. He'd brought Lulu's coat and purse. I hopelessly tried to shove my hair into a white cap, then Koivu and I donned protective suits and gloves. We spread a plastic sheet over my desk, then set the items on it. Koivu checked the coat's side pockets. One contained a white handkerchief, and the other was empty. In the breast pocket was an object about the size of a bug-bite stick. Koivu pulled it out.

"Well, well. Pepper spray," he said.

The purse was black leather, a little larger than a paperback and with red embroidery. Even though I wasn't the best person to evaluate the prices of purses, I had the impression that this one was expensive. I snapped open the ornate latch. Inside were two compartments with a zippered pocket between. One of the compartments had another small zippered pocket and a cell phone sleeve.

"Lulu's phone. Excellent." It was a clamshell model, which looked more like a compact than a phone. The makeup bag was so large it filled half the purse. In the pocket next to the phone was a ring of keys and a separate car key, and the middle zippered pocket contained a collection of medications: prescription pills, an allergy inhaler, a couple of sleeping tablets, heartburn medication, and a condom.

"She was ready for anything," Koivu said, trying to be funny, but then he realized how lame he sounded. Ultimately Lulu Nightingale hadn't been prepared for whatever happened last night in her dressing room.

In the other compartment of the purse was a small wallet and a thin calendar. I quickly flipped through it. It was obviously her private calendar, because the entries were sparse. The previous week Lulu had visited her hairdresser, and this week she only had her appearance on *Surprise Guests* marked. Today she was supposed to get her nails done at noon.

In the wallet were a couple of credit cards, three different airline bonus cards, a social security card, a library card, and one hundred and sixty-two euros and fifty cents in cash. There were also a bunch of Lulu's calling cards. *Making your wildest dreams come true. Lulu Nightingale, the Blue Nightingale.* The card had a phone number and Lulu's web address. We would also have to check her website, along with her calls and e-mails. Earlier in the morning I'd sent off requests for access to all of this, which had become routine in homicide cases.

The wallet didn't contain any actual personal effects, no photographs or other people's business cards. There weren't even any receipts or postage stamps. The calendar didn't have a phone list or an address book. I opened Lulu's cell phone but couldn't get past the PIN code. I tried her birth date in various forms, then the combination of her building and apartment number, but without any luck. We'd be able to get information on her calls from the phone company, but it would be interesting to see whose numbers she kept in her contact list.

The makeup bag held all kinds of expensive brand-name products, which were more familiar to me from advertisements than my own cosmetics collection. The eye-shadow applicators had been wiped clean after use. The liner pencils were freshly sharpened: bright red for the lips, dark violet for the eyes. The bag also included perfume, a travel size bottle of hair spray, two different blush compacts, and other small containers. I estimated that the total value of the contents of the makeup bag was more than two hundred euros. When I told this to Koivu, he shook his head.

"Why do you women allow yourselves to be ripped off like that? Did Lulu at least get to deduct her makeup as a business expense?"

"Puupponen can look into that. I—" Just then Ursula burst into my office. Sometimes she didn't knock or ring the buzzer, presumably because she wanted to catch me gorging on candy or talking about personal business on the phone.

"Wow," she said when she saw the contents of Lulu's makeup bag spread across my desk. According to Ursula my estimate was on the low side: Lulu's foundation cream alone cost almost two hundred euros. A few years ago, I'd suspected Ursula of subsidizing her brand-name obsession by leaking details about investigations to the press, but I'd never found any real evidence. Apparently, she also had rich male companions who enjoyed giving her expensive gifts. Ursula didn't hide the fact that she had a number of older gentlemen under her thumb, though she never gave any names—of course, these men likely preferred discretion. Maybe that was what Mauri Hytönen meant about paying for sex.

"The autopsy is at three, so I can do interviews until then. I tracked down Iines Iivonen, who was the one implicated in Lulu's procurement case. We'll have to go all the way to Hämeenlinna if we want to see her. She earned a year for aggravated assault, and she's been serving it since October. So she won't know much about Lulu's recent activities."

"Let's ask for local help in questioning her."

Ursula reached out to stroke the soft fur of the coat's collar. "Sweet coat. Of course, you don't have any furs. Your husband wouldn't approve."

My reply was interrupted by our unit secretary, Eija, who'd stepped in to deliver the approved search warrant for Lulu's apartment. Koivu immediately called Forensics. I packed all of Lulu's belongings except her phone and keys back into their plastic bags, and we dropped them off at the evidence room on our way to the parking garage. Koivu drove while I arranged interviews. Puupponen and Ursula would start with Tero Sulonen at noon, and I arranged myself a meeting with Nordström for three. Riitta Saarnio didn't pick up her phone. So I called the number of the family doctor I'd been given yesterday.

"She's at home with a nurse. I'll visit her this evening, but I can already tell you she isn't in any shape to be interrogated today. She's still in shock. Let's talk again tomorrow."

There was nothing I could say to that. Ilari Länsimies's phone was busy, so I left a message on his voice mail. Koivu rolled around the Punavuori neighborhood of Helsinki searching for a somewhat-legal parking spot. In the end, we had to leave the car a few blocks away from Lulu's building. As we slipped and slid along Iso Robert Street, I couldn't help remembering a time thirteen years before.

"Koivu, do you remember that building?" I asked, pointing to a postwar apartment building that rose above us. Koivu nodded.

"We went there together to search Tommi Peltonen's place," he said. "Antti moved into Peltonen's apartment, and you lived there for a while too. I was in my first job after the academy and all jazzed that I'd made it right into the Helsinki Criminal Division, which I thought was the best gig in the country. And then I had to go and follow a girl to Joensuu! Well, at least things worked out in the end . . ."

I wrapped an arm around Koivu. There was no need for words. Koivu knew what the gesture meant. I released him as we turned the corner onto Punavuori Street. The Blue Nightingale was located on the top floor of a six-story building, and the entry was in the courtyard. From the street, there was no indication that an escort service operated inside. I wondered what the law said about the use of a residential apartment for business purposes. I imagined it was OK, since people cut hair and gave massages out of their homes.

Even though the building had an elevator, I started climbing the stairs. I could feel my morning run in my thighs, since I hadn't taken the time to stretch properly, and I no longer recovered as quickly as I had ten years ago. Koivu followed, puffing and panting. Forensics hadn't arrived yet, but we went ahead and began donning our protective suits in the hallway. The nameplate on the door simply read "Nightingale" in Finnish and English. Apparently Lulu had paid some consideration to her neighbors' sensibilities. Although on this floor there was only one other door, with a nameplate that read "National Federation of Bicycle Repair Shops." It had never occurred to me that such a thing existed.

Lulu's door had both a standard Abloy lock and a high-security deadbolt. The key to the latter was easy to find in the bundle from her purse, but the former required three tries. Just as we got the door unlocked, my phone beeped with a text message from Hakkarainen saying they were a block away and looking for a parking spot. I wrote back to tell them to drive into the courtyard if the van would fit through the archway.

When I opened the door, the day's newspapers and pile of junk mail settled at my feet. Even though it was daytime, the entryway was completely dark. Koivu fumbled for the light switch. When he finally found it, dozens of red stars lit up on the ceiling and walls. The lighting made Koivu's face blaze pink as if he had a fever. He tried again, and a normal yellow overhead light came on.

There were two doors on the left side of the hallway and one on the right, all closed. The end of the entryway opened into an arched vault outlined by red vinyl curtains. Without any need for discussion, we moved in that direction.

"So this is the Blue Nightingale," Koivu said as we stepped through the curtains into a large room the size of a standard one-bedroom apartment. Lulu had combined the living room, dining room, and small library so the Blue Nightingale stretched the width of the building. The windows also had red curtains over black blinds. No daylight could get in. The main illumination came from reddish spotlights, which could be dimmed from the brightness of sunshine to perfect darkness. On the wall to the left of the arched vault was a row of cabinets extending to the outer wall. The four-poster bed was so large that four people could have made love on it with ease. On the bedposts were metal rings. In the middle of the room was a device that looked like a weight bench, with padding and four legs, as well as more metal rings. Next to it was a low divan. On the right side of the room was an enormous black bathtub with two steps leading up to it. Behind the bathtub, half-concealed by a curtain, I could make out a set of wall bars. On chains dangling from the ceiling was a set of hooks.

The sound of the doorbell interrupted our search. It was Hakkarainen and Mikkola, with the photographer, Kerminen, lurking in the background.

"What are we looking for?" Hakkarainen asked as he pulled on a protective cap. It made him look like an aging actor playing a doctor heading into surgery.

"Lulu Nightingale. Her whole life should be here, her work and her home. What do you think, boys?" I couldn't help but grin at young Mikkola's expression as he looked around Lulu's studio. Give him twenty years and that expression would be gone. By then he'd think he'd seen everything. But no matter how jaded he got there would always be some new, incomprehensibly brutal crime that would shock him and remind him just what kind of evil people are capable of.

The second key I tried in the lock of the cabinet was a hit. Inside were enough clothes to fill the pages of a porn magazine for a year's worth of issues. Vinyl, rubber, leather, a gas mask, and a real nurse's uniform, along with various corsets and garters. There were also an adult-size onesie and a baby bonnet. Who manufactured those?

The next cabinet was full of shoes, including a pair of Nokian rubber rain boots and a pair of yellow wood clogs. In the third cabinet were wigs and masks, adult diapers, and a liter-size baby bottle with a giant nipple. The fourth cabinet was organized like the shelves of a hardware store, neatly filled with ropes, chains, locks, five different sets of handcuffs, and one set of ankle cuffs. Whips and clamps were in the final cabinet, along with a wheeled cart carrying a CD player and a small TV/VCR. Everything was carefully arranged to be easy to find. Still, the room had a strange feeling, as if the slaps and kisses exchanged there still echoed within the walls, as if the smell of all the bodily secretions still hung in the air.

"Should I take pictures of all of this?" Kerminen asked. I said yes, even though I knew copies of the prints would end up in break rooms all over the police station.

"This Lulu was a smart woman," Hakkarainen suddenly said. "Look, Kallio. There are at least three panic buttons hidden around the room. She could have her bodyguard here in an instant."

I went back into the hallway, then tested the keys on the lone door on the right side of the entryway. The lock was another Abloy, and once I got it open, I walked into another world, leaving the others to wonder at the possibilities of the Blue Nightingale. The room on the other side of the door was all brown and beige, decorated with a cold asceticism. Bed, desk, armchair, and television. One wall was filled with cabinets. The first, when opened, revealed shelves full of books. The second held normal clothes: jeans, jackets, and sweaters. The third was for underwear and more shoes. At the back of the room was the entry to the bathroom. Inside, I found its shelves weighted down by rows of makeup and hair products, and light bulbs surrounded the mirror like that of a theater dressing room. The medicine cabinet held the same medications as Lulu's handbag. There were two boxes of condoms but no sign of contraceptive pills, so maybe Lulu used an IUD. I decided to search the bathroom more carefully once I'd been through the whole apartment. I walked back out into the hallway and, after again playing with the keys, found that one of two doors on the left side of the entryway led into a bathroom that was clearly part of the Blue Nightingale. The light was dim, the tiles black and red, as was the toilet, the sink, and the bidet. Somewhere Lulu had even managed to find black toilet paper. The other door led into a perfectly normal kitchen, which was decorated in the same Scandinavian style as the bedroom. Around the table were chairs for three, and on it the fruit bowl held a fresh pineapple and a couple oranges. Curious, I opened the refrigerator door. Light yogurt, fat-free buttermilk, several cups of cottage cheese, and various juices. Lulu and Tero probably shared the fridge. In the lower section were a couple of bottles of sparkling wine and one of expensive champagne. In the cupboards, I found muesli, nutritional supplements, pasta, and two bottles of Fernet Branca, one opened, one sealed. I collected those for analysis.

"Are you hungry?" Koivu had snuck up behind me. "God what a place. It sure makes your imagination run wild."

"Save it for tonight with Anu. Now what do we have here?" I'd noticed another door between the cupboards.

The servant's quarters behind the kitchen appeared to be Tero Sulonen's kingdom. The room was about ten by ten feet, with space for a narrow bed, a TV and DVD player, an armchair, and a serving cart that seemed to function as a table. The room smelled of sweat and aftershave. Koivu looked in the clothes cabinet crammed in the corner.

Next to Sulonen's bed was a red lamp. I asked Koivu to wait, then returned to the business side of the loft and pressed one of the panic buttons. Because the doors connecting the rooms were open, I heard a buzzing from Sulonen's room. When I went back into Sulonen's room, Koivu said that the light had also turned on.

"You look around here while I search Lulu's bedroom. Maybe her customer records are there," I said.

I went back into Lulu's room. The door had been set to relock automatically, and this time I noticed that there was also a chain on the inside. The desk had a locked cabinet and four drawers, the topmost of which was locked. I tried an appropriate-looking key from the key ring, and the cabinet opened. Inside were a laptop and some file folders. I grabbed a plastic sack from my crime scene kit, but before I logged the items I took a quick look at the first folder. It was full of bills and receipts, all in careful chronological order. As I flipped through I found a paystub for Tero Sulonen's February wages. His gross pay was two thousand euros a month, and the Blue Nightingale also paid the appropriate taxes and social security. Sulonen's official title was security guard.

I left the laptop untouched, since someone else would be able to figure out the passwords much more efficiently. The unlocked drawers contained normal office supplies like envelopes, pens, and stamps. The bottom drawer also had a stack of letters, all addressed to Lulu Mäkinen. The sender was a Horst Beckenbauer from Zurich. They were written in German, so I didn't waste my time struggling to read them. Instead I put them in the sack.

My phone rang, and I recognized the number as Ilari Länsimies.

"Detective Kallio here."

"Hello, Detective. You called."

"Yes. Can you come in for an interview at one o'clock?"

"There's no way I can come to the Espoo Police Station today," Länsimies said tersely. "Two o'clock might work, but I can only give you half an hour. I have a meeting here at three with Mining Counselor Raivionpää, so it would be best if you came here." Länsimies spoke in an imperious tone, but then his voice softened. "I can promise some great coffee. Talking about serious business doesn't have to be unpleasant. Come to Westend. You'll be my guest."

I shook my head but said, "OK. I'll see you there." At least I'd have time to prepare my questions for Länsimies on the drive over, and on the way back I could get ready for Nordström. I hung up the phone, then unlocked the top drawer. There I found three thousand euros in cash and five thousand US dollars, along with five large desk calendars. The most recent was from this year. When I opened it, I found what I was looking for—at least partially. This was clearly Lulu's client calendar, but unfortunately, there were only initials.

P. K.: sado session, wants restraint and BJ. J. T.: baby games. A. G.: erection issues, try oil massage. The addresses section of the calendar was empty. Lulu had to have a full client list somewhere. Only having a copy on the computer hard drive was risky, but I didn't see any disks anywhere. I carefully checked the contents of the wardrobe, but I didn't find any disks there either.

I asked Hakkarainen to also search the desk, since he was better than me at finding false bottoms and hidden compartments. I moved on to the cosmetics—it wouldn't have been any wonder if Lulu had hidden her disks there. The rows of bottles were out in the open. Boxes of tampons, panty liners, pads . . . Wait a second.

I grabbed the box of maxi pads and shook it. Instead of the sound of soft, absorbent cotton, I heard a faint metal clinking. Reaching into the package, I found two disks and one mini CD. There were no labels on them. I placed each in a plastic baggie and recorded them in my list of evidence. Hakkarainen knocked around on the desk and then stood up.

"This is just like a politician's head. Solid wood. But out in the sex lair we found at least thirteen different fingerprints and a pile of hair, short and long. Should I send everything to the lab for DNA tests?" Hakkarainen asked.

"No, there's no point spending that much money yet," I said. "Just look at the fingerprints for now. Although they won't prove anything unless we find the same prints in Nightingale's dressing room at the TV studio."

From out in the other room I heard Koivu guffawing. Outbursts like that usually only came from him when Puupponen told a truly terrible joke. The laughter drew closer, and then Koivu stepped into the room.

"Maria, wait until you hear what a tender heart Tero Sulonen has. The cabinets are full of all the best legal nutritional supplements, from vodka to protein powder, and then there's a little less-legal stuff too. 'Roids, I mean. But Mr. Bodybuilder is also a poet. Listen to this: 'Your golden hair, beyond compare, sets my heart ablaze, each time I gaze.'"

"You made that up!"

"Did not. Look for yourself!" Koivu offered me a notebook. Sulonen's handwriting was rounded and childish, like a first-grader tentatively practicing his letters. "There's a whole stack of notebooks, and there's no question about who his muse was."

I read a few of the poems. Some of the rhymes were off, but Sulonen forced them through, perhaps thinking that rhyming verse was the only real kind of poetry. In places, he crossed out stanzas and wrote new ones, but for the most part the poems were carefully transcribed. There was something tender and sincere about them, like the accounts of first love you saw in the pages of teen magazines. I thought of the bodyguard sitting in his room writing clumsy poetry and watching the light in case he had to rush to Lulu's aid.

"Put them back in Sulonen's cabinet. Searching his room is a little questionable anyway, since he isn't an official suspect yet. We'll come back later if we find some solid evidence against him. Let's head back to the station now. I want to get a look at Lulu's computer and these disks I found. Hakkarainen, let us know when you're done." It was about time to let Tero Sulonen back into his home. Lulu Mäkinen's next of kin were her parents, and they'd have to be the ones to decide what to do with the contents of the Blue Nightingale.

I was sitting in the car when Puustjärvi called. "We found just a couple of interesting things on these tapes. We already knew that Länsimies was in and out of the dressing room hallway, along with Riitta Saarnio. But Tero Sulonen wasn't sitting in the control room the whole time. The tapes show him going into Lulu Nightingale's room with a glass," Puustjärvi said.

"A glass? But not a bottle?"

"No, just a glass. I'll print out some stills for you. Wasn't Sulonen supposed to come in for questioning today?"

"He should already be in the building. Check with Puupponen and Honkanen. They promised to handle it."

I suggested to Koivu that we stop for food on the way to Länsimies's house. We ended up at a Turkish buffet in Tapiola. Koivu piled his plate with kebabs and rice while I settled for the vegetarian offerings.

"At this point I'd put my money on Sulonen, especially since he obviously worshipped Lulu," Koivu said, then wiped garlic sauce from the corner of his mouth.

"Yes. But why kill Lulu at the TV studio when he could have done it any other time? Why make it an obvious murder? Why not stage the death as an accident? And besides, there was so much hope in those poems. Or at least acceptance of the situation. Lulu was Lulu, and Sulonen was content with getting to live with her."

"I'm no literary critic. But I can only imagine how frustrating it would be to have the woman you love banging other men while you're just the guard dog. You remember my ex, Anita . . . the one from Joensuu. Remember how messed up I was when she cheated on me? Maybe Sulonen killed her at the TV studio because he thought he wouldn't be a suspect if it happened outside their home."

"He didn't seem like a cold-blooded mastermind, but what do I know? Hopefully Ursula and Ville also think to ask him about Oksana." I took a bite of my meal and just so happened to get a chunk of hot chili pepper. My mouth felt like it was on fire. It was so bad I had to go grab a glass of buttermilk from the buffet table to relieve the burning.

"Think I'll be able to get home by five? Anu has a hair appointment and I promised I'd take over childcare duty. She doesn't get out much without the kids."

I coughed, then cleared my throat. "We'll shoot for that. Depends on how talkative Nordström is, but first we have to handle Ilari Länsimies. You know much about him?"

"Yesterday Anu was saying he's like a poor man's Jörn Donner. Not quite as smart or charismatic, and Finnish speaking besides. Didn't he do some other programs before *Surprise Guests*, mostly cops-and-robbers shows? I don't watch that stuff."

"For a while he hosted a financial show and reported on foreign news on the radio. If I remember right, he was on the Espoo City Council for a while, back when the Liberal People's Party still existed. Now he's unaffiliated. His wife has a shoe boutique in Helsinki. I went there once and felt totally out of place. There wasn't a single pair of shoes under a hundred and fifty euros."

Back in the car, I read through the information about Ilari Länsimies that Puupponen had found on the web. The man had been in the public eye for decades. His father had been a diplomat, and Länsimies had spent his youth in the United States, Ireland, and New Zealand. At some point, he'd earned his doctorate too, and his dissertation dealt with relations between Finland and the US during the Paasikivi administration, right after World War II. My father, who was an amateur historian, had asked me to get it for him for Christmas when it was published ten years ago. I'd have to remember to ask him what he'd thought of it.

Now, at fifty-five, Länsimies was a lieutenant in the army reserves and a doctor of political science. But he reported his profession as "private entrepreneur." West Man Productions was owned by Länsimies, his wife, and Riitta Saarnio. Länsimies also owned one-third of the shares of his wife's shoe store, Boutique Rosella. The couple had two children, a married daughter who lived on the outskirts of London, and a son who worked for Nokia in Singapore.

Länsimies's house in Westend was easy to find. A gate blocked the driveway, so I got out of the car and pressed the buzzer on the call box. Länsimies responded almost immediately.

"Yes?"

"Detectives Kallio and Koivu."

"Come on in," Länsimies said, his tone welcoming. The gate opened, and by the time Koivu got our car parked in the carefully plowed driveway, Länsimies had already opened the front door. The house had two stories and was relatively new, with a backyard that abutted the sea.

We walked up the few steps to the porch. Länsimies was dressed in a dark-gray three-piece suit with a black tie. I caught a faint whiff of his aftershave as the front door closed behind us. After shaking our hands, he took our coats and hung them up. "I didn't get much sleep," he said when he saw his reflection in the entryway mirror. On television he wore makeup, but now his skin looked gray, with blue shadows under his eyes. "The advertisers are furious about what happened. We have a contract for ten more episodes, but the network president asked me to come in to talk to him tomorrow. We'll see what happens. This way. Please, come in. We'll go to my office."

Länsimies led us upstairs. Light flooded in through the skylights, illuminating a large landing with a stately fireplace. He opened the door on the south side of the room and led us into his office, its dark walls and heavy furniture a contrast to the previous brightness. It was what I would call a masculine room. The desk was next to the window, giving Länsimies a view of the sea. Over a seating area with room for five hung a photograph of Länsimies shaking hands with Ronald Reagan, who was wearing a Stetson. Under it on the table was a thermos pitcher, three coffee cups, and some tempting chocolate pastries. Länsimies pulled out a chair for me and then sat down beside me. His hair had a slight wave to it, and while he had a touch of gray at his temples, that only made him more attractive.

The corner of Länsimies's mouth went up in amusement when Koivu brought out the recorder. I hadn't managed to begin the actual interview before my phone rang. The display said it was Puupponen, so I answered.

"Hi. I checked all the criminal records. They're all clean except Länsimies has some speeding tickets. Then there's Hytönen. He's got a tax evasion charge going to appeal. The District Court only fined him, and the prosecutor wasn't satisfied. And that isn't all. Guess who the plaintiff was in that assault case against Nightingale and Sulonen? Mauri Hytönen."

5

"I didn't lie. I've never been a client of Lulu Nightingale. You didn't ask if I knew her from anywhere else." Mauri Hytönen sounded amused. I'd excused myself and left Länsimies's office to call him. I'd walked downstairs to the entryway, poking my head into the living room on the way. Light-brown leather furniture, colorful Indian textiles, and wooden carvings. Impeccably stylish. There wasn't a single magazine lying around or a dry flower in a vase, not to speak of dirty dishes.

"Didn't you think it might be worth mentioning that you and Nightingale went to court for assault?"

"She was the one who attacked me, her and that brainless gorilla, who somehow didn't recognize me at the TV studio. It's been two years since then, so why should it matter? I didn't kill her. Maybe she had HIV and thought it was best to off herself before it got her."

"You knew full well I wouldn't have let you go home if you'd told me about this incident."

"It never even crossed my mind. And why are you coming on so strong? I didn't even know Lulu was going to be on the program. That's the whole idea. *Surprise Guests*!"

Over the phone Puupponen had given me a summary of the assault case. Two years earlier Mauri Hytönen had approached Lulu Nightingale at the Mikado and announced out of nowhere that he wasn't interested in whores like her, that he held a higher standard. In a fit of pique, Lulu had slapped him across the face, and one of her large rings had left a gash on his cheek. He then started screaming at her, which drew the attention of Tero Sulonen, who at that time was still working as a bouncer there. Sulonen hit Hytönen several times and literally threw him out of the restaurant, resulting in a dislocated thumb. According to witnesses, Hytönen didn't put up a fight, so the court found Sulonen guilty of excessive force.

"You're planning on leaving the country for work soon, right?"

"Yes. At the end of next week, I'm supposed to go to Tarttu in Estonia. We're working on a remodel there. Am I suspected of something?"

"How about murder?" I said and hung up. Now I had less than half an hour to question Länsimies before his guests arrived. The fact that Hytönen had known Lulu and Tero Sulonen beforehand wasn't enough to arrest him, but I still didn't like that he was going to be two hundred and fifty miles away from Espoo.

One thing was certain: my unit wasn't going to have the weekend off. That would hit those of us with small children at home the hardest. Autio's boys were already in high school, and, as he told it, mostly just needed him to drive them to hockey practice.

I returned to the office, where Koivu was keeping Länsimies company. They were talking about soccer. I'd read that in his youth Länsimies had played in the Elite League, but he'd never made it onto the national team. He still had the solid frame of an athlete, and nowadays he played water polo and tennis with partners from the upper crust of society.

"People are made to be in motion. What do you do, Detective?"

"I jog when I have time. I like that I don't need all that gear or have to depend on other people—all I have to do is walk outside," I replied. Maybe letting Länsimies ask some questions was the best way to get him to talk.

"Whose idea was it to invite Lulu Nightingale to come on *Surprise Guests*?" I asked once we'd covered the benefits of various trail surfaces for running. Länsimies preferred a sawdust track, while I liked dirt.

"Probably me. Riitta and I always confer about the themes. The criminalization of buying and selling sex is coming up in Parliament soon, and there are strong feelings on both sides. I'd read some of Lulu's interviews. I thought she had a rare courage and directness, so I got in touch with her. I need guests who are willing to speak openly."

And who interest your viewers, I thought. Finland sure had changed: fifteen years ago, being a stripper was a source of shame, and now taking your clothes off in public was a sure road to fame, landing you interviews alongside politicians and philosophers. But had any of that really reduced the country's prudishness and narrow-mindedness? Maybe the repression had just changed form.

"Did you meet with Lulu before the day of the program?"

"Yes, a couple of times. The final guest plays a key role. She has to be able to turn the show's mood on its head one last time. We don't have musical guests or a studio audience, so we have to rely on the power of speech. Riitta was with me for the first meeting, but Lulu and I were alone for the second one, the day before yesterday, at Lulu's studio. She'd wanted to show it to me. Quite a place. I assume you've been there by now."

"Was it hard to talk Lulu into coming on the program?"

Länsimies smiled as if to say that everyone wanted to be on television.

"She liked the idea of getting some publicity for her business, and it would give her a chance to voice her opinion about criminalization. She was really hoping to testify in Parliament, and she intended to say so on the show, but she never got the chance. It's too bad, really. In this job you meet a lot of people, and you learn to keep your distance. But I liked Lulu. She was serious about her profession. She wanted to give people pleasure." Something flashed in Länsimies's eye that I couldn't quite read.

"You, Riitta Saarnio, and the makeup artist knew that Lulu Mäkinen would be the final guest on the show. What about the others, the camera and sound crew?"

"I might have hinted to them that we'd have a professional sex worker on at the end, but they never see the guests before taping. It heightens the surprise. Nuppu puts on the mics when she goes to get the guests. Except not this time."

"So it appears you were the last person to see Lulu alive."

"Let's not jump to any conclusions, Detective. Wasn't the last person to see Lulu alive the one who killed her? I've been wondering: How did they do it? The newspaper said the police aren't releasing the cause of death for reasons having to do with the investigation."

"Correct."

"But that bottle of Fernet Branca has to have something to do with it, right?"

Ilari Länsimies was used to being the one to ask the questions. So was I. We were like two cats stalking each other, but I was at a disadvantage because we were on Länsimies's turf. I still didn't answer the question about the bottle, but that was because I couldn't, since Lulu's cause of death was still unknown. Not that I'd mention that to Länsimies. Apparently, my silence began to irritate Länsimies, because he glanced at his watch and stared at the phone he'd placed on the table as if hoping it would ring. He hadn't poured us a second cup of coffee, apparently thinking the interview would only last long enough for one. Koivu had eaten the chocolate pastries while I'd been on the phone.

"Nordström didn't let any of us near the body. In retrospect I realize that he was a poor choice for the show. Too curt and dry. You cops are just so hard to get to comment on anything. In fact, he was the fifth one I asked. The chief of police had other commitments." Länsimies appeared resentful. Apparently in his mind getting to be on his show should have been everyone's dream.

"Tell us about your visit to Lulu's dressing room before the show."

"I always stop in on our guests to make sure they're comfortable and to build rapport. I visited Lulu a little before nine. She was putting some finishing touches on her makeup, and she looked amazing."

"Was she sober?"

"I didn't know her well enough to tell. She didn't appear visibly drunk, and I didn't see any open bottles around. Of course, there are always risks with a live show. Once we had to drop a poet because he showed up hammered. Riitta and I had to improvise a bit on that one. Lulu did seem to be enjoying herself, and I could tell she was confident."

"What about her bodyguard, Tero Sulonen?"

"What about him? She told me that he goes everywhere with her. That was fine with me so long as he stayed out of sight of the other guests."

"Wouldn't it have been easier for Sulonen to wait in Lulu's dressing room?"

"He asked to be in the access control room. I'm not sure why. Maybe someone had threatened Lulu, and Sulonen thought he could keep an eye out from there . . . Apparently, he couldn't, the poor devil." Länsimies spread his hands. "Hiring him may have been one of Lulu's few miscalculations. Muscles aren't enough in the protection industry. I learned that in the United States. Real pros have to have sharper instincts, like the secret service did when that guy tried to kill him." Länsimies gestured at Reagan. The picture was twenty years old, and Länsimies's hair was wavier and not gray at all. The actor-president was dressed casually, just like Länsimies. Horses stood in the background.

"You can't get into the studio without a key, and the security cameras see everyone coming and going. Finding the perpetrator should be easy," Länsimies said and smiled at me in a way that could be interpreted as either encouraging or demeaning.

From my brief conversation with Puustjärvi, I'd understood that no one unauthorized had entered the television studio during the taping. However, Sulonen hadn't been in the control room the whole time, and maybe the moment when he was away taking the glass to Lulu was exactly when the killer arrived. Locks didn't keep out professionals, and if someone intended to kill Lulu at the TV studio, they would have looked into the security arrangements beforehand.

Lulu's position and expression indicated poisoning. Ursula would soon be observing the autopsy. I hoped we'd have the cause of death today. But if it did turn out to be poisoning, that could mean anything from premeditated murder to suicide.

My phone beeped. The brief text message said, *Unavoidable delay. Can't come until three thirty. Lasse Nordström.* I stifled a curse. Nordström wanted to show me that he would dictate the schedule for his interview. Let him try.

"Did Lulu Nightingale give any sign that she was afraid of this TV appearance or its possible consequences?"

Länsimies shrugged, but he seemed irritated. "I thought this was already clear. Lulu was happy to come on. I didn't have to talk her into it."

"When you were doing background for the show, did she ever mention anyone threatening her?"

Länsimies laughed. "That was exactly Lulu's agenda: if prostitution was made legal, the human traffickers and mafia thugs would go away and the girls"—Länsimies waved his hand dismissively—"or women, workers, whatever the PC term is, could do their work in peace. I assume she'd received threats, but she didn't tell me anything specific. I'm sorry, but that's really all I know. You should ask her bodyguard."

Länsimies glanced at his watch again. It was already ten to three. "I really must ask you to leave now. My next appointment starts soon. And tonight I need to stop in to see Riitta, the poor thing. Only she and Nordström saw the body. It was such a terrible shock for her." Länsimies wore an expression of sympathy. But I didn't want him meeting with Riitta Saarnio before we'd had a chance to question her properly.

Länsimies stood up, signaling that it was time for us to go. I said I'd be in touch as necessary. His handshake was warm, and he even slapped Koivu on the back like they were old friends. *We're on the same side,* the gesture seemed to say.

A handsome black limousine with tinted windows was already waiting outside the gate. I guessed this was Mining Counselor Raivionpää's ride. Raivionpää had just moved up, from CEO of his family's forestry company to chairman of the board of directors. His name had come up as a possible conservative candidate for the upcoming presidential election, but apparently his health wasn't good. He was one of those old-fashioned business leaders who liked to keep a low profile.

From the car, I called Riitta Saarnio's house and talked to a nurse, who promised not to let anyone in. Saarnio's husband was also home, and he wanted to talk to me. It wasn't until he introduced himself that I realized I was talking to none other than Arto "Hatchetman" Saarnio, the infamous corporate raider.

"The doctor just left. Riitta's doing a lot better. Unless she takes a turn for the worse, you can interview her tomorrow." Arto Saarnio had the matter-of-fact voice of a person who was used to delivering bad news. "We have a medical certificate that protects her from having to undergo an interrogation today."

"Right. I'll come tomorrow morning then, along with Detective Pekka Koivu. It would probably be best for your wife not to allow any visitors, not even Ilari Länsimies, until after we speak with her."

Arto Saarnio laughed. "It would be my great pleasure to bar that man from my home." That sounded interesting.

Because Nordström wasn't anywhere to be found at the station, I went to see Puustjärvi. He was just putting the finishing touches on Lulu's parents' interview record, and Autio was trying to get in touch with Lulu's sister but had only reached her voice mail. Maybe she was on her way from Salo to comfort her parents. I sat down on the corner of Puustjärvi's desk and asked how things had gone in Inkoo.

"If the term heartbroken ever applied to anyone, it would be these people," Puustjärvi replied, his voice full of empathy. "They live in a duplex just outside Inkoo and both used to work at the harbor. They're on disability retirement now. The father has a bad back and the mother's got a heart condition. They have a spitz—it's old and lame too. They said they'd known for years that things wouldn't end well for their daughter. According to them, she got mixed up with the wrong crowd in Zurich. Fortunately, their other children have done well for themselves, but Lulu only caused them sorrow. They'd been praying for her to turn respectable, then this happened."

"Did they have any ideas about who might have done it?"

"No. Lulu hadn't visited them in three years. She did keep in touch with her sister, the one who lives in Salo."

At this point, Autio joined in. "The sister works at Nokia and is married to an engineer. Kallio, you should have seen the parents' house. It was like being in a time warp. The furniture was all at least thirty years old, and there was a cross-stitch of that painting with the fighting wood grouse on the wall. And there were other cross-stitches all over the place, including on Lulu's dad's slippers. I guess Lulu inherited her mother's craft gene; she just took it in a different direction." Autio snorted at his own joke. "At first, I was amazed by all the flowers, but they turned out to be fake and covered in dust." Autio brushed off his jacket as if ridding it of the memory of the Mäkinens' home. Today his suit was dark gray, and, as always, wrinkle-free. His tie had dark-blue flowers on a light-blue background.

Lulu's parents were no help in terms of the criminal investigation. However, as the next of kin, they would have to arrange their daughter's funeral and empty her apartment. Or would that be Tero Sulonen's job? Who would buy Lulu's costumes and sex toys? One of her colleagues?

Had the Tax Administration allowed her to claim her ropes and whips as business expenses?

Defenders of the sex industry were often asked if they would want their own daughters to be prostitutes. That question did two things: first, it exposed the assumption that sex workers were always women. Second, it revealed how people tended to divide humanity into "us" and "them" and that their daughters had nothing to do with the "others" who could be bought and sold. I no longer hesitated in answering that question. When I thought of Iida, I said no.

My phone beeped, and I looked at the message because I saw it had come from Ursula. *Prelims from the morgue. Lulu's blood is bright red, indicating cyanide. Tubes tied. Signs of violence postmortem.*

"Jesus!" I exclaimed, loudly enough to make Autio spit out his coffee. "The pathologist suspects that Lulu died of cyanide poisoning, but someone beat her up *after* she was dead too. Autio, find out ASAP how a regular person could get their hands on cyanide. Can it be ordered online? Hopefully the lab results on the liqueur bottle and the glasses come back soon. It matters whether the poison was in the bottle or the glass."

"Cyanide . . ." Autio shook his head. "Maybe it was suicide, and we'll find a note on the computer or those disks."

"Yes, go through the computer too. Haapio is working on the passwords. We were lucky we could get him for a few hours." Haapio was the department IT expert. He worked mostly for Narcotics and White-Collar Crime, but I'd managed to talk him into squeezing us into his schedule. "I'm going to question Nordström now and put off a press conference until tomorrow morning, assuming the autopsy report is complete by then."

Nordström, press conference, computer . . . The words swirled in my brain. I needed some fresh air, but our office windows didn't open. And I didn't feel like going outside, because that would look to Nordström like I was waiting for him. So I threw together a quick interim report for the public relations officer and asked him to announce the morning briefing. By the time Koivu and Nordström finally walked into my office, I'd managed to call home too and tell Antti not to count on me for anything over the weekend. He was supposed to be in Vaasa again starting Wednesday, so we'd need to ask his mother for help.

Nordström was a large man at nearly six foot six. He'd been just as broad-shouldered during college as he was now, but the belly was a new addition. Maybe squash had taken a back seat to the demands of the job. He was wearing jeans and a sports coat, and his cowboy boots added another inch to his height. When he shook my hand, I intentionally shook back as hard as I could.

He sat down on my couch without being invited to do so and patted the seat next to him. Instead of joining him I took the chair across from him, and Koivu pulled his own chair over so he could set his laptop on my desk.

"Well, Kallio, have you figured out what poison killed our songbird?" Nordström said. "And don't try to tell me it wasn't poisoning. The convulsive state of the body was obvious."

"The autopsy is still ongoing. Let's start officially now," I said as I started the recorder. "March eleventh, four thirty p.m. Present Detective Lieutenant Maria Kallio and Sergeant Pekka Koivu. Please state your full name and birth date for the record."

"Nordström, Lasse Henrik, born August sixth, 1962. Shoe size twelve and . . ." Nordström stopped when he saw my face. "Come on, Kallio, we don't have to be so formal, do we? We're all cops here."

"You of all people should understand that we have to do this by the book. Did you know that Lulu Nightingale was one of the other guests on *Surprise Guests* that night?"

"No, and I didn't know anything about any of the others. Am I being questioned as a suspect or a witness? I assume you know the difference."

"Your current status is witness," I replied. That meant Nordström had to tell the truth if he wanted to avoid being charged with perjury. Cop or not, we were going to interrogate Nordström to the fullest extent.

"Did you know Lulu Nightingale, AKA Lulu Mäkinen?"

"I knew who she was, but I didn't know her personally. I assume you two keep tabs on potential future clients too. It isn't that abnormal for a whore to end up dead." Nordström grinned at Koivu, who returned a forced smile after a moment of hesitation. Lasse Nordström wasn't going to fall for any "good cop–bad cop" games, but male solidarity might be an inroad we could use. Koivu knew the tactic, and we'd used it before. My job, of course, was to play the bitch.

I asked Nordström to tell us about what had happened after Riitta Saarnio had stumbled screaming into the studio. He squinted like a cat that's caught a mouse and is waiting for praise.

"It's instinct, you know that. When there's an emergency, you rush to help. Civilians tend to panic. So I knew that, as a law enforcement officer, I had to take control of the situation. I ordered the others to stay put and went to investigate. When I found Lulu, she looked dead, and there was no pulse or respiration. I tried to revive her, but it was obviously pointless."

"You tried to revive her? You did chest compressions?"

"Yes, and rescue breaths."

I remembered Ursula's message about signs of postmortem violence. That was probably the result of Nordström's attempt at CPR.

"When that didn't help, I called emergency dispatch. I knew the Espoo guys, and gals, would respond, but I couldn't have guessed that a detective lieutenant would rush to the scene. Don't you trust your people?"

"Did anyone else go in Lulu's dressing room?"

"No, I didn't let anyone else in. Her bodyguard tried to get in, along with Ilari Länsimies, but I locked the door from the inside and didn't open it until your patrol arrived. Then I thought I'd done my part, even though the studio was still pretty chaotic."

Nordström had to understand the meaning of what he was telling us. He had been alone with the body, so he would have had every opportunity to hide or stage evidence. I looked at his fingers, which drummed on his broad, muscular thigh. They were delicate, out of proportion with the rest of his solid frame. He had a cleft chin, which many women probably found sexy. But there was no ring on his left hand, which surprised me. I'd been under the impression that Nordström was married and had at least two children. "This is a pretty strange case. If I were you," he continued, "I'd look into the relationship between Lulu and her bodyguard. Maybe someone bribed him to kill her, and he decided to do it in a place where there would be other suspects. I've worked enough investigations into the connections between these girls and organized crime to know just how cheap their lives can be. Like that one you posted the notice about in the paper. You aren't going to find her. She might have survived if the police hadn't interfered, but once you started questioning her, they would have had to silence her. The underworld has its sources, probably even in this very building. Who can stay perfectly clean on these salaries?" Nordström leaned toward me and put his hand on my arm. He was playing the good cop now, trying to convince us he was on the right side. But I shook his hand off. My shoulders hurt—I must have been tensing them unconsciously.

"OK, that's enough for now. Interview terminated at four fifty." Koivu switched off the recorder, and Nordström gave me a confused look.

"That was the official interview. Now let's move on to the unofficial part, between colleagues." Giving Nordström a crooked grin, I set my feet up on the table with the soles of my shoes facing him. Koivu thought for a second, then stood up and asked if we wanted any coffee. We both did.

"So, are you really claiming you didn't know Lulu Nightingale, even though you're a lead investigator on sex trafficking at the NBI? You all must have had Lulu under surveillance."

Nordström sighed and leaned forward so he could reach the tips of my shoes. "Maria, Maria." He shook my shoes, but I didn't move my legs away. "I said I knew who Lulu Nightingale was. We weren't tracking her, but the Helsinki PD was. After that one procurement case, Lulu never hired anyone else and tried to stay inside the law."

Koivu arrived with the coffee. Nordström glanced at his suspiciously and then tasted it.

"Is your department cutting back on coffee appropriations too?" he asked. I thought the coffee was remarkably weak too, but I still poured a splash of milk into mine.

"You said the life of a prostitute is cheap. Who would have wanted to take Lulu's life?"

Nordström quickly finished his coffee but sat in silence for a long time. Fortunately, when the coffee came he'd let go of my foot.

"You must know what the situation is like all over the metro area. Girls come and go. Some are junkies, some are just coming over the border looking for a better life, and some . . . some are just children sold into slavery by evil bastards in the former Soviet states. There's something for every taste, if you know where to look. I'd start looking for Lulu's murderer among the people who are threatened by a woman working independently and therefore might serve as an example to other girls."

"Names?"

"If I had those, they'd already be behind bars." Suddenly Nordström stood up. "I have to pick up my car from the garage. I'll let you know if my sources hear anything about Lulu. And Maria, you look tired. Put your subordinates to work and go home and get some rest. Aren't your kids still pretty young?"

"Their dad is watching them. What about you?"

"The twins are with my wife. I mean, my ex-wife. Next week I get to play daddy again for the weekend."

Nordström gave a handshake just as crushing as when he arrived, then turned and opened the door. When he was halfway through, he turned back.

"Oh yeah, and Kristian says hi. He's working as a consultant for Europol. He said he can't believe a girl as smart as you is slaving away for peanuts in Espoo. He said he expected more of you." Nordström closed the door hard after him. I couldn't help but smile. Even after twenty years, Kristian hadn't forgiven me for doing better than him in school. We were just like so many valedictorian girls and unindustrious boys: two decades after graduating, the good-for-nothing boys enjoyed high-paid positions and the girls worked themselves to death for next to nothing.

"What's he hiding?" Koivu's question interrupted my thoughts.

"What do you mean?"

"I was watching his gestures. His hands fidgeted, and he was generally tense. I don't think it was just irritation about being interrogated."

"Are you thinking that maybe after his divorce he started paying for it?"

"Or before. He's a cop, and you know that sometimes the job can offer certain benefits."

"Tell me more."

To my surprise Koivu blushed. "Think about it. A girl gets caught soliciting on the street or in a bar. What would be better than making a deal with the police? And Nordström could have visited Lulu without breaking any laws, just to question her, and still be worried about how that looks."

"The thing that confuses me is that he refused to give us any names. Surely he knows who runs the meat markets in the city. We'll have to figure it out ourselves, since he won't tell us. Let's have Puupponen and Ursula dig into it." I stretched my shoulders. A session on a rowing machine would do them good. "Will you call Pastor Pihlaja? Let's try to talk to her tomorrow right after Saarnio. Send me a text when it's scheduled, OK?"

Koivu nodded. I told him to go home, then went to have a chat with IT. Haapio hadn't even cracked the passwords yet.

"What about the disks?"

Haapio grinned. "This little tart of yours knew what she was doing. These are all protected with a PGP program. Maybe they were only in those tampon boxes to keep them from getting destroyed by accident."

"What's PGP?"

"Encryption. We'll have to try to crack the keys, and there's no guarantee they're the same as the passwords on the computer. How many hours of overtime do I have budgeted for the weekend?"

"Six," I pulled out of thin air, since I hadn't even thought about that yet. Kaartamo was going to have my head for this, but there wasn't another option. We had to get Lulu's computer open.

When I arrived home, Antti was reading to Taneli. Iida was playing with her Barbies on the living room floor. Everything was normal and peaceful, and a shaft of light from the kids' room fell on the entryway floor. Antti had left me a little salmon lasagna, which I ate and washed down with buttermilk. Then I took the laundry from the clean basket, folded it, and put it away, and I even ironed a couple of Iida's shirts. It was a nice change of pace after a day of nonstop talking.

"Mom, what's a whore?" Iida asked from the floor, still immersed in her doll play.

I froze. One of our parenting principles was that we would always answer our children's questions, no matter how uncomfortable that made us. But how could I explain this in a way that an eight-year-old would understand?

"A whore is a person who has sex with other people for money. And sex is the thing men and women do together to make babies."

"Oh, like sleeping together," Iida said, apparently satisfied with my explanation. Her game continued, but after a few moments, she said, "Can kids be whores?"

The true answer would have been yes, unfortunately, but I lied and said that they couldn't, though I disliked bending the truth. It seemed as though someone at school had been talking about Lulu's death. In the headlines, she had been referred to as a sex worker or an owner of an escort service, but how people were talking about her was something else entirely.

"Let's go read now too. You have practice tomorrow at ten, so you need to be asleep by nine. Dad's taking you. I have work."

"Boring! Why can't you both ever be home at the same time?" Iida grabbed *Poor Iris* from the shelf. She loved Anni Swan's books for young girls. Reading with her curled up on her bed, we came to the part about the death of Iris's friend Ulla, which I cried over simply because Iida did.

After the children fell asleep, I started getting ready to go out.

"Where are you off to now?" Antti asked over the top of his book.

"Work." I wanted to watch the tape of Tero Sulonen's interrogation, read the autopsy report, and prepare for the press conference in the morning.

Antti gave me a long look.

"Don't you have working hours at all? Or are you really this bad at organizing your time? You have to sleep sometime too!"

I didn't have the energy to fight or even to slam the door behind me. And I didn't want to disturb the children and the neighbors. But I was angry, and because of this I drove faster than I should have and in the garage nearly managed to hit the wall in front of my parking spot. How many resolutions had I made about working nights and weekends, and how many times had I broken them? I tried to convince myself that I had a right to be away from home for work too, just like Antti was more and more all the time. But something inside nagged at me, telling me my logic was flawed.

Although it was the weekend and therefore Patrol was busy, the rest of the building was quiet. Only the most urgent cases kept anyone working: serious drug offenses and homicides. The upper floors were dark, and in our unit's hallway only one light burned.

Ursula had left a copy of Sulonen's interview tape and the autopsy report on my desk. First I glanced at the latter. Kirsti Grotenfelt, who in the parlance of our unit was still "that new pathologist," even though she'd been in the position for more than two years, was a better writer than her predecessor. The lab results hadn't come in yet, but Grotenfelt was already sure we were dealing with cyanide simply based on the color of the blood.

There had been bruising on Lulu's chest that was consistent with Nordström's attempt at CPR. On the right clavicle was a bite mark and there were welts on the inner thighs, the source of which I tried not to contemplate. Lulu's medical history included two broken ribs, both within the past two years, a tubal ligation the previous year, and two abortions when she was a teenager. After that she'd taken birth control pills. There were no indications of sexually transmitted disease in her official health records.

I remembered what Autio had said about Lulu's childhood home. Had the little girl who grew up surrounded by cross-stitch on the walls found her dream job? Why had Lulu chosen to sell her body? Why had she chosen a profession that now made her just one more dead whore in so many people's minds? Why had she chosen to be someone a lot of people were glad to be rid of?

6

"You receive a lot of benefits from your job: room and board, a car. And what else?" Ursula Honkanen asked intently. Tero Sulonen stared at her like a stone statue. His face was covered in sweat, and he kept dabbing it with a paper napkin.

"That was all . . . It's all in my contract."

Ursula snorted, and her red fingernails tapped the tabletop. The video captured them sitting in Interrogation Room One, a cramped cellar room where the interrogators and their subject were so close to each other that they fit in the same camera frame and could have hit, or kissed, each other. The table was less than two feet wide. Ursula was the more active questioner, as usual, since she enjoyed interrogations and presumably the power that went along with them. She didn't know about the poems he wrote. We'd found them at the same time the video was being made. Ursula was going to rake Sulonen over the coals.

At twenty-eight, Tero Sulonen was younger than I'd imagined. He was from the Vantaa suburbs north of Helsinki, from one of the drearier housing projects. His parents had moved south from Iisalmi in the 1970s, and his mother was the child of a family of Karelian evacuees. After finishing the required years of comprehensive school at the standard age of sixteen, he'd spent a couple of years unemployed before taking a security guard course and beginning work as a guard at a warehouse. Then followed a few gigs as a bouncer before he ended up at the Mikado. Ursula listened with a look of amusement as Sulonen explained his background, and Puupponen recorded the main points.

"I'm going to ask you again, because I don't think you fully comprehend. Did you and Lulu Nightingale have a sexual relationship?"

Sulonen's blush was visible even on the grainy, washed out image.

"No," he said firmly.

"Did you want one?"

Sulonen's head began to sink and his lips pursed as he wiped his brow again.

"Why are you asking that?"

"Did you lust after Lulu Nightingale?"

The water running down Sulonen's face was no longer just droplets of sweat.

"I offered to marry her and support her so she wouldn't have to do it anymore . . . But she just laughed and said she liked her work and the freedom it gave her." Now Sulonen wept openly, shaking and sobbing. I fast-forwarded the tape because no one said anything for a while.

Once Sulonen calmed down, Ursula returned to the events of the night of Lulu's death. According to Sulonen, Lulu had been in a good mood all day. She didn't have any clients and had slept in until noon before going to the gym and having a massage. Then she started her makeup.

"Lulu was so thorough. I don't understand how dolling yourself up can take three hours, but that's how long Lulu spent because she didn't want to rush."

"Women," Puupponen could be heard saying with a sigh, presumably trying to take the good-cop role, but Ursula's glare silenced him, and Sulonen didn't seem to be listening anyway.

"She sang to herself and said that this was going to be the show of her life, that people were going to remember this for a long time. That a sex bomb was going to set off a news bomb on live TV."

I tensed at the same moment as Ursula did on the tape. *Don't screw this up!* I found myself screaming at Ursula in my mind.

"What did Lulu mean by that?" Ursula continued calmly, but I could see that the tapping of her fingernails on the tabletop had grown feverish.

Sulonen stared for a long time and then shook his head. "I don't know. She didn't tell me everything. I've learned that I shouldn't be too curious."

Ursula tried to press for more. "Did Lulu intend to out one of her important clients? Was she planning to strip or something?" Sulonen didn't have an answer. He just repeated that Lulu was in a good mood and that he didn't believe for a second that she'd committed suicide.

"Not Lulu . . . She loved life. And when I find out who did this to her, I'm going to do the same thing to them . . ." Sulonen had to wipe the tears away again.

Puupponen changed the topic to Lulu's clients. Sulonen claimed he didn't know much about them. They'd set the studio up so that the customer wouldn't realize that anyone was on the premises besides himself and Lulu. When someone came over, Sulonen would sit in his room watching movies with headphones on, watching for the light alarm, hoping that Lulu wasn't getting into any trouble.

"I wasn't interested in them. I'd seen enough at the Mikado. Why would I have wanted to see a bunch of horny guys getting off anyway? That seems kind of perverted."

"How could you not be interested? Didn't you realize you could make money by getting information on Lulu's customers? I'm sure they would have been only too happy to pay to keep their little adventures at your establishment secret from their wives or bosses," Ursula said, taking over the conversation again. Puupponen closed his mouth and didn't ask whatever question he'd had ready. Sulonen believed Lulu's customer records were on her computer, since he'd seen her looking at them before, but he'd never tried to see for himself.

"What would I have needed money for? I had a job and everything I wanted."

I thought of his servant's room at the back of a sex studio. Maybe that was the peak of Sulonen's life up to this point.

"Since she had you, Lulu apparently thought she needed protecting. Why?"

"Sometimes clients got difficult. It didn't happen often, though, because Lulu was careful about who she took on, and she had a lot of regulars she trusted."

"What happened when someone got difficult?"

"Then Lulu pressed the panic button, and I intervened."

"The cavalry arrived, is that it?"

"No, just me. What cavalry?"

Puupponen snorted and then tried to stifle his laughter, but Ursula's face was still steely.

"Forget it," Ursula said with a sigh.

"There were a couple of clients she needed me for. One wanted me to put on a uniform and watch while Lulu disciplined him. That turned him on. I didn't like it. Once he asked for me to kick him. He paid extra, and Lulu gave me a bonus. And then there was another one who wanted me to wrap him and Lulu up like mummies and tie them together. But I wasn't involved otherwise." Sulonen wrung his hands as he talked, but Ursula's eyes radiated a genuine curiosity.

"Did Lulu really keep a full-time bodyguard just because of a few clients? That can't be the whole truth."

"I'm not lying! Of course the mafia threatened Lulu, tried to make her work for them. Fucking Russians. As if Lulu was just some cheap street whore stealing their business. Every time someone new came on the scene we had to negotiate with them all over again. And I couldn't even get a concealed carry permit because of my convictions. We had to be careful. And now they finally got her. They must have followed us . . ."

"So you suspect that the Russian mafia killed Lulu?" Puupponen and Ursula asked at nearly the same time. Sulonen just nodded and swallowed his tears.

They gave him some time to calm down before continuing the questioning. I paused the tape for a minute and got myself some coffee. My footsteps echoed in the empty hallway differently than they did during the daytime, and the air smelled of cleaning fluids. The custodian had already been through and wouldn't come again until Monday night. There were no cookies in the break room, just old, soft crispbread. When Lähde had been around, the cookie supply never ran out. That was the only reason I missed him.

Once I had my sad little snack, I returned to the video. "What kind of threats did Lulu get? And who threatened her?" Ursula asked. Sulonen talked about anonymous phone calls and slashed car tires. Once someone had dropped a bag with a bloody heart in it through the mail slot.

"Lulu said it was a pig's heart. I almost puked when I saw it."

"According to our information, no police reports were ever filed about these incidents. Why?"

"Lulu didn't want to. She said she wasn't going to be intimidated, and she had me to protect her. But then this happened . . ." Sulonen's voice cracked again.

I shifted the chairs in the media room around so I could put my feet up. The idea that the Russian mafia was behind Lulu's death was perfectly plausible, but why would they have done it at a television studio, and why use poison? On the tape Sulonen gave more information about their security arrangements, including the fact that Lulu never even went to the corner store for cigarettes without him. Usually Sulonen went out alone for the cigarettes and everything else.

"Who bought that bottle of Fernet Branca? You or Lulu?"

"What bottle?"

"The one in her dressing room."

"Not me. Lulu liked bitters like that, but I didn't know she had a bottle with her . . . Was that what she needed the glass for?"

Ursula didn't reply. Instead she asked, "Had you ever met any of the people at the TV studio before that day?"

"No. I did see a couple of them from the control room when they went in for makeup. It looked like the old lady argued with the makeup artist about her hair. And then there was that cop who started giving orders after that one lady screamed. I tried to get to Lulu, but that bastard wouldn't let me!"

"You really didn't recognize Mauri Hytönen, the man you and Lulu were convicted of beating up two years ago?"

Sulonen's face took on a look of disbelief, and I could almost see the thoughts reordering themselves in his brain. "Lulu was dead. How could I have noticed anything after that? Was that prick there? Did he kill Lulu? Goddamn it!" Sulonen stood up, walked to the door, and kicked it hard enough to leave a dent in the laminate. "Where is he now? You have him in a cell, right? Just give me a little time with that bastard and I'll . . ." Sulonen clenched his fists and grimaced like a weightlifter preparing for a push press. Ursula stood up and, for a moment, appeared uncertain.

"Try to calm down. Hytönen will be interrogated in good time. But first I want to know why you lied. Sit back down."

Sulonen stood there breathing heavily for a while but then let Ursula gently push him into his seat. Maybe Ursula trusted that Sulonen wouldn't hit a woman. Puupponen watched, ready to intervene if necessary. Ursula was tall but slender, Puupponen was muscular but small for a cop, and Sulonen weighed almost as much as the two of them together. And a bodyguard/bouncer might very well have better self-defense skills than a police officer.

"What do you think I lied about?" Sulonen asked.

"You claimed you were in the control room the whole time. But on the surveillance tape you can be seen walking down the dressing room hallway with an empty glass in your hand. Were you on your way to see Lulu? Or perhaps someone else?"

The panic that appeared on Sulonen's face was also a surprise to his interrogators. Sweat began pouring from his forehead again, and he didn't say anything for a long time.

"I never went in any hallway," he finally spluttered.

"The camera doesn't lie. Puupponen, roll the tape!" Ursula said, her eyes fixed on Sulonen's face as if preparing for another outburst of aggression. My subordinates were well prepared—the video was a great idea. I'd have to remember to praise them for that. Sulonen sighed when he saw himself walk quickly into the frame. The glass in his hand was familiar to me, since it was the same one I'd seen on the table in Lulu Nightingale's dressing room: a thick, heavy-looking water glass. The one in Sulonen's hand was empty.

"There you are. What do you think, Puupponen, should we take Tero here to lockup so that he can think about whether he should keep lying to us? We can hold him for probable cause. Which one of us should call the lieutenant?"

Sulonen shook his head, clearly trying to invent an explanation. Finally, he found it:

"Lulu called me. Look at my phone. I can show you." Sulonen punched at his phone and then showed it to Ursula. "See? Lulu called me yesterday at 8:58 p.m." She asked me to bring her a glass. I asked why and she said she was thirsty and didn't want to mess up her lipstick by drinking straight from the bottle. I didn't know what bottle she was talking about. In the control room on the table there was a glass—I don't even know if it was clean—and I just took it and rinsed it out in the bathroom on the way. I swear I rinsed it out! Could something have been on it . . . something that killed Lulu?"

Sulonen didn't receive an answer to his question. Instead Ursula asked what happened next. Her lips were parted, and her eyes shone like a woman in love. She was expecting a confession, but at Sulonen's reply her expression turned to disappointment.

"I knocked on Lulu's door. She opened it just a crack, so I only saw her hand. She whispered that she couldn't come out of her room because someone might see her, and she told me to get out of sight fast. And I did . . . and then I never saw her again."

So Lulu had had a bottle with her! Sulonen began crying, so I fast-forwarded. Ursula interrupted the interview and went outside, apparently to confer with Puupponen. When the conversation started up again, it was brief. Puupponen informed Sulonen that he was free to go. Sulonen exited quickly like a dog fleeing before someone kicks it. I rewound the tape and turned off the VCR.

It was almost eleven o'clock. Tomorrow would be another long day, so I needed to go home and get some rest. Antti was probably already asleep. I visited the ladies' room and splashed cold water on my face, ignoring that what was left of my mascara would run. Who was going to see me? Then I went to fetch my things from my office. When I'd gone to the media room, I'd left my office door open because no one except the cops in my unit and the custodian had access to the hallway. That's why I screamed when I ran straight into a man standing in the doorway.

"Ouch!" Puupponen said, trying not to laugh. "You weren't frightened, were you?"

"Of course I was!" I said, attempting to calm my breathing. I was embarrassed that I'd reacted so strongly. "What are you still doing here?"

"Looking at porn online. What else would a bachelor be doing on a Friday night?" Puupponen grinned. "Actually, I was looking online for more info about Lulu Nightingale and that Oksana girl. Johns can find prostitutes online now. Lulu even has her own website. From which I found out, among other things, that her favorite food is oysters and her favorite drinks are Cava and Fernet Branca."

"Excellent! So anyone could have known that."

"Exactly. I also found the phone numbers for some Russian women offering companionship for lonely gentlemen. Should I call and ask around a bit? Sulonen suspects the mafia. What if Lulu knew who killed Oksana and was going to out them on TV?"

Puupponen's face was tired, but enthusiasm still burned in his eyes. He rubbed his chest. "I'm going to have a bruise, but that's what I get for creeping up on you. I really am sorry."

"Don't sweat it. Ville, this is your second night up. Don't you think you should get some rest before your interviews tomorrow? After you're done with Anna-Maija Mustajoki, you should talk to as many of these friendly Russian women as are willing."

Puupponen grinned. "Ursula can handle the interviews. She likes being in the driver's seat."

I smiled back. "Your charm might be more effective in this case. Come on, I'll drive you home."

The next morning, it was hard to get out of bed even though the sun was shining with the promise of melting snow. Iida demanded to have her pink tights for practice, and of course they were in the wash. And then she complained about the bun I put in her hair.

"Antti, are you going to the library today?"

"Yeah, I thought I might."

"Could you try to find Anna-Maija Mustajoki's memoir? It came out last spring. I think it was called *Everywoman*."

"Does it have something to do with work?" Antti took Taneli's skates, with pieces of fabric rigged as blade guards, off their hook and put them in a tote bag. I admitted that it did, and I couldn't read Antti's expression when he heard my answer. "I probably won't make it to that antinuclear power demonstration then," he said when he saw me putting on my black pinstripe pantsuit.

"No, probably not. I'm sorry." I'd put on enough makeup to look presentable, and now I pulled my own hair back into a bun. At press conferences, it was best to focus the listeners' attention on something other than my appearance.

As I drove I thought through what I would say, and when I arrived at work I was surprisingly calm. The lab results on the glass and the Fernet Branca had come in. The bottle had contained such a large dose of cyanide that it could have killed an entire soccer team. The remaining drops of Fernet Branca left in the cup had also contained cyanide. There was no need for further speculation about the cause of death.

About forty reporters and photographers showed up to the press conference. As I stepped in front of them, I heard one of the tabloid reporters whispering to a journalist from a local radio station. "Hopefully this isn't another one of those information sessions where they inform us there's no information to share."

I told them that we had established Lulu's cause of death but that for investigative reasons we weren't revealing it yet. No one had been arrested, but interviews were continuing at a rapid pace. I tried to choose my words carefully, because the media was an indispensable tool for a detective. That is, when it wasn't our worst enemy. It depended on the journalist—some were still interested in finding out the truth, while others would rather devote themselves to chasing scoops.

When I finished talking, a flood of shouted questions washed over me.

"Do you know why Lulu Nightingale was killed?" asked the same local radio reporter, followed by someone from the STT newswire. "Does Nightingale's death have anything to do with the prostitution allegations against the Russian Trade Representation office earlier this year?" A tabloid reporter asked about Lulu's clients. For these people, Lulu Nightingale wasn't just another anonymous dead whore. I couldn't help remembering another press briefing I'd held around Christmastime about a homeless wino who had been killed by one of his drinking buddies. Only one reporter had showed up.

When the press conference finally ended, I was relatively pleased. At least they hadn't ripped me to shreds.

I picked up Koivu at the Westend bus station and drove the two miles west to Haukilahti. The Saarnio family's house sat on a hill set back from the bay, but when we drove up the driveway, we found that there was a view of the water. The weather was fantastic, and the ice was full of skaters, pedestrians, and fishermen at their holes. I would have liked to be one of them. A blackbird landed on a bird feeder. I hadn't heard its trill yet, because spring was late. Every year that sound managed to cheer me up.

I rang the Saarnios' doorbell. Riitta Saarnio answered. She looked feeble, and it seemed difficult for her to shake our hands. Still she'd managed to put on some makeup, and she was wearing cotton trousers, a cream-colored knit blouse, and house slippers. The straight hair that extended to her shoulders was half-brown and half-gray. Riitta Saarnio seemed like one of those women who insisted on presenting a tidy outward appearance regardless of what chaos might be reigning inside.

We were led into a large living room, and Mrs. Saarnio motioned for us to sit on the sofa. She politely asked if we wanted tea. I said thank you but no for both of us, even though I knew Koivu was always hungry and thirsty. It was clearly best to get this interview over with as quickly as possible.

"I'm a little embarrassed I broke down like that," Saarnio said apologetically as she set a bowl of fruit down in front of Koivu on the coffee table. He took a banana and opened his laptop.

"Discovering a body can be a shock for anyone, even a professional," I replied.

"But I shouldn't have run into the studio like that and ruined the whole show! I should have just announced that the final guest was ill. Ilari would have managed. He always does."

I interrupted Saarnio for a moment so that I could turn on the recorder, even though it bothered me to do so since she'd begun talking on her own. But this was an official interview, which meant we had to go by the book. Saarnio took a seat in a chair across from us. She told us that she had arrived at the studio around six, at which point Länsimies informed her that Lulu didn't need makeup since she would handle it herself.

"I think Nuppu was a little offended at first since she takes pride in her work. But she's a single mom, and her toddler was sick, so she didn't want to leave her with the babysitter any longer than necessary. Nuppu is a good, affordable makeup artist, so we try to be flexible. I didn't mind letting her leave early. Even though my title is producer-director, I don't always have to be watching what Ilari and the cameramen are doing. Mostly I try to make sure they don't focus only on Ilari and the most beautiful female guest all the time, and that they remember to capture the other guests' reactions to what the speaker says. Ilari agreed to sending Nuppu home too when I said I could bring in the final guest."

Saarnio confirmed that only she, Länsimies, and the makeup artist had known whom the guests were, but she claimed that Länsimies chose the topic of prostitution himself.

"I wasn't as enthusiastic about it. We have enough sex talk in the media already. There's more to life than that. And, to tell the truth, I wasn't very excited about having Lulu Nightingale on our show. I would have preferred someone who hadn't chosen the profession quite so happily. Lulu gave such a one-dimensional picture of things—or she would have if she'd had a chance to speak."

"Do you and Länsimies often disagree about topics and guests? How did you two end up working together?" Riitta Saarnio and Ilari Länsimies didn't seem like the most natural pair. I might have expected a man like Länsimies to choose some cute young thing who worshipped him as an assistant, but Riitta Saarnio didn't seem like a mere assistant. She did own 35 percent of West Man Productions after all, so theoretically she and Länsimies were on equal footing.

"Ilari and I have known each other and worked together for years. I've spent most of my career in TV documentaries, as a producer for various companies. But the last one went under after the last round of cuts at the Finnish Broadcasting Company. I happened to run into Ilari at a cocktail party, and when we were trading news, he suggested that we start our own production company. You know we don't just produce *Surprise Guests*, we also have a cooking show and a series about celebrity pets. We just produce those, though. Other people do the hosting and directing. I'm really thankful for Ilari's suggestion, because finding work as a fifty-five-year-old woman in the media sector isn't easy, and I didn't want to be forced into early retirement."

The devil in me said that the wife of Arto "Hatchetman" Saarnio would hardly have suffered from privation even if she was out of a job, but the feminist in me understood a woman wanting to earn her keep.

"Ilari and I rarely disagreed since he wasn't interested in only interviewing vapid celebrities all the time either. We've had guests like the president and the CEO of Nokia, and that's the standard we try to maintain. *Surprise Guests* is a talk show designed for adults, or, to put it more bluntly, for middle-aged adults." Saarnio gave a sudden smile, and her face was momentarily radiant. "I think Ilari wants to influence how people think, and this prostitution show was a message to Parliament. Ilari has a lot of friends there."

"Did you meet Lulu before the program?"

"Once. Usually one visit with a guest is enough, but Ilari also went to Lulu's . . . office. My meeting with her was here at our place. Appearing together anywhere public wasn't an option because the guests have to be a surprise. Lulu was quick at repartee, and she could back up her opinions. Ilari was happy since beautiful, smart women are the guests he prefers."

"Why didn't you participate in the second meeting?"

"It wasn't necessary. Ilari was the one hosting the show," Saarnio said tersely.

"Did you see Lulu before the broadcast?"

"Briefly. I was waiting for her at the door at eight thirty. Her bodyguard was a surprise, but I decided to let him in without asking Ilari because Lulu demanded it. The bodyguard wanted to go to the control room, and I didn't see anything wrong with that. We don't use it much, and it's really just left over from when that floor of the building was a law office. The previous owner had all the security equipment installed, and we inherited it as part of the sale."

"Did you talk to Lulu?"

"Just as much as was necessary to show her the dressing room. She seemed excited to have the chance to talk to such a large audience. Poor girl. Was it a very painful death?" Saarnio's composed facade collapsed all at once, and she began to shake. "I can't bear to think that we were making a television program while someone was dying alone just down the hall . . ." She began breathing rapidly, and it looked like the beginnings of hyperventilation. She leaned back and closed her eyes, obviously concentrating on getting her breath under control.

"Tell us how you found the body, then we'll be done," I said gently after a few moments. Koivu took a plum from the bowl. Behind me I heard padded footfalls, and a large, dark-gray cat appeared. Its fur was long and bushy, and a white stripe decorated its nose on one side. The cat jumped onto its owner's lap and began to purr. That seemed to help Saarnio finally calm down.

"There isn't much to tell. I knocked on Lulu's door when it was time. When she didn't answer, I knocked again. I peeked in the women's restroom, since sometimes guests end up in there if they're overly nervous. It was empty. When she didn't answer the third time I knocked, I opened the door. She was lying there on the floor in that strange position, and her face was twisted. I knew immediately that only a dead person could look like that, and . . . Then I don't really remember. I just had to get out of there, so I ran into the studio and . . ." Saarnio was shaking again, and the cat stood up, looking offended. It rubbed its face against Saarnio's cheek and then curled up again.

"So you had a key to Lulu's dressing room?"

"I have a keycard that opens all six dressing rooms."

"Do you have the only one like that?"

"No. Ilari and Nuppu have ones too. Guests receive cards for their own rooms, which they turn in when they leave. Of course, sometimes they forget, and it's a pain for us because reprogramming the locks is complicated and expensive." Saarnio seemed to calm down when she could talk about something other than Lulu's death. Suddenly her expression changed again, first to one of confusion and then to horror.

"Nuppu's keycard . . . She left in a hurry and forgot her purse on the table. She called later and asked for me to put it out of sight for her. I did, but the keycard and the rest of the contents of the purse were out on her makeup table for at least half an hour, out where anyone could have taken it. I wonder if Nuppu ended up picking up her purse. We'll have to check if the card is there. Shall I call her right now?"

"No need. No one is being allowed into the studio yet. Our officer on guard can check the purse once we have Ms. Koskela's permission." I took a deep breath. This was a good discovery, maybe even a decisive discovery. A lost keycard could mean that someone unauthorized could have accessed Lulu's dressing room. But at what point was the poison placed in the bottle? Lulu hadn't left her room. And at what point would this unidentified person have entered the studio?

Could he have been waiting since earlier in the day?

"Did anyone visit the studio before the broadcast? For example, any delivery or maintenance workers?"

"Thursday? No . . . Although I wasn't there the whole day. Ilari and I didn't come in until ten, because on production days it's good to sleep in. We spent a couple of hours reviewing plans for the show, and then Ilari went home to rest. I handled the technical arrangements with the sound and camera crew and then went to Tapiola for a massage. I guess someone could have visited while I was out . . ."

The sound of footsteps and then a cough came from the hallway, as if Arto Saarnio wanted to announce his presence before stepping into the room.

"That's all the time the doctor allowed. We can't overtax my wife."

Mr. Saarnio had probably listened to our conversation. He walked over to his wife and placed his hands on her shoulders. The cat stood up to greet him, and Mr. Saarnio gave a little smile as he petted it. His wife had closed her eyes and looked calm again. A ping from Koivu's computer indicated that the interview record had been saved. "I mean what I say, Detective Kallio. We've tried to be cooperative, so I expect you to do the same. Can you do anything to prevent all these reporters from calling us? I don't want any more headlines like this." He showed us a tabloid with the headline "Leading Businessman's Wife Finds Dead Prostitute." I'd only had time to read the morning paper, so these articles were new to me.

"That is unfortunate, but we have free speech in this country, and that headline is technically true." I stood up. I shook hands with Mrs. Saarnio and then her husband. The cat jumped down onto the floor and followed us, along with Arto Saarnio, to the front door. I bent down to pet it.

"Beautiful animal."

"Miisi is smart too. She walks on a leash just like a dog, which is good, because otherwise we couldn't let her out at all. That would be against the law after all." Arto Saarnio smirked, and his face filled with laugh lines.

"Don't risk it. The fines can be steep," I replied and smiled back, although what I probably should have done is confront him about the job losses at Copperwood. I wouldn't dare tell my sister Eeva that I'd been friendly to "Hatchetman" Saarnio.

"What now?" Koivu asked as I started the car and drove down the slippery hill to the main road.

"Time to go to church. That's all there is for now," I answered and steered the car toward Tapiola. Pastor Terhi Pihlaja had agreed to meet with us between a wedding and funeral.

7

I'd gradually learned to like the square, modernist concrete edifice that was the Tapiola Church, despite my gloomy first impression. So many memories were connected to it now, though, both beloved and brutal. I'd been to funerals here for Antti's father and my coworker Juhani Palo. Antti's cousin's wedding last summer belonged to the good memories. I hadn't met Terhi Pihlaja during any of these services, however.

When we entered the foyer of the church, organ music was playing in the chapel. Judging from the dress of the congregants, I concluded this was a funeral.

"Hello!" Pastor Pihlaja, wearing her clerical garb, was already walking toward us. "One of my colleagues is handling the current service, but I'm up again in an hour. Let's head over to the parish and we can speak in my office. This way, please."

Pastor Terhi Pihlaja's office was cluttered, with papers and books heaped on the desk and floor. At least the chairs were empty, but there were only two of them. Pihlaja fetched a stool from another room and placed it across from us, then sat on it. Koivu shifted papers away from one corner of the desk to make space for his laptop. One of the papers, a confirmation class schedule, fell at my feet. A painting of the Madonna and Child graced the wall, looking ornate and Catholic in these ascetic Lutheran surroundings. Pastor Pihlaja was thirty-one and after her ordination had worked first in Lohja and then here in Tapiola. She happened to live just a few buildings down from Antti and me, and she said she'd seen me out running sometimes.

"I stick to Nordic walking. My knees can't handle jogging. Writing sermons is easier outside while exercising than sitting here at my desk. I imagine being a police detective is similar to being a pastor—you often meet people in their moments of greatest distress."

"Absolutely. You at least get to celebrate baptisms and weddings. And sometimes you get to go on TV talk shows. Why did Ilari Länsimies invite you on his program?"

"Some time back we both presented at a seminar on the relationship between the church and the media. I wrote my thesis on it. At the seminar, I criticized news coverage that always paints the church as an institution built around prohibitions and used gay marriage as an example of an area in which attitudes are changing. That was probably where it started. I had to think about it for a long time, but somehow Länsimies talked me into it. He's good at that. I almost felt hypnotized."

"Why did you hesitate?"

"Some of my congregation disagree with me, but I prefer to foster cooperation rather than deepen divides between people who think differently, although of course I must have the courage to speak my mind. And it was quite a coincidence that Lilli and I were invited for the same program, even though we didn't end up having a chance to meet."

"Did you know Lulu Mäkinen?"

Pihlaja's eyes went wide. "Don't you know? Lilli and I grew up together. We were in the same class. We went to elementary school and middle school together in Inkoo, and high school in Virkkala. Lilli lived in town, and I lived out in the countryside, so we only saw each other at school and on the bus and didn't really run in the same circles. I was a good churchy kind of girl, and Lilli was . . . well, different. Even when she was young she wanted to stand out from the crowd and be something."

"What was that something?"

"Famous. A star. Nowadays every other teenager dreams of fame, but fifteen years ago it wasn't like that yet. Lilli wanted to travel the world and meet important people. She went to Helsinki to watch bands play and tried to get backstage. I imagine I thought I was better than all those tough girls who came to school Monday morning with hickeys on their necks. I was a condescending hypocrite." Pastor Pihlaja smiled, but the smile was strangely introspective, not meant for me and Koivu.

"Did Ilari Länsimies know that you and Lulu were classmates?"

"How would he have known? Of course it would have added to the drama of the show, but poor Lilli never got her chance to speak."

"Did you keep track of Lulu's career?"

"Not actively, but I knew about it. Once I even visited her website, out of curiosity. But I just thought there was something sad about it."

I continued to ask Pihlaja about more details of Lulu's childhood. To hear her tell it, Lulu had despised her parents' way of life and their little country village, which luckily for her was only an hour from Helsinki.

"I guess the Mäkinens were genuinely poor. My brother went over there sometimes since he played on the same soccer team as Lilli's brother. I remember my brother commenting on how old and worn out Lilli's brother's cleats were. Lilli started working summers picking strawberries when she was just in middle school, and in high school she was a cleaner in some building. It was the kind of hard work that messed up her fingernails. It's funny how much you can remember when you try. And there's no denying that Lilli was a memorable person." Pihlaja fell silent for a moment, looking past me into the middle distance.

"And she hitchhiked . . . Once we picked her up on our way to Helsinki. My mom and I were going to buy new winter coats, and Lilli was outside in a storm at the Degerby junction. She'd only been able to get a ride that far. Mom took pity on her and asked my father to pick her up so she wouldn't end up with some truck driver. I think Lilli hated me even more after that—the daughter of a cantor would never dream of hitchhiking and had enough money to go all the way to Helsinki to buy a coat. Yes . . . I can remember her saying I looked like someone's aunt in that coat. And I probably did. It was a navy-blue quilted overcoat. Oh heavens, you should have seen me after she made fun of me in front of this boy named Masa. 'Terhi doesn't dare to wear anything but old potato sacks so no one has any sinful thoughts.' I remember that night I cried myself to sleep. I guess Lilli realized somehow that I had a crush on Masa. She always had a good eye for relationships between people."

"What was she like at school?"

"Average. She didn't try very hard at anything but languages. She probably thought that would be useful in the future. She always copied her math homework from these popular guys Jussi or Pave, and even back then people talked about what she did for the boys in return, but you know how teenagers talk. At that age, everyone is still confused by their sexuality and thinks that everyone else is more experienced." Pihlaja glanced at her watch and then began to riffle through her papers. She finally found the one she was looking for on top of her computer.

"My funeral sermon. Good thing I found it! I have pretty good diary entries from high school, and I can look at them if you need more information about Lilli when she was young. I do remember that Lilli didn't like that there were different rules for boys than for girls. People called her a whore even back then, but she just laughed at them. She walked her own road. That's how Lilli was."

"Did you ever see each other after graduation?"

"No. Lilli went abroad somewhere right after, maybe to Switzerland or somewhere like that, and I went to Helsinki to study theology. We haven't had any class reunions. It's sad we never had a chance to meet again. I could hardly believe it when Riitta Saarnio rushed into the studio like that and started screaming that Lilli was dead. I'd thought a lot about her choice of profession after agreeing to go on the program."

I saw Pihlaja's cheeks flush. "I wanted to see her with my own eyes, but that policeman wouldn't let me. Did she suffer?"

I didn't answer and just scanned the papers and books stacked around the room. Some of the books were church manuals, some theology, but I also saw poetry and a P. D. James mystery set in a seminary. The top drawer of the desk was open, and I saw a packet of tissues and a lipstick. Although Pastor Pihlaja seemed open and cooperative, I couldn't shake the feeling that it was partly an act. Maybe that was just me, since I usually felt uncomfortable around clergy. I imagine I was afraid they would demand that I explain my religious views, which I avoided thinking about because I just didn't know. Antti was a confirmed atheist, but I wasn't able to think that simplistically. Sometimes I prayed, but I never had a clear idea what I was praying to. At least Antti had agreed to baptizing our children to please the grandparents. Some of our kids' godparents were what people referred to as fairy godparents since they didn't belong to the church and so couldn't officially fill the role.

"Those diaries might be helpful—I wouldn't mind hearing more from them. Do you remember any particularly close friends Lulu had during school?"

"There was a girl named Niina Räsänen, but I haven't seen her since school either. I imagine Lilli's parents would know better. Do you have any other questions? I want to spend a few minutes meditating before the funeral. This was a difficult situation. A thirteen-year-old girl who died of leukemia."

"What are you going to say? That it was God's will?" I asked, perhaps more pointedly than intended. Koivu shot me a surprised look, but Pastor Pihlaja just shook her head.

"God isn't cruel. He can be stern but not cruel. Those are two different things. You police have to trust in facts to solve crimes. You can't rely on mysteries. But in my work, you see that not everything can be explained. Anyway, I'll have time to look at my diaries tomorrow night. I'll call if I find anything interesting." I gave Pastor Pihlaja my card, and then we left her in peace. Through the crack in the door I saw her taking a seat at her desk, bowing her head of shiny black hair, and clasping her hands. I hoped she would find words to comfort the family of the dead girl.

I didn't have to be the bearer of bad news to families much anymore—that task fell to others—but I still encountered sorrow. In my bag, I carried pamphlets from various support and crisis services, which I distributed as necessary. Sometimes even the interviews we conducted seemed therapeutic since they gave people an opportunity to talk about their deceased loved one, but the deaths I encountered were usually violent and sudden. I hoped I could help by finding the truth, even though it was often brutal and increased some people's agony. Still I believed it was better to know.

"What did you think of that?" Koivu asked as we walked to the car. "Quite the coincidence. Could Pihlaja have guessed that Lulu would be on the program too? And taken the cyanide with her just in case? Getting it isn't very hard. Butterfly collectors always have it. Apparently Autio's brother collects butterflies, and Gideon was shocked when he found a hundred grams of calcium cyanide in his brother's shed."

The sun shone brightly, but the car's thermometer read negative six degrees Celsius. I could have been getting a nice tan out on the ski track right now. We went back to the station to write up a summary of our interviews, which didn't seem to have cleared up anything. I still wasn't able to get into Lulu's computer or disks. That was frustrating.

Ursula and Puupponen sat in the break room arguing about something, but they stopped when they saw me and Koivu. They had just come from questioning the cameramen and the memoirist Anna-Maija Mustajoki.

"She didn't have any contacts with Lulu, and she said she hadn't even heard of a prostitute named Nightingale. She doesn't read any of the gossip rags. She generally seemed kind of uptight. And the cameramen confirmed what we already knew: they never went into the dressing room hallway."

Puustjärvi and Autio were in Salo questioning Lulu Mäkinen's sister. Ursula wanted to continue interrogating Tero Sulonen since she thought he was our strongest suspect.

"Mark my words, somebody bribed that dude. Whores blackmail their clients all the time. I bet some disgruntled john chose for it to happen during the television show so there'd be other suspects besides Sulonen."

"So the poison was in the Fernet Branca bottle, but how the hell did it get in there?" I asked. "And whose bottle was it? Did Lulu bring it with her? I'll ask Helsinki to see if they can find out if Sulonen or Lulu bought any Fernet Branca from one of the state liquor stores near their apartment recently." Forensics had processed the two plastic bags from Alko found at the Blue Nightingale, but neither had contained a receipt.

"Hey, Ursula, you feeling lonely?" Puupponen said with a grin. "I made a list of every woman I could find offering 'companionship.' We'll interview them today."

Ursula nodded but seemed impatient. I'd heard she transferred to Violent Crime from White Collar because white-collar crime investigations were years-long desk jockey affairs that rarely entailed any action or drama. What had she thought she'd find here? Continuous gunfights and cat-and-mouse games with serial killers?

Ursula took the arm Puupponen was offering, then turned as they were leaving.

"Have the phone records arrived yet?"

"Puustjärvi and Autio are handling them. Come see me at ten tomorrow, and we'll see where we are. Let's keep our fingers crossed that today is peaceful. We don't need any more work."

I hadn't eaten since breakfast, and my stomach was growling. The drop in blood sugar made my hands tremble. My emergency salmiakki stash in my office seemed tragically unsatisfactory given the circumstances. I grabbed a glass of juice from the machine, which helped just enough for me to feel safe driving home.

When I opened the front door, I heard talking and laughing coming from the living room, and a moment passed before I realized that Antti was on the phone. Something in his tone of voice made me pause there in the entryway, although of course I should have walked in and made my presence known.

"Yeah, that would be great, but let's see what Maria's work situation is like . . . Yeah, that case has her all tied up, and of course she can't think about anything else . . . Yes, you're right, and you know how much I'd like to stay . . . Exactly, and it's only two weeks until then. It's going to be a blast . . ." A strange trepidation shot through my body. Who was Antti talking to in such a flirtatious tone?

Dropping my bag loudly on the floor, I forced myself to walk into the living room. The way Antti flinched when he saw me only made me feel worse.

"Maria's here. Call if you hear anything new about Paris. Thanks . . . You too. Bye!" Antti hung up the phone but didn't immediately look at me. "You're home early. I thought you'd be out all night again. That was Virve. We were talking about our conference in Paris. It's coming up in two weeks."

Of course I remembered. I would have gladly gone with Antti, since we hadn't gone anywhere farther than Helsinki alone together in years. But I had to save my vacation time for the summer to make our childcare work.

"Both copies of Mustajoki's memoir were checked out, and there's a waiting list, so I went to the bookstore." Antti handed me a book, its cover a collage of action shots of Anna-Maija Mustajoki at various ages. "We can probably deduct it from our taxes since it's work related. How's the investigation going?"

"Slowly. How're the kids?"

"Taneli's napping. He skated hard at practice, and then we were outside all afternoon. Iida's in our room reading. There's chicken pasta in the fridge if you haven't eaten. You up for a sauna today?" Antti drew me into his arms, but something about it felt awkward. "Virve's throwing a party on Friday, and she asked me to stay for it. It would be nice to get to know some of the people from the university a little better. I can ask Mom or Marita if they're available to come watch the kids. Do you have to work tomorrow?"

"Yeah." I pulled away and went to heat up the pasta in the microwave, even though that always dried it out. Iida padded into the kitchen carrying Venjamin. We'd tried to teach the cat that he wasn't allowed at the dinner table, but when he smelled the chicken, he jumped out of Iida's arms and tried to climb up. Iida laughed, and I dropped a piece of chicken on the floor and ordered the cat to stay there.

"I did a good single loop today, so now I know that one and the toe loop and the Salchow and the waltz," Iida said, planting her feet together in the loop-takeoff position. "Watch, Mommy, it's like this!" Iida's arm whacked the door of the refrigerator when she jumped, and Venjamin fled in terror. "Mom, why is it so cramped here, and why don't I have my own room? I hate sleeping with Taneli!"

What was I supposed to say to that? I remembered how wonderful it had been when I finally got my own room at the age of twelve. Before that I'd always shared with my sisters, Eeva and Helena. My room was just a tiny closet in the attic, but it had been mine alone, with a door I could lock. Now my parents lived in a big empty house in Arpikylä, and we were crammed into this two-bedroom apartment. That's how life went.

Antti had closed the bedroom door, and I could hear his tapping on the electric piano as he played with headphones on. His regular piano was banished to his sister Marita's house because an apartment building and his intensity of playing weren't a good match. I still had my bass, but I rarely played it anymore, and when I did it was usually unplugged.

Our jam sessions were mostly a thing of the past, since we only would have had time for it after the kids were asleep, and then we needed to be quiet. I'd started longing for the days of being with my band in a grungy garage and turning the dials up to eleven. We weren't always good, but the music was our own. Sometimes I played along with my favorite bands, and the children had a good laugh at my karaoke routine.

Once Iida and Taneli fell asleep, Antti and I took a sauna. In my postsauna languor, I started to read Anna-Maija Mustajoki's memoir. The much-talked-about sexual encounter only lasted a few pages, and for some reason reading it made me feel embarrassed. The male prostitute whom Mustajoki had visited had been a clumsy, frightening junkie with bad teeth. The act itself was a nauseating rut. In 1968, attitudes had been more conservative, and Mustajoki hadn't been willing to talk about her experience publicly. Now she was trying to make it clear that the purpose of her memoir wasn't to present a glossy portrait of herself.

I flipped back and forth through the book, trying to find something to latch onto, something that somehow related to Lulu Nightingale's death. In one chapter, Mustajoki wrote about the role of human trafficking in international crime and the systematic subordination of women, but she presented facts and figures, not individual cases. She was an insightful and humorous writer who didn't really reveal anything about herself. I did notice a few familiar names: Mustajoki and Ilari Länsimies had served on the same Foreign Ministry cultural policy workgroup in the early eighties. Mustajoki described Länsimies as one of those politicians brought up during the Kekkonen era who had more ambition than competence. Länsimies had made the mistake of siding with Ahti Karjalainen in the wrangling surrounding the 1982 presidential election, effectively resulting in an end to his political career.

Antti lay next to me reading his own work papers, and I felt as if we were lying in separate beds, in separate realities. The good-night kiss we exchanged was only a formality. Without it, we both would have started to be afraid.

The morning was bright again, but the snow in the yards and parking lots looked brown and tired. A large icicle hung over the downstairs door, so I stretched up to knock it down before it fell on someone's head. A slight scent of earth thawing hung in the air even though the temperature was still well below freezing. Soon the willows would begin to redden, and the birch branches would turn violet, even though the trees would still have to wait most of a month to leaf out. I felt like I was living on solar power: everything would go fine as long as the sun continued to shine.

I was at the police station well before ten, but I wasn't the first. Ursula was already there and opened her door when she heard my footsteps in the hall. I let out a cry when I saw her bruised face and her right hand, which had a large bandage around the thumb.

"Morning, Maria. I'm going to need to take some sick leave. But I wanted to see you before heading home."

Ursula wasn't wearing any makeup. I'd never seen her au naturel before, not even in the gym. Her skin was pale, and a dark bag hung under the eye that wasn't purple from bruising. Ursula was still at the age when she looked younger without makeup than with it.

"What happened to you?"

"I got beat up last night." Ursula's voice trembled. "Can we go sit somewhere? I haven't slept all night, and I'm feeling a little unsteady."

"Let's go to my office," I suggested and took Ursula by the elbow, apparently not cautiously enough, because she let out a gasp of pain. I let go. "Who did this to you?" I asked once we were sitting on opposite ends of my couch.

"Two men in Helsinki. They just wanted to scare me. They thought I was a prostitute trying to muscle in on their territory. They were Russians or something. Their Finnish sucked."

"What on earth were you doing?" Ursula's short hair stood up at odd angles, and one of her long nails had broken.

"Puupponen and I couldn't really get anything out of the women we talked to. It was the wrong tactic—I told Ville he should have set up dates with them, but he said that would take too long. Better to talk to them on the phone as a cop. But no professional is going to talk to the police. This one girl named Agnuska said she'd known Lulu, but that was all we got. I was so irritated when Puupponen stole my idea about surfing porn sites, and then you praised him for it! Anyway, I had a date on Friday, so I couldn't stay at work, and Ville ended up doing my stuff for me. The date was shitty too. He was just another asshole from Patrol. Then yesterday I got the idea to go over and test the waters at the Mikado, since that was where Lulu and Sulonen met, and I thought someone would have information about her and Oksana. I still think that Sulonen is guilty. Someone paid him off."

"Ursula, you have to tell me before you go out and do things like this! The idea was good, but you can't do it alone." I tried to keep my voice calm. Shouting wouldn't help since the damage had already been done.

"I didn't take any ID with me, not my badge or my driver's license, since I didn't want there to be any chance for someone to find out who I am. I thought in an emergency I'd just claim I was a reporter. It wasn't my first time at the Mikado, and last time I was there I saw Assistant Chief Kaartamo. I think he was looking for company, not working, because he beat it fast when he saw me. But that was last year. Ow!"

Blood had started to trickle from Ursula's nose. I went to grab some tissues from my desk and noticed that my salmiakki box was empty, so I tossed it in the trash. Ursula put her head on her knees, and her spine poked through her shirt in a series of vertebral hills.

"It was a normal night at the club, and there were other cops around. I definitely recognized one guy from the NBI. I remember him from a seminar. Pretty good-looking guy. I was constantly having to turn guys down—of course it's easier to get them talking if they like the merchandise." Ursula was obviously trying to act calmer than she was. "In the restroom, I attempted to talk to a few of the Estonian girls, but they said they didn't know anything about anyone and that they didn't have a clue about any Oksana. I claimed I was an old friend of Lulu's from Zürich." Ursula straightened up and took the tissue away from her face. The bleeding had slowed.

"The second time I was in the restroom, trying to avoid this one drunk guy, I heard Russian coming from one of the stalls. There were two girls in there. I'm sure they said the name Oksana, but that's all I could catch. I spent a long time on my makeup, hoping they would come out. That was probably a mistake. One of them did eventually, a short redhead about forty years old. Her Finnish was terrible. Finally, I had to get out of there because it must have started to look suspicious, with me just sitting there sipping the same Garibaldi and not leaving with anyone. And every time a guy got irritated, it attracted attention."

The nosebleed had stopped, and Ursula lifted her face again. Suddenly there were tears in her eyes.

"I walked to the taxi stop, but there wasn't a single car around. So I thought I'd take a bus. When I got to the little park in front of the Scandic Hotel, two thugs jumped me. I swear, they came out of nowhere. They both started hitting me, and they had some kind of blackjack or something. One held his hand over my mouth, and I bit him hard. They said the Mikado was 'Mishin's' territory, that independents weren't welcome, and that I had better remember that. I tried to scream and left a good scratch on one of their cheeks, but they were pros. It only lasted a minute—they just did their job and disappeared."

"In the middle of the city? And no one intervened? Were there any eyewitnesses?"

"I guess there was probably someone around, but you know how it is. Would you intervene in the middle of the night if you saw two big brutes beating a woman dressed like a whore? And there weren't any cops around. I do remember that one of the guys had a coat with a fur collar. I probably still have hairs from it in my pocket. I was afraid my cheekbone was broken, and I finally got a taxi to take me to the ER, even though the driver complained the whole time about me bleeding on his seats. I said I fell. The nurses asked me if my boyfriend had hurt me and whether I wanted to call the police. I almost laughed. Of course, I couldn't tell them I was a cop, so I said I was a waitress. They gave me a sick leave order until Wednesday. There was a line at the ER, so I didn't get home until six, and I couldn't sleep, so I took a shower and came here."

I sighed. Of course, being a police officer entailed the risk of bodily harm, but it was stupid to take those risks heedlessly. My mind and my body carried reminders of violence, some of which had resulted from my own recklessness and inexperience. In the center of my left palm was a scar from my summer as a sheriff in my hometown of Arpikylä, and I could still remember how it felt when I was pregnant with Iida and a murderer threatened me with the sharp end of an ice skate. A couple of years ago I'd been threatened with a gun, and the bomb that went off in the mailbox of our old house could have blinded me or one of my family members. I knew how vulnerable a person really was, and how little the police could do to protect anyone. I looked into Ursula's eyes.

"You've notified the Helsinki PD, right?"

"No. What good would that do? There's no chance those two are here legally, just like Oksana. They're probably using fake names."

"But every assault has to be reported! Don't you have any sense? We have procedures for undercover work!" I'd been able to stay calm but now began shouting, and my voice bore a strange resemblance to my mother's when she caught me drinking whiskey back in high school.

"I didn't do anything illegal! I can sit in a bar, can't I?"

"Did anyone ask you your price?"

"I told one guy I cost five hundred a night. And what do you know, he would have paid it! I might just go ahead and change jobs . . ." Ursula tried to grin, but it turned into a grimace.

"Damn it, Ursula! That's selling sex in a public place, which is a crime. I'm going to have to report you to Kaartamo. Do you realize that we could both end up out on our asses if this goes sideways?" I stood up and walked to the window. If Ursula didn't file a crime report, we could sweep this all under the rug. But I was worried about the NBI agent. If Ursula remembered him, he probably remembered her. And if he said anything this would turn into an official misconduct case. For a moment I wished that Ursula hadn't told me any of this, but she had.

Kaartamo would be overjoyed to finally get rid of me.

8

Ursula stayed for the morning meeting. She didn't actually want to take any sick leave, though she was certainly entitled to it. She must have understood that losing even one detective would be a huge problem for the rest of us. We agreed that she wouldn't do any interviews and could just handle IT issues, lab results, and background research. Ursula told the rest of the unit she'd fallen cycling.

"You were wearing a helmet, right?" Koivu asked. He and Ursula got along passably these days, even though he hadn't really forgiven her for accusing him, without cause, of sexual harassment a couple of years back soon after she joined the unit. I'd thought Ursula had learned from that episode.

We compiled the results of the previous days' interrogations and forensic studies. The Fernet Branca bottle had only had Lulu's fingerprints on it.

"We know the cause of death, the circumstances of the death, and the place of death. All we're missing are a couple of minor details like a perpetrator and a motive. Ideas?" I asked once Puustjärvi had finished his summary. Autio immediately opened his mouth.

"My three votes are for Saarnio, Länsimies, and Sulonen." In honor of Sunday, Autio was wearing a black pinstripe suit and a pink shirt. He looked completely out of place in the cluttered break room, which the custodian hadn't visited since Friday morning.

"So you believe the theory that the perpetrator was someone in the studio. On what basis?" I asked as if I were his teacher.

"Only they knew Lulu would be on the program. All of them had access to Lulu's room. Saarnio or Länsimies could have arranged to deliver the Fernet Branca to her room and poisoned it ahead of time. Sulonen could have done it at home."

"It's easy to think of motives for the bodyguard, but what about Länsimies and Saarnio?" Koivu asked.

"Länsimies is easy. Blackmail. He'd been one of Lulu's customers and didn't want anyone to know." Autio poured himself more coffee.

"In that case, why did he invite Lulu on his show?" I asked.

"Hey, what if Lulu threatened to tell on live TV what a terrible lover Länsimies was and that's why he had to kill her?" Puupponen grinned, but then the smile turned to a yawn. "Maybe Lulu blackmailed Länsimies to get on his show so she could advertise her services, but then Länsimies had misgivings about what she would say."

"But what's the sense in killing her during his own TV program?" Koivu asked.

"It's the ultimate reality TV!" Puupponen said. "And what about Saarnio? Isn't her husband some kind of big-shot businessman? Those are exactly the kinds of guys who visit whores. What if Riitta Saarnio discovered a relationship between her husband and Lulu? Do we need to check whether she happens to be a butterfly collector, perhaps with some poison stashed in her gardening shed?"

"I can guess what her husband collects," Koivu added, and he and Puupponen guffawed like two teenage boys. Ursula grinned at me as if wanting to comment on how childish the men were being, and the gesture was so out of character for her that I found myself bewildered. Ursula wasn't usually interested in "us-girls" networking, preferring to make alliances with men.

"What about Nuppu Koskela, the makeup artist? You interviewed her, right?" Autio asked Puupponen. "She doesn't have any connections to Lulu, does she?"

"None we've discovered so far. She seemed much more interested in her daughter's ear infection than in murder."

"Wait until you have kids," Puustjärvi said to Puupponen, and once again I had to play kindergarten teacher and remind my subordinates to stay on topic.

"What about Nuppu Koskela's keycard? Is it accounted for?"

"We found it on the makeup table under a powder box. We sent it for fingerprint analysis," Puupponen said.

"Good. Let's move on to our other main line of investigation then: What if Lulu Nightingale was killed because she'd stepped on the toes of some pimps? We have at least one name to start with: Mishin. Ville, start figuring out who he is. Autio—Gideon . . . You be Ville's partner, maybe for the next four hours. Ursula has to rest."

"I don't need—" Ursula said.

"No, you have to take it easy. You should really be at home."

Around noon I realized it was time for me to go home too.

Two assaults and one rape had happened the night before, so my unit would have to add those to the pile. We knew who the perpetrators were already—the assailants were in Holding and the rapist was the victim's ex-boyfriend—so completing those preliminary investigations would be purely routine.

I decided to leave talking to Kaartamo until tomorrow. God, how I missed Taskinen. The conversations and the lunches, even though those hadn't happened often enough. I didn't dare e-mail him about Ursula's screwup, because I feared it might end up in the wrong hands. I needed someone to talk to. So in the car I called my friend Leena.

"Have time for a cup of tea tonight? Or take the kids out for a walk?"

Leena had moved to a neighborhood on a bay to the west of us, and during the cycling season we'd made a habit of riding back and forth between each other's homes.

"No dice. I'm baking like a madwoman for Aunt Allu's funeral. Are you going to be able to make it?"

"Oh right, the funeral!" Leena's godmother, her aunt Allu, had died two weeks earlier, after a brief illness. Allu had owned a car dealership, and she'd had incredible stories about the early days of her business in the 1960s. Some men simply refused to do business with a woman. But Allu had smashed the glass ceiling with a sledgehammer, and Leena and I had often talked about how much her example meant to us. "I'd love to come."

"Five o'clock Wednesday at the Tapiola Church, then food afterward at our place." Allu didn't have any family of her own, so Leena and her mother were the next of kin.

"Any chance the priest doing the service is named Terhi Pihlaja?" When Leena said yes, I decided I'd definitely be there. I could almost call it official business.

That afternoon we took the whole family skating outside, although Iida complained about the lumpy ice. Antti was adorably clumsy in his size twelve and a half skates. Iida tried to teach him a loop, but it was next to impossible in hockey skates. I helped Taneli work on his spirals. Finally the adults had to give up because our ankles hurt too much.

"Julia said Taneli has a lot of talent. The angles and trajectories come naturally for him," Antti said as we were hopping up and down to stay warm on the edge of the rink. "Iida has more dedication than ability, so maybe we should think about moving her from individual to synchronized."

"Oh, let her enjoy her ice princess dreams a little longer! I really don't think we need to start thinking too far into the future. Let's at least wait until next winter. By the way, when was the last time someone put snow down your shirt?" What followed involved considerable rolling around in the snow, and despite the chill, I felt good once I lay defeated in a drift, pinned under Antti. At least we still knew how to have fun together.

In the morning, I felt guilty for how chipper I was when I saw the exhaustion on Puupponen's freckled face. But he had an enthusiastic glint in his eyes, because he'd managed to dig up a considerable amount of information about Igor Mishin, a Russian citizen with permanent residence status in Finland.

"Was he the one who was responsible for the pimping scandal at the Russian trade office last fall?" Koivu asked.

"No. Our Igor isn't guilty of anything. He owns an import business. He sells pickles and frozen *kulebyakas*."

"What's a kulebyaka?" Koivu's gastronomical knowledge didn't extend far beyond Finnish and Asian cuisine.

Puupponen looked at him and chuckled. Ursula joined in, and I couldn't help smiling too.

"Meat pies, dunderhead," Ursula cackled. "He runs a meat pie company."

"More like a fur pie company," Puupponen said and started laughing again. Once he'd regained his composure, Puupponen told us that both the Helsinki Patrol Division and the National Bureau of Investigation had Mishin under elevated surveillance and that they'd interrogated him a couple of times for pandering but hadn't found enough evidence to charge him. Mishin lived in the Eira neighborhood, not far from the Blue Nightingale. Rumor had it he was one of the big fish in Helsinki's prostitution business.

"It's a good system. He forces the restaurants to buy his food and charges them astronomical prices, which is really protection money," Puupponen said. "And if things start to get too hot, he can just skip back home to St. Petersburg. He actually owns his own helicopter. And a bakery and apartments all over Helsinki, supposedly for short-term bakery workers. Because sometimes there's so much demand for kulebyakas that they have to import temporary workers. Since Finns don't know how to bake them right."

"We still have to do more looking into Mishin's girls," Autio added. "Today I'll review all the temporary bakery workers' permits and contact the visa office. He probably has illegal immigrants working for him too, but our Oksana might be one of the girls with legit papers."

"Do we know whether Mishin's goons have killed anyone before?" I asked. Autio didn't know. For now we'd have to leave it at that.

Immediately after the morning meeting, I went to see Assistant Chief Kaartamo. His office was impeccably clean, probably due to his secretary's efforts.

"What's the big emergency?" Kaartamo didn't invite me to sit, but I did anyway. My chair was lower than his, so I had to look up at him.

"One of my subordinates, Ursula Honkanen, had a bit of a screwup." I tried to keep my voice from trembling when I spoke to Kaartamo, but it wasn't easy. Kaartamo listened to me with his arms crossed, his gaze fixed on the surface of his desk. There was already a lot of gray in his thin hair, and he'd recently switched his glasses to square frames. Kaartamo wore a suit, but unlike some of our more fashionable colleagues, his suits often looked too tight and shabby.

"Didn't we have some trouble from Honkanen a few years back?" he asked once I was finished.

"Yes, but we straightened that out with a couple of conversations and a short sick leave."

"So Honkanen hasn't filed a criminal report?"

"No, but I think she should."

Kaartamo uncrossed his arms and leaned forward, squeezing the edge of the desk with his hands.

"Well played, Kallio. You brought this to me so I'd get dragged into the muck too. I'll talk to Honkanen."

"If I hadn't notified you, I'd be guilty of misconduct!"

"Exactly. I said it was well played. Is Honkanen in the building now, or is she home recovering?"

"She's here even though she shouldn't be."

"Send her up right now. Forcing people to work when they're injured doesn't look good." Kaartamo's voice was pure ice. I stood up and left, feeling like a cat who'd been shooed away from the dinner table. Ursula was in her office, working on the computer.

"Go talk to Kaartamo. March!"

Ursula had tried to cover her bruises with makeup and been reasonably successful. A scarf tied as a hairband covered the worst contusion on her temple. Ursula never wore anything like that, so to me it looked out of place.

"What does that mean?" Ursula's voice was uneasy.

"I don't know. Go find out."

Suddenly Ursula jumped up and snapped at me.

"I just had to go and tell you . . . I was so messed up from not sleeping. I should have just kept my mouth shut. You're such a goody two-shoes, you've probably never even had a parking ticket. Your life must be so boring."

I didn't have the energy to argue, so I just left. When I closed my own office door, it banged more loudly than normal. In my e-mail inbox, I found an edited draft of my article for a book the Ministry of Social Affairs and Health was publishing about domestic violence. Since this was still considered a women's issue, and I was a female violent crime detective, I'd been asked to write one of the chapters. I thought that was like putting responsibility for motor vehicle theft on the car owners, rather than the car thieves. Still, editing was a nice change of pace. I was about to send out my new draft when the phone rang. It was Iida's teacher.

"Good afternoon, Maria. I'm calling to let you know that Iida will need to stay after school for detention today. She bit a fifth grader named Miro Miettinen during recess."

"She bit a fifth grader?"

"Yes. She bit the back of his hand hard enough to break the skin. We had to take him to the health center. The hand will heal, but Iida is going to get some time to think about why she did it."

"Did she say why? Did the boy say anything?"

"No. I'd like to ask you to talk to Iida about the incident at home and contact me again if you find out something. Of course, we tried to talk to the other students, but so far we aren't clear about what started the incident. We do know that Miro's friend reported to the recess monitor that Iida was biting. Miro is a full head taller than Iida, but her bite was so strong that he couldn't shake her off him. You can call me this evening if necessary. We need to get to the bottom of this."

I was so thrown off that I initially sent the edited article to the wrong e-mail address. Then I had to send a message to apologize. Iida wasn't usually violent. When she was a little younger, she sometimes pushed Taneli if he messed up her games, but that had stopped once she'd started school. And now to attack a boy three years older—why would Iida do something like that?

When I was younger, I hadn't hesitated to tackle opponents larger than myself on the soccer field, but I'd never attacked someone for no reason. I knew girls got in fistfights these days, but I thought that didn't start until puberty. Early in the winter Koivu had questioned three fourteen-year-old girls who'd kicked a classmate badly enough to put her in the hospital. The reason they'd given was that the girl was "too snobby."

Puustjärvi knocked on my door. He had good news.

"IT got into Lulu's computer! They're going through the files now, but at least one has the word 'customers' in the title. I'm going to head down there right now and see if we can get any names."

"Excellent. Let me know if you find anything significant. It'll be interesting to see who's in there."

"Probably just normal Finnish men whose wives don't put out or aren't interested in experimenting," Puustjärvi said bitterly. A few years ago, he'd told me about his one-night stand with Ursula, and I think he still regretted that. At last year's department Christmas party, he'd come over to talk to me about it, and I assured him I'd forgotten about the whole thing, which I almost had.

I tried to reach Antti, since it would be good for him to know Iida would be coming home an hour late, but he didn't answer the home phone or his cell. Maybe he was swimming. I went to eat with Koivu and vented my astonishment about Iida's behavior.

"Tell her that her godfather is going to come give her a talking-to," Koivu said, then scarfed down his stroganoff and three large boiled potatoes. "I only had a roll for breakfast," he explained when he saw my expression. "Anu said we should ask her brother's girlfriend's sister about Oksana. I guess she's been running with a pretty questionable crowd. I'll handle it."

"Good. I think we'll start seeing some progress now that we have access to Lulu's computer." A piece of carrot was stuck between my teeth, and I tried to get it out with my tongue. When that didn't work, I had to resort to a toothpick. My phone started ringing—it was Kaartamo.

"I need you right now," he said without asking if I was available.

I glanced at my plate, which was still half-full of veggie pasta. All I could do was heap some on my fork, shove it in my mouth, and mumble a quick good-bye to Koivu. As I climbed the stairs, I wondered whether this would be the last meal I'd ever eat in the department cafeteria. Maybe I would be relieved of duty and eventually fired after some messy administrative proceedings.

Kaartamo stood in the middle of his office, and Ursula sat in a chair near the window.

"Close the door," Kaartamo said. Once I did, he began speaking. "I'm only going to say this once, and then this matter is closed. Ursula Honkanen never visited the Mikado. She fell cycling."

"But we can't just . . . We have to report the assault—"

Kaartamo interrupted me. "Listen up, Maria. I'm taking full responsibility for this decision. You can feel free to hide behind me if this ever comes up again. I hope you'll keep your mouth shut and not gossip about this at your knitting circle or soccer club or whatever it is you women are doing these days. Loose lips could cost you your job too. Dismissed."

I stared at Kaartamo for a moment and didn't like what I saw. Then I turned around and walked out, slamming the door behind me. I didn't bother to wait for Ursula. At the bottom of the stairs I kept right on walking out of the building. The people waiting in the lobby to collect passports and driver's licenses stared—my expression must have been quite a sight.

"Hey, Kallio, where's the fire?" yelled a young officer from behind the glass of the crime reporting desk.

I walked through the parking lot to the few pine trees that remained of the forest that had once grown here. Their bark was already turning red as it did every spring, and cones dotted the ground. I picked one up and crushed it between my fingers. The wind picked up and blew my hair into my eyes. I hadn't gone back to my office for my coat and was now cold. Kaartamo had decided to take the easier way, but it was the wrong decision. I didn't believe we'd get caught, yet that possibility did exist. Should I take the initiative and start looking for a new position as a village cop?

A great tit twittered in one of the trees. Soon a blue tit flew up next to it. The wind felt as if it were coming straight from Siberia, and spring seemed further away than ever despite the other signs.

Back inside, I grabbed some hot cocoa in the cafeteria and then walked up the stairs to get my blood flowing again. Puustjärvi and Ursula were sitting in the conference room, working in seeming perfect harmony through Lulu Nightingale's computer and disks, all of which had now been accessed. In the end, it turned out that Lulu's passwords weren't anything special: the computer password was "Paavo" and the disk password was "Anita"—her parents' names.

"We've already found a few familiar names," Puustjärvi said. "I'll try to get a summary together for the morning report, and then we can talk about which ones we should pull in for questioning. One is a former government minister, and there are a couple of CEOs and a hockey team owner."

Ursula said that on the disks were some sort of combination diary/notebook with more details about Lulu's encounters. I left them to work and went to consult with Puupponen about a rape case he was investigating.

"Typical story. The woman was a little drunk and accepted an invitation from a neighbor for a nightcap. The man claims she kissed him first. The woman says she never agreed to sex. The case is going to Katri Reponen to consider charges. It'll be interesting to see what the defense is like. There aren't any witnesses, but the woman has injuries that make her story more convincing than the man's, at least to me."

"It's good this is moving along. We have access to Lulu's computer now, and we're likely to have a new list of names for interviews. Well done," I said and patted Puupponen on the shoulder. Then I tried to reach Antti again, with as little success as before. I thought about Tero Sulonen. Maybe he would be able to tell us about these people in Lulu's notes.

All of a sudden Ursula burst in without knocking.

"Maria, I found something strange!" The largest bruise on Ursula's face had begun to turn yellow around the edges. A few years ago, one of the makeup trends had been black eye shadow that made everyone look like junkies. When would that be replaced by bruises to make everyone look like battered women?

"What is it?"

"There are notes here about Lulu being questioned twice by Lasse Nordström. Listen. 'That Nordström fucker grilled me again today. He showed up at the door in the middle of the day and demanded to talk to me. Wasn't it enough for him to make me come down to the

NBI office? I don't have the information he wants, and even if I did, I probably wouldn't tell him. I'd prefer to protect girls like Svetlana and Oksana.' The entry is from February of this year. But Nordström said he hadn't had any contact with Lulu."

"Yes, he did. Does she mention this Nordström's first name?"

"No. But it would be an incredible coincidence if there was another prostitution investigator named Nordström. I can check, though." Ursula seemed overly enthusiastic.

"Yeah, find out and then let me know."

I looked up Lasse Nordström's number, and when Ursula came back to tell me that there wasn't another agent or detective in any of the Helsinki area police forces with the same last name, I called the National Bureau of Investigation.

"Where should we meet, Lasse? You lied in your interview. You do have a connection to Lulu Nightingale. You interviewed her once at your office in Tikkurila and once at her home. There's no point denying it, since it will be in your case files."

There was a moment of silence on the other side of the line, and then Nordström started to laugh. It sounded forced.

"No, Kallio, you're wrong. Those documents aren't public yet. We're in the middle of a huge operation, and you'd better not screw it up."

"I interviewed you as a witness, not as a suspect. That's definitely recorded in our reports. That means you can't lie."

"I don't have anything to do with that whore's murder. I just happened to be unlucky enough to be on the same TV program. Are you going to believe me, or do I need to get our bosses involved?" I could imagine how Lasse Nordström looked sitting in his office, free hand clenched in a fist, brow furrowed, lips pursed. I felt my own body tense, and my voice dropped an octave.

"Don't you try to threaten me. Besides the fact that you knew Lulu, apparently you also know something about the woman who disappeared from Jorvi Hospital a few days ago. Oksana. You haven't mentioned anything about that either. What time are we meeting tomorrow? How about first thing in the morning, at nine o'clock?"

Nordström didn't speak for a moment. He clearly wanted to choose the best option for himself, the one that would require the most concessions from me.

"Tomorrow is a bit busy. I could give you an hour . . . How about six thirty at my apartment in Helsinki on Kulma Street? Will you be coming alone, or shall I make breakfast for three?"

"I'll have Koivu with me, so make extra. He's always hungry!" I hung up, then returned to the conference room, where the whole unit had gathered around the computer.

The men stared wide-eyed at Ursula's screen.

"This can't be right," Koivu finally said.

"There have been rumors," Autio said.

"A bunch of bullshit," Ursula said angrily. "Who made this and why? We'll have to check the porn sites to see if we can find it there. Come look, Maria. It's a crazy mashup of Lulu and the president."

"What?" I pushed my male colleagues out of the way and looked at the screen. The picture was bright and showed President Tarja Halonen as the receiving partner and Lulu as the giving partner, and although Lulu's face was covered by her blond hair, the body and tattoos were easily recognizable. The president was looking directly at the camera. "Someone had a good laugh. Is there any more material like this?" I asked. I felt nauseated. I knew that in theory anyone could be the victim of revenge porn, but I would never have expected something this extreme, even from the people who held a grudge against the president for having been chairwoman of the Seta LGBTI rights organization earlier in her career. I was a member of that organization myself—why should that matter?

"This is one more reason to bring Sulonen in for questioning. Puupponen, you go at him again. I'm going home to count my children. One of them is going to get a little talking-to. Koivu, I'll pick you up at six o'clock tomorrow morning. We're going to have a chat with Lasse Nordström. And, Ursula, good job finding the notes about him and Lulu."

Then I left the room without looking back. I stopped by the grocery store on the way home. I still didn't know where Antti was. I arrived in front of our building at the same time as he was getting back from picking up Taneli at day care. Antti's bicycle had winter tires with sharp metal studs, but it still made me nervous when he rode with one of our children on bike paths without gravel.

"I got your message just as I was about to call the school because Iida hadn't come home yet. What happened?"

"She got detention because she bit a fifth-grade boy."

"Why on earth?"

"Didn't she tell you?" The three of us crammed into the elevator. Usually I used the stairs, but the shopping bags were heavy.

Iida sat in the kids' room, scribbling something in a notebook. It looked like her religion homework. Antti stayed to help Taneli out of his snow clothes while I went to talk to my daughter. I lay my hand on her hair and bent down so I could look her in the eyes.

"Iida dear, why did you bite that big boy?"

Iida turned her gaze to the floor. "I only bit him a little."

"We don't bite people at all. What happened?"

"I don't want to tell." Iida squirmed away. "I have to do my homework, and I want to be alone!"

"OK, but we'll talk about this later," I said, then went to the kitchen to unload the groceries and start dinner. The vegetable and fish stir fry was a snap. Antti could have a go with Iida—I'd noticed that sometimes she would open up to him and tell him things she didn't want to say to me. Maybe that was because he was gone so much these days.

I'd just started on the salad when Iida came into the kitchen. She had a doll in her arms and was bending its arms and legs in figure-skating poses and not looking at me when she said, "Mom, I bit Miro because he called me a whore. He's said that a lot before, but I didn't know what it was, but now I know because you told me. And I don't sell anyone baby making so he can't call me that!" Iida's voice trembled, and tears filled her eyes.

"You're absolutely right, dear! Why didn't you tell me or the teacher?" I swept my daughter up into my arms. Her hair smelled of baby shampoo, and her body still had the softness of a child.

"Those fifth-grade boys always call people names. They call the boys in our class fags and they call Roosa a fat-ass dyke."

"Dad and I have always said it isn't OK to call people names, and if someone does call names, you need to tell. I'm glad you told me now. You still shouldn't have bit Miro, although I understand that mean names are upsetting." Iida nodded and started to cry in earnest.

After dinner I called Iida's teacher, and I had to restrain myself from shouting. So far, we'd had a model working relationship with Iida's school.

"No one should be allowed to call eight-year-olds names like that, and definitely not eleven-year-old boys! I expect the school to take this seriously. According to Iida, this isn't new behavior from these boys. This has to stop. I'll continue teaching Iida that she should tell a teacher when something like this happens. Because this is exactly the kind of thing that happens when no one tells. Iida isn't the problem here." I felt like a mother lion protecting her cub. I didn't want my children to live in a world where verbal sexual harassment was a part of little kids' everyday lives.

After I hung up, my phone rang again almost immediately. It was my work ringtone, "Cops Are Heroes" by the Rehtorit.

"It's Hakkarainen from Forensics. Listen, we just made an interesting find in Lulu Mäkinen's car. In a bag in the spare tire we found a small bottle, which seems like it's what we've been looking for. Cyanide, I mean."

9

"Can't you understand I had to keep quiet about my connection to Lulu Nightingale? Nothing about the operation we're working on can leak to the media. We've identified the members and funders of one of the two main gangs running prostitution in the metro area, and now all we need is proof. We don't want the local cops bumbling into our investigation."

Lasse Nordström sipped his coffee. This was his third cup since we'd arrived. I poured more milk into my own, because the coffee Nordström had made was bitter and as thick as tar. Maybe coffee was like alcohol: as your tolerance grew, you had to increase the dosage.

"As a detective, you have to know how important homicide investigations are, Lasse. If I was your boss, you'd be on administrative leave until Lulu Mäkinen's murder was solved. You were questioned as a witness! The law is very clear that lying under those circumstances is a crime."

Some of Nordström's coffee went down the wrong pipe and he spent a while coughing. Koivu spread butter on his third piece of bread and piled salami on top. He'd crawled out of bed five minutes before I picked him up.

"You aren't my boss, Kallio, and my boss has already talked to your boss. I met Lulu Nightingale twice. We weren't interested in her, only in whether she'd been forced into working for one of the pimps."

"Mishin?" I asked quickly. Nordström looked startled but didn't reply, and I immediately regretted my slip. Ursula's adventure at the Mikado couldn't come out under any circumstances.

"Well, had Lulu been threatened or blackmailed?" I asked when Nordström remained silent. He glowered at me and snorted.

"Don't ask stupid questions, Kallio. It's a miracle she stayed alive as long as she did. No one's life means much to these Russian pigs. When they aren't trying to bribe me, they're threatening me. The image Lulu gave of her profession in the media was nonsense. There's no limit to the ways they're willing to exploit women, and sometimes it's just human trafficking plain and simple. The girls don't have any choice, and within a couple of years they're all used up. They talk about savings and gifts for the family, but in reality the money just goes to pimps and drugs. If you ask me, they gave Lulu's bodyguard two options: either kill Lulu or take a bullet in the brain. You're wasting your time looking for other perps."

As soon as I'd heard about the cyanide turning up in Lulu's car, I'd issued an order to have Tero Sulonen picked up, but so far, we hadn't been able to find him. He hadn't visited his apartment since Lulu's death. Nordström didn't know about the cyanide, and I didn't intend to tell the media for a while either. First, we had to figure out how it ended up in Lulu's car.

"Why do you assume someone bought off Sulonen?"

Nordström laughed and then stood up, walked to the bay window, opened one sash, and lit a cigarette.

His apartment was different than I'd expected. It had a large but old-fashioned kitchen with a window that opened onto an inner courtyard. The bathroom was tiny, and I wondered how Nordström even managed to close the door. Maybe he didn't have to since he lived alone. The best part was the combined living and bedroom, which had high ceilings and a stage-like elevated platform against one wall where Nordström slept. At one end of the platform was a small recess where Nordström kept his reading chair. He had a lot of books and an ample art collection, including statues and paintings I wouldn't have thought someone on a cop's salary would be able to afford. Maybe Nordström had received an inheritance. Or could the money be from somewhere else? I remembered what my coworkers had said about some of our colleagues who looked the other way when it came to prostitution. Finnish cops were considered honest, but maybe there were those among us who were ready to sell themselves for the right price. Nordström had always known whose songs it paid to sing.

Solidarity among criminals was just a romantic notion cooked up by movie scriptwriters. Eat or be eaten, that was the reality. "Of course, we've made inquiries about Sulonen, and he's no Boy Scout. When he was a bouncer he was also a pimp and small-time crook." Nordström blew smoke out the window. He looked strangely out of place in the rounded recess, too big and bulky for such a small yet elegantly designed space.

Nordström had set out breakfast in the kitchen but asked us to sit in the living room. Would the discussion have felt too intimate if we'd sat around the kitchen table? Lasse Nordström seemed like the kind of man who always wanted to be in control.

I wanted the same thing. I'd worn my most masculine outfit, a black pinstripe pantsuit. My blouse was white, and my hair was tied back in a bun that had been exasperating to put up so early in the morning. My heels gave me an extra two inches, but that didn't help at all next to Nordström. He'd intentionally put me in a low armchair, which was comfortable but left me nearly two feet below his eye level.

"So you visited Lulu's studio? Did you see anything there that might help move our investigation forward?" I asked, trying to make my voice sound pleading. Koivu gave me a confused look. Would the damsel-in-distress act work on Nordström? It was a waste of effort. Nordström saw right through me.

"If I knew anything that would help you, I'd tell you, but I don't."

"What about Oksana? Who was—is—she?"

"I don't have a clue. These girls come and go, since most of the customers want variety. Maybe someone bought her as his personal plaything and then lost his cool when he didn't get what he expected for his money. Maybe Lulu Nightingale's murder will solve itself once we finish our operation. Then everyone's going to want to sing. I'll tell you what I hear then."

"What do you know about Mishin's bakery workers' visas? Are they in order?"

Nordström didn't answer for a while, waiting until he was done with his cigarette and then stepping down from the recess to get his next cup of coffee.

"If I'd know what a hullabaloo would come from going on Länsimies's show, never in a million years would I have agreed to it," he said with a sigh and then took a sip of coffee. "Don't you understand that when we take Mishin out of the game, his competitor will try to establish a monopoly? Then we'll surround him too. That will give us a couple of years of quiet before the next set of clowns can build their organizations. Maybe by then the lawmakers will come up with some new rules that aren't quite as difficult for us to enforce. But, Kallio, if you and your people mess up our operation, you're going to have trouble."

Koivu stood up and walked past Nordström to the bathroom.

Nordström moved right up next to me, leaned over me, and hissed, "You should have come alone. Off the record. I don't want all this ending up in your report." Nordström crouched so we were on the same level. "Remember that everyone has their price, and that price isn't necessarily monetary. You have two children. What if someone threatened to hurt them if you looked too close?"

Nordström's gaze was cold, and I could smell the coffee on his breath. When the bathroom door banged behind Koivu, Nordström stood up.

"I need to get going." He grabbed the sandwich tray and coffee pot and carried them into the kitchen. I frowned at Koivu, who made a face back and pointed at his stomach. He would have liked another sandwich. "You two aren't stupid," Nordström said as he walked back into the room. "You already know that Lulu Nightingale had clients in high places, men who naturally avoid the prostitution run by the mafia because they don't want to be blackmailed. But wasn't Nightingale just as greedy as all the others? And we know that things always end badly for people like that. Look at her client list and think about who would be the most likely suspect—or who would have enough money to buy off Sulonen." He smiled and politely opened the door for us.

"'My dad is stronger than your dad!' What the hell!" I huffed as we walked out of the arched gateway onto the street. The wind was blowing in off the sea, and the Kruununhaka neighborhood felt bleak. Still, I wondered what it would be like to live in the very heart of Helsinki, so close to all the shops and theaters and cafés, not to mention the sea itself. But it wouldn't work with the kids. I thought about what Nordström had just said. Was that meant as a threat to me, or had he been telling me indirectly about his own choices? What was he trying to tell me?

"Kaartamo isn't going to be much help," Koivu said. I didn't answer. Even Koivu didn't know that Kaartamo and I were colluding to cover up Ursula's misconduct. I would have wanted to vent about the situation to him, but I couldn't. I felt completely alone, and I didn't like the feeling. I was used to sharing my work worries with my colleagues, especially Taskinen, and my family worries with my girlfriends. It was crazy that I was going to a funeral to see my best friend because otherwise I wouldn't have time. Life shouldn't be like this.

After the academy, I'd worked on the Helsinki Vice Squad, which was soon disbanded. Prostitution had been completely different in the mideighties. Instead of drugs, alcohol had been the big problem, and the women and girls were locals. Compared to how it was now, everything was much more innocent and amateurish back then. But the fall of the Soviet Union and the recession in the early nineties had set off an explosion in the sex business, with no end in sight. Even though Nordström and company were fighting it, I feared that soon Finland would be offering flesh for every taste: yellow or black, twelve years old or four hundred pounds. And of course, rich men could always travel to fulfill their needs in countries where parents were willing to sell their children to tourists in hopes of raising their standard of living.

We started driving west, back to Espoo. Of course downtown Helsinki was backed up, and we had to wait at the traffic light in front of the Ateneum Art Museum for several minutes. Koivu whistled and tapped the dashboard, and I caught him glancing at the women who walked by, despite the heavy winter coats that concealed their bodies. The sun had risen, and there might be some time later in the day when a coat would feel excessive.

"Maria, look! Isn't that Sulonen?" Koivu suddenly shouted. I braked and saw a broad-shouldered man with a crew cut disappear into the tunnel down to the metro station.

"Shit!" Koivu threw his door open. "I'm going after him. I'll call you. Try to get some local backup. Now we've got that SOB."

I saw Koivu careen down the stairs, nimble for such a large man. Immediately I called Helsinki Dispatch and gave our location, along with Sulonen's description. I wished I'd gotten a better look, since all I could tell them was that he was wearing a black leather jacket. I parked in front of the Helsinki Central Railway Station and set out my official identification. Then I headed for the nearest set of stairs down into the tunnels. I clipped my phone to my belt, and the hands-free earpiece was still in place. Koivu answered almost immediately.

"Do you have a visual on Sulonen?"

"Yeah. He just stopped at a newsstand to buy some gum. Do you think he's dangerous? Can I try to take him alone?"

"Wait for me or the uniforms. I can see two of them coming out of the metro, but they probably don't know Sulonen."

"Now he's going into the record store," Koivu announced, which made me feel better. The store in question was small, and getting out of it without being noticed would be difficult.

"Go guard the door, but stay inconspicuous. He doesn't know you. I'll be there in one minute." I sped up and caught the two patrol officers, whose nametags said Montonen and Konkola, at the top of the escalator. I briefly laid out the situation, and then the three of us walked to the record store, where Koivu was browsing the heavy metal section right next to Sulonen, who was currently looking at the latest release from Timo Rautiainen and the Neckshot Trio. Sulonen would have looked right at home in a heavy metal band.

"Hi, Tero. Could I have a word?" I said, and Sulonen spun around with a start. When he saw me and the uniformed officers, he dropped the record as if it were something shameful.

"Oh yeah? About what?" Bags hung under Sulonen's bloodshot eyes.

"I have some questions for you. Let's take a drive to Espoo. We've been trying to reach you, but you haven't been answering your phone."

"It's broken." Sulonen's voice was full of fear. I stepped closer.

"Come on. We have a car right upstairs."

I tried to interpret Sulonen's expression, but I couldn't tell whether he was terrified or just surprised. Koivu took up a position to one side of Sulonen, and Montonen and Konkola followed behind. They were both tall, Konkola well over six feet, with a shaved head. Montonen had a flat top spiked up like a punk rocker. Sulonen looked small in front of the three of them, and I didn't dare think about how I looked. We all walked toward the stairs that led up to the railway station square, but as we passed the ethnic store before the stairs, Sulonen turned, pushed Koivu, and took off running in the other direction. A couple of seconds passed before our brains kicked in and all four of us took off after him. Konkola and Montonen had long legs, but they bumped into people as they ran. I soon caught up to them and watched as Sulonen climbed onto the railing of the upper level of the tunnel area, intending to jump down to the metro entrance. Sulonen threw himself over the railing and spread his arms like wings as he fell toward the large compass rose inlaid in the floor. Someone screamed as his body hit the ground. We rushed down the escalator, shoving people out of the way. Sulonen stood up, tenacious as a comic book hero, and headed for the longer escalator down into the metro, but his left leg wouldn't hold his weight. It was easy to catch him.

"You feel better now?" Koivu asked Sulonen, who grunted in pain. "What the hell were you thinking? We're going to have to get a damn stretcher and an ambulance. Is it broken?"

Sulonen shook his head. "I'm a good jumper."

When I looked at his eyes more carefully, I realized he'd had something more than alcohol.

A crowd gathered to watch as Sulonen was carried on a stretcher to an ambulance, with the Helsinki officers accompanying him. I said we would interrogate him later and warned them to keep an eye on him.

Our ride home was glum. We'd caught Sulonen, and that was good, but it had turned into a clown show. There was no reason for him to have been injured, and that just added another complication. There was sure to be a long wait at the emergency room in Töölö, and that would be a huge waste of Montonen and Konkola's time. And we wouldn't be able to question him until the next day at the earliest.

"Was he trying to kill himself?" Koivu asked as I merged onto the Turku Highway.

"I don't know. It would be nice to know where he's been sleeping and who's been helping him. And see the contents of his wallet. We'll have to call and ask Montonen to take a look. With any luck, Sulonen's injuries won't be serious."

I'd let the rest of the unit know we'd be late for the morning meeting. When we arrived, I found Puupponen with a swollen cheek. Apparently one of his teeth had started oozing pus during the night, and he had an appointment with a dentist in the afternoon. Puustjärvi had already read through the lab results for the cyanide bottle.

"It was found in the middle of the spare tire in the trunk of Lulu Nightingale's car. Whoever hid the bottle there was careful. There weren't any fingerprints on it, and they only found Lulu's and Sulonen's prints in the trunk."

"And the glass had the same fingerprints. Sulonen's smart enough that he would have known we'd wonder if his prints weren't on the glass since he took it to Lulu's room." Koivu looked contemplative. "But why did Sulonen take the glass to Lulu at all? If Lulu brought the alcohol, to keep herself calm or something, why didn't she ask for a glass immediately? And why did she ask Sulonen for it instead of Länsimies?"

"How could anyone from outside have known that Lulu had the bottle of Fernet Branca with her? Or turn it around: If someone brought the bottle for Lulu, how could they be sure Lulu would take a drink? I just keep coming back to the same two people—besides Sulonen—who had the opportunity to kill Lulu: Riitta Saarnio and Ilari Länsimies." I squeezed my pencil so hard it snapped.

"Keep it together, Maria," Koivu said.

Puupponen hummed "Somebody Put Something in My Drink" by the Ramones, and I scowled at him. After making assignments for the day, I went to my office to prepare my remarks on rape investigation for the Women's Police Day event happening next week. If things kept going this badly, I might have to cancel my appearance. I wondered why rape was considered a women's police issue, since all cops had to investigate them, but I realized that if I were a victim, I'd probably want to talk to someone of my own gender instead of a man. On the other hand, some had suggested that in rape cases female police officers were actually harder on women and more likely to blame them than male officers were. Maybe we knew better than men how defenseless a drunk woman on a dark street was, but that still didn't give anyone the right to attack anyone else or blame the victim when it happened.

After working for half an hour, I went to get some coffee, even though I could still taste Nordström's tar in my mouth. Someone had left a tabloid on the table in the break room, so I quickly leafed through it. There was only one mention of Lulu's murder investigation, buried on an interior page.

Someone had also left one of the celebrity rumor rags on the table. On its garish, patchwork cover was a picture of Mauri Hytönen. The interview filled two pages, and in one of the pictures Hytönen was posing with a blond bombshell. The woman had more makeup than clothing. Hytönen repeated everything he'd said on TV and added, "Modern women demand too much from men. Even in sex men are just supposed to focus on pleasing women and forget their own pleasure. And feminists know exactly how to exploit the pressure society puts on men. I'm happy to pay to be able to think about my own pleasure and determine how I get it."

The next page picked apart the details of the latest celebrity divorce. This time it was the woman who'd cheated and the man who was dishing. Did publicly rehashing divorces and infidelity make them easier to deal with? Did it insulate the person from the pain of their own experience? Maybe Mauri Hytönen was being honest when he bought sex since he didn't want commitment. Wouldn't that be easy: no unnecessary emotion, no unnecessary entanglements. There was no space for children and families in that world, though.

I'd just sat down at my desk again when the phone rang. The display said "Unknown Number." I answered, and a familiar voice came from the receiver.

"Hello, it's Arto Saarnio. Is there any chance you have a free moment, Detective? I'm leaving a meeting and happen to be just around the corner, and I'd like to discuss something with you."

"Right now?"

"If it isn't too much trouble. I'll be there in a few minutes."

"I assume this has something to do with Lulu Nightingale's death?"

Saarnio sighed. "Yes . . . or, well . . . I'll tell you when I get there. I assume you have someplace we can talk without being overheard."

"Sure. We can meet in my office." As I tidied up the worst of my piles of papers, I wondered if Arto Saarnio suspected his wife. Jogging down the stairs to meet Saarnio in the lobby, I realized my muscles were tense with anticipation.

"Hatchetman" Saarnio's camel-hair overcoat was unbuttoned, and underneath he wore a perfectly fitted dark-gray suit. The shade of the red stripes on his white shirt repeated in his matte red tie, and his black shoes were so shiny I could practically see my reflection. The only deviation from his meticulously conservative appearance was the gray two-day stubble, obviously professionally maintained. An eighth of an inch more and it would have looked unkempt.

Saarnio attracted attention in the police station lobby. The people picking up their passports and renewing their driver's licenses stared openly, and I saw an old man clench his fists.

He shook my hand, but his smile didn't reach his eyes. After exiting the elevator he walked down the hallway with his gaze fixed forward as if wanting to avoid eye contact. He didn't speak again until my office door was closed.

"I assume you understand, Detective Kallio, that what I intend to tell you is absolutely confidential?"

"Mr. Saarnio, I assume you also understand that that depends on what you say. Please, sit." I motioned for him to take a seat on the couch. He gave a strained laugh at my retort and rubbed his stubble for a moment before he began to speak.

"I didn't come here to confess to murder. I . . . believe it or not, I've been forced to have a lot of painful conversations with crying people in my life, but nothing has been worse than this."

"I think I might know something about those conversations. My brother-in-law was the CIO at Copperwood." The words slipped out of my mouth before I had a chance to think them through.

"I remember him. Jarmo Vesterinen is a good man. I'm sure he'll find new work in his field if he's willing to leave Joensuu for Helsinki or go abroad. Of course, you have every reason to be disgusted with me for his sake, and what you're about to hear isn't likely to change that attitude. You see, I was one of her clients."

"Lulu Nightingale's?" I was already groping for my tape recorder. This would now have to be an official interview. But Saarnio shook his head.

"No, not her, the other one you're looking for. Oksana Petrenko. It's so banal that I don't know how to tell you . . . Although I assume that, as a police officer, you hear all sorts of strange stories." Saarnio tried to smile again. I didn't smile back. He stood up and took off his coat, which he set carefully next to him on the couch. I caught the forest scent of his aftershave, with a slight hint of salt.

"Well, my wife and I haven't had a sex life for years. Riitta has made it clear that I can meet my needs however I see fit just so long as it doesn't attract publicity or become a nuisance for her. The only problem was that I didn't want to. A man in my position has to choose his mistresses carefully, and I've always thought prostitutes were somehow pathetic. I didn't want to get involved in anything like that." Saarnio interrupted his story and asked if he could have a glass of water. I grabbed a water bottle from the cabinet and poured it into a mug, although I didn't know how fresh the water was. At least it was wet.

"I met Oksana last August. We were hosting guests from a Swiss subsidiary, and they assumed that we would arrange female companionship for them after dinner. I knew this from previous experience. Usually our executive vice president has handled these matters since he has more interest in that industry. It isn't anything out of the ordinary. People still think that the more important the man, the more women he has to have." Saarnio smiled at his own thoughts and sipped more water. A bead of sweat had stopped in a furrow on his forehead, and he wiped it away.

"We spent the evening in the company's sauna suite, although only a couple of the Finns actually used the sauna. Oksana was one of the girls who had been invited to attend. Her English was quite poor, so the Swiss were more interested in the other girls. One of my subordinates was seriously drunk—he was fired soon after when he refused to go to AA—and he hit Oksana. I intervened and made it clear the girl belonged to me, and of course my employee had to acquiesce. I know Russian, because I'm from the generation during the Kekkonen era who handled business in the East—it was safer to do business without interpreters listening in. And that's how it started, even though nothing happened that night. I just talked with her on the balcony and then took her home."

"Where did she live?"

"The girls shared an apartment in Punavuori, then they moved near the center of Espoo, but they met clients all over the place. The suppliers arranged several short-term leases, supposedly for contract workers. But Oksana and I met at hotels. It felt so stupid slinking around the hallways, afraid of getting caught!"

"Hatchetman" Saarnio and a beautiful young woman—the headlines were easy to imagine. It was a titillating topic: Finland's most hated man buying sex and cheating on his wife, who was also a public figure because she directed Ilari Länsimies's show. But Arto Saarnio had decided to take the risk, apparently caught up in a late midlife crisis.

"But I'm not one of these men who can buy sex just as sex. Oksana was an intelligent girl. She'd studied economics at the University of Kiev."

"So she was Ukrainian?"

"Her family was transferred there in the seventies from the St. Petersburg suburbs. The father was a party official and a raging drunk. Oksana has four younger siblings who needed clothes and shoes. When she was offered the opportunity to go to Finland to work as a waitress, she thought it would only be temporary. She'd been here nearly a year before we met. Turned out the work wasn't just waitressing."

"Did she have a visa?"

"No, she was here illegally, which is the beauty of human trafficking—for the traders, that is. Who can an illegal immigrant turn to when she's beaten and her money is stolen? Oksana had forged papers."

It felt absurd having the Hatchetman lecturing me about human trafficking. I'd imagined that for him people were just line items that only mattered if they could be used to reduce expenses or produce increased revenues for shareholders.

"Oksana knew how to listen. These past few years have been demanding, and I've had to make a lot of decisions that weigh heavy on me. I haven't been able to talk about them to anyone, not even Riitta. Oksana was removed enough from the situation but understood how the economy works. She still remembered the socialist era and how difficult it is to build democratic capitalism. Maybe that's why I fell for her like an idiot. She was so understanding."

"So you had a relationship?"

"A relationship . . . that doesn't seem like the right word. Of course, I paid her, and I gave her gifts, jewelry and clothes. And she had other clients, although . . ." Saarnio thought for a moment and then didn't finish the sentence.

"Was Oksana's garnet ring from you?"

"If it has the inscription *Nad Oksanu, A.* I bought it in Amsterdam. I thought no one knew me there so it would be safe to have it personalized. Was she wearing it, then? Of course I didn't have any big plans, but I wanted to help her. Oksana wanted to stop selling herself. I promised to help her get a visa and a residence permit, and I made it clear my company could arrange an honest job and an apartment. But Oksana said she couldn't take any risks. The girls were all being blackmailed, and their families were in danger. The situation was impossible: she would have had to return to Ukraine to apply for a legal visa. Meanwhile, the men she worked for had threatened to kill her."

"What men? Do you know any names?"

Saarnio shook his head. "Oksana didn't tell me. She wanted to protect me—I would have been too tempting a target for extortion by the mafia."

I suspected Saarnio hadn't wanted to know. "When did you last see Oksana?"

"Wednesday a week ago. I tried to convince her to leave, but she said her pimps wouldn't let her get out of the country alive. Do you know what happened to her? Who cut her like that?"

I looked at Saarnio and tried to figure out whether he was telling the truth. What if he was the one who'd attacked Oksana and knew that now she was dead? But then why would he have come here to tell me he knew her?

"Did your wife know that you were a regular client of Oksana Petrenko?"

Saarnio looked me straight in the eyes. "I've wondered that myself. What if Riitta was confused? What if she thought I was Lulu's client . . . Maybe she noticed me being more distant than usual but also, sometimes, as happy as a schoolboy. I'm sure it seemed strange. I don't know what she knows . . . Poor Riitta."

Saarnio sighed, leaning back and crossing his hands behind his neck. The stubble was a clever trick, almost entirely covering up the slack skin beginning to form below his jaw. I poured myself more water and asked again about Oksana Petrenko's pimps. Finally, he mentioned one name.

"Sometimes Oksana talked about a Mishin. She said it wasn't a good idea to make trouble for Mishin."

"How did the executive vice president you mentioned arrange for the girls that first night?"

"Apparently one of Oksana's roommates, Svetlana, was an old acquaintance. Of course, I can ask, although . . . He can't know anything about any of this. And I can give you all the addresses I know Oksana lived at. At first, I thought I'd hire a private detective to track her down, but then it seemed best to turn to the police, especially after what happened on

Surprise Guests. Riitta and I don't sleep in the same room anymore, but I hear her screaming in her sleep. She has nightmares about finding Lulu Nightingale that night. Could that be a sign of a guilty conscience?"

"Has she seen her doctor again?"

"Riitta? No. Soila, our daughter, tried to get her to go, but she wouldn't. To think, my daughter is eight years *older* than Oksana: What did I think I was doing?"

I remembered Oksana's injuries. It wasn't out of the question that she'd done it to herself. Thinking about the way her genitals had been mutilated made me shudder. The poor girl. Maybe she'd thought the pimps wouldn't want her anymore. But where was she now?

I asked Saarnio a few more questions about his wife. Previously we'd thought that Riitta Saarnio only had an opportunity, but now she also had a motive, even if it might have been based on a mistake.

"Did you ever talk with your wife about Lulu Nightingale?"

Saarnio took a sip of water before answering. He dug a pill out of his coat pocket, put it in his mouth and swallowed, then wiped his brow with a red checked handkerchief, which matched his shirt and tie. It was hard to believe that the man sitting before me was the same one I'd seen on television looking so calm and cool.

"Riitta told me early last week what the topic of the show would be. She said she didn't like it. She and Ilari had argued about it. Riitta didn't want Lulu Nightingale on the show because she thought it was offensive to present prostitution as an acceptable profession. She asked what I thought, and when I didn't agree with her quickly enough, she stormed out of the room shouting that she knew what I'd been up to. We didn't talk about it anymore after that, but . . . Detective Kallio, tell me: What do I do if my wife murdered Lulu Nightingale because of me? And what if those mafia thugs murdered Oksana because I wanted to give her a new life? What the hell do I do?"

10

I had to use the authority of my office to convince Saarnio to agree to retell what he knew about the pimps for the official record. I told him we would also have to question his wife again. Saarnio looked like a sick old man when he heard that, but there wasn't anything he could do about it. He'd made his choice when he'd come to see me. I also wrung Oksana's last address out of him. It wasn't far from the place she'd been found.

"And if you find Oksana, please let me know. Is that something I can ask you to do? Do you think I should hire a private investigator after all? Maybe Oksana's coworkers would trust a PI more than a police officer."

"That's your decision. But let's make a deal: I'll tell you if I hear anything about Oksana, and you'll tell me if you hire a PI. Agreed?"

To my surprise, Arto Saarnio extended his hand and said, very formally, that he agreed. After that he left, likely heading back to his corporate office. I stared after him as he walked out of the lobby, my head in a daze. He had just given me a motive for Riitta Saarnio. It was flimsy, but it was possible. Or had Arto Saarnio just used me? Could he not admit to his wife that he was cheating on her and was sending me to do his dirty work? Well, that's what I got paid for, shining lights in the dark corners of people's lives. I would have to set up a meeting with her as soon as possible.

I arranged with my counterpart from the Patrol Division to send a pair of uniforms to downtown Espoo. I would be very interested in having a chat with Svetlana and Oksana Petrenko's other colleagues. The women's prison in Hämeenlinna had confirmed that Lulu's former employee, Iines, hadn't been in contact with her old boss during her time in their facility.

Montonen called from Helsinki while I was about to leave to grab some lunch. Sulonen had a couple of broken ribs, but he didn't need to stay in the hospital.

"Should we bring him over to you? He's sitting with Konkola in the van right now. He's come down off his high, so he's just sort of dazed and depressed. He keeps repeating that he didn't do anything."

"If you have time to drive him over here, I'd appreciate it."

"We're busy," Montonen replied, "but this is the kind of job Konkola and me spend most of our time doing. Next week we're headed to Turkey to deport some Kurds. We'll be there overnight, and I doubt we'll get any sun or see the beach."

Out the window I could see the shrinking snowbanks along the Turku Highway. There'd been pussy willows in the thickets since January, and now more of them were appearing. My stomach rumbled—a lot of time had passed since breakfast at Nordström's.

I knocked on Ursula's door, but she wasn't there. I found her in the cafeteria downstairs sharing a table with Assistant Chief Kaartamo. They seemed to be having a good time. Kaartamo's face was flushed with enthusiasm, and Ursula's eyes glittered. The neck of her sweater was open so that it revealed one of her nicely shaped shoulders. Fortunately, Liisa Rasilainen and Mira Saastamoinen waved at me from their table under the ficus, so I took my carrot soup over to their table and tried not to think about Ursula and Kaartamo. Liisa talked about a domestic violence case she'd been dealing with that morning: some day-care workers had filed a report about a three-year-old boy with bruises all over his body.

"A mother and a stepfather, both unemployed. Apparently they're big fans of visiting Estonia, and they had hundreds of cans of beer at home. We notified DCFS, and the case will be headed up to you," Liisa said. "How's the murder investigation going?"

Time and time again I'd tried to lure Liisa and Mira over to my unit. Both were competent and assertive women with decent senses of humor. Mira had taken some time off for maternity leave, and now she complained about being out of shape.

"When will the soccer fields thaw out? I've got to get some playing time in soon," she said, and Liisa and I nodded. The department women's soccer club was a lifeline I never missed unless absolutely necessary.

Ursula was still giggling with Kaartamo when I walked past again. I told her that Sulonen was ready to be interviewed, and I wanted the job handled as soon as possible.

"But Ville left for the dentist. He'll be gone all afternoon. And I was supposed to . . . But yes, I'd be happy to take another pass at him. He tried to throw us off with all that Russian mafia garbage."

"Honkanen is an enterprising girl," Kaartamo said. I thought about the half-finished presentation sitting on my desk and sighed. I told Ursula I could join her for Sulonen's interrogation.

"But I want to do the talking!" Ursula said testily. "I had a good rapport with him last time."

"Sure, you talk, I'll listen," I said, although I thought Ursula's "rapport" on the video looked more like hectoring.

We asked the officer on duty in Holding for Sulonen's belongings. The cell phone was locked, and his wallet was little help. He had twenty-three euros, a bank credit card and another credit card, customer loyalty cards from a supermarket and a gas station, and a social security card. Two photographs, one of Lulu, which seemed like a passport photo, and another of Lulu and Sulonen in coats, apparently at the door of a restaurant. The paper of that picture was glossy, like it had come from a celebrity gossip magazine.

"No library card," Ursula noted. "Sulonen must not be interested in anyone's poetry beyond his own. And it shows." While waiting for the morning meeting, Ursula had recited some of Sulonen's poems to Puupponen, and both had ended up doubled over with laughter. At which I'd pointed out to Puupponen that he should be more supportive of a fellow writer, which left him blushing and Ursula confused. The others didn't know about Puupponen's novel manuscript.

We picked up Sulonen and escorted him to the interrogation room. He walked with difficulty—apparently his right ankle was sprained, and his ribs obviously hurt when he moved. He entered Interrogation Room Two tentatively. His hands shook, and his eyes were bloodshot, but he didn't smell of stale booze like people usually did after a bender. He did, however, stink of sweat.

He sat down slowly in the chair we offered and hiked up his trousers, which had no belt.

"So how's our poet doing?" Ursula asked. "You really loved Lulu. It must have hurt when she didn't take your proposal seriously."

Sulonen blushed, and I tried to stifle a yawn. At some point, I'd have to do something about Ursula's interrogation tactics.

"Have you been reading my poems?" Sulonen shouted. "You have no right! Those were meant for Lulu!"

"I really admire how in tune you are with your inner teenage girl," Ursula said. "Now, why haven't you answered any of our calls? Where have you been hiding?"

Sulonen looked at me as if begging for help. I stared back, giving him my most maternal look. That would have to be my role in this discussion. The evil bitch and the kind mother figure. Sulonen's sweatshirt had stains on it that looked like mustard. He shifted and groaned, his hand moving to his ribs.

"Where have you been hiding?" Ursula repeated.

Sulonen looked at the table. "I couldn't stay there! The place felt so empty, and all of Lulu's things were there. And the cops left a mess everywhere. I couldn't clean, so I went out. To see some friends."

"Why didn't you answer the messages we left?"

"I turned my phone off because of all the reporters. I just wanted to be left alone. I went to see friends." Sulonen groaned again. His face drained of color, and he grabbed the edge of the table as if he felt faint.

"What friends did you go see?" Ursula asked, but I interrupted.

"When did you last eat?" I asked Sulonen, and Ursula shot me an annoyed glance.

"Eat . . . I don't know. I haven't felt like it."

"You can have a sandwich if you tell us who you got it from," Ursula said. Sulonen clearly had no idea what Ursula was talking about—or else he was a good actor. "We found your little stash in the car. You were pretty careless."

Sulonen was so pale his skin looked almost blue. "I don't understand what you're saying," he spluttered.

"You were careless about what was used to kill Lulu. We found it."

Sulonen's head dropped to his chest. The hospital had probably given him strong pain medication, and if he hadn't eaten in days, it was no wonder he was feeling ill. Despite Ursula's glare, I ordered a pause to the interrogation. I got Sulonen two glasses of juice and a ham sandwich, which would raise his blood sugar. Sulonen stared at me suspiciously, but he began cautiously drinking the juice. When he grimaced, I remembered he had wounds in his mouth too.

After eating, Sulonen denied hiding anything in the car.

"I didn't drive it very often by myself. It was Lulu's car. Or, actually, the company's."

"You're a grown man, and you don't even own your own car. Last time you bragged about how Lulu gave you everything you needed. But you didn't even get your own car." Ursula looked at Sulonen in amusement. "Which one of you drove to the studio?"

"Me. Lulu wanted to concentrate . . ." Sulonen took a bite of sandwich, his movements still tenuous. He swallowed before continuing. "Lulu'd had a little to drink too, some wine or liqueur. Fernet Branca, I mean."

"Why didn't you tell us before that Lulu drank Fernet Branca?"

"I don't remember everything! I'm so confused. Guess how much I've slept since Lulu . . . I wished I'd died in that jump, but no. I don't care about anything anymore."

"Did you always have Fernet Branca at home? Do you drink it?"

"Yeah, I guess . . . We had bottles of the stuff. I don't drink it, though. A bodyguard can't drink. Sometimes I have a couple of beers when we're free and Lulu's at home taking a break."

"Did you see Lulu take a bottle of Fernet Branca with her to the TV studio?"

"No! She had a big bag full of stuff, makeup and hair spray and things like that."

Ursula then tried to squeeze Sulonen for information about Lulu's guests over the days preceding her death, but Sulonen claimed he didn't know any names. Lulu hadn't mentioned anyone bringing her a bottle of bitters as a gift.

"Did you think you were saving Lulu from sex with other men when you offered to marry her? But Lulu didn't want saving. Right? And that's why you killed her?"

Sulonen's intake of breath was so sharp he nearly choked on a piece of sandwich. These days men rarely played Prince Charming, so we women were usually the ones who thought our love could save the men, could make a new person out of the drunk, the wifebeater, or the murderer. The more brutal the violence the man had committed, the more torrid the fan mail received from women. Now I'd met two exceptions in one day: Arto Saarnio and Tero Sulonen. But, beyond that one similarity, these two men didn't seem to have much in common.

"Where were the car keys during the TV show taping?" Ursula continued, ignoring Sulonen's coughing. Tears filled his eyes, and finally I slapped him on the back, at which he howled in pain, and I cursed my thoughtlessness. Whacking a person with broken bones! Fortunately the piece of bread came loose. Sulonen swallowed it and then washed it down with juice.

"They were in my pocket, but the other set of keys were probably in Lulu's purse."

I tried to remember the contents of Lulu's purse. Yes, the keys were probably there. Would the killer have had time to deposit the cyanide bottle in the car after poisoning Lulu? No, because according to the security camera footage, no one had left the studio. What about Lulu herself? Could she have left the bottle in the car without knowing what was in it?

"You didn't tell us about your friends. Who have you been staying with?"

"Pate Mustajärvi. I mean Antti Mustajärvi. But everybody calls him Pate because of the singer from Popeda, you know? He's in Sörnäinen. I mean he lives in the town of Sörnäinen, not in the prison. I can give you his number, but he doesn't know anything. He was at work. He's a bouncer at the Helsinki Club. We go to the same gym."

Sulonen continued to deny his guilt just as doggedly as he had before, despite Ursula's merciless hammering. I listened and wondered whether friendliness might work better. I was also concerned that Sulonen had been released from the hospital after receiving little more than first aid. He seemed physically and mentally unsound.

Ursula placed a printout of the picture of Lulu and President Halonen on the table.

"What do you know about this? Who took this picture?" Sulonen stared at it, looking bewildered.

"I don't know. I've never seen this. It's strange. The background is just like our place, but the president has never visited. Lulu would have said something if the president . . . Is this a real picture?"

"I'm asking you," Ursula said icily, but Sulonen didn't have an answer.

After an hour and a half of ineffectual talk, I gave Ursula a questioning look and motioned for her to join me in the hall. I closed and locked the door behind us, even though I didn't expect Sulonen to try to escape a police jail with a guard on duty.

"I think he's close to breaking," Ursula said. "Let's keep him here for the night."

"Sure, that's fine," I said. I had my own ideas, though. At the end of the day I could come talk to Sulonen informally, just the two of us. Ursula would be annoyed if she heard about it, but what did that matter? I was the boss.

We ordered the guard, Officer Koskinen, to take Sulonen to a cell. Koskinen complained that they were full, because Narcotics had made a big bust the night before. "I guess we can find a spot for your guy, but tonight had better be quiet or we're going to have issues."

I asked Koskinen to guard Sulonen well, because he was injured. He should take any complaints seriously. Then I returned to my office and looked up the pictures of Oksana. Even though it made my stomach turn, I enlarged them so I could see every detail. Blown up three times larger than normal, the genitals looked strange. The pubic hair was like a thick forest, with a deep gash cut through it like a hastily constructed logging road. The cut resembled a clumsily performed episiotomy. Now that I had the victim's name, I could request assistance from the Ukrainian police. Maybe Oksana had gone back to Kiev.

"I'd prefer to protect girls like Svetlana and Oksana" was what Lulu's note had said. My impression was that Oksana was a common name in Russian-speaking countries, but this could easily be the same Oksana. Maybe Sulonen would know.

I picked up a ruler and held it like a knife. I mimicked inflicting Oksana's injuries on myself, slash by slash: face, breasts, stomach, groin. I shuddered. Arto Saarnio had meant well but had only caused more evil, just like he did in his professional life. Layoffs were always justified by the excuse that they allowed other jobs to remain in Finland. Which didn't make much difference for the people who owned the bulk of the shares of Copperwood, since they weren't Finns anyway. In twenty years, once wages in China had climbed too high, everything would be moved to the next country with the cheapest labor. The rich countries would make sure there were always places willing to undercut wages. Tonight, I'd have to call Jarmo and Eeva and ask how they were doing, but now it was time to tie up all the loose ends I could before the end of the day.

Autio had promised that he and Puustjärvi would interview Oksana's roommates, if they could track them down. That would be stepping on Nordström's toes, but I didn't care. If the National Bureau of Investigations couldn't handle their cases, that was their problem. The patrol who'd gone downtown to look for the girls hadn't reported back. I called the switchboard and had them connect me to Officer Haikala.

"No one's answering the door. We've been waiting in the stairwell, but there's no sign of them. One of the neighbors was home, and she said there's been a ton of traffic in and out of the apartment for weeks but that it's been quiet for a few days now."

"Is there a building superintendent?"

Haikala laughed. "What's that? We're in a rental building. I guess there's probably a maintenance man somewhere, but we don't have authority to go in anyway, do we?"

That was true. I ordered the patrol to stand down and asked Autio to figure out who was renting apartment G 122. Then I went to talk to Sulonen. Holding was quiet. Officer Koskinen said he'd just checked on Sulonen, who'd asked for more juice.

"I'll take it to him."

"And here's the pain meds the doctor prescribed. There's also an order to give him sleeping pills if needed," Koskinen said. Koskinen's cousin, Sake, was a detective colleague of mine in the Tampere Police

Department, and we got along well. I always looked forward to seeing him at seminars.

After his fifth sleepless night, Sulonen might be ready to talk, but it would be torture, and I didn't want to sink that low or go against doctor's orders. I took the juice and painkillers, and Officer Koskinen opened the cell door at the back of the hall for me. I'd only been in this particular cell once before, but I remembered it well because someone had tried to scratch a replica of Hugo Simberg's *Wounded Angel* on the wall. The result resembled three drunks stumbling along, but that was a perfect fit for the wall of a holding cell. In addition to the drawing, the usual Bible verses, curses, and upside-down spiders decorated the walls.

Sulonen lay on a bunk under a blanket, but when the door opened, he tried to sit up. It was slow.

"Hi, Tero. You asked for something to drink. Here you go, and some pain meds. Why did you have to try to run away in the station tunnel like that? You could have really hurt yourself."

"I haven't slept at all since Lulu's death. It's like I'm looking at the world through plastic, and I don't understand . . . I don't understand anything. What did they find in our car? I guess some kind of poison, but what?"

"Does the name Oksana Petrenko mean anything to you?"

Sulonen thought for a moment and then nodded. "She's that blond chick from Russia or somewhere who got put in the hospital, right? Yeah, Lulu knew her, because she commented on the newspaper story."

"What did she say?"

"'Fucking bastards' or something like that. She was even thinking about calling the pigs, but then . . . She was too afraid! But what if she did and they killed her . . ." Sulonen pounded his fist on the bed and then realized a split second later how much the motion hurt.

"Tero, calm down! Did Oksana work for your company?"

"No! Lulu never took on any Russians. It was too big a risk. But Oksana visited us once. She asked something about the Finnish police, but I didn't really understand. They spoke English. Lulu was like that.

She always wanted to help people in the life, even though she herself was proud of being an independent entrepreneur and not anyone's employee. Girls like that can't pick their clients."

Sulonen finished his juice. Above his head I read, *Marko here again, missing my lady and the kids. Sorry I screwed up again.* The date was from seven years previous. The walls hadn't been painted since then—it was considered pointless given that they'd just be vandalized immediately. Maybe the inscriptions entertained the prisoners. I read them with interest myself. During college, I'd always thought it was lame when they painted over the most interesting compositions on the bathroom walls. Once, in the mid-1980s, I'd even written a snatch of Pelle Miljoona's "Academic Boy" on the wall of a restroom in the Helsinki University Main. At the time, I was already a police officer and a law student. It had felt like the appropriate level of rebellion.

"Did you read my poems?" Sulonen suddenly asked, pleading in his voice. "Did the police take them? Can I have them back?"

"Of course. We're just reviewing them," I said, pitying Puustjärvi, who'd been assigned the task. He was supposed to just skim them to make sure they didn't contain any threats against the author's muse. Sulonen was our strongest suspect, after all.

"Lulu . . . Lulu only got to read the best. I couldn't help it. The poems just came to me. They wouldn't stop coming."

"Writing poetry is a wonderful hobby," I said distractedly. I was still thinking about Oksana. Had she asked for advice about how to counter Lasse Nordström? Sulonen continued speaking, but I became increasingly inattentive. I didn't snap out of it until he shook me by the arm. "Are you listening? When we got to the studio, Lulu looked confused when she saw one of the other cars and said, 'Oh, that asshole's here too.'"

"Whom did she mean?"

"I wasn't sure. For a second I thought it might be Länsimies—she thought he was a prick. But then I remembered that it was his show, so of course he would be there."

Would Lulu have recognized Nordström's car? That was a risk: the guests might recognize each other before showtime if their cars gave them away. Nordström didn't advertise that he was an NBI agent, but what about Mauri Hytönen? He ran an HVAC company and might have had a decal on his car.

"Why does that other one have to be so mean all the time?" Sulonen asked. "The other woman? As if it were a crime to love a person. Why does she think I killed Lulu? You don't believe that, do you?"

I smiled and told Sulonen to get some sleep.

"Sleep? I might as well be dead. Then at least I'd be in the same place as Lulu." Sulonen sniffed. Tomorrow we'd pump him again for information about Lulu's individual clients. I could imagine how much Ursula would enjoy that. Fortunately, Puupponen would be the one to handle the questioning with her.

I was happy to leave work that day. The bitch cop/mother cop act had paid off after all. God, Ursula and I actually worked well together. That was irony for you.

Autio called just as I pulled into my apartment building's parking lot.

"It's about that apartment downtown. The lease ran until today under the name of a limited liability partnership called Machine Brothers LLC, who rented it for temporary workers. The keys were returned yesterday. Now the apartment should be empty. Should I track down the company or get the maintenance man to let me in? There might be some clues."

I cursed. If these were professionals, there wouldn't be anything left in the apartment that could be useful to us. I asked Autio to find out who owned Machine Brothers, even though I didn't think he'd have much luck. I decided to send Nordström an e-mail to ask him what he knew about the company.

I tried to call Eeva and Jarmo. No one answered their home phone, but I finally reached Eeva on her cell. She was picking up their daughter, Aliisa, from her music lesson.

"This isn't much fun," she said. "Of course, the kids don't want to move, and I don't either. But where is Jarmo going to find a job in Northern Karelia? He's talked a little about setting up a consulting firm, but mostly he's just been moping. And drinking beer."

"Jarmo isn't usually much of a drinker, is he?" I couldn't remember seeing my sister's husband drunk since the Midsummer holiday in 1995.

"Now he is. A six-pack doesn't even last two nights."

Eeva's voice was tense. She'd always been the most fastidious of us Kallio girls, and any upcoming visit still sent me into a cleaning panic. Eeva always had a hard time accepting it when things didn't go according to plan. Before hanging up we arranged for Aliisa to come spend some time with Iida during the summer. They got along well, because in addition to playing violin, Aliisa was also a figure skater.

After dinner, Antti went to the library with Iida, and I stayed home with Taneli to tidy up, even though mostly we just played with the Legos that were spread all over the floor. The phone rang just as I completed a monster from outer space.

"Hi, it's Marjatta. How are you all doing? The papers have been making it sound like you've got your hands full."

"I do." I wondered why my mother-in-law was calling my cell phone rather than the landline or Antti's phone.

She asked whether Antti was home, and when I said no, she replied, "Good. I think it's best to talk to you about this first. Tauno would have wanted this, and I talked about it with him many times. I intend to move in with Marita. I don't need much, and Marita's boys will be moving out soon for the army and school. I'll split Tauno's legacy between her and Antti—the money from selling the house in Inkoo and the stocks. You won't have to keep scraping by paying that terrible mortgage, and you can buy a proper home."

My breath caught. I didn't know what to say.

"I know what Antti thinks. He's too proud to accept help. Stupid boy. The rest of the money will be yours eventually, but I'm a tenacious old lady, and I might live another twenty years yet. In the meantime, you're wasting your lives with him going back and forth between different sides of the country. The children need their father. With my husband's money, you'll be able to buy a house, and Antti can spend some time unemployed if he needs to. What do you say?"

I found myself blinking, and tears weren't far off. "Marjatta, that sounds lovely, but you have to talk to Antti, not to me. This is about his father's money."

"But that boy is so stubborn!"

I laughed, which made the tears fall onto my cheeks. "Yes, he is. And he likes his work in Vaasa. I don't know if he'll want to give it up. Of course, I can tell him your proposal, but wouldn't it be best for you to talk to him yourself?"

Marjatta still wanted me to broach the subject first. I understood why. Antti's relationship with his mother wasn't a simple one. In the later stages of Tauno Sarkela's illness, she had leaned on Antti for support and tried to convince him to clear up some longstanding quarrels with his father, which Antti wouldn't even talk to me about. I'd tried to play the mediator between mother and son, since my mother-in-law seemed to think I was a sensible, level-headed person. Antti had a habit of shutting down during difficult situations, and his mother's truculence didn't help. The best thing now would be for me to forget my own feelings about the matter, although of course I hoped Antti would accept the money.

I didn't bring it up immediately once Iida and Antti got home, and I waited until the kids had gone to sleep before telling him about his mother's call. He listened quietly, but he fidgeted the way he always did when he was nervous or irritated.

"Why does my mom have to use you as a go-between?" he asked once I was done.

"I asked her to call you directly, but she refused. But it doesn't matter. Think about it. This is a great solution! The kids can have their own rooms, and you can have an office that isn't just a corner of the living room table."

"Well, yes, that would be nice, but does Mom really think I'd leave my job in Vaasa? I like what I'm doing. I don't want to live on my inheritance. It would be a waste of my education. Would you consider moving? We could get a really nice house in the Vaasa area with that much money."

"There aren't any positions open, and I happen to like my job too."

"But we're always living on your terms, Maria!" Antti stood, shoved his feet into his shoes, and grabbed his coat. "I'm going for a walk. I have to think. None of this is as simple as it seems," he said, and then he was gone. His wanting to be alone was his typical reaction to conflict. I was used to it, but it still irked me. Why couldn't Antti talk it out with me for once? I remembered the way he had laughed with his colleague, Virve, on the phone. Workplace romances were common enough, and I'd been in danger of getting mixed up in something like that with Taskinen more than once. I had to admit that Antti had had good reason to be jealous a couple of times when I'd felt too much for someone other than him, but I'd never actually acted on those feelings. I'd always trusted Antti, but now I didn't know anymore. What had Mauri Hytönen said about men's sexual needs?

I'd thought the recent tepidness of our sex life was simply due to lack of opportunity. We were both rarely home at the same time, and by the time the kids were asleep we had hardly any energy left. I didn't need anything special, just the touch of the person I loved. I thought about Lulu Nightingale's arsenal. Did I need to get some naughty lingerie or a nurse's costume? The very thought depressed me.

I didn't know what Virve looked like, only that she was ten years younger than me and a prodigy who earned her doctorate in economics before the age of thirty. I realized I was imagining her as an assertive blond like Ursula.

Antti had left his phone on the table next to his wallet. First, I opened his wallet. This was no big deal—I'd taken money from it countless times before. The same familiar pictures were there in their plastic covers: me at our wedding, Taneli and Iida's most recent day care and school pictures. I felt under them just in case. I found one more picture, but it just showed our kids a couple of years ago. Taneli's eyes looked as big as an alien's.

There were also sixty euros in the wallet, Antti's credit card, and a stack of library cards. Under those I found a restaurant receipt, but it wasn't from Vaasa—it was from Nykarleby, a small town about halfway between Vaasa and Espoo. Strange. Antti hadn't mentioned going there. The receipt was from the previous Wednesday at 9:30 p.m. Antti had paid for a bottle of red wine, two pepper steaks, and two coffees with cognac. What on earth was this? Why hadn't Antti mentioned going to a town I'd never been to before? I felt my breathing accelerate and my heart rate pick up. What was he up to?

I put everything back in his wallet just as I'd found it and set it on the table, then picked up his phone, which was unlocked. But what would it prove if Virve's name was in his contacts or even if he'd called her? They could just be talking about work. What about text messages . . . Oh hell, what was I doing? Violating my husband's privacy, that's what. I felt dirty. Was I really this big an idiot? I put his phone down, then took a shower, scrubbing myself with a brush until my skin shone. The feeling wouldn't go away, however, even when I got out and put on a clean nightgown. I got into bed to read and wait for Antti. He came home twenty minutes later, his hair wet from the snow outside. He told me that he was going to see his mother in the morning. An issue this big deserved a face-to-face conversation. I understood that well enough.

I could hear that Antti couldn't sleep either. We lay awake in the same bed without touching each other. That felt much worse than being alone.

11

On Wednesday morning, I woke up at six to have time for a jog. The sun was already rising, and the light cast the trees in sharp relief against the horizon in a red-and-yellow line. The sky was a dazzling blue, and a half moon hung above the trees. I ran about three and a half miles, greeting the familiar people out jogging or walking their dogs. It was cold and windless, which increased the stench from the exhaust of the cars as they idled at each intersection. It was a beautiful day for a funeral.

When I returned from my run, I wasn't as depressed as I'd been when I woke up. Antti had already made coffee, and I ate a hearty breakfast after showering. He would take the kids to school and then head for Vaasa after seeing his mother. Then she would come watch the children in the afternoon.

"I was thinking about staying over on Friday for Virve's party," Antti said. "Maybe it's good for me to have some time to myself to think things through."

"What's so hard about accepting free money?"

"That's exactly the point. I didn't earn it! What right do I have for things to be so much easier for me than someone else just because my dad's family happened to have money and he had a good job?"

Of course, I understood Antti's logic. He'd always felt guilty about his father's family being so rich. I hoped he didn't think I was pushing because I wanted us to take his inheritance. If Antti accepted the money and we used it to buy a house, it might be a good idea to sign a postnup. Apparently, there was still a little bit of the lawyer left in me.

"You'll be fine with the kids, right? Mom's happy to help. She enjoys getting into our business now that she doesn't have Dad to care for anymore."

I was surprised at the bitterness in Antti's voice, and Virve's party had me terrified. Why did I think it was just going to be a party for two? I vowed to myself that I wouldn't call Antti's cell phone on Friday night. I still had my pride. The kiss we exchanged before I left for work was a formality, but we didn't dare go without it. We weren't actually fighting, after all.

I scraped the frost off the side mirrors and thought about Iida's teacher's promise to speak to Miro Miettinen's teacher. She'd said that, sadly, it was difficult to do much about a child's behavior if the parents weren't cooperative. Maybe Miro was from a family where name-calling like that was allowed. Antti was right. A child didn't choose their parents or the values they were raised with. I'm sure Iida and Taneli would have liked to have parents who were home more often.

Snow began falling gently, and the car ahead of me slid every time it braked. Maybe its driver had taken a risk and switched to summer tires already. In the morning meeting, we went over a report from Helsinki. No one at any of the state liquor stores in south Helsinki remembered Lulu Nightingale or Tero Sulonen buying any Fernet Branca. I decided to widen the search to every Alko outlet in the metro area, even though it felt like a waste of time. Then we worked on profiling Lulu's murderer.

"The situation is unique, because no one could get into the studio without ending up on the security tape. On the other hand, we can't rule out Lulu Nightingale having brought the Fernet Branca herself. Her handbag was plenty big enough for a liquor bottle to fit. It's a shame it doesn't really show up on the security camera. If Lulu brought the bottle, then the killer had to rely on chance. If he didn't act until they were at the studio, it must have been spur of the moment. So what kind of person are we looking for?"

"Someone who takes risks," Ursula said.

"And someone who can seize an opportunity," Puupponen added.

"A gambler." Puustjärvi's voice was more assertive than usual. "Someone who's willing to bet everything on one card. He must have risked everything before and won."

"A professional," Koivu said. "For a professional, breaking into Lulu's car would have been no sweat. The fact that Lulu died at the TV studio was pure chance."

"She said it in one of the interviews I read on background," Puupponen said. "Lulu, I mean. She said that she didn't drink much alcohol but that when she did her favorite was either ultradry champagne or Fernet Branca. So anyone could have known that."

We stared at each other in frustration. This was going nowhere. I stood up to get a cup of tea. I was sick of coffee.

"Have the DNA results come back?" I asked Puustjärvi.

"They're still processing. I've been riding the lab," Puustjärvi replied. "This is their top priority."

After the meeting, Koivu and I drove to the West Man Productions studio. Riitta Saarnio had asked to meet us there. In the light of day, the studio looked like a boring box, which fit in well with the car dealerships and warehouses that had sprung up in the fields that had once blanketed the area. Koivu rang the bell, and Riitta Saarnio came to let us in. She was dressed all in black, which heightened the paleness of her skin, and the blood red of her lipstick didn't help. Even though her voice was calm, I got the feeling she was trembling inside.

"Luckily no one else is here yet, so we can chat in peace. I don't want my personal business being spread around." Riitta Saarnio led us to a room I'd only glanced into in passing while investigating the crime scene. It was part office and part conference room: in the middle of the room was a table with four chairs around it, and in the far corner of the room was a workstation with a computer and a filing cabinet.

"I can't believe my husband did this to me," Riitta Saarnio said after sitting at the head of the table. Her lipstick had already started to spread to the lines running vertically above her mouth, making her upper lip look like it was bleeding.

Arto Saarnio had told his wife about our discussion, so I was saved from having to reveal the ugly truth. On the other hand, that robbed me of the opportunity to surprise her. Koivu set a voice recorder on the table and rattled off the routine interview information while I watched Saarnio. The tremor that plagued her during our first interview still bothered her. Her hands wouldn't stay in one place. Her pink nail polish was flaking, and the backs of her hands were more wrinkled than her face and neck. She gave the impression of holding herself together with the final shreds of her strength, but I couldn't allow pity to prevent us from questioning her.

"During our previous meeting you said that you didn't know Lulu Nightingale, but you met her while you were preparing for the show. Would you like to change your testimony now?"

"There isn't anything to change! I didn't know Lulu."

"Did you know about your husband's relationship with a prostitute named Oksana Petrenko?"

"No, I didn't. I mean I didn't know who the woman was, but I suspected Arto had a relationship with someone. He would stare off into space and looked like a lost sheep. Men always look like idiots when they're in love, or at least Arto does. I haven't forgotten how he looked when we started dating."

Riitta Saarnio clearly had to struggle to maintain her self-control. She tried to hold onto the table, but her hands wouldn't comply. I thought of my aunt who had Parkinson's disease.

"I don't know what I'm more shocked about, the fact that Arto was seeing a prostitute or that he thinks I had something to do with that other whore's death. How could he do that to me after thirty years or marriage! 'Riitta dear, I know this will come as a shock to you even though you gave me permission. I've had a long-term customer relationship with an escort. Or did you already know? You just suspected the wrong woman, right?' I've never heard anything so outrageous in all my life! And then he goes on to say, 'You have to tell the police everything. If you're guilty, I'll do everything I can to help you. Because I'm guilty too.'" Riitta Saarnio suddenly began to laugh without a trace of mirth.

When the conference room door opened, the laughter broke off.

"Riitta?" Ilari Länsimies's head appeared in the door, followed by the rest of him. "Oh, you aren't alone. I'm sorry. Hello, Detective Kallio and . . . was it Koivu?"

"Ilari, would you mind leaving? This is a private conversation."

"Ah, another official interrogation. Your investigation seems to be moving quite slowly. Have you even made any arrests?" Länsimies tried to sound relaxed, but his voice had a sharp undertone. "Once you catch the murderer, I'd love to invite you on the show, Detective Kallio. This Friday's ratings will probably set another record, but I doubt I'll be able to offer quite such a sensational climax as last time. Good day to you all!" Ilari Länsimies turned and closed the door behind him. His footsteps echoed in the hallway for a moment. When their sound disappeared, Riitta Saarnio continued.

"I imagine my husband told you that I gave him permission to handle his sexual needs just so long as it didn't become public. What else could I do? But I still believe that he respected me, that he wouldn't . . . or at least that he would be too afraid of ruining his social standing. All he has is work, work, work. He golfs and reads just so that he can say he has hobbies. He thinks that reading a novel instead of work documents on a plane softens his otherwise hard image. And the golf course is the perfect place to network and make business deals. That's why I play with other women instead of him."

"Did you—" I tried but failed to interrupt Saarnio's flood of words.

"Maybe I should be thankful Arto chose whores instead of mistresses so I don't have to endure what happened to my friend Raila, whose husband traded her in for a younger model. He's just like Arto, a man whose mind only has room for work. Raila raised the kids alone, took care of the house. She ran the whole show. Then her husband started having kids with his new wife and, just imagine it, wrote a book about the joys of fatherhood at age sixty! Because now he knows how to appreciate it! Guess how Raila and Raila's children feel about that!" Saarnio looked at Koivu's hands, which were tapping away at his computer, and then at my left ring finger. "Both of you are married. God help you."

"I've already experienced what you're talking about," Koivu said suddenly. "It was just a girlfriend, but it still hurt. You can get over it. It might not feel like it right now, but you'll recover."

Koivu didn't have a habit of sharing his personal life with suspects, but this helped calm Saarnio, even if tears did well up in her eyes. "Yes, I know I'm not alone in any of this, and now Arto's slut has disappeared too. But there are always more where she came from."

Apparently Arto Saarnio hadn't told his wife how attached he'd become to Oksana, probably thinking that a casual relationship was easier to forgive. Once again, I remembered Antti's flirtatious tone on the telephone and felt empty inside.

"A couple of questions related to that night's show. Lulu came to the studio in her own car. Do you know how the other guests arrived?"

Riitta Saarnio took a moment to think. "Usually I'm the one who gets the travel reimbursement requests, but we never got to that this time. We'll have to take care of it at some point, since everyone has to be paid! Thank you for reminding me. Let me think . . . the priest, Terhi Pihlaja, came by bus because she had an easy connection. Anna-Maija and Nordström came by taxi . . ."

"Do you know Anna-Maija Mustajoki?"

"Only as well as one can during a night course in French conversation at the community college. We're just acquaintances. Hytönen also came in his own car."

"What kind of car?"

"I don't know. I let him in, but I wasn't paying much attention."

"Where were you last Wednesday night, on the ninth of this month?"

Riitta Saarnio didn't reply immediately, clearly thinking about what I was asking.

"Last Wednesday . . . that's easy. I was at the French conversation class I just mentioned. It goes from six to seven thirty. Afterward I drove Raila home—she's in it too—and stayed for a cup of tea. Raila's been having a really hard time, and she needed a friend. Is that the same night Arto's little girlfriend was attacked? I know what you're thinking!" Saarnio's voice rose again, and she looked at me with eyes full of hatred. Koivu intervened.

"We have to ask these questions. We'll also need the phone numbers of the friend you mentioned and the teacher of the French conversation class." Koivu smiled in a way that he usually reserved for children, but it worked on Riitta Saarnio too, and Koivu got the contact information.

"How long did it take you?" Saarnio asked Koivu as we collected our things. "Getting over the shock of being cheated on, I mean."

"The first six months were the worst," Koivu said and shook Saarnio's hand. After a moment's hesitation, she also shook my hand, but she let go quickly as if my hand were ice cold.

As we started walking down the hall toward the front door, Ilari Länsimies came to meet us. Maybe he'd been waiting for our conversation to end. He was his calm, smiling self again, and the agitation he'd had on the day we questioned him was gone.

"You haven't been doing a very good job of keeping the media apprised of the progress of your investigation," he said. "The people have a right to know, and all of us mixed up in this need to have our reputations cleared. You've got us on tenterhooks. As I said, our ratings next time are sure to set a record. We're going to have to shorten the conversation because so much ad space has been sold. But if the price of that is that we're all under suspicion, it's too much to pay."

"And what is the topic of the next show?" I asked. I hadn't had a chance to read the TV guide.

"Finland's relationship with the superpowers, Russia and the United States. And I'll sell you a state secret, Maria: one of the guests is the director of the Institute of International Affairs. I can trust the police with that kind of information, right?" Now Länsimies's smile contained some flirtation, and although I knew he was intentionally using his charisma on me, I had to concentrate to keep it from working. Länsimies knew he was good, and I'd always liked men who knew their business, whether it was guitar playing, sailing, or wooing the public.

"That's a big topic," I replied. "But can you be sure I won't leak it online, Ilari?" I couldn't help smiling, and I used his first name since he'd used mine.

"I can't. But what would life be without some risk? And why would we attack little issues when only the big ones matter? There's already enough pointless drivel on television." Länsimies snorted and pointed to one side. The door to the studio was open, and I saw the set for a cooking show: a gas stove, an electric stove, and a hot plate with a perky chef couple conjuring up a festive version and a light version of the same dish. I'd never seen the program because it came on at Taneli's bedtime. The aroma of curry and coriander wafted in from the studio, but the spotlights were off and the cameras rested under their covers. Had the cooking show used Fernet Branca recently? Or had there been a bottle in the program's storage space waiting for use?

"One question, off the record," I said and moved closer to Länsimies, as if we were friends. "How did Riitta Saarnio act when you met with Lulu Nightingale?"

Länsimies snorted. "Sad to say, she wasn't very professional. A producer shouldn't let it show when she doesn't like a guest. That's why I decided to leave her out of the second meeting. Riitta didn't complain at all. She was negative about the whole prostitution topic, but it's my program."

I nodded. We still couldn't eliminate Saarnio from our list of suspects. Then something else came to mind.

"Did you see Mauri Hytönen's car?"

"Oh, you mean the van with the name of his company plastered across it in giant letters? I saw it when I went outside for some fresh air before the broadcast. It pissed me off. Hytönen's HVAC company probably wouldn't mean anything to our other guests, but there was still the chance. After the fact, I read in the paper that Lulu knew him. That was quite a coincidence. It probably would have meant an interesting discussion . . . But let's follow up on the idea of you coming on the show after you've solved Lulu's murder. I can count on you, right?"

Länsimies extended his hand to make it a deal, and I didn't have much choice but to take it. Then he escorted us out, walking so close to me that I could feel the heat from his body and smell the clove scent of his aftershave. He opened the door for us. Outside the sun was shining, and it blinded me for a few seconds. The sunlight felt good, but I couldn't linger. We had to keep moving.

"You drive. I have a couple of calls to make," I said to Koivu as I opened the car door.

"Maria, you were flirting with him!" Koivu exclaimed.

"With whom?"

"With whom! What, you think I mean Riitta Saarnio?"

"No, you were the one who was being more than sympathetic to her! Let's just let Länsimies believe I'm helpless against his charm. Then he'll think he has one up on us when he doesn't." I gave Koivu a wink, but he didn't reply.

I called our investigative secretary to ask her to check on the schedule for flights to Kuopio. Then I checked with my mother-in-law to make sure she was free the next day. I kept the call brief because I wanted to hear from Antti himself about what he'd arranged with his mother.

"Hell hath no fury like a woman scorned," Koivu said contemplatively as we turned onto the Ring II beltway.

"Except the fury of a scorned man, as we've learned," I replied. Koivu snorted. An elderly man skied along the edge of a field, and I thought I recognized him as one of our neighbors from our previous house. He and Antti had broken the trail to Central Park together each winter. Now the man's kicks were sluggish, as if his skis weren't sliding properly. He disappeared behind an embankment.

I hesitated for a moment before speaking my next words. Koivu was one of my best friends, and he'd stood by me when I'd freaked out over my high school crush, Johnny, while investigating a murder and then later over one of our suspects, Mikke Sjöberg. Koivu knew Antti, but his loyalty was to me. "Pekka, do you think Antti could cheat on me?"

Koivu was so startled that he jerked the steering wheel and had to quickly correct to keep us in our lane.

"Why would you ask something like that?"

"Well, because . . ." I felt stupid explaining my suspicions. In the bright light of day everything felt differently than it had the previous night.

"No, I've never thought Antti was the type of guy to screw around. He was probably just flirting. Everyone does it. You should just ask him directly. You two have always been able to talk. Men hate being spied on, and they hate beating around the bush. Should we stop at a café? I need a snack. Or no, let's go straight to lunch."

I had to get my presentation finished before the funeral and talk to Puupponen about the job in Kuopio the next day. Puupponen could make sure Hytönen would be in town. I'd let our friend from Vesanto slip out of my grasp far too easily. But even with all this to do, I agreed to catch a quick bite with Koivu in the cafeteria. For me that meant a turkey salad, and for Koivu it was pork chops and baked potatoes.

"I could lay money on Arto Saarnio being our poisoner," Koivu said through a mouthful of meat and gravy.

"Why? He wasn't even at the studio."

"This morning we talked about the killer's profile. A risk-taker. Saarnio is definitely that."

"On the contrary—he's a cold, calculating corporate raider. There isn't any risk in what he does. He helps businesses 'recover' by firing people. When Saarnio is done, you always have the same thing: a company with a good balance sheet and a bunch of people with no jobs and their lives in ruins. He doesn't take any risks himself. But think about Riitta Saarnio. She sensed that her husband had found someone new. What if Lulu Nightingale said the wrong thing before the broadcast, something that made Mrs. Saarnio think that Lulu was her husband's lover? And if Oksana knew Lulu, she might have told Lulu about her relationship with Arto Saarnio."

"But Lulu would never reveal something like that to Mrs. Saarnio. Lulu was a professional!"

"Yes, she was, but what if she suspected Riitta Saarnio was the person who cut up Oksana?" I realized I was talking too loudly, and the passport officials sitting at the next table were staring. "Damn it. We just don't know enough about Lulu! Hopefully Ursula's had success with Sulonen today. Who truly knew Lulu? Who knew what she really wanted?"

"Who knows anyone, really? I never would have guessed that you'd suspect Antti of unfaithfulness," Koivu said. I couldn't think of a sufficiently witty retort.

Back upstairs, I conferred with Ursula about Sulonen. According to her, they'd found out all kinds of dirt about Lulu's clients, and she would be happy to go interview some of the more important ones.

We both agreed we should let Sulonen go. When one of the tabloid reporters called, I had to confirm that we had made an arrest but that it hadn't led anywhere.

After throwing together the rest of my presentation, I changed my violet sweater for a black blazer and a silk polo shirt that matched my pants. I tightened my bun and made sure my lipstick was appropriately subdued. Katri Reponen had arranged for flowers from both of us. We were going to the funeral more to support Leena than for Aunt Allu, but flowers seemed appropriate for honoring the memory of such a unique woman.

Katri was already waiting by my car by the time I got there. Even though we worked in the same building, we saw each other with distressing infrequency. Sometimes Antti's mom joked that she mostly saw her friends at funerals, and now I seemed to be in the same situation.

We talked about work while we drove. The prosecution for Lulu's murder was probably going to fall to Katri. That is, as soon as I found someone for her to prosecute.

Leena was in the church lobby welcoming everyone as they arrived, and we shared a long hug. There was already a lot of gray in her dark hair, and it looked good on her. The youngest of Leena's children was now in middle school, so her life seemed much freer than my own.

"I'm surprised you're having the service for Allu in a church. I thought she was an atheist. That's why I bought such bright-red roses." Katri showed the bouquet, which easily could have been for a wedding. I thought it fit Allu perfectly.

"She rejoined the church when the Espoo Diocese got its first female bishop. The church had changed enough for Allu to be willing to associate with it again. According to Allu, a person could change her mind just so long as her heart stayed where it belonged. Are you coming to the reception after the service?" Leena asked, turning to me.

"For a while. Antti left for Vaasa, so I'll need to relieve his mom since I'm going to need her tomorrow too."

Katri and I sat at the back of the chapel. As the organist began the prelude, I felt someone approach. When I turned, I saw that it was Anna-Maija Mustajoki. We greeted each other awkwardly, although it shouldn't have been a surprise that Anna-Maija was here too. Allu had once sat on the board of the Finnish Feminist Association.

After the prelude, Pastor Terhi Pihlaja approached the altar. I was curious to hear what she would say. I abhorred priests who spouted empty words and hollow comfort, and the ones who couldn't defend their own views and just hid behind verses from the Bible. Sometimes my pique amused me, because it laid bare the fact that I still had feelings about the clergy speaking well.

Eulogies had the same initial routine as interrogations, which have to be carried out before the pastor could move on to her own words.

"Aila Viitanen was a woman who walked her own road. She had the courage to do things that others didn't dare try. She didn't care about what society thought. Yet she was not indifferent to the individual. She was a warm and caring person, who was loved and will be missed. I had the pleasure of getting to know Aila Viitanen the year before last when she called me to ask to rejoin the church, which she had left in the 1950s. But she wanted to talk to me before she made her final decision. That conversation led to a correspondence that was both fruitful and challenging for me, and I hope for her. Aila did not shrink from offering criticism or admitting her uncertainty, but she still had the courage to return to the bosom of the church she had been baptized into."

Pastor Pihlaja elicited smiles in the congregation as she described how irritated Allu was about the sensation caused by *The Da Vinci Code*. "Don't people know D. H. Lawrence anymore! In its time, *The Man Who Died* was the great rebellion against the doctrines of the church, but I think it's nice to imagine Jesus not being deprived of all earthly pleasures." Apparently Pastor Pihlaja trusted that mourners gathered to see off Allu Viitanen wouldn't complain to the diocese about her radical opinions. Tears welled in my eyes simply because this was just how Allu would have wanted herself to be talked about. The selection for the hymn, "Spirit of Truth, Show Us the Way," was also very Allu. I hadn't sung it in years, but now I realized how well the words applied to my own work too.

Anna-Maija Mustajoki was there, and she laid flowers on the casket with three other women, who were all sobbing openly. Katri and I were more restrained. Leena was weepy but calm. She'd had time to accept what had happened. Allu would be cremated later, so after the presentation of the flowers, we left the church and migrated over to Leena's house for the reception. In the line for the buffet, I ended up next to Anna-Maija Mustajoki again.

"How did you know Allu?" Mustajoki asked, and I couldn't avoid answering.

"I'm her niece's friend."

"Leena's? She was like a daughter to Allu. I thought the police only went to the funerals of victims to monitor suspects, but I realize you have private lives too." Mustajoki moved through the crowd to a table by a window, and I followed her. The others had questioned her, so I didn't have much of a picture of her.

"When will Lulu Nightingale be buried?" Mustajoki asked once we were in the corner of the room where our words would be drowned out by the general murmur.

"I don't know. As far as we're concerned, she can be buried any time."

"I imagine I'll read about it in the paper. There's no way they'll leave the poor woman in peace. I would have liked to have met her. It took me years before I recovered from that terrible encounter I had with that boy prostitute." Mustajoki spooned a large piece of tuna fish cake into her mouth.

"Did they succeed in keeping you all from knowing who the other guests would be?"

Mustajoki laughed. "Yes and no. I'd watched the show enough to know Länsimies's tricks. I was sure there would be a sex worker and a sex customer, and then someone else who wanted to criminalize it. But I expected some sort of Christian conservative, not an intelligent female priest. Instead of a police officer I thought Länsimies would invite some official from the Ministry of Justice, but maybe Nordström was a natural choice. I'm an inquisitive person, so I kept my eyes and ears open. When my taxi arrived in the parking lot, I saw an HVAC company van and wondered if it belonged to someone who was working in the building or a guest. I tried to suss out the situation."

I nodded and sipped my coffee.

"Of course, I knew what role Länsimies had chosen for me: the old fat feminist who wants to deny men their physical pleasures. That was why I wouldn't let them put my hair up in that bun. Länsimies had obviously given the makeup artist instructions. But I wanted to choose my own image."

"I read in your memoir that you had met Länsimies before. And you were in the same French conversation group as Riitta Saarnio."

"Yes, and Riitta was the one who asked me to come on the show." Anna-Maija wiped tuna filling off her jaw. "I hadn't seen Ilari in years. He's irritating, mostly because you can't help liking him once he turns on his charm."

I understood what Mustajoki meant. Länsimies was always present in the moment, and he enjoyed attention. That sort of self-confidence appealed to many women and reassured most men.

"There was a tense mood in the makeup room. The makeup artist was clearly concerned about something. I guessed there were problems with the schedule. Riitta, who came to bring me into the studio, was nearly hysterical, and I didn't think having one member of the staff missing was enough to explain it. I kept thinking something had gone wrong, like one of the guests had canceled or something. Länsimies was as self-absorbed as always."

Anna-Maija Mustajoki seemed like a woman who was used to making observations, so I simply let her talk. She described what she'd heard in the hallway before going on camera.

"Someone was talking on a telephone. It was a woman's voice but so quiet I couldn't make out the actual words. Länsimies was going from door to door. He told me we were going to make this the best show of all time and asked me to be assertive and provocative. Someone went to the restroom. Someone knocked on a door and then went away."

That must have been Sulonen bringing Lulu the glass. Lulu's dressing room had been next to Mustajoki's, so these observations were important.

"I've thought a lot," she suddenly said, "and I'm not sure whether I'm imagining it or if I really heard Lulu fall. I did hear a strange thud from the neighboring dressing room, but I didn't pay any attention to it. I was more focused on planning what I would say. I just thought that you never could know how each person prepared for something like this—maybe someone was doing push-ups to release their tension."

"When did you hear this thud?" As far as I knew, Mustajoki hadn't mentioned this in her previous interview.

"Just before Saarnio came to get me, about nine fifteen. Now my indifference haunts me. What if I'd mentioned the sound to Riitta and we'd gone to see what happened? Could we have saved Lulu? Don't sugarcoat it. I can handle being responsible for another person's death."

12

All I could tell Mustajoki was that I didn't know. Cyanide worked quickly. Did a time of death of 9:15 p.m. shut out any suspects? No.

I went and exchanged a few words with Leena, and then decided to leave. Pastor Pihlaja stood outside in the yard, trying to call for a taxi.

"I can take you. We're going in the same direction," I said.

"Thank you! Sometimes not having my own car is a problem. I feel like in the second largest city in Finland I should be able to get by with public transportation." I unlocked the car with the remote control, and Pihlaja took the passenger seat.

"I liked your eulogy," I said, even though I didn't know if that was quite appropriate to say.

"Thanks. This one was easy and hard at the same time. Easy because I knew Allu and could talk about her in more detail than if she were a stranger. Hard for the same reason. Back in seminary, we argued about whether a priest could cry at a funeral since she's supposed to be there to comfort everyone else. But after the tsunami, even the bishops cried. I was afraid I'd start bawling there by Allu's casket, but thankfully God gave me the power to control myself."

"I imagine you have counselors you work with since you see sick and dying people so much."

"Yes, of course. Although in the church there are still people who believe trusting in the power of God is enough. And maybe for some it is. But I need human support too."

I'd turned the heat up full blast because the windows had frosted over. Pastor Pihlaja took off her gloves and unbuttoned her coat. I wondered whether the white collar of her clerical clothing ever felt constricting or if it gave her strength to stay in character the same way my police uniform did, although I only wore it infrequently, mostly just when lecturing or attending formal events.

"I've needed to call you. I read through my old diaries. It was brutal. You think you've grown up and learned so much, but then you just see yourself repeating the same mistakes and entertaining the same fantasies as you did in high school. My entries from that period are detailed. Apparently instead of listening in class, I just recorded by own thoughts."

"I was always thinking about bass lines for my bandmate Jaska's terrible songs or daydreaming about boys instead of listening to the teacher," I said.

"I thought about boys too, but for me it never ended up turning into anything beyond my daydreams. But Lilli had the courage to act. She quickly got a reputation for being easy, but also for being able to get anyone she wanted. By the end of high school, she had a real Helsinki boyfriend, an economics student who would come pick her up from school in his car. And not just in any car: a BMW. I was jealous of her, jealous of how easily she interacted with the opposite sex and how she looked, even though I wrote that she was a painted whore and that I'd rather be smart than look like her."

"You mentioned a woman named Niina Räsänen. Lulu's friend. We've tried to reach her, but she lives in Basel nowadays. Did Lulu and Niina go to Switzerland together?" I asked.

The pastor thought for a moment. "Yes, that's just how it happened. Lilli went first, and then Nina followed. I heard about it from our common acquaintances, but I doubt they know much about where Niina's ended up either," Pastor Pihlaja said.

"Is she involved in the sex industry too?"

"No. She and her husband run a small farm, and they have three kids."

"Were you surprised when you learned what Lulu was doing before she died?" I asked.

Pihlaja thought for a moment. I glanced at her and saw confusion in her eyes. I kept getting the sense that there was something she didn't want to tell me.

"I don't know. I just hoped that she'd chosen it herself, not because she needed money for drugs."

"If it's any consolation, our lab didn't find any traces of drugs in her system. Just alcohol."

We sat in silence at a traffic light, and I had a chance to take a good look at her profile. At least at funerals she didn't wear her normal red lipstick, and her makeup was generally inconspicuous. Her face was relaxed and plain but pleasant.

"Lilli was ashamed of her parents. During the spring we graduated, her family bought a cabin in Barösund. We happened to be at the store at the same time, buying food for our graduation parties, Lilli with her mom and me with mine, and Mrs. Mäkinen started proudly telling us about the cabin. It had its own sauna and everything. But Lilli just complained: the cabin didn't have electricity or running water, and the shore was half a kilometer away. Lilli told me that as soon as she got her graduation cap, she was gone. And leave she did. The very next day she jumped on a ferry to Sweden."

I merged onto the West Highway. Traffic was backed up in the opposite lane because of an accident, apparently a fender bender that set off a chain reaction. There were three cars off to the side, the middle one with the rear bumper and the hood crunched, the first one with the rear bumper bent, and the last one with the hood dented. Police and an ambulance crew were already on the scene. I looked to see who was on duty and recognized Officers Haikala and Suomalainen. The word "Police" on Suomalainen's jumpsuit was so worn that only the *L* and the *I* were readable. Pastor Pihlaja muttered something to herself. Once we'd passed the scene of the accident, she asked whether I thought anyone had been hurt.

"It depends on the speed. The people in the middle car got the worst of it, but likely no one died in a collision like that. Let's hope for the best."

"Exactly. I was thinking yesterday about what kind of eulogy I would give for Lilli. I realized I couldn't condemn her even though I don't approve of prostitution. We can denounce phenomena, but with individual people it's more difficult. Allu and I agreed that Mary Magdalene's reputation doesn't need rehabilitation. It doesn't matter whether she was a prostitute or not. She loved Jesus, and he loved her. That's the heart of everything, love. Maybe in her own way Lilli offered love to people who weren't receiving it elsewhere. But who loved her?"

I thought of the way Tero Sulonen worshipped her and the way she used him. Love could be cruel when "the one" thought you were nothing of the sort. And then there were the people who felt like they were meant for each other but didn't nurture their love or let it become crushed under the impossibility of circumstance.

"How do you define love? Doesn't Lulu's choice of stage name tell us what she thought of her profession?" I replied.

"Sure. Love might have been part of it for her, but the fact of the matter is most prostitutes don't voluntarily choose the profession. Luckily there are some things you can't buy—like grace and mercy. Right after I graduated from seminary, I was a chaplain at the juvenile detention center in Kerava. There were a lot of kids there for whom the entire concept of grace and mercy was foreign. When I said that grace even applied to murderers, they were just confused."

I thought of a few killers I'd met who believed the only way to make amends for what they'd done was by dying. I didn't agree, and I couldn't even imagine supporting the death penalty. Maybe my belief in the possibility of redemption was akin to Pastor Pihlaja's belief in grace.

I dropped her off a couple of blocks from my own apartment. As I drove the rest of the way home, I promised myself that after we solved this case I'd make time to talk to her again.

The smell of crepes wafted in the hallway outside our door. My kids were crazy for their grandmother's crepes. Iida complained that I didn't bake *pulla* or make crepes enough. I'd tried to teach her how, but it had required patience. My own mother had usually shooed us girls out of the kitchen because we were more of a hindrance than a help. I tried to remember that and do it differently, not always with success.

Taneli had already eaten his fill and was playing with Legos on the living room floor. Iida was still at the table, and Marjatta was loading the dishwasher. I grabbed the last crepe and spread some strawberry jam on it. I enjoyed simple treats like this.

"We had pea soup too, but the children finished it off," Antti's mother said. "Was the funeral nice?"

"Yes, thank you. I'm glad you're able to come again tomorrow. I have to take a quick trip up north."

Marjatta dried her hands and then took off her apron. Whenever she came she brought her own apron and slippers. During her husband's illness and after his death, she'd lost several pounds and her hair had turned completely gray. Antti and Iida had inherited her hair type, so they would probably go gray as well.

"Antti stopped by today, but he said he still couldn't decide if he's willing to accept the money. I asked him if I should give it to a pack of stray dogs instead. And I reminded him that after I die, you'll get it all anyway. Maria, is everything alright with you and Antti?"

I assured her it was, since my mother-in-law was the last person with whom I wanted to share my suspicions.

After the kids fell asleep, I called Antti. He was outside walking, and in the background, I could hear the sounds of cars and people shouting. Our call was brief since neither of us had much to say. I didn't ask whether he was alone or with someone. I didn't want to know.

We nearly missed the plane to Kuopio in the morning because a huge snow storm had blown in overnight and made a complete mess of traffic. The weather report had warned us, but apparently no one listened. Fortunately, the plane was a little late too for the same reason, and we made it to the airport just in time. At first the flight was bumpy, but the sky cleared as we traveled north, so I could track the ground beneath us as the sun came up. The route roughly followed Highway 5, and I was able to pick out the city of Mikkeli and the Juva Hotel below. That brought back warm memories of the previous summer and the ForestStock rock festival held behind the hotel. My parents had watched Iida and Taneli so that Antti and I could go out and dance like teenagers. Maybe we should go to another rock concert.

Puupponen ate my muffin as well as his, because the very idea of a sweet snack on a plane made me feel nauseated. I was lucky and didn't end up with the motion sickness that sometimes plagued me on morning flights. The Kuopio airport was next to a lake, and the ice was still so thick that I counted eight ice fishermen without turning my head. Puupponen was dozing, so I nudged him in the ribs as the plane descended.

"Ville, we're home."

A rental car was waiting at the airport. Puupponen wanted to drive, and he knew the local roads. We'd agreed to stop by and say hi to his parents in Kuopio if we had time. At the intersection outside the airport, Puupponen turned right. If he'd gone left, we would have ended up in Arpikylä, where I was from, but that wasn't where we were going.

The Puijo Observation Tower stood proudly on its hill and against the light-blue sky. The road wound through empty, endless forests, with only the occasional house. The price for this kind of natural beauty was that everything was a long way away. Puupponen's uncle lived in the village of Tervo, which was along our route to Vesanto, so I got to hear about their fishing trips. I leaned back and enjoyed the sparkling of the snow in the trees. Even though we were driving along a main road, the snowbanks were clean, and they were three times bigger than those in Espoo.

Puupponen had brought a map of Vesanto. Supposedly finding Hytönen's business would be easy. We drove down a long, steep hill toward the main village, then passed a narrow lake. After the church, we turned left toward the lake. On the right, we passed a three-story school building that was now abandoned. It looked hospitable but sad. After another quarter of a mile we came to a relatively new warehouse building with "Hytönen HVAC" on the sign. When I saw the van in the parking lot, I remembered that the same one had been parked next to the door of West Man Productions last Friday.

Puupponen had verified that Hytönen would be in the office. As we got out of the car, he came to meet us.

"This is a great honor. It isn't often we have visitors all the way from Espoo," he said, extending his hand. His sweater and jeans looked like they'd been purchased at the local village clothing store; they looked comfortable and sensibly priced. Hytönen was an entrepreneur who clearly knew what was worth paying for and what wasn't. How far away was his world from Arto Saarnio's, once all was said and done? Small businessmen suffered from the cutbacks that people like Saarnio orchestrated, because they often resulted in a loss of subcontracting work.

"Come on into the office. I'm sure you could use some coffee. Minttu, hold all my calls. Say I'm in an important meeting," he yelled to the young woman sitting in a glass booth in the lobby, who nodded to indicate she'd heard him.

"Minttu is a good girl. She went to the polytechnic in Kuopio, but then she decided to come back home. Her boyfriend works for me too. It's important to provide jobs for local kids so the place doesn't end up having just a bunch of old people." Hytönen opened the door to the office. The coffee pot was full, and there were three rose-patterned cups and saucers on the table, along with cream, sugar, a braided loaf of pulla, and, thankfully, sandwiches. After the bumpy flight, the thought of salami and rye made my mouth water.

Hytönen invited us to sit and poured our coffee while I took the chance to look around. On the wall of the office was a diploma, and I saw that Hytönen had been voted businessman of the year in Vesanto in 2001. The wall calendar had pictures of rally cars. Apparently Hytönen didn't trust electronics, since he had forty-some-odd phone numbers written on a sheet of paper taped to the top of his desk phone. Binders organized in alphabetical order bore client names. In addition to coffee, the room smelled of oil, tobacco, and aftershave.

"So little Mauri Hytönen is an important enough suspect to bring in detectives all the way from the capital. My goodness. And so officially," Hytönen said as Puupponen placed the recorder and his laptop on the table. "I thought I might turn into some sort of celebrity when I agreed to go on that show, but I never imagined anything like this. Soon they'll be asking me to run for president, since I'm so brave and I tell it like it is."

"I read one of your interviews. Have there been others?" I asked as I stirred two lumps of sugar into my coffee.

"Practically all I've done is talk on the phone and give interviews! A porn magazine even asked if I'd come and talk about the best places to get girls in Tallinn. And ever since the show, all my employees' wives keep calling and asking what their husbands have been up to with me in Estonia. I just say they should ask their husbands themselves. I've never roped anyone into anything, and the few who have gone with me I made swear to use a condom. I don't want my workers bringing home any unpleasant surprises. But Jesus, it isn't like I'm going to turn them in to their wives! What do you think, Detective? You're married. Would you want to know if your old man was out having adventures?"

"I would, but I'd want to hear it from him. Let's move on to that fight you got into two years ago with Lulu Nightingale at the Mikado. We've read the file, but some details are still unclear to me. Why did you insult Lulu in the first place?"

"She overpriced herself. So I thought she needed a lesson. It's a buyer's market." Hytönen brushed a crumb out of his mustache. "And, OK, I was drunk. I'd just been in a tough negotiation, and I was pissed because the selection at the Mikado that night was pathetic. But I didn't want Lulu even though she came and rubbed her tits in my face."

"But you knew who she was?"

"Yes, she was already a celebrity in those circles. She had a website and everything. Don't get me wrong. In a way, we were on the same side. We both wanted more freedom. But I didn't think Lulu was doing it as a service to the masses. She wanted to control men. I wouldn't be the slightest bit surprised to find out she'd been blackmailing customers. There's a motive for you."

I looked out the window. In the parking lot, workers loaded plastic pipes into another, larger van. Behind the building was a ski track, which looked to be in good condition. Hytönen poured himself and Puupponen more coffee, but I declined a second cup.

"If you've read the court files, you know it was an open-and-shut case. Lulu and her bodyguard confessed, and the whole thing could have been handled through mediation instead of a trial. I never would have pressed charges, but the restaurant staff called the police. The whole mess was unnecessary. And I didn't have any desire to have anything to do with those people ever again. People complain about the police being underfunded, but you still have money to fly around Finland asking stupid questions. On the private side, no one would have the resources for that."

I took another sandwich and waited for Puupponen to chime in. He'd talked to Hytönen before. When he didn't say anything, I decided to give them an opportunity to talk. "Where is the restroom?"

"In the hall. We don't have a separate women's bathroom because Minttu's the only one here. Second door on the left."

Even though I wasn't a shrinking violet, the Hytönen HVAC restroom gave me the creeps. It was clean, the fabric hand towels appeared recently changed, and the sinks shone. But there was no way to escape the pinup calendars. One hung above the sink, and another on the door so you could see it if you were doing your business sitting down. The third was behind the toilet itself, clearly intended for those who stood. The March girl, who had silicon breasts the size of soccer balls and a French bikini wax, posed leaning on a drain pipe. The calendar was German. Maybe it was a business calendar. I wondered how Minttu felt when she used the restroom. When I left, I intentionally turned the wrong way and ended up in the warehouse, which was full of pipes, couplers, and electrical wire. I didn't know half of their names or uses, which, as a woman, I was comfortable with. The average man, however, might have become agitated and felt inferior if he couldn't immediately identify each kind of wire. Antti was pretty handy, but he despised service stations because the other men there always expected him to want to talk about alloy rims and engines even though he wasn't interested in things like that. Still, sometimes we talked about building our own house. I sensed that despite it all, that was Antti's dream, the traditional test of manhood. But now when that dream was within reach, he was rejecting it.

On the bulletin board in the warehouse there were also pictures of scantily clad women. I walked toward the booth where Minttu sat. She was tall and thin, and her short hair was dyed in a black-and-white 1980s style. She had a nose piercing. Her crop top seemed too skimpy and thin for an industrial workplace, and her ribs poked through the tight fabric. She looked at me with suspicion and then leaned her head out the window of the plexiglass box.

"What do y'all think Mauri did? Because he didn't kill nobody," Minttu said angrily. I noticed a tongue stud as well. "Mauri's a great boss and he's never tried nothin' with me. He gave me a job and didn't ask if Late and me were going to have kids, even though all the other places did and I never thought I'd find no job. He does what he does, but he ain't no murderer. Y'all should leave him alone!"

"So you enjoy working here?"

"Yes! And I've got a full-time job, just like Late. Nobody else from my class has a steady job, except of course Assi since she's got a farm. Y'all don't understand what a gift from God Mauri is for this village. And it ain't against no law if he does go see women in Estonia! I know you big city folk want to make Mauri a laughingstock since he's from the country. But you listen here: that man would have more women to choose from here than he could count on two hands, but he wants to live the way he lives, and so he does."

"And these decorations don't bother you at all? I mean all these pictures of naked women?"

"Them's just pictures. No one touches me, cuz everyone knows I'm Late's girl. We're gettin' married in June, and Mauri already promised to be Late's best man."

Minttu's skin was gooseflesh, and I was cold too. Someone had opened the warehouse door, and there was a draft.

"Does Late go to Estonia with Mauri?"

"They're leavin' for Tarttu today! But I trust Late. He's a one-woman man. Guys like that do still exist!" Minttu slapped the window jam as if to drive home her words. "Guys stay faithful if you're nice enough to them and you don't nag about everything. Mauri's second wife was so horrible. She screamed about every little thing, like leaving the toilet seat up and stupid stuff like that. And she didn't even let him watch hockey. Thank God me and Late like the same things. Why don't you go back to Helsinki and look for murderers there!"

Minttu pulled the window shut in front of me and started tapping angrily at her keyboard. In front of her was a pile of bills. Apparently, she also handled the company's payments. A man in coveralls walked toward me, gave me a glare, and continued on into the warehouse without a word. I decided that Puupponen had had enough time alone with Hytönen and decided to go back in the office. From the hallway I could hear laughter.

Puupponen's accent was significantly more pronounced than when he was in Espoo, and he actually seemed to be exaggerating it. Apparently talk had turned to hockey, in particular the coaching situation for the Finnish national team.

"I played for KalPa in the juniors, but I was kinda slow getting to the puck," Puupponen was just saying. "I tried hard, though, because I thought players got the girls."

"Did it work?" Hytönen asked. Puupponen didn't reply and cast me a pointed glance. It seemed my entrance had been poorly timed. I sat back in my seat and sucked down the weak coffee, which didn't help with the chill. Great, all I needed was to catch a cold.

I made Hytönen retell his account of the night at the TV studio, and he swore he hadn't seen anyone but Länsimies and the makeup artist, Nuppu Koskela. "Didn't you think that this kind of fame might put your business at risk?" I asked him.

Hytönen laughed. "All press is good press. If some tight-ass gets their HVAC work done somewhere else, what do I care? I've got more demand than I can handle. Soon I'm going to have to hire more men. Before you know it, they're going to pin a medal on me for all the jobs I'm creating."

"You seem to have extensive experience with Finnish sex workers. Do you know a girl named Oksana?" I stared into Hytönen's eyes, and I saw his face twitch.

"You must mean that girl they found all cut up down your way."

"That's the one. How often do you use girls who obviously have pimps, or does that matter to you?"

"I'm an entrepreneur, and I understand the laws of business." Hytönen's voice was suddenly tense, and his dialect had disappeared entirely. "I also understand that a businessman shouldn't ever get involved in anything that could lead to blackmail. I want my contacts to be safe. So yes, I know who you mean. I knew Oksana. She's associated with a guy named Mishin, who controls the Helsinki market. And he isn't a man you mess with. I keep my distance from those thugs. But you aren't going to find Oksana. She made a mistake when she went to the hospital and let the police find her. She's probably at the bottom of the Gulf of Finland with weights around her feet."

Hytönen stood up and walked to the coffee maker, but he didn't pick up the pot.

"Detective Kallio, I know the risks of my hobby. That's why I want it to be legal, so that the women can be better protected. We're heading to Tarttu today, where I have one of my regulars, Birgitta. She's a nice girl who likes money and is studying Finnish at the university. We have a mutual protection agreement, which nobody knows about, because the pimps in Tarttu don't want any independent entrepreneurs on the market either. I understand that, even though in my business a little competition can be a good thing sometimes. My prices may be a lot higher than what the Estonians charge, but my company is a reliable supplier and my boys do good work. That's why Finnish companies use me. In the same vein, I don't pay for the services of women who don't live up to my standards. That Nightingale lady was just running a scam. Find out who she didn't satisfy or who she was cheating, and you'll find who killed her. Now, if you don't have any more questions, I'd like to get back to preparing for my trip. I need to send Minttu to buy some presents for Birgitta. She likes our Finnish salmiakki."

Hytönen extended his hand as if to end the discussion. For a few moments we sized each other up. I didn't take his hand. Instead I asked about Mishin, but Hytönen denied knowing him. It occurred to me that we'd need to question Nordström again, and Tero Sulonen's bank accounts would need a close inspection. If Sulonen suddenly seemed to have a lot of extra cash, that might start clearing things up.

Once I felt as though Hytönen realized that he wasn't going to be ordering me and Puupponen around, I stood up and declared the interrogation over. Puupponen turned off the recorder, and I looked at Hytönen. His black mustache and hair looked dyed. Maybe he suffered from premature graying. Otherwise he seemed youthful, and his face had hardly any wrinkles, just some scars from adolescent acne. His body was slim and athletic. The thick gold chain that hung around his neck seemed somehow un-Finnish, and it would have been out of place on a job site. I imagined Hytönen used it to show off his success.

"Just let me know if you ever need any tips for finding female companionship," Hytönen said to Puupponen as we were leaving, and Puupponen blushed. He didn't say a word until we were five miles out of town. I thought about Puupponen's love life. Was his lack of a girlfriend a problem for him, as I'd sometimes sensed?

"I'll call Mom and have her put some food on. We can have lunch there," Puupponen finally said and started fumbling with his hands-free headset to the point that it seemed more dangerous than simply picking up the phone. The call was short, and he just said he was coming with his boss and that we wouldn't stay long.

Puupponen's parents lived in an apartment complex on the north side of Kuopio. Now retired, his father had worked for the railroad, and his mother had been a secretary at the police station. At their front door they greeted me as an honored guest, and they refused to call me anything but Detective Lieutenant. Puupponen's mother was particularly excited to learn how her son was doing as a police officer in the big city, so I took every opportunity to praise him, along with the fresh dill flavoring of the beef stew she had made. It appeared he'd inherited his sense of humor from his father, who dropped puns left and right in his thick dialect, while Puupponen's mother glanced at me now and then, apparently worried that her husband's jokes might be too risqué. In the end, we had to rush to get to the airport, but as luck would have it, the plane was late again. After takeoff, Puupponen took out his laptop and began the interview report. I tried to nap but failed. All I could think about was what Hytönen had said, and seeing Ursula and Kaartamo together in the cafeteria at the police station.

I checked my phone after we'd landed—there were four messages, but I decided to let them wait. Once we were sitting in the privacy of the car, I asked Puupponen if he knew anything about Kaartamo and Ursula's relationship. Puupponen had a good, professional relationship with Ursula, better than any of the rest of us did.

"Come on, Maria, do you really not get it?" Puupponen said with pity in his voice. "It's easy to understand why Ursula is fawning over Kaartamo. She wants to get into the noncommissioned officers course, and so she's going over your head to Kaartamo in hopes he'll recommend her." Puupponen swerved to avoid a car abandoned by the side of the road, its rear driver's side smashed in. The radio said that four people had been killed in the storm, along with dozens injured. Thank God not a single fatality had occurred within our jurisdiction.

"Why does Ursula think I wouldn't recommend her?"

"Because you don't like her."

"I don't approve of some of her methods, but I think she handles most of her work well enough. Why is she so damn intent on imagining that I'm trying to get in her way? Especially after I stood behind her in that—" At which point I cut myself off since Puupponen didn't know about Ursula's adventure at the Mikado. "I would definitely recommend her for the NCO course, although it certainly wouldn't help with our staffing shortage."

"Kaartamo is plenty willing to take payment for his services," Puupponen said. "Maybe we should warn Ursula."

"Payment?"

"I've gone out for drinks with Kaartamo after work parties a few times, and I know how he operates. Ursula thinks she's a tough chick, but I don't think she's quite cynical enough to sleep with Kaartamo just to get him to sign off on a training course."

"Do you really think Kaartamo—" I began, but then the phone rang. It was Mira Saastamoinen.

"Hi, Maria. I finally caught you! Where have you been hiding?"

"On an airplane coming back from Kuopio."

"I'm over at the Big Apple Mall. There's an investigation underway. A man was shot in the head, and the whole thing stinks to high heaven . . ."

"In what way?"

"Well, first of all we have no idea what the weapon was. It couldn't have been any normal firearm. And second, there's the victim . . . It's Tero Sulonen."

13

Puupponen immediately turned us toward the mall. It felt inconceivable that someone had been shooting in the middle of a crowded shopping center. Professional criminals didn't usually take risks like that. Even though the snow had let up, traffic was still a mess, and along Ring II there were more stranded cars that had yet to be towed away.

I called Koivu, who had taken command of the unit in my absence and organized the morning meeting. The DNA results from Lulu Nightingale's body had come back. The National Bureau of Investigation crime lab had nearly set a record with their turnaround time. But the results weren't anything surprising. They'd found one of Tero Sulonen's hairs on her blouse, there was nothing under her fingernails, and her vagina had been free of semen. There was a small blood stain on her skirt, but it was her own blood.

"Ursula and Autio are questioning Lulu's clients. That's taken a fair amount of persuasion. Do you trust Ursula not to leak to the press again?" Koivu asked. A few years earlier we'd suspected Ursula of leaking the identity of a prisoner, but we'd never found any hard evidence. "Some of them deny any connection to Lulu, understandably. Lulu's notes won't hold up in court because we don't have any pictures or other evidence yet. We still haven't found Lulu's safe deposit box."

"And now Sulonen has been shot, the same day we really start interrogating Lulu's customers. Damn it! We should have kept him in a cell. At least he would have been safe."

"Calm down, boss," Puupponen interjected.

The area around the Big Apple was full of police vehicles: three of our cruisers, a forensic van, and another unmarked Saab, which I recognized as Kaartamo's. "What the hell is he doing at a crime scene?" I muttered to myself. I also spotted a TV news van. A shooting in a mall was unheard of in Finland. In the afternoon, the Big Apple was full of schoolkids. In a few years, Iida would be hanging out along with them.

An ambulance was parked right next to the freight elevator, and suddenly the elevator door opened. Men carrying a stretcher rushed out. The victim's head was bandaged and he lay on his side, a temporary IV already inserted into a vein. We moved out of the way, but I caught a glance of a pale face with eyes staring, wide open but empty. The paramedics loaded the stretcher into the ambulance and jumped in behind it, and the vehicle took off at full speed, sirens blaring and lights flashing. I hoped Tero Sulonen would survive, although I didn't know whom to petition for that favor.

The escalator on the second floor of the north side of the mall was cordoned off. I stepped over the tape and flashed my badge to the guard posted to keep civilians out of the upper floor. It seemed that whoever was in charge of the crime scene had asked the mall security for assistance. Maybe it would have made sense to call in the military.

Assistant Chief of Police Kaartamo seemed to be the one holding the reins. He was in the middle of an intense phone conversation when we walked up. He hadn't cleared out the mall yet, so curious onlookers were jostling to see what was happening, even though there was no longer anything to see, just an outline on the floor where Tero Sulonen had fallen. It felt somehow surreal, like something was out of place. Then I realized the reason for the strange feeling: the only sound was the muted buzz of conversation. The music and advertisements that usually echoed through the halls of the mall had been shut off. Good. At the moment, I didn't really need an ad for cheap coffee or the latest pop hit.

"Kallio, what are you doing here?" Kaartamo shouted. "I thought you were up north."

"Not anymore." I scanned the crowd for Mira Saastamoinen and spotted her just rounding a corner.

"Hi, Maria! They just took Sulonen to Jorvi Hospital. The bullet left a nasty mark. The whole back of his head is a mess."

"Bullet? You just said you didn't know what the weapon was."

"We don't, because no one heard the shot or saw the gun."

"A pistol with a silencer?"

"No, it's something higher caliber," Mira's partner Akkila said. "The wound looks more like something a rifle would make. The bullet might still be in his head."

Mira and Akkila had been in the mall, on a coffee break at the time of the shooting. They had been the first to respond to the mall security guard's call for help. The eyewitnesses were still sitting in the coffee shop: a middle-aged woman in a leather jacket who was clearly trying to look younger than she was judging from the highlights in her carefully tousled hair, a teenage boy, and a young mother with a baby in a sling. They'd been walking near Sulonen when he suddenly groaned and collapsed. The boy said he thought Sulonen must have had a heart attack. "You know those bodybuilders." The middle-aged woman was the first to notice the blood and started shouting for security. The young mother said all she could think about was protecting her baby. But there was no sign of a shooter.

The ballistics experts would be able to determine where the shot had come from. I watched the familiar bustle of the crime scene, the measurements, the interviews, the searching. I wasn't alone in this, even though I felt devoid of strength despite Puupponen's mother's nourishing stew. I looked up at the third floor. People often leaned on the railing and looked down at the main level. Could someone have fired a shot from there without anyone noticing? But where would they go? Next to the movie theater was an elevator and stairs, which lead down to the parking area. The shooter would have been able to flee, practically before any alarm had been raised. An hour had passed since then. He could be anywhere.

What was the profile we'd just constructed? This shooter was a person who was willing to take risks. But was this even the same person who'd killed Lulu Nightingale? What if Sulonen had been running his own blackmail operation, and this is where it had led?

I walked over to Kaartamo. He was talking on the phone again and nodding.

"You're right. No, there's no cause for worry. This is an isolated case, and the man who was shot had connections to the underworld and a recent murder. There isn't any insane shooter on the loose. You can put the public's minds at ease. I can come too if necessary. Yes, this is a significant-enough operation, which I'll be taking responsibility for. She's a perfectly competent girl, but maybe I'll still—" Kaartamo gave a start when he noticed me. Kaartamo knew exactly what I thought about his habit of calling female professionals "girls."

After a moment, he got off the phone and turned toward me. "Listen up, Kallio, we need to have a meeting. That was the minister of the interior. He's worried about public safety. We need to get this case solved fast. As of this moment all vacations are canceled for everyone in the department, and every last person with a badge is going to come down here and start questioning this crowd. God damn all these traffic accidents tying up our men. We can't even get help from Vantaa because there are so many of them. I can handle the press conference. You just focus on investigating Lulu Nightingale's murder. You have information on Sulonen from that. Is there anything you've uncovered recently that will help with this?" Kaartamo appeared agitated. Usually he enjoyed being at the center of attention and getting to show what a tough guy he was. "And we need to get in touch with Nordström's crew," he hissed. "They know more about these whores' clients than we do. This could have turned into a code red. Thank God our shooter only needed one shot." Kaartamo's chatter was getting on my nerves. I walked over to the window of a barber shop to call my mother-in-law.

"Hi, it's Maria. How's it going?"

"Everything's fine. We just had Karelian stew, Taneli's favorite."

"Good. Can you plan to stay the night? I don't know how long I'm going to be here. You're going to hear about it on the news anyway, so I'll tell you now. There's been a shooting at the Big Apple, and I'm going to have to start the investigation. The victim is one of the suspects in another case I'm working on." After she confirmed that she could stay, I said, "Say hi to the kids. I'll call when it's time for good-night hugs if I'm not home by then."

I mentally riffled through the contents of the cupboards and decided we'd be able to manage until tomorrow. Then I climbed the spiral staircase to the third-floor landing in front of the movie theater. Based on the direction that Sulonen was walking and the angle of the shot, it appeared probable that the shooter would have been standing right here, outside the theater. I put my hands in my pockets and tried to imagine having a revolver. I could have aimed it from inside my jacket, and probably even a sawed-off shotgun too. But a rifle . . . I couldn't conceive of any way that would be possible.

My phone rang. It was Mira. I saw her standing in the coffee shop downstairs, and she waved at me. I could hear her voice in the receiver very faintly over the noise of the shopping center.

"Update from Jorvi. Sulonen is in surgery, and the bullet is still in his head. His condition is critical. He's suffered severe damage to his skull and his brain. They promised they'd tell us when they know more, but so far it looks like the operation will last several hours. I asked them to call you directly."

"Thanks," I said, although I didn't know what Kaartamo would say. It was true that we needed to have a meeting. In an operation this large, with this many people to interview, responsibility had to be shared. It was strange that Kaartamo hadn't immediately asked the NBI to join the investigation.

In situations like these, civilians were usually helpful and cooperative. If someone saw the shooter, they would say so, as would the dozens and dozens who had just thought they'd seen something. But the doors of the mall hadn't been closed when the alarm was raised, and that probably meant the perpetrator had escaped. Maybe the security cameras would tell us something. Hopefully they'd been set to record.

I walked back to Kaartamo, who was currently giving a statement to a TV reporter. His tone was soothing, just like when he'd spoken to the interior minister on the phone: this wasn't an act of terror or the action of a mass murderer, just an attack directed at a single individual, Tero Sulonen. But when the reporter asked about the status of the Lulu Nightingale murder investigation, Kaartamo sicced him on me, and I had to explain that the investigation was proceeding but that no one had been arrested beyond temporary detentions for questioning.

Once I got rid of the reporter, I suggested to Kaartamo that we have all the trash cans inside and outside the mall searched in case the shooter tossed the gun or some article of clothing on his way out. Kaartamo glared at me and said that would cost too much, but then he agreed to call out the Guard to help. The soldiers could sort through the trash.

"Let's head back to the station," I said to Puupponen. I called Koivu and asked him to bring the unit together, since the attempt on Sulonen's life suggested that we needed to focus more resources on the Helsinki pimps. It was already six o'clock, but now was a time for overtime if there ever was one.

The lower level of the police station was already quiet, and the officer at the desk waved as we passed. When I saw my reflection in the mirror in the elevator, I flinched: my skin was pale and blotchy, my lipstick had worn off, and my bangs were sticking up. I looked like a sloppy middle-aged woman. Puupponen didn't look much better: under his freckles he was pasty, and I could smell the sweat coming from under the arms of his wool sweater.

Puustjärvi was making coffee in the conference room, and Puupponen and I had grabbed cardamom sweet rolls and sandwiches on the drive in. Even Ursula obviously hadn't been getting her beauty sleep lately, because she couldn't stop yawning. Mascara had flaked under her eyes, and her bruises had turned yellow under her makeup. Even she wasn't capable of looking completely put together after an intensive week of investigation.

Lulu seemed to have had a steady, rich clientele, a clientele who had a lot to lose if their escapades were ever found out. These weren't your average johns; they were the pillars of society with money to pay for their predilections.

"Do you have any idea where that picture of Lulu and the president came from? Maybe she had a customer who had a fantasy about that," I said to Ursula, who laughed.

"Not a clue! The IT guys say it's an obvious forgery. These days you can photoshop almost anything."

"The IT guys? They don't have that picture pinned up on their wall yet, do they?" I asked, fearing the worst. "I'm going to hoist every last one of them up a flagpole by their balls—and you by the ovaries—if that picture ends up in the press. What did you find out from the interviews with Lulu's clients?"

Ursula blushed. "Endless requests for confidentiality and assurances that it was just a temporary relationship, which Lulu had handled with perfect professionalism. Nothing indicating any blackmail. Most of the clients didn't know anything about Sulonen. At most they knew that Lulu had a bodyguard but never saw him. But most of the men whose names show up in Lulu's customer list claim the list is false."

"Puustjärvi?"

"You already heard about the DNA results from Lulu's body, and there isn't anything new from the other forensic analysis or Lulu's computer. And the damn bank secrecy laws won't let us get at her safety deposit box information." As he spoke, Puustjärvi stood up to get more coffee.

"Did Lulu have a will? Who's her lawyer? Is that in our files? Who defended Lulu in the trial against Hytönen? Talk to him. Petri, what about the liquor stores?"

"Their product tracking system isn't detailed enough. The EAN codes don't reference individual bottles. Our only hope would be cross-referencing all the receipts in the system with credit card records. But the court isn't going to give us a warrant for that since we don't have an actual suspect. We can't ask them for information on the booze purchases of half of Finland." Puustjärvi sat down, and coffee splashed from his cup onto the table and his pants, eliciting a muffled curse.

"But there is still a murder victim! Let's get Lulu's card information. See if you can get it through. I'll sign off on it," I said.

"But what if she paid cash? I always do that when I shop at Alko, for this very reason," Autio suddenly said. "And I never use any kind of customer loyalty cards."

"I think it would be nice if Alko had a customer card. Every tenth vodka bottle free? Sign me up!" Puupponen said, trying to lighten the mood, but we only laughed out of a sense of duty.

"Let's see who Patrol tracks down from the mall. Autio and Puustjärvi, you two go through the preliminary interview reports and try to sift out the most reliable witnesses. We'll focus on them first and then move on to the flakier ones. Mira Saastamoinen is our point of contact. Ursula and Puupponen, you handle the actual questioning, and Koivu and I . . ."

My phone rang, emblazoned with Kaartamo's name like a threat. I considered it best to answer.

"Where did you disappear to? I said we needed to meet."

"I'm back at the station. You seemed to have things under control."

"Come to my office. Nordström will be here soon too. We need to talk now."

Normally violent crimes came straight from Patrol to my unit, but bad luck had caught me on the plane from Kuopio when the call came in, and the location of the crime had caused Kaartamo to intervene.

"I'll come as soon as my own meeting is done. Why are you getting Nordström mixed up in this?"

"He's the NBI's specialist on this, and he's a good man! And we won't wait for you forever."

I'd had just about enough of people who constantly needed to prove how much power they had. To make it worse, Kaartamo was one of the old-school cops who thought the department should be run like the army. Most of the leadership thought differently nowadays, and habits had changed. Despite Kaartamo's bluster, I took my time wrapping things up with my unit before heading upstairs to his office.

Kaartamo and Nordström stood at the window, drinking orange Jaffa soda. Kaartamo motioned for me to sit. Neither man shook my hand. I didn't like the setup, because Nordström was still one of my suspects for Lulu Nightingale's murder. And I didn't have any interest in getting mired in an interagency power struggle.

Nordström sat down next to me and pulled his chair over close enough to touch me. He was wearing faded blue jeans and a denim jacket the same color. His T-shirt said "Hawaii." Kaartamo's suit was wrinkled, and there was mud on his shoes. He glared at me in irritation before sitting down behind his desk, which was cluttered with papers. His cell phone beeped to indicate a new text message, but Kaartamo didn't look at it.

"You finally came. Just don't say you have to rush off to take care of your kids now."

"I won't. Which of us is going to lead the investigation into Sulonen's attempted murder now, you or me? That's mostly what I came here to check." I stood up and walked to the window. Kaartamo's office had a view of the parking lot and the small strip of pine forest that remained between the police station and the next building. It was already dark, but the ice crystals on the tops of the cars glittered brilliantly. It was getting colder.

"You will," Kaartamo said, "but I'll set the pace. We can't let the investigation get in the way of the NBI's big sting."

Nordström nodded in satisfaction.

"If everything is supposed to be so hush-hush, why did you go on that TV show?" I asked Nordström. "I would have thought you'd avoid publicity before your big moment. Or did you think you'd get more glory if you were already recognizable?"

Nordström stared at me, his jaw clenched, but then he poured himself more Jaffa. "Relax, Kallio. We're all on the same side. I might even be able to solve your case for you. I was just sitting here thinking about which of the pimps would use a paid assassin, and I always come back to the same name. Mishin." Nordström's expression wavered a bit. Some people reacted that way when they talked about their lovers, but Nordström's archenemy seemed to arouse even stronger feelings.

"How about the NBI gives us Mishin's stooges? You have files on them, I presume. What happened here is probably the standard story: they gave Sulonen the dirty work, to knock off Lulu I mean, but he got too greedy. Mishin's boys wouldn't stand for that," Kaartamo said and gave me a stern look.

"Sometimes Mishin uses a guy named Yevgeni Urmanov as his enforcer," Nordström said.

"He's wanted in several cases, but nothing seems to stop these fuckers from getting into the country on fake passports. Do you have any eyewitnesses for the shooting?"

I said that the interviews were still in process. Nordström threw out a few more names and promised that his undercover detectives would keep their ears open. I couldn't believe what I was hearing: even though Nordström himself was technically a suspect for Lulu's murder, he was assigning his own subordinates to do their own investigation of the same crime! Usually I avoided leaking insider information to the press, but now I really wanted to. What would that nice fellow from MTV3 say if he heard about this?

"When are you going to run this big sweep of yours?" I asked, trying to keep my tone neutral, even though it kept slipping toward a snarl.

"Wouldn't the vernal equinox be an appropriate time? Good Friday? That would be smooth. So it would be better if you could idle your investigation until then and leave Mishin alone. All the better if we can file murder and attempted murder charges against the lot of them. Or will it be two murders? What's Sulonen's prognosis?"

"We don't know yet. Are you saying we can go ahead with our murder investigation just so long as we stay silent as a mouse so that your shiny operation doesn't get messed up? Doesn't it seem like maybe our priorities are getting a little out of whack? We're investigating a homicide, in the worst-case scenario as many as three. You haven't forgotten Oksana Petrenko, have you? Doesn't that take priority over everything else?"

"It isn't quite that simple, Kallio," Kaartamo replied for Nordström. "I've already informed the interior minister of the situation. The most important thing is to stay calm and avoid involving innocent people in the investigation. The mafia wanted this murder to be highly visible, and they probably murdered Lulu in particular to send a message to other independent prostitutes. Mishin is becoming dominant in the metro underworld, and we need to stop that. You do want to be involved in this, don't you?"

Kaartamo was talking like George W. Bush trying to convince the rest of the western world to support his bombing campaign in Iraq. I believed him just as little as I believed George double-idiot. Now Nordström stood up and walked over to me. I took a step back.

"I'm going to do my own work," I said, "and I'm going to do it as best I know how. I am a team player, but I'm not going to sit this out on the fucking bench. And I don't like your position here, Nordström."

"I assume you remember, Kallio, that your own position is tenuous, given your subordinate's shaky grasp of the rules of policing," Kaartamo snapped, and Nordström glanced at him with interest. I could have kicked Kaartamo. Nordström set his hand on my shoulder. It felt heavy.

"Maria, Kaartamo is right. The people behind this are mafia thugs. The local police can't handle them. But if we keep each other informed, we'll get this done." He emphasized the word "we" as if trying to shut out Kaartamo. I still didn't know whose team Nordström was really playing on.

"You can go," Kaartamo said like a school principal ending a scolding. I was only too happy to comply. After leaving the room, I kicked the elevator door a couple of times, even though it only hurt my own foot. Still, it helped. I walked down the stairs wishing I'd brought my portable CD player to work. A good dose of some loud punk music would have lifted my spirits, but I'd have to wait for that drug until I drove home. I made a quick call to say good night to the kids over the phone. Mom-on-the-phone wasn't a role I particularly liked.

The conference room was all in a ruckus. Mira Saastamoinen was explaining something to Puupponen, and Liisa Rasilainen just said a quick hi before making her exit. I poured my thirteenth cup of the day and sat down. My head ached.

"I have Sulonen's phone records," Puustjärvi said from the door. "Someone called him at nine this morning from a pay phone at the train station in Helsinki. Yesterday, after he was released, he called Mauri Hytönen and three of Lulu's customers, along with Riitta Saarnio—and placed a call to that same pay phone at around three."

"That's an hour before the shooting. OK, let's get someone to canvass the guards and the ticket workers at the train station. Who are we looking for?"

"A legal cell phone we could have tracked," Puustjärvi said. "This person didn't want us to be able to track his calls."

"A pro would have just swapped SIM cards," Autio said. "Would it be worth dusting the pay phone for prints? Even though it's been most of a day, we still might find something . . ."

I understood what Autio meant. We had to cling to every speck of hope. We had to seize every possibility. Criminal investigation was thorough and boring. It was like water slowly wearing away at rock, and when a hole finally formed, even that only grew slowly, never dramatically. "Our friend Hytönen didn't mention Sulonen's call," I pointed out. "What time was it at?"

"Two fifteen."

"So right after we left! And the one to Mrs. Saarnio?"

"A little before three."

"Find out what the calls were about." I massaged my temples, but it didn't help. I was headed for a migraine if I didn't get some fresh air, some painkillers, or both. My purse was in my office, and I had some ketoprofen tablets. Once again, I cursed the windows, which didn't open, and headed back to the conference room. Puupponen grabbed me by the sleeve, smiling like a kid who wants to make his mom happy.

"There's something consistent here," he said. "Five sightings of a man in a long, black overcoat. On the heavy side. Average or below-average height, wearing a wide-brimmed hat to cover his face and a black scarf pulled over his chin. The girl at the ticket counter at the theater noticed him walking fast past the theater toward the stairs. It's unlikely that anyone's making this up since the sightings are all so similar. On the other hand, it could be someone innocent who just attracted attention by dressing oddly."

"Did anyone see him with a gun?"

"No. One of the witnesses said he was holding his hands in his pockets and looking down into the crowd. But the interviews are just getting started. Should I sit these witnesses down with a sketch artist?"

"Yes. How many witnesses are still in line?"

"Fifty-two. The fifty-third is so drunk they took him to a cell to wait for his turn in the morning. He was saying something about a crossbow. Sounded a bit far-fetched. But his BAC was through the roof. What happened with Kaartamo?"

I shrugged. Even though I trusted Koivu and Puupponen, I still wished Taskinen was around. "You clearly need a hug," Puupponen said suddenly and pulled me into his arms. He was right. I hugged him back until I heard an amused voice.

"Now I know why you two went to Kuopio together. Did you even go to Vesanto? Are they renting rooms by the hour somewhere up there now?" It was Ursula—her tone was joking.

I pulled a face at her, and Puupponen said, "How'd you guess? And are you still up for that trip to Mikkeli tomorrow?"

Ursula laughed, and I managed to join in for a few seconds before my phone rang. It was Antti.

"Hi. You aren't home, are you?"

"No, work. We have a situation." My phone started buzzing with another call, which I had to answer. "I'm sorry, I can't talk now. I'll call you back, dear—" but Antti had already hung up. On the other line came a voice I didn't recognize.

"This is Dr. Miasofia Hietamäki from Jorvi Hospital. Am I speaking to the right person? Is this the head of the Espoo Police Violent Crimes Unit?"

"Yes."

"We have a patient here by the name of Tero Sulonen. He's just come out of surgery."

"Did he survive?"

"Yes, but it's hard to predict how he'll do going forward. The damage to his brain was significant. We're keeping him in a coma for now so he won't be available for questioning for several days, possibly weeks. We'll just have to see how quickly he recovers. But you'll be interested to know we found the projectile he was shot with."

"Projectile?"

"Yes. The object in question is about eight millimeters in diameter, steel and round like a ball. I've never seen anything like it, and neither has my colleague who happens to be a sport shooter. According to him it isn't from any normal firearm."

14

The department ballistics expert, Kaide Söderholm, was already on his way to bed when I called him.

"Jorvi . . . ? Now . . . ?" Söderholm asked with a yawn, and I thought I heard his jaw pop over the phone. "Is this about the Big Apple case? Have you found the weapon?"

"No, but the docs dug the bullet out of the victim. This may be the key to cracking the case. I'll see you in half an hour at the hospital."

My hands trembled, and it wasn't just from the exhaustion and the coffee. It was the same familiar excitement that always came over me when a case started to resolve itself.

"Keep things going here. I'm headed to Jorvi. I'll have to keep my phone off there, but leave me a message if anything significant happens. I'll come back here after I'm done," I told Koivu, who had taken his glasses off and was rubbing his temples.

"A man of average or below-average height?" he said. "What about a woman dressed in men's clothing? Anna-Maija Mustajoki has pretty broad shoulders."

"And large breasts. Those aren't so easy to hide. We're looking for a man, Koivu. If you think of the people at the TV studio that night, only one fits the profile: Ilari Länsimies. Mauri Hytönen is in Tarttu, or at least he should be. He hasn't answered Puustjärvi's calls."

"Oh, we all know where he is," Puupponen said wryly as he walked by. "There's a sixth eyewitness report of a man skulking around the third floor. That pretty much clinches it. They all more or less line up. By morning we should have a sketch to circulate."

"Good."

"Two of the witnesses said that there was something familiar about the person they saw, but they weren't able to place it. One said that the face seemed like it was out of place."

"That could be a lot of help. Anything else?"

"It is strange that none of the eyewitnesses heard the shot. Even with a silencer there would have been some noise. A couple of witnesses on the lower floor were sure the shot echoed through the whole mall, but people always imagine hearing things after the fact," Puupponen said and then excused himself to go question his next witness.

I grabbed a chocolate cookie and then ran down the stairs to the parking garage. I drove up to the outdoor parking lot, got out, and took a few deep breaths of fresh air. My eyelids didn't want to stay open, but I refused to give in. The clock said 10:00 p.m. I turned on the radio to keep me company. A reporter was talking about the shooting at the Big Apple and asked anyone with information related to the incident to contact the Espoo Police. The department tip line had been jammed all evening. Kaartamo had handled the press release and promised to do the briefing in the morning as well, but he wanted me there too. Maybe it would be good for me to look like I knew I would after a night of barely any sleep. It might give the media the impression that the police were really toiling away on the case.

After the news, Celine Dion sang the theme from *Titanic.* I quickly changed the station, but the song reminded me of my grandmother, who had been widowed in the war before her thirtieth birthday. She'd found comfort in the belief that she would see her husband again after this life. I hoped that was true, although I didn't know if I believed in the afterlife. There were enough unknowns in this life to try to understand. Lately my own beliefs had been on my mind more than usual. I'd written it off as a midlife crisis, a final realization of my own mortality. Because of my profession I couldn't escape the knowledge of how fragile life is, but so far, I'd succeeded in running away from thinking about whatever came after.

Leena's aunt Allu had rejoined the church, and Tero Sulonen believed that after he died he'd go to the same place as Lulu. Was that just an attempt to delude themselves, to postpone the inevitable? Was hope bad if it helped people endure? I remembered a colleague who had killed himself after his lover was murdered. Had he done it to be with her? In that case hope for a reunion was dangerous because it pulled the person away from life.

It was easier to think about ballistics than metaphysics. I inserted a CD of the Boys and sang along with "Punk Rocker." As they lamented society overtaking young rebels, I realized how well the words fit my own life. I was a career public servant who rarely picked up her bass guitar, and the closest I ever came to a mosh pit was dancing with my kids in the living room, much to their amazement.

At the hospital's front desk I asked for Dr. Miasofia Hietamäki and received directions to her office. Söderholm was already there and looked more like an old rocker in his jeans and battered leather jacket, or maybe a younger version of the author Samuel Beckett, than a top forensics expert. He was inspecting a clean steel ball in a plastic bag. Hietamäki was flipping through a stack of pictures taken of the back of Tero Sulonen's head.

"This had to come in at high velocity because it penetrated the skull and the outer layers of the brain," Hietamäki said.

"What was the range?" Söderholm asked me. He smelled of cigarettes, and the slender fingers that held the plastic bag bore yellow nicotine stains. The smell was almost welcome in the sterile environment of the hospital.

"Twenty or thirty meters. We haven't established the shooter's exact location yet, but we're narrowing it down."

"OK. Is there a computer here I could use? I have to check my records."

"Go right ahead," Dr. Hietamäki said, gesturing toward her own computer. "Or wait. I can't let you see these files." She sat down quickly and clicked several times until only the desktop was visible.

Söderholm dug in his pocket and found a pack of cigarettes. He opened it and placed one in his mouth. Dr. Hietamäki inhaled sharply and was just about to say something when Söderholm turned in his chair and grinned.

"I'm not going to light it. I just think better this way. I'm a true addict. Even hypnosis didn't work on me. Or I just didn't want it to work."

Turning back, he opened a web browser and began typing and humming to himself.

"You said on the phone that Sulonen will probably live but you couldn't predict anything beyond that. What did you mean?" I asked. Sulonen had only been free for one day, and Koivu was currently trying to track his movements.

"The projectile likely damaged the speech centers of his brain. We'll just have to monitor the situation. We're keeping him in an artificial coma for at least three days to give his brain a chance to heal. It's very likely that after he wakes up he'll suffer from at least partial memory loss."

Dr. Hietamäki perched on the edge of her desk, her back to Söderholm.

"Unfortunately, my colleague who shoots recreationally is in another surgery. I'm also on call, so I may have to leave at any moment. We've tried to locate Sulonen's next of kin, but we can't find anyone. He lived with a woman, but she hasn't replied either."

"Sulonen lived with Lulu Mäkinen, also known as Lulu Nightingale. She's dead."

Hietamäki frowned. "Yes! Why didn't I make the connection before? I was just thinking about saving my patient. Do you think he's a security risk?"

I'd wondered the same thing. For Sulonen's sake, it would be best to spread the word that he was barely alive and wouldn't regain consciousness for a long time. On the other hand, we had to keep patient information confidential, and there didn't seem to be anyone to ask for permission to release it.

"I'd recommend a guard," I said, remembering Oksana. She'd disappeared from this same hospital in broad daylight. If professional criminals were behind this case, they could do the same thing to Sulonen. "I'll just go ahead and arrange it."

"Bingo!" Söderholm suddenly said. "I was right. I thought this might be it. Come have a look, ladies. Here's your weapon, and it's a dandy." Söderholm moved away from the screen and pointed to the image as proudly as if it were his firstborn.

At first, I didn't register what I saw. The picture showed a sort of slingshot with a solid, ergonomically molded handle that went on the hand like a glove. A heavy-duty elastic band was connected to the handle, just like the slingshots I used to shoot rose hips at my sisters when I was a kid.

"It looks like a slingshot," Hietamäki said.

"Exactly. It is a slingshot, but it's no ordinary slingshot. This is an Italian hunting slingshot. I tried one once. In Finland they're illegal, but there are EU countries where they haven't been able to outlaw them yet. They're used for hunting birds, since they don't cause as much destruction as a shotgun and there's no sound to scare off the birds. That ball is just the right size."

"But can a slingshot nearly kill a grown man?" I asked incredulously.

"The range was just about right. A slingshot is easy to hide in a jacket pocket, and it's hard to notice: no gunpowder smell, no bang. The shooter had to have it visible when he was aiming, but he could have it hidden again before the ball even connected with the target." Söderholm's eyes shone with excitement. "Maria, promise me that when you catch this guy, you'll let me question him. I want to know where he got this and how he came up with the idea to use it. I've never seen anything like this before." The cigarette hung from the corner of Söderholm's mouth like he was a French film star. I was afraid he might bite it in half in his excitement. "I'll take the ball to the evidence locker. I'll have to do some more investigation to confirm everything, but I'm relatively certain this was a slingshot. That's unfortunate in the sense that it wouldn't be in any database, but illegal firearms aren't either."

"Do you think the selection of weapon points to a professional criminal? Do you know if slingshots are legal in Russia?"

"I'll check. I think this points to someone with a sense of humor. Like I said, send him over to me when you nail him. Is it OK if I get my report to you tomorrow? Our youngest has had an ear infection for almost a week, and I haven't slept much because my wife's on the night shift. She's home tonight, though." Söderholm looked at Dr. Hietamäki and asked, "Do you also do cancer operations?"

"Brain cancer, yes."

"Too bad. You could have shown me some scary lung cancer pictures. Maybe that would help me kick the habit. I've gotta go light up now. See you ladies later!"

Söderholm waved and left. Tero Sulonen had been moved to intensive care, and after some arguing, I received permission to see him. I didn't quite know why I wanted to, especially since only his face was visible with all the bandages and tubes. He looked strangely small in his hospital bed. I walked over to him. The machines said his heart was beating and his lungs were breathing, although to look at him I wouldn't have known whether he was alive or dead. When I placed my hand next to his face, I could feel the warmth of his skin.

"Tero, don't give up. You still have poems to write. You at least need to write one to remember Lulu by. Stay alive."

Sulonen's belongings had been moved to storage to await forwarding to the police. I borrowed some gloves and a hair cap before looking through them. The jacket was stiff with blood, but I still shoved my hand into the pockets. Nothing. The pockets of his jeans were also empty. Sulonen's underwear had Mickey Mouse pictures on them. His wallet and cell phone were in separate bags.

"I'm taking these," I said, and the nurse on duty didn't object. I wrote her a receipt and set off driving through the darkness back to the station. Of course, Sulonen's phone was locked, but we could always try to crack the PIN code.

My stomach growled angrily to let me know that it objected to its diet of coffee and pain pills. I would have paid a lot for a glass of buttermilk. Antti had tried to call my phone again, but he hadn't left a message. I didn't have the energy to think about him right now. All my brain could focus on was the investigation at hand. I broke the speed limit as I drove, enjoying the empty streets and the stars twinkling beyond the lights of the city.

Only Koivu was in the conference room, talking on the phone. I peeked in the refrigerator and found some milk. I'd given up drinking milk as a sixteen-year-old and only used it in coffee these days. Now I forced myself to drink a glass, even though it felt harder to do so than eating blood pudding. Turning on the conference room computer, I checked the date. Then I pulled on a fresh set of gloves and got to work on Tero Sulonen's phone. Maybe the PIN code would be 1511, Lulu's birthday. I tried that first. I was right.

We could check Sulonen's phone records, but we might find other interesting things on his phone itself, such as a contacts list or text messages. I opened his contacts. The first name was Lulu. Then Maki, O-P, and Pate. Dearlulu. Taxi. And that was all. I looked at the numbers. Lulu was the same cell phone we already had for Lulu Nightingale. But what about Dearlulu? I opened the detail screen, and it showed me a completely new number. So Lulu had a second cell phone. Where was it now?

I went to the computer and opened the phone database. At first, I didn't see the Dearlulu number, so I moved to the restricted number database. There it was, registered to the name Lilli and T. Sulonen. I wanted the call logs for this phone too, but I'd have to wait until tomorrow. I tried calling it from Sulonen's phone, though I didn't expect anyone to answer. After a few rings the voice mail picked up.

"Please leave a message after the beep" was the message, said in Finnish and English. Lulu's voice was easy to recognize.

I didn't leave a message, although I felt like screaming for joy. Someone had Lulu's other phone, and as soon as we received a warrant, we'd be able to track it down. The murderer wouldn't be so stupid to have kept the phone, would he? Maybe he'd just thrown it in the forest. But what sense would that make if the phone contained information the murderer didn't want getting out? Or had Lulu hidden the phone somewhere, and if so, where?

The call log on Sulonen's phone told us what we already knew. As I browsed through it, Koivu, who'd finished his own call, sat down next to me.

"Is there any more coffee?" he asked, shaking his thermos. He checked the coffee pot and found it empty. "Damn it. What idiot finished this off and didn't make more! I could really go for a meat pie and a cold beer." Koivu grabbed a filter from the cupboard, filled the water reservoir, and then loaded so much coffee in that my stomach began complaining just at the thought of it. "Mauri Hytönen says hi. He was around Heinola when Sulonen was shot. His employees can vouch for him. And he wouldn't have been able to get to Espoo in time after you left his office anyway unless he had a helicopter since he wasn't on your flight."

"But why did Sulonen call him?"

"He wanted to know whether Hytönen knew beforehand that Lulu would be on the TV show. I guess he was trying to solve the case himself. Of course, he accused Hytönen of being the killer and threatened him, but Hytönen just laughed it off. He'd had to catch a ferry then so couldn't call us. Do you really think it's wise to let him go running around Estonia?"

"I don't think Hytönen is our man. Even if he might have connections to the Russian mafia." I put my fingers on my temples and rotated them to get the blood flowing in my face. "What about Mrs. Saarnio? What did she say?"

"She didn't answer her cell or the home phone. Should we go pay her a visit? I did leave a message telling her what it was about."

"I think that's enough for tonight. I have a hard time imagining Riitta Saarnio running around with a slingshot. Try again in the morning. Do you know how many more interviews are left?"

"Ville just said they've got nine left in line. According to Mira, more have volunteered since they started, but they're scheduled for tomorrow. Respectable people are already asleep."

The lights of the conference room felt bright, and outside all I could see was darkness because the windows faced the woods. On the tables were dirty coffee mugs and plates with crumbs of pulla and bits of parsley. One coffee cup had a piece of chewing gum stuck to it.

"Forensics went to the train station, and Rasilainen and Airaksinen went with them. They didn't find anything to write home about, though, since all the staff on the morning shift had gone home. Rasilainen and Airaksinen are going to handle that tomorrow. One of the guards or someone at the ticket booth might have noticed a person hanging around the pay phones, since everybody has a cell nowadays." Koivu glanced hopefully at the coffee maker and then at the open door. "So, Maria, what happened with you and Antti? Have you cleared it up?"

"No. I'm probably just imagining things." I felt bad about having shared my stupid suspicions with Koivu. I avoided his gaze, but Koivu took me by the arm. His grip was so tight that I had an urge to shake myself loose.

"Maria, there's one thing we've learned in this job. You never know anyone perfectly," Koivu whispered, and his voice made me meet his kind, blue eyes. Then he let go and went back for his coffee. He asked if I wanted any. I declined. It would be best to head home, even though the kids were already asleep. Antti's mom would sleep on the floor in the kids' room. I'd asked her to take our bed, but she said she was still spry enough to sleep on the floor.

I checked the latest interview records on the intranet, but there wasn't anything significant in them. I was just turning off the lights in the conference room when someone barged in.

"Is there coffee here?" It was Hakkarainen from Forensics. "What are you going to ask us to do next? A pay phone in the train station? Jesus Christ! I've never seen so many fingerprints. Granted, we did get a hit: our old friend Köpä Nykänen. He's been a wino since the sixties. Strange he's still alive. But I don't think he's who we're looking for. I checked the registry, and all he's ever done is petty theft. The other prints didn't match anything. Do you want us to take DNA too? We found a hair or two and some flakes of skin. Kaartamo's going to love it when he hears how much this is going to cost him."

"Forget Kaartamo. We'll talk again in the morning." I stifled a yawn, but I didn't entirely succeed, and Hakkarainen caught it too.

"When is Taskinen coming back?" Hakkarainen asked. I told him when Taskinen's leave ended and that I didn't know anything more than that. I walked downstairs slowly, stretching my thigh muscles. My mouth opened in a yawn every tenth step.

Suddenly I heard a commotion in the lobby. The duty officer's booth was open, and a young woman was screaming and weeping in front of the desk.

"You have to help me before they kill me too! Put me in jail! Can't you just fucking arrest me? I just took twenty euros for a blow job!" The girl pulled out the bills from between her breasts. I moved closer, but stayed behind the doors into the lobby. The girl's eyes were almost black, her pupils almost entirely dilated. Sweat and tears had smeared makeup across her cheeks. She was wearing a short leather jacket, a top that barely covered the bottoms of her breasts, and tight red satin pants. The four-inch heel of one of her boots was bent. A vein pulsed rapidly in her neck.

"Calm down," Officer Nyyssönen said in a fatherly tone from behind the desk. He could tell the girl was high too.

"But Lulu and Tero are already dead, and that Russian girl, and I'm next! They're after me! You have to believe me!"

Hearing these familiar names made me move closer. I opened the glass doors and waved to Nyyssönen.

"I'm going to have a little talk with this young lady. She seems like she might have some information about my case. Come on in," I said to the girl. "Are you friends with Lulu Nightingale and Tero Sulonen?" I asked as I escorted the girl through the doors. In response, she burst out wailing. I took her to sit in the waiting area. Her age was hard to place because her body was thin and haggard, her face prematurely lined, but the breasts hanging free under her top had the perkiness of a teenager's.

She cried for a while. "Am I at the police station now?" she finally asked.

"Yes. I'm Detective Lieutenant Maria Kallio. I'm investigating Lulu's death. Who are you afraid of?"

The girl didn't answer, but at least she looked at me. Her short hair was greasy and matted to her head. The ends were blond but her roots were dark brown.

"My mouth is really dry," she complained.

"Have you been taking speed?" She didn't answer. "Wait here. I'll get you something to drink. Nyyssönen, make sure she doesn't go anywhere!" The duty officer had one window into the lobby and another into the space between the two outer doors, where people could come at night to report crimes. I grabbed a Coke from the machine in the downstairs break room. After a moment's thought, I got a second bottle too.

The girl leaned back in her chair and wiped the sweat from her brow. When I handed her the bottle I'd opened for her, she grabbed it and immediately drained half of it, and then sat still as if waiting for the liquid to take effect. I sat down next to her and thought with longing of my soft bed.

"Who are you afraid of?" I asked again.

"Them . . . those men. They beat me up once. You can never know which guys will be nice and which ones will hit you. And I never go anywhere with Russians!" the girl said.

"What's your name?"

"I don't have a name," the girl said. A small purse was visible under her jacket, with the strap over her shoulder. Maybe it had her identity papers in it.

"You have to tell the police your name. You know that."

"Will I go to jail if I don't tell? But that's where I want to go," she said, some defiance in her voice now.

"Yes, you will. And they'll take away all your things."

The girl's hand instinctively flew to her purse. "I didn't dare stay at the train station," she said. "I jumped on the Kirkkonummi train, but just before Leppävaara a conductor came. I ran and got off the train. I didn't think they could find me here in BFE Espoo . . . I knew there was a police station in Kilo because of the jokes in school. What's the heaviest police station in Finland? The Kilo police station . . ." The girl giggled, then hiccuped and sat up straighter.

"I'm a whore. I sell my body at the Helsinki train station and around there. It's illegal, so arrest me. My name is Pamela. And I knew Lulu, or I did . . . I wished I could be like her. I asked her for a job, but she said she didn't take druggies." The girl drank some more Coke. "I'm so tired of everything, being afraid and everything. I just want to die."

The crying started again. With some patience, I was finally able to drag the story out of her. About two weeks earlier, two Russians had lured her into their car, saying they were customers and promising Pamela two hundred euros if she'd service them both. Then they drove her out of town, dragged her out of the car, and beat her as punishment for trying to turn tricks on their turf without permission. If she didn't stop, the next time would be her last. "But I couldn't just stop. Where would I get money?"

"Drug money?" I asked, although I knew the answer.

"And today they were there again. I saw them! It was the same blond liar in his fur coat!"

I remembered what Ursula had said about her attackers: one had worn a coat with a fur collar. It seemed as though Mishin's thugs were on the case again. I called Holding, where the officer on duty said they had a cell open. Even though the police station wasn't a hotel, I thought it was best to keep Pamela for the night. She tried to object, but it was just for show, and she claimed that she didn't remember her name or address because she was so tired. We found her ID in her purse with her makeup, money, phone, and condoms. Pamela Donna Lahtela, born 1987, Helsinki. I left instructions for Patrol to find out more details about her and where she lived, and asked the officer on guard to give her something to eat. In the morning, she'd be facing amphetamine withdrawal symptoms, and I couldn't predict whether she'd be able to talk then.

Espoo was quiet. There was no movement in the apartment building parking lot, and our windows were dark. I managed to open the door almost without a sound and got it closed without any loud banging. I knew my mother-in-law was a light sleeper like most people her age. My care went to waste, though, because no sooner did I have my shoes off than a god-awful racket started in the entryway. It was Venjamin, expressing his disapproval for my coming home so late. Luckily the door to the children's room was closed—apparently my mother-in-law hadn't wanted the cat jumping on her or curling up with her. I picked up the silly animal so he'd be quiet. His soft fur felt good against my face, and he almost immediately began to purr. I took him with me into the kitchen and closed the door before giving him some milk and frozen fish. I washed up and then I climbed into bed. The cat jumped up on my feet. We both tried to get comfortable, and Venjamin ended up behind my knees. I'd have to avoid rolling over.

I woke up just before six. Venjamin meowed in irritation when I pushed him off my stomach, where he'd moved during the night. My phone had been on silent, and I'd thought the buzzing on the nightstand would wake me up, but I was wrong. Three calls had come in, two from Puupponen. He'd also left a message, so I let it play.

> *Hi, Maria. I'm just leaving. It's 1:00 a.m. Arto Saarnio called to say he got our message on their landline. Mrs. Saarnio is missing. He didn't come home until midnight, and he couldn't find her anywhere.*

The third call was from Arto Saarnio. The voice on the message belonged to an anxious, tired old man.

> *I'm sorry to bother you so late at night, but this really isn't like Riitta. I've already called all the hospitals, but there's no sign of her and she isn't answering her phone. Can the police track it? Can you call me when you get this message?*

Saarnio tried to make it sound like a command but failed.

I went to put the coffee on and sent Puupponen a text message letting him know that I'd be at the station soon. I didn't dare drive without caffeine in my bloodstream. I glanced briefly at the morning paper. The incident at the mall took up two columns on the first page, with speculation about the weapon and the connection to Lulu Nightingale's murder. If I could have chosen, I wouldn't have released Sulonen's identity yet, but the choice was Kaartamo's. I gave Venjamin more food because he was meowing at me and tried to keep him from pulling open the belt of my bathrobe. As I was pouring myself a cup of coffee, I heard the door open. It was Taneli.

"Mom, are you going to be home tonight?"

"I'll do my best, honey. You should go back to sleep. You don't need to be up for two more hours."

"Is Dad going to be with us then?"

"No, he's coming home tomorrow. Grandma will be here." Taneli pouted, and I picked him up. Just then my mother-in-law appeared in the kitchen.

"Ah, I see we're already up. Did you get any sleep at all?"

"A few hours. Can you be here tonight again if they need me at work?"

Marjatta's steel gray hair was disheveled, and her expression was the same as Iida's when she was cross. I wondered whether Iida would wrinkle like her grandmother as she aged, in a crisscrossed spiderweb of lines.

"Where is Antti? Isn't he coming home for the weekend?"

"He has some kind of party in Vaasa. He'll be home tomorrow. I may be able to come home at the normal time, but if you can just be prepared . . ."

"Is a party more important to him that caring for his own children?" she asked incredulously. Instead of replying, I focused on my coffee and tried to whip up a sandwich while Taneli hung on my legs.

Finally, I convinced him to get back in bed. As I stroked his hair, I hoped Iida wouldn't wake up.

Back in the kitchen, my mother-in-law sat at the table spreading marmalade on a piece of bread. Venjamin batted at the tassels on her slippers and had managed to pull a couple of threads loose. Marjatta didn't seem to notice him.

"You haven't had time to talk to Antti about the money, have you?" she asked.

"I've tried, but he wanted time to think. I'll try again once he gets home."

When I went in the bedroom to dress, Marjatta followed me. I felt uncomfortable removing my bathrobe in front of her, but I had to. Work was calling. And I didn't presume to be ungracious to her because what on earth would we do without her?

"Is everything OK between the two of you?" she asked sternly. "Or is there something you aren't telling me? Is Antti moving to Vaasa?"

"No! Why would you think that?" I managed to hook my bra despite my hands' shaking. Had Antti hinted something to his mother that he hadn't told me? Marjatta didn't reply; she just watched as I pulled on my trousers. Makeup would have to wait for the women's restroom at the station.

"I'll call when I know when I'm coming home. Take this," I said and pulled a fifty euro bill out of my wallet. "The cupboards are bare, so take the kids out for pizza so you don't have to waste time shopping. Thank you. You're a lifesaver."

In the car, I plugged in the hands-free and cursed when the cable got caught in my hair and the buttons of my winter coat. I looked up Arto Saarnio's number. He answered after the first ring.

"Hello?"

"This is Detective Kallio. Good morning. I just got your message. Have you heard from your wife?"

"No! I've called all her friends and coworkers, but no one knows anything. This really isn't like Riitta, but she's been really mixed up since the killing at the studio and all the rest of it. I'm extremely worried."

"Is her purse and wallet at home? What about her car? Her passport?"

"The car is gone, along with her wallet. Wait . . . I'll check the safe." I heard Saarnio set the phone down on the table. I'd called the landline. I was at the Turku Highway interchange when he finally returned.

"Her passport is here, and I don't think anything's missing from her closet, although I have to admit I don't know all her belongings. Her toothbrush is here, along with her skin creams and nightgown. It's like she didn't come home from work at all. I heard on the news that Lulu Nightingale's bodyguard was shot at the mall. Riitta's disappearance couldn't have anything to do with that, could it?"

15

I pulled off at a bus stop. Traffic was still light, so I threw a quick U-turn and headed back toward Olari. I would have plenty of time to run by West Man Productions to see if Riitta Saarnio's green Renault Megane was in the parking lot. At the same time, I checked in with the department to make sure no one had heard anything new about her.

The industrial area was quiet, and the parking lot at the TV studio was almost empty. The only vehicles were a beat-up black van and behind it a passenger car, which turned out to be Riitta Saarnio's. I rang the buzzer for West Man Productions, but no one answered. I tried Riitta Saarnio's and Ilari Länsimies's work numbers. Länsimies answered his cell phone, and his tone of voice told me I'd woken him.

"Riitta? She stayed at the studio yesterday after the show. I left pretty soon after we'd finished. The ratings were amazing, just like I said, well over a million. It was an all-time best for *Surprise Guests*."

"Who comes to the studio first?"

"A cleaner comes every morning, around eight. Has something happened to Riitta?"

"We don't know."

"Arto called me during the night, but I didn't take him seriously. I assumed Riitta took one of the guests home or stayed to watch tape."

"How did she seem yesterday?"

Länsimies reported that the whole crew had been on edge because the previous show's bad memories still weighed on everyone. They'd all been at the studio in the morning and then gone home to rest. They returned to the studio by five—so Riitta Saarnio could have visited the Big Apple in the meantime. But would she be able to make herself look like a man? When women dressed up as men, they looked younger than their true age.

I asked Länsimies who handled their property management, but he didn't remember the name of the company.

"That's Riitta's department. I have three keycards to the building, so I've never needed their assistance. Can't you wait until the cleaner shows up? I've got a meeting at eight, and I can't cancel it. It may be Riitta took a sleeping pill and fell asleep on the sofa in the dressing room. Maybe she wanted to attract Arto's attention. I understand they've been having . . . difficulties." Länsimies laughed in a way I didn't like. How much had he heard of my conversation with Riitta Saarnio on Wednesday?

"Try to remember the name of the property management company," I said irritably. We could get the name of the company from the police property database, but I wanted Länsimies to have to do something at least. He promised to call me back when he found the information.

The studio door was steel. With a glass door, I could have broken in. Next to it was a narrow window, but it was too small for me to fit through. And the lock's angle relative to the window made it so my arm wouldn't have been able to reach it even if I did break the glass.

I didn't feel like sitting around in my car, so I went to the station. Traffic was picking up, and the steady stream of headlights gradually began to dim in the brightening morning. Was Antti already awake? I selected his number on my speed dial but didn't press the call button. He wasn't his best early in the morning either. Instead I notified Arto Saarnio that I'd found his wife's car.

"Thank you, Detective Kallio! Why didn't I think to go check? But shouldn't someone go inside? What if Riitta had some sort of medical emergency . . ."

"I'm trying to get the name of the property management company right now. If that doesn't work, we'll get a member of the crew to come over."

"What about Ilari?" When I told him about Länsimies's meeting, Saarnio gave a deep sigh. "I have an important negotiation today too, but nothing is more important than finding my wife. Wait . . . I'm sure that Riitta has a spare keycard here somewhere. Just a minute . . ."

I turned into the police station parking lot. The road was slick with ice, and my wheels started sliding during the turn. I only managed to right the car at the last second to avoid hitting a woman with a stroller.

"Detective, are you still there? I have the keycard. I could go over to the studio right now to check."

It was almost eight o'clock, and the unit meeting was supposed to start at eight thirty. I told Saarnio I'd come with him and then called Puupponen to tell him that plans had changed. Driving back to West Man Productions, I felt like environmental enemy number one. It was insane to burn this much gasoline.

I was only there a couple of minutes before Arto Saarnio, who appeared to have left immediately. His face showed that he hadn't slept, and his stubble was longer than usual and seemed to have more gray in it than before. I put on a pair of disposable gloves before opening the door and handed another pair to Saarnio. He gave me a serious look and then pulled on the gloves.

The keycard opened the door with no trouble. I turned on the light in the hallway and yelled, "This is the police. Is anyone here?" No answer.

"Riitta!" Arto Saarnio called, but the silence held. It was like a thick, invisible poison gas, and I found it difficult to breathe. The doors of the dressing rooms were all half-open, and a strong smell of aftershave wafted from one of them. I continued to the combined office and conference room, where I'd talked with Riitta Saarnio the time before. I turned on the light, and Arto Saarnio followed me through the door.

His wife was there, lying collapsed on the table.

"Keep your distance," I told him. At first, he hesitated, but then he took a step back. I approached Riitta Saarnio and took her wrist. Her arm was stiff and cold. She had obviously been deceased for several hours. I tried to find a pulse even though I knew it was futile. Riitta Saarnio's face was turned away from me, so I walked around the chair to get a look at it. Her grimace was one of agony and rage, like an animal caught in a trap. Was I imagining it or was there a smell of bitter almond coming from around her mouth?

"Is she . . ." Arto Saarnio couldn't finish the sentence.

"I'm sorry, but she's dead. No, don't touch her yet! Maybe it would be best for you to leave the room."

Saarnio did as commanded. Then I called the station and asked them to send Forensics. That was when I noticed the letter. It was on the floor next to the body, as if it had fallen there during Saarnio's final furious struggle against death. I bent down to look at it and, to my surprise, saw my own name.

> *Please deliver this to Detective Maria Kallio.*
> *I killed Lulu Nightingale and her bodyguard, who tried to blackmail me. I thought my husband was Lulu Nightingale's client, and I couldn't stand the idea. The bodyguard must have seen when I put the poison in Lulu's glass. I'm taking my own life the same way I did Lulu's. I'm sorry.*

The letter was written on a computer and printed on West Man Productions letterhead. The signature was easy to read, and her name was even printed below it.

I left the letter on the floor. After the photographer had been here I could have a closer look. The room was cold, as if the heating had been turned off. The computer was turned off, and all the piles of paper were in order. A glass, apparently the one Riitta Saarnio had drunk the poison from, had rolled under the line of cabinets, but there was no sign of a poison bottle. I realized it would be best for me to leave too, in order to avoid contaminating the scene, because I wasn't wearing shoe covers.

I found Arto Saarnio in the hall. He stood still, his face empty. His phone was in his hand, but he wasn't talking into it.

"Forensics will be here soon. Let's go sit in there for now." I motioned to the dressing room where Lulu Nightingale's body had been found. Had the previous night's guest known which room he was in? I pulled two chairs up to the table.

"How did Riitta die?" Saarnio finally asked. I didn't reply, and he seemed to understand my silence. When I asked when he'd last seen his wife, he had to think.

"Wednesday morning," he finally said. "When I came home in the evening, she was already asleep. We have separate bedrooms. And yesterday morning I took the eight o'clock flight to Stockholm. Riitta was still sleeping when I left."

I'd spoken to Riitta Saarnio myself Wednesday morning, so I probably knew more about her state of mind than her husband. On Wednesdays Riitta had her French conversation course. We'd have to call her girlfriend who went with her—and Anna-Maija Mustajoki.

"I told her about Oksana on Tuesday night, and she completely lost it. It's understandable, but I had to do it. I thought it might be a new beginning for us. I loved my wife," Saarnio said wistfully. "She's been dealing with depression for a long time. I thought her doctors had finally found the right medicine, but telling her about Oksana was definitely the wrong medicine."

"So your wife had mental health problems?"

Saarnio looked at me again, and the expression in his eyes was focused and thoughtful. "If you believe depression is a mental health problem. That's what caused her lack of sexual desire too. And I didn't help the situation at all by cheating on her. When I told her the truth, she seemed to have this hysterical fear that my misadventures would end up in the papers. She said she could accept everything else, but not that her private life might be dragged out into public."

"How long has your wife been depressed, Arto?" I'd done it unconsciously, but calling him by his first name felt natural now.

"Ever since she lost her previous job. She was sure she'd never find work again because she was over fifty. Ilari's production company really was a lifesaver, although I don't like the man himself that much. But he and Riitta got along, and Riitta got to do what she's really good at."

Saarnio's phone rang, and he answered. Even though he appeared calm, I knew it was just the initial stage of shock. His brain still couldn't comprehend what he already knew and what he confirmed calmly over the phone.

"Yes, it's true. All of my meetings for today are canceled. Move everything tomorrow as well. We've found Riitta . . . she's dead." Saarnio paused, and I could hear the intense torrent of words his announcement caused. He listened without reaction. "Don't tell anyone who doesn't absolutely need to know. Just say I'm unwell. I don't know much yet, not even the cause of death. And . . ."

It was my phone's turn to ring, and I recognized Ilari Länsimies's number.

"Hi, it's Ilari. I have the name and number of the property company."

"We don't need it anymore."

"So you've found Riitta? That's good. I can leave for my mee—"

I curtly cut him off.

"I got a keycard from Arto Saarnio. I found Riitta in her office, dead. Naturally we'll want to interview you and the other members of the staff as soon as possible."

For once Länsimies shut up. Thirty seconds passed before he replied. "Dead? What the hell? I heard yesterday that Lulu Nightingale's bodyguard was shot too. Is the Russian mafia going after all of us? God, do I need a bodyguard now? Or a gun . . ."

The doorbell rang. I told Länsimies the police would contact him later in the day, hung up, and then went to the door. The forensics team marched in with Mikkola in the lead, and I gave them the necessary instructions.

"This place has been busy lately," said the photographer, Kerminen. He'd been at the studio the previous week. "Is this program so bad that someone dies after every episode?"

I put on proper protective clothing and went back into Riitta Saarnio's office. Saarnio was wearing dark clothing—black trousers, low-heeled lace-up shoes, and a thick blazer. I remembered the description of the Big Apple shooter. Could a man's overcoat and a wide-brimmed hat make her look like a man?

It would be easy if the solution was right here: Riitta Saarnio as the murderer and a suicide note admitting what she'd done. A handwriting expert would have to verify that the signature was Saarnio's, and a linguist would need to compare the language in the suicide note to that which Saarnio used in her other letters. That was complicated, however, because a person in an abnormal mental state might use completely different language than she would normally. Sometimes handwriting changed too.

Arto Saarnio still sat in the dressing room. I asked him to make sure I could reach him later in the day. Once the letter had been tested for fingerprints and copied, I wanted him to see it.

"Do you have anyone you can ask to be with you? Would you like us to notify your children?"

"I'll inform them myself." The Saarnios' daughter, Soila, lived in Brussels, and their son worked in Oulu. "Aleksi can probably fly home. Can you even tell whether Riitta was killed or if she . . . or maybe it was a sudden illness?"

"Not at this stage."

I shook Saarnio's hand and then walked out into the dazzling spring sunshine, which revealed just how dirty my car windows were. That seemed like a minor issue at the moment. I now had a second body on my hands, Oksana Petrenko was missing, and there was no guarantee that Sulonen would recover. Were the mafia pimps really so skilled and powerful that they could stage Riitta Saarnio's suicide? I stopped at a traffic signal and made a quick call to the department's public relations officer to arrange a press conference for one o'clock. Arto Saarnio was about to find himself in the headlines again.

Someone honked behind me. I hadn't realized the light had changed. My lack of sleep was having an effect on me, as was the shock. Riitta Saarnio's wasn't the first body I'd found, but you never get used to it. Still, now wasn't the time for emotional reactions. I had to act.

Focusing on driving, I managed to get to the police station parking garage in one piece.

My team was waiting for me in the conference room. I began by telling them about Pamela Lahtela coming in to the station the previous night and Riitta Saarnio's death, then reminded them that it would be premature to shut off any avenue of investigation. Puupponen stared at me dumbfounded, and Koivu's yawning stopped dead when he heard about Mrs. Saarnio's fate. Sorrow flashed in his eyes. Only Ursula understood my reference to the man in the fur-collared jacket.

"What news do we have about Sulonen?"

"Sulonen's condition is the same," Koivu said.

"They're keeping him unconscious, and they can't be sure how severe the brain damage is. Sulonen's pal Pate confirmed that Sulonen crashes at his place sometimes. He claimed that Sulonen never would have killed Lulu in a million years since he was so crazy about her. Apparently Sulonen was trying to solve Lulu's murder himself because he didn't trust the police. Which suggests that Sulonen found out something important enough for someone to want him silenced," Puupponen said.

"I've been trying to trace Lulu's other cell phone, but it's turned off and calls just go to voice mail. We'll have the warrant for full access today." Puustjärvi looked satisfied.

"Keep going with that. Ursula, what about Lulu's customers? Anything new?" Ursula smiled, but it was cruel.

"I'm starting to believe we're looking at two or three separate crimes. Sulonen would have been a rich man if he'd started extorting Lulu's clients. If buying sexual services becomes illegal, we're going to have an interesting new criminal group on our hands, made up of regular dads, corporate executives, and politicians. Apparently rather a lot of them are willing to risk their reputations and their marriages to follow their little soldier's orders. And some of them are awfully obedient."

"Did Sulonen try to blackmail anyone?"

"He contacted a few of Lulu's regulars, apparently trying to cover his back. He asked for money or he'd go to the press. Three different men told me the same thing. I asked why they didn't file a police report, but they were all afraid of publicity. Maybe they should have thought about what they were getting into earlier," Ursula said in a moralizing tone that was rare for her.

Puupponen had compiled a summary of the interviews from the mall. He said he'd even managed to sleep for two hours in the department lounge. His freckles glowed against his pale skin, which was stretched tight across his cheeks. He sipped an energy drink as he talked.

"The reports of the figure on the third floor all line up. Unfortunately, no one got a close look at him, and no one saw the actual shooting. Petri started looking at the security camera footage yesterday and will finish up today." Puupponen motioned to Puustjärvi, who was leaning back in his chair and seemed to be sleeping but perked up when he heard his name.

"Yep. I watched the upper-level tape first, but that particular spot is in a dead zone. It's like our shooter knew. But the mall has a good enough camera system that he must have been caught on tape somewhere. And I'll check the parking garage logs. Oh, and one more thing about Lulu Nightingale's computer. We noticed some deleted files on the hard drive, which we can try to recover if you want us to. But we haven't found any notes about the Russian mafia or any more diary entries."

"OK. Autio and Ursula, question the West Man Productions staff again. Start with Ilari Länsimies. I'll handle Arto Saarnio myself. Meet back here at three thirty. And remember to eat during the day," I said as if I were their mother. Autio and Puustjärvi were the same age as me, but the others were younger: Koivu by about a year, Puupponen by ten, and Ursula was only thirty. Sometimes I wished for a really experienced, hard-boiled sixty-year-old detective who'd lived through the time when matching a fingerprint was the greatest technical achievement conceivable in police work. Most cops that age had taken early retirement by now, since the work was so emotionally demanding. When you added to that the constant development of investigative methods and the increasing brutality of the criminal underworld, it was no wonder that few field officers managed to make it to full retirement age. But no technical wizardry could replicate the human brain's ability to imagine standing in someone else's shoes.

As the group was disbursing, I remembered one thing:

"Oh yeah, Riitta Saarnio's autopsy. Koivu, be ready for that. I don't know if they'll have time for it today, but I'll have them notify you."

"Thanks a lot," Koivu said, playing the martyr. "Today we're having Anu's niece's birthday party."

"Yeah, and I need to take my dog to the barber. Don't even, Koivu," Puupponen said.

"When did you get a dog?" Koivu retorted, and I was happy that they were still able to rib each other. Thankfully the announcement of the news conference had made the media requests quiet down. The tabloid headlines didn't hold back. "Terror at the Mall: Eyewitnesses Tell All" and "Is a Serial Killer Hunting Prostitutes?" They certainly knew how to attract readers. I quickly glanced over the articles, which already felt like old news. Riitta Saarnio's death had turned everything in a new direction.

Pamela Lahtela's personal information was waiting on my computer. She'd started with shoplifting in elementary school. Then she became a ward of the state at age fourteen, and now she was a runaway from a youth home. A year ago, she'd gone through drug treatment. I called Holding, where the officer on duty said Pamela was still sleeping, but according to their notes she hadn't fallen asleep until six in the morning.

"Sleeping? Are you sure?"

"Yes. I even went in the cell to make sure she was OK, and she was breathing normally."

I decided to let Pamela sleep as long as she needed, because I had plenty of other things to do. The first reports from Forensics were already in by ten o'clock. In Riitta Saarnio's purse they'd found a small bottle with a white, strong-smelling liquid at the bottom. I'd have to ask Arto Saarnio who'd been treating his wife and ask for a statement about her mental state. When a copy of the letter found next to Riitta's body showed up on my desk, I called her husband. He didn't answer his phone, but I left a message to call me back. Almost immediately he did. I told him about the letter, which I wanted him to read, and he said he'd come right over. That was also a common reaction: people in shock tried to bury their grief in frenzied activity and motion. Some people went to work just to pretend that everything was still the way it had been. But there was no way to escape pain forever, and when it came, it overwhelmed everyone.

I checked my salmiakki supply, but it was still empty. Damn it. How was I going to survive this press conference without my brain-boosting licorice elixir? I tried to make myself look more chipper with powder, mascara, and lipstick. I used three times more highlighter than usual. As I was smoothing the color on the lines around my eyes, someone began ringing my door buzzer. I pressed the button to unlock the door. Outside stood Kaartamo.

"What's this press conference you set up without telling me? I just spoke with the public relations officer, and he said you're going in front of the reporters at one. Didn't we agree I'd handle PR for the Big Apple case?" Kaartamo's face glowed red like the ancient director of the ski association after news of the Lahti doping scandal came out.

"Yes, we did. Didn't he tell you this is about another case?"

"What damn case?"

I gave a mental sigh. Our department public relations officer was a competent person, but he didn't like people stepping on his toes, which Kaartamo did constantly. "Riitta Saarnio, the producer at West Man Productions, was found dead today at the TV studio. We have to issue a statement."

"So we really are chasing a serial killer. Maybe it's about time we called in the SIS and NBI. If Nordström's theory holds up, we might be facing an enemy that's bigger than we can handle."

"I think it's premature to get Security Intelligence involved. There isn't anything about the case that indicates a threat to national security. And aren't you already in contact with Nordström? You could ask him how much the NBI really knows about Lulu. That would be a big help." I wondered whether the National Bureau of Investigation knew about the connection between Arto Saarnio and Oksana Petrenko.

After a moment's consideration, Kaartamo said, "Fine then, let's hold a joint press conference at one. But before then I need you to brief me on everything we have so far. What do we know about what happened yesterday at the mall?"

"We have numerous eyewitness accounts but no suspect. Sulonen's condition remains critical."

"Lunch at twelve thirty in my office," Kaartamo said, turning a deaf ear to my objections. I suspected I wouldn't keep much food down in his company.

Arto Saarnio was quiet but calm. He said he'd notified his children about their mother. His daughter was trying to make it back to Finland for the weekend. We talked about practicalities, such as the release of the body. The thought of the autopsy clearly wounded Saarnio, but he understood the necessity. He reminded me of a soldier who knows that in order to win the war, killing the enemy is unavoidable. Was that how he justified firing people too? Did he think that some had to suffer so the others could carry on?

I handed him the letter.

"Does this signature belong to your wife?"

Saarnio first read the whole letter, and the rest of the color drained from his face once he understood what it said. Otherwise he didn't reveal his agitation.

"Yes, this is Riitta's handwriting. Her signature has stayed the same all these years. I remember her practicing it when we got engaged. She claimed that writing beautiful, round letter *A*s had always been hard for her . . . Her maiden name was Riipinen." Saarnio paused. "It's just so hard to believe that what's written here could be true. I can maybe imagine about Lulu Nightingale, since I'd suspected as much, but the other attack . . . Riitta never could have done something like that. But why would she lie about it?"

"Does the phrasing sound like something she would write?"

"I don't know!" Saarnio suddenly turned in his chair to hide his face from me. When he finally spoke, his voice was husky.

"I drove her to this. I'm the one you should put in prison."

I allowed Saarnio to calm down before asking him about his wife's doctor. Saarnio gave me the information willingly. All during our conversation he didn't ask anything about Oksana, as if the girl had ceased to exist even though a few days ago she had been so important to him that he'd been willing to endanger his privacy for her.

After Saarnio left, I went downstairs to buy some salmiakki. Puustjärvi ran to catch me in the hall; he had news.

"A car matching the description of Riitta Saarnio's was seen in the parking garage at the mall," he said. "We don't have a license plate, but the make, model, and color match. And the time is right, a little before five."

"Does the witness report seem reliable?"

"Mira Saastamoinen did the interview. Ask her. I'm about to review all the security footage for that area. My eyes are about shot, though." Puustjärvi rubbed his temples. He was used to careful work with his hands from tying fishing flies.

"Would you rather do interviews?"

"No, I'll finish what I started. But you can bet I'm taking all my comp days once this thing is solved. Soon the twins are going to be asking who that nice man is," he said, with rare jocularity for Puustjärvi. Apparently, all was well on the home front again.

Puupponen and the sketch artist sat in the conference room, and when Puupponen saw me walk by, he yelled for me to come look at the composite drawing from all the eyewitness reports.

"Hi, Kallio! Doesn't this remind you of someone familiar?" the sketch artist asked enthusiastically. "Everyone talked about a face with no expression. But if you look closely, doesn't this look a lot like our neighbor to the east? Putin, I mean."

"Putin? Does he have a brother in the mafia?" Puupponen asked, and then he realized at the same moment I did:

"Oh, damn it to hell! Of course, he was wearing a mask!"

16

Puupponen and I spent some more time with the sketch artist, but we concluded that our guess must be correct. We would have to interview the eyewitnesses again and ask them if their determination of the sex of the person leaning on the railing in a black coat was based on facial features or body type. That would be Puupponen's job.

Kaartamo had ordered chicken fajitas. Usually I liked them, but now I had a hard time forcing the guacamole down. Kaartamo spit salsa on his tie when he heard our theory about the Putin mask. In contrast, Riitta Saarnio's letter delighted him immensely: now we could wrap up the preliminary investigation and send the case to the prosecutor to decide what to do next. Our case closure statistics would go up.

"I think it's premature to announce Riitta Saarnio's confession. I'm not convinced it's authentic. Let's wait to hear from her doctor." I'd left a message for Dr. Erkko-Salonen, but she hadn't called me back yet. "I propose we tell the facts and not exaggerate anything. We can call a new press briefing when there's more to report." I forced myself to swallow some chicken and tortilla.

"The most important thing is to calm the public down. We don't have mafia assassins rampaging around Finland. Is it hard for you to accept that the perpetrator is a menopausal woman with a screw loose? Why invent bogeymen?"

I didn't bother reminding Kaartamo that the previous day he'd been 100 percent behind the mafia theory. Regardless of any of that, we'd have to do our best to present a united front to the media. Afterward I'd have to ask a couple of reporters I knew what their informants were telling them.

Kaartamo said he'd start and I could answer the detailed questions. That was fine with me. I visited the women's restroom to add some powder and touch up my lipstick. I'd already put my hair up in a tight bun before lunch. Kaartamo put on a clean tie, although he complained that red flowers weren't the best choice for an official event. According to him that tie was more appropriate for after work.

I was nervous as we marched into the auditorium, where the members of the media waited. Even though I often felt small standing in front of the cameras and microphones with the public relations officer, I would have preferred that to trying to manage Kaartamo. He couldn't help hinting that the police were hot on the trail of the killer.

"Has anyone been arrested yet?" asked the Channel 4 reporter. Kaartamo gave a self-satisfied smile but didn't reply. When one of the tabloid reporters asked him for a comment on his statements about the mafia the previous day, he blushed in embarrassment and redirected the question. The reporter tried again and Kaartamo lost his cool.

"Do you really have to whip people into hysteria? The situation is completely under control."

"But as far as we know, Riitta Saarnio didn't have any connection to the prostitution business. What would be the motive for her killing?" I didn't recognize the reporter, who sat in the front row. Maybe he was from one of the regional papers. They rarely sent reporters all the way to Espoo, instead relying on the newswire. The fact that this reporter was here was significant. His question caused a commotion in the crowd. What could be juicier? "Hatchetman" Saarnio's wife mixed up with pimps and whores.

"Mrs. Saarnio discovered Lulu Nightingale's body," I said for clarification. We couldn't ignore the fact that Tero Sulonen had called Riitta Saarnio the previous day, though. The TV lights blazed right in my eyes. I could feel my skin sweating under my makeup. My armpits were damp.

"Is there any information about the weapon used to shoot Tero Sulonen?" The MTV3 reporter directed this question to me. Kaartamo opened his mouth, but I cut him off.

"We do know what it was, but we can't comment yet for reasons having to do with the investigation. As Assistant Chief of Police Kaartamo already explained, we're close to a breakthrough. The killer has made too many mistakes. We may be able to provide more information tonight or tomorrow at the latest. We'll be sure to keep everyone in the loop. Your cooperation is important. I'm sure you'll want to interview eyewitnesses from yesterday's incident and Riitta Saarnio's coworkers. We'll appreciate any tips the media can provide. We're all on the same side in this case."

"We haven't heard anything about that missing Russian woman in a while. Have the police determined her identity? Does she have any connection to these crimes?" the MTV3 reporter asked.

"We do know who she was, but unfortunately I can't comment," I replied. At the beginning of the briefing I'd put my phone on silent, but it kept vibrating in my pocket and causing static in the reporters' microphones. Now I turned it off completely. I answered a few more questions and then let Kaartamo talk. Once the briefing was over, the reporter from MTV3 hung back to talk to me.

"Care for a smoke?" he said, even though he knew I didn't smoke and I knew that neither did he. I agreed, and he asked his cameraman to stay behind. Normally smokers were sent outside to the parking lot, but for emergency situations—in other words, for bribing people we were interrogating or building trust in relationships—we had a couple of places in the building where smoking was allowed, even though it was a gross violation of the indoor clean air laws. I took the reporter to the smoking cell in Holding and told him to give me one too so the officer on guard wouldn't wonder what was going on. Then I closed the door.

"I don't know if this means anything," he began, "but yesterday I was chatting with a political reporter I know. He was pretty worked up about all this attention surrounding Ilari Länsimies. According to him, Länsimies's name has been getting attention in a slightly surprising context lately."

I immediately thought of the mafia, but the reporter continued.

"Some powerful people want Länsimies to return to politics. They want him to run for president."

"Powerful people?"

"It's worked before, bringing in a presidential candidate from outside the normal party machine. Think about Martti Ahtisaari. I don't know if this has anything to do with anything or whether the rumor is even true, but that's what I hear. Apparently Länsimies is on board because he never really fulfilled his political ambitions." The reporter gave a wide smile. "A lot can happen in a year, as we saw in the last election. But I'm not a political expert."

"I'll remember this." The ventilation in the smoking cell was terrible, and even though the room lacked any textiles, the oppressive stench of thousands of cigarettes clung to the walls and the cement furniture. My hair would stink for the rest of the day. "I'll call you as soon as I can talk about the weapon from the Big Apple," I promised in return. "And let's have a beer once this case lets up. My treat."

After the reporter left to file his story, I went to see how Pamela Lahtela was getting on. She was awake and looked even more miserable than she had the night before. Her pupils were almost normal, but she was perspiring and shaking uncontrollably. When I opened the cell door, she jumped up and rushed so close to me that for a second I thought she meant to attack me.

"Why am I here?" Her breath smelled of vomit. "I didn't do anything. You have to let me go!"

Pamela was a runaway from a youth home, and that was enough by itself to hold her. According to information collected by the welfare authorities, her mother had left about ten years ago, and her father, whom she'd lived with, was a serious alcoholic. In the past, she'd been able to skip the line for drug treatment because of her age. However, her eighteenth birthday was only a few weeks away.

"They were here during the night, the Russians! I couldn't sleep because they were coming!" Pamela explained. "I was waiting the whole time for them to take me. I want to get out of here. I'm not safe anywhere!"

Pamela had been on the run for almost three months, since the week before Christmas. I asked where she'd lived.

"What do you mean lived? I don't live any fucking place. When you're on speed you don't get tired. And the winter has been warm. There's always someplace to crash. I'm used to being free. Let me out of here!"

"How did you get to know Lulu Nightingale?" I sat down on the bunk, but Pamela continued pacing the floor. Four steps in one direction, four steps back. Amphetamine made a person move compulsively.

"I saw her in an interview in a newspaper when I was still in that Nazi concentration camp they call a youth home. I thought that I wanted to be like her, with my own studio and everything, and then no one could hit me. I could choose my johns too. I . . . I called her, since her number was in the phone book. She told me to come over, and I did."

"When did this happen?"

"When there was that flood at the Market Square. I almost jumped in to swim, it was such a fucking cool thing to see . . . And I like water. Sometimes guys take me to hotels with showers and bathtubs. Once at the Tower there was a claw-foot tub. It was so sweet." Pamela's eyes glinted, and for a moment she looked her age.

"You met Lulu in early January, then?"

"I guess so. She said I could come visit, but when she heard that I work the train station and that . . . Then she didn't want me. She told me to go to the Pro Centre, that they could help me to stop using. She said bad things would happen to me, that whoring and speed don't go well together. That the Russians wouldn't look the other way for long. And she was right." Pamela sat down next to me and took my wrist. "She knew she was in danger too, and she was the best! Why didn't her bodyguard protect her? Is he dead now too?"

I stared at Pamela. The previous night I'd been so tired I hadn't understood how illogical her speech was. Still, how could she have known that Tero Sulonen had been shot when we hadn't released his name before today's press conference?

"Pamela, who told you that Tero is dead?"

"It was Tero who was shot at the mall, wasn't it? It had to be Tero. He arranged the meeting there, even though he was afraid. He said the guy was totally insane."

"What guy? What are you talking about?" I felt like shaking the girl. She stood up and made for the water faucet. She drank but then spat out the water.

"Fuck, this tastes like shit! Don't you have more Coke?"

"You can have more when you tell me what you know about Tero Sulonen." There wasn't time to wait for witnesses. Pamela could repeat her story later in an official interview.

"Are you stupid? I was there in the train station when Tero was talking on his phone. I saw him hanging around near the flower stand and went to express my condolences about Lulu. He's always been nice to me, and I thought maybe he'd give me a few coins or buy me a cup of coffee. But Tero said he didn't have time to talk since he was waiting for a call. He pointed to this guy at the pay phone and said he was a fortune-teller because his cell phone was about to ring. And it did."

"What did the guy at the pay phone look like?"

"I don't really know because his back was to us. He was just a man, I guess. Not tall. Expensive coat and nice hat. I thought it was weird that someone like that wasn't using a cell phone. I didn't see his face, because Tero told me we had to get out of there when he hung up. We ducked out onto the platform. Can I have something to drink now? My mouth is too dry to talk anymore."

The guard had orange Jaffa, which would have to do. While Pamela was gulping it down, I asked her what Sulonen had said during the call. She finished it off, then wiped her mouth with the back of her hand.

"Tero told the guy that he wouldn't tell anyone what he knew about Lulu's death if he got enough money. Then he said OK, he'd come to the Big Apple at five and meet the man in the bathroom at the movie theater. So it was Tero who got shot, right?"

I nodded because the information was already public. It was hard to imagine Pamela inventing this story, even though she did seem to have delusions about the thugs who'd beaten her.

"I didn't know Tero that well, but I think he was afraid. He told me he didn't actually want the money, that he wanted revenge for Lulu. He asked if I knew anybody he could borrow a gun from, but I didn't. Then he left."

My own mouth was dry too, after Pamela's story. I called Liskomäki from Patrol to join me and took Pamela to an interrogation room. She repeated her story on tape without complaint. Her description of the man on the phone at the train station matched the eyewitness accounts from the mall, but the man Pamela saw had a normal build, unlike reports of the mall shooter being more heavyset. When asked, Pamela couldn't swear that it was a man, but based on the clothing, she assumed so. Her testimony that the man was a Russian seemed, under closer inspection, to be her own invention, which lined up with her paranoid delusions.

I asked Liskomäki to call the child welfare authorities, who could take Pamela into their care. Hopefully they could get her a bed in a treatment facility. The fate of a junkie prostitute on the street was too easy to predict. Pamela swore at me as I left, but I couldn't release her. I let her swear but decided to track her down later. Hakkarainen and Mikkola from Forensics were waiting in the conference room.

"Weren't you supposed to be off?" I asked Hakkarainen.

"No. I'm saving vacation days for this summer so that my wife and I can go to Australia for a month. Mrs. Saarnio's office was quite the interesting place. The last time we'd searched it with the same thoroughness as everywhere else and didn't find anything, but this time there were all sorts of new things. Like this." Hakkarainen produced two plastic bags from behind his back. One contained the glass I'd seen under the cabinet in Riitta Saarnio's office.

There was still the slightest drop of liquid in the bottom. "We already sent a sample to the lab," Mikkola said. "But look what we have in bag number two! Ta-da!" Mikkola lifted the second, larger plastic bag containing the slingshot.

"They found this in the trash at the Big Apple. It just came in. Of course there weren't any prints."

"What? Why wasn't I told about this?"

"We tried to call, but you didn't answer! Someone said you were in a press conference. Is this what Söderholm's been going on about in the break room?"

"It must be, and you'll be friends for life if you call him and tell him to come have a look at it. How much strength does it take to shoot this thing? Do you have some gloves?" I asked because my own kit was in my office. Mikkola handed me a pair. I verified that they didn't intend to dust for prints again, then pulled them on and took the slingshot out of the bag. It was surprisingly heavy and sturdy. I placed it in my left hand. It was a little too big for me. Then I pulled the rubber tubing back like a bow string. The slingshot bucked a little when I let go. I looked for something I could shoot. Paper clips were too light. "Take this," Hakkarainen suggested and handed me a five-cent coin. The ball taken from Sulonen's head was slightly smaller across than the coin, but significantly heavier. I pulled back the rubber tubing and aimed at the conference room wall. I tried to hit a dark stain on the wall bequeathed to us by my former colleague Lähde. He'd leaned against the white wall wearing a jacket with oil on it. It had never come out completely, and there wasn't money to repaint the wall over something so minor.

The slingshot was surprisingly accurate, and I hit within two inches of where I'd aimed. The coin banged against the surface and then ricocheted forcefully, landing on the floor several feet away from the wall. When I went closer, I saw a dent in the wall less than a quarter-inch deep.

"Here, let me," Mikkola said, and aimed at the door.

"Don't you dare," Hakkarainen said, and just in time because right then Puustjärvi walked in.

"Dumbass," Hakkarainen said to Mikkola. Puustjärvi grabbed a cup of coffee and joined in our baffled admiration of the slingshot. These grown men reminded me of Taneli when he got a new toy car. Puustjärvi rubbed his eyes. Staring at security camera tape was boring, but luckily, he knew the time to pay special attention to.

I went to my office and tried to think. How could Länsimies have first tried to kill Sulonen at the Big Apple and then run a live television broadcast as if nothing had happened? I could also ask how he could have performed on live TV while waiting for the poison he'd given Lulu Nightingale to work.

I called Ursula to check in about how the interviews with the West Man Productions crew were going. They'd just finished with the cameramen and Nuppu Koskela. They hadn't questioned Länsimies yet. I remembered him mentioning an important meeting, which seemed to be taking an awfully long time.

"Try to get Länsimies down here for questioning and notify me when he arrives," I said to Ursula. "If necessary we'll move the three thirty meeting. What have the other staff members said?"

"They're all in shock. According to them, Riitta Saarnio was the last person at the studio. Länsimies left with one of the guests, a Foreign Ministry official in charge of military affairs. The technical crew stayed to break down their equipment. Nuppu Koskela was the last one to talk to Saarnio. She was really upset. And of course the survival of the show and the whole company is jeopardized now."

"OK. Try to get hold of Länsimies."

Ursula grunted something. She must have been driving. Was Länsimies avoiding us? What if he'd already fled the country? Should I alert the border stations? But no, I didn't have any evidence yet, nothing but speculation based on an overheard conversation. That wasn't enough to draw conclusions from. And if Länsimies intended to run for president, wouldn't he try to keep his background as clean as possible?

A call from the psychiatrist who'd treated Riitta Saarnio, Iiris Erkko-Salonen, interrupted my ruminations. First, we arm wrestled over patient confidentiality. Finally, she agreed to confirm that Riitta Saarnio had been suffering from depression for an extended period of time, and sometimes it affected her ability to work. But she disputed the idea that Saarnio could have been a danger to anyone but herself.

"Had she threatened suicide?"

Erkko-Salonen hesitated. "Saarnio had mentioned it as a possibility. After her daughter's family moved to Brussels, she became increasingly unhappy. I think her grandchildren had helped her enjoy life a little more."

I thanked the doctor, then hung up. Ursula and Autio managed to break away from their interviews for our meeting. Koivu said that Sulonen's condition remained unchanged, although the signs on the

EEG were grounds for optimism. There was hope that his speech centers hadn't been damaged, but the doctors predicted paralysis of his lower extremities. At least his legs weren't moving yet. His arms did, though.

"He probably knows who shot him," Koivu said. "He wouldn't have gone to that mall without a reason. The shooter must have arranged a meeting and used the situation to his advantage." The others muttered in agreement. That had been our working hypothesis all along: the attempted murderer had called Sulonen from the pay phone at the railway station.

Ursula and Autio had established a timeline of Riitta Saarnio's movements the previous day, but independent evidence was sparse. When the cameramen had arrived after five, Riitta Saarnio had already been at the studio.

"OK. Let's focus on Riitta Saarnio as our prime suspect, but keep the other lines open. Expand the circle of interviews to Mrs. Saarnio's friends. Honkanen and Autio can take that on. Why don't you drop by Länsimies's house too? Notify me when you find him. Everyone else, continue with what you've been doing. I'll continue with Arto Saarnio."

"What is his status, Maria?" Puupponen asked. "Are you treating him as a witness? What if he's behind all of this? Maybe he's running a prostitution ring and the whole thing about falling in love with Oksana Petrenko was just horse puckey. Maybe he wants to find the girl so that he can take revenge."

"Saarnio could have gone to pick up his wife from work on Thursday night and slipped the poison in her glass," Koivu added.

"Saarnio came in on the last flight from Sweden," I snapped with more of an edge in my voice than was necessary.

"Has anyone checked that?" Koivu snapped back. "Finnair or SAS?"

"How about you check both of their passenger manifests?" I tried to keep my voice calm, but I was at my limit. I missed my children, and it was insane that both their father and mother were putting everyone else ahead of them.

"OK, *boss*," Koivu said, adding a sarcastic emphasis to the final word. I pulled a face at him, but all I got back was a cold glare.

"When is Riitta Saarnio's autopsy?" I asked him in an attempt to get us back on track.

"Not until Monday morning. Nice way to start the week. Can I skip the morning meeting?"

"Go ahead."

My exhaustion was so intense that I decided to just go home. I'd just have to arrange with my sister- and mother-in-law to take the kids if Länsimies came in later for questioning. The sun was still high in the sky as I drove home. The willow branches were taking on their usual ruddy spring color, and there was violet in the birches. Little streams ran along the roads, and I could almost hear their murmuring in the car. I called Marjatta to tell her I'd stop by the store to pick up some groceries.

It felt good to do something normal. How many gallons of milk did we need? Was there any yogurt left? What about cheese? A new brand of hard cider had appeared on the shelf, so I grabbed a couple of bottles to give it a try. Antti thought drinking cider was perverse, that it tasted like artificial flavoring. But I liked it, and I was waiting for someone to invent a salmiakki cider. Salmiakki vodka went down my throat so smoothly that I only let myself buy it in exceptional circumstances. I bought Venjamin some kidney, which was his favorite. Whenever I heard the way he purred eating it, I forgot the sharp scent of urine it gave off. Iida wouldn't pick him up as long as the smell lingered on his breath.

As I pulled into the parking lot at home, a text came from Koivu informing me that Arto Saarnio had been on the final Finnair flight of the day from Stockholm. He also said that he was headed home too. His wife, Anu, was at her wit's end after the past few days, even though she was well aware of how consuming police work could be. Even so,

I'd never led such a knotty and multilayered investigation—usually only one homicide happened in Espoo per year. Statistically the city was safe, especially given its size. Finnish homicides usually happened in smaller localities, and my home area of Northern Karelia was listed depressingly high in the rankings. Killings there were usually the result of showdowns between drug users or drunks.

At parents' night for Iida's class, someone had mentioned a study that claimed it was possible to predict as early as age eight whether a child would become a criminal later in life. The other parents had pressed first the teacher and then me—they knew what I did for work—about whether something so disturbing could be true. Iida's teacher carefully responded that studies like that were done so that the indicators could be spotted early enough to intervene. And that the parents of the problem cases usually didn't show up for parents' night. I thought of Pamela and wondered what she had been like as an eight-year-old. I was in a debt of gratitude to her, and I had to pay her back somehow.

I was inside my apartment building when Söderholm called. "This slingshot is a nice piece of work," he said enthusiastically. "The Crime Museum would probably like it for their collection."

"I have no doubt." I struggled to keep my balance as I opened the elevator door while carrying the grocery bags.

"I hear you play bass guitar. We're going to have an opening in our band, since Kantola is moving to Tampere. Any interest in coming by for an audition?"

"What kind of music?"

"Police punk," Söderholm said with a laugh. "The other guitarist is Montonen from the city. He mentioned that you and he just ran into each other at an arrest."

"It's not the worst idea I've heard today. I'll think about it and give you a call," I said as I stepped out of the elevator.

At my own front door the children rushed at me with glee, and Marjatta poked her head out of the bathroom to say she was washing

Taneli's good rain pants, which had been waiting in the laundry hamper for days. I hadn't even remembered them. She agreed to take the children in at her house in Tapiola if anything surprising happened. Before leaving, she asked again whether I'd talked to Antti, and I claimed I hadn't had time. That was almost true.

I made pasta with ham, which we all liked, and I drank half a bottle of beer with it, even though I wasn't sure if I'd need to drive again today. I baked brownies with Iida and cleaned up the kitchen, read them an Astrid Lindgren story they both liked, and then mended a tear in Iida's skating tights. I didn't try to reach Antti—let him enjoy his party in peace. Of course, I knew that wasn't the real reason I didn't call. I was afraid if I did he wouldn't answer at all or, if he did answer, he'd be evasive and tell me half truths. I didn't want to make him do that.

Ursula called at around eight.

"Hi. We caught up with Mrs. Länsimies at her shoe store this afternoon. Mr. L. is at a Ministry of Transport and Communications seminar in Kuopio today and tomorrow. Mrs. L. doesn't think Mr. L. will be accepting calls because he doesn't want to comment to the media on his business partner's death. According to her he's a very sensitive soul."

"That's a new side to him. Did she know when he's coming back? Is he flying or driving?" It was hard to imagine Ilari Länsimies sitting on a bus or train.

"He's flying into Helsinki-Vantaa at 4:25 tomorrow. Shall we go welcome him home?"

"Definitely. I'll call in the morning to let you know if I can come along. If so, Autio can stay home. OK? Now go on home—you need some time off too."

"Actually, I have a date tonight. So never say there's no such thing as a free meal. Because now there is," she said mysteriously and hung up.

The kids begged to be allowed to sleep in Mommy and Daddy's bed, and eventually I gave in. Since the lieutenant from Narcotics was on duty, I went ahead and shut off my phone. Taneli fell asleep first, while Iida spent another half hour sitting up reading. After she nodded off too, I went into the living room and took out my bass guitar, which I plucked at absentmindedly as I channel surfed. Confirming Antti's return time tomorrow would have been a good excuse for calling him, but I resisted the temptation. I'd have plenty of time to call him in the morning. When the evening news ran their tape of me and Kaartamo, neither of us looking our best, I cracked open a bottle of cider. Venjamin climbed onto my neck and started grooming my hair. His paws kneaded my shoulders pleasantly, but when he brought out his claws, I had to push him off. I fumbled through some basic scales on my bass guitar and fantasized about playing with the amp turned all the way up. Sometime after ten, I crawled in between the kids, and Venjamin followed me. I had a dream in which Vladimir Putin had decided to run for president of Finland too.

In the morning, the sky was still gray. The three of us woke up slowly, since skating practice didn't begin until ten. It was amazing that the club had managed to land such a good ice time for the small skaters, since the hockey teams usually took the best times.

Over coffee I listened to my messages. Koivu had left one saying that some reporter had tried to sneak into the hospital to take pictures of Tero Sulonen, and that one of the tabloids had a long piece about my murder investigation. Apparently the reporter thought it was turning into a catastrophe as the bodies piled up.

Paparazzi just didn't care about rules. Bare breasts weren't enough to sell papers anymore, so tabloids always featured stories on adultery or child pornography. Even the local papers were feeling the pressure of increasing competition and had started printing pictures of the bloody corpses of victims of bombings and natural disasters. I had to admit I would welcome any headline that could keep our investigation off the front page.

I buttered bread for the kids to take as a snack to practice. I was glad not to have to wake up Marjatta, since my subordinates seemed to be doing fine without me. For once I could focus on my kids—Iida was worried that she wouldn't be home in time to see the entire women's long program in the World Figure Skating Championships. She'd even made a small Finnish flag out of a piece of an old sheet, which she intended to wave for Susanna Pöykiö. Iida jabbered on about how much she loved all of our national team skaters, and it broke her heart that only one Finnish skater had qualified to represent Finland at the world championships.

"But next year we're sure to get two places since Susanna is tenth after the short. Mom, could we go watch sometime?"

"Once you're a little bigger and you can sit in an arena for hours on end," I promised, even though I knew I'd have to answer for that promise later. Iida had an excellent memory for these kinds of things.

Suddenly the door opened. I was surprised—my mother-in-law usually rang the doorbell, and she wasn't even supposed to come over today. But instead it was Antti.

"Oh, are you home already?"

The children rushed at their father. Taneli grabbed onto Antti's long legs and Iida threw her arms around his waist.

"Did you fly?" I couldn't quite bring myself to go kiss him. I wouldn't fit between him and the kids anyway, I told myself.

"No, I took the first train. It left at five thirty. I've been up all night," Antti said and leaned over the children so he could plant a kiss somewhere around my left ear. His breath smelled sour. "It was a fine party, but I missed home. Virve thought I should talk to you as soon as possible too."

My hand, still holding the butter knife, froze. *Now it's happening. Antti is leaving me.* Even though I'd had my suspicions, I'd never imagined anything this dramatic. My throat clenched, and my hand shook so violently that I smeared butter across the cutting board. Did Antti have to say it in front of the kids? I didn't want them to see me cry, and I could tell that I was going to cry. I felt like I was going to vomit.

"I was talking to Virve and Jouni about our situation, and Virve said that I would be an idiot to not accept Mom's offer. I finally saw the light, and we celebrated a bit, even though the party was really for Virve and Jouni's engagement."

"Engagement? Virve and . . . who's Jouni?"

"Virve's boyfriend. They've been together for years. I guess I sort of convinced them it was worth finally tying the knot. They're planning a summer wedding. Virve actually asked if Iida would want to be a flower girl, since neither of them have any young relatives the right age."

"Yes!" Iida squealed. I sat down on a kitchen chair. Contradictory thoughts and emotions tumbled through my brain, and I didn't know whether I should laugh or cry. How did I think I was going to solve a crime if I suspected my own husband of infidelity for no reason?

"How have I never heard about this Jouni before?" I asked.

"Haven't you? Well, I guess he travels a lot too, so that's why Virve and I have spent so many evenings moping together. Of course, next they'll start having babies, and then I'll get to play babysitter in Vaasa instead of being with my own kids. Because I'm not going to leave this project hanging, even though the travel is a bear. But otherwise I'll be a good little boy and do as Mother says, take the money and say thank you. Do you have time tomorrow to start looking at houses? Maybe we can find a nice little cramped row house, since I know that's your favorite."

Antti sat down next to me and wrapped his arms around me. I leaned against him and wondered whether I should tell him what I'd thought. I decided that I would someday, but not now. Now it was time to enjoy the warm feeling that slowly spread from my body to my mind as Antti first kissed my forehead. And then he kissed my lips.

17

I was sitting on the edge of the rink watching Iida attempt a single axel when my phone began to vibrate in my pocket. I recognized Arto Saarnio's number. I stood up and walked out to the hallway to talk. My muscles were stiff, and I was frozen to the bone. During the two years of being a figure-skating mom, I still hadn't gotten used to just how frigid empty ice arenas could be.

"Hello, Detective, this is Arto. Saarnio, I mean. Do you have any news about my wife's death?"

"The investigation is ongoing. She died of cyanide poisoning, just like Lulu Nightingale. I'd like to ask you to keep that information confidential."

"Could Riitta have found the bottle of poison used by Lulu Nightingale's murderer and decided to use it on herself? Where else could she have gotten cyanide? And, I have to ask, isn't cyanide poisoning a very painful death?"

"Yes, but also quick." I heard the music change in the arena. Now the children were practicing to the soft rock strains of Antti Tuisku. Iida's trainers had mostly ignored her requests for some real rock 'n' roll. They did play Apocalyptica sometimes, because a lot of international-level skaters were using it in their competition programs.

"This may be a complete shot in the dark, but an acquaintance stopped by yesterday to pay his respects. Jaakko Aarnivuori—maybe you know him? He's an old army buddy, now on the boards of Nokia and Nordea. He dropped some interesting hints about Ilari Länsimies."

Jaakko Aarnivuori's name stopped me short. It had been in Lulu's customer records—apparently Aarnivuori liked being whipped. Ursula and Puupponen had laid bets on how much a tabloid would pay for that information.

"I'm desperate to believe that Riitta was not a murderer, so I may just be grasping at straws here. But I think you should hear this, although not over the phone. Are you at work?"

"No, I'm at the Matinkylä Ice Arena."

"Can I meet you there? Someplace private? I wouldn't want my children hearing what Jaakko told me."

"I'll be here for another hour. We can talk outside in your car. Call me when you're in the parking lot, and I'll come out."

I was irritated to not have a voice recorder with me, but at least I had a notebook at the bottom of my purse. I hopped in place for a minute to get my blood flowing again, then I returned to the arena. Most of the other mothers were better equipped than me, wearing everything from expensive furs to full ski outfits. In addition to Antti, there were also a few other dads in the stands.

Iida's group was currently practicing their pirouettes. Next would be Taneli's turn on the ice, and Iida would head to the dressing room to cool down and stretch. I always got a kick out of watching the under-fives group, since many of the children barely knew how to walk properly, let alone skate. This time, however, I would have to put work ahead of my amusement.

When Arto Saarnio called, I told Antti I had to go. "But tomorrow we'll go look at houses," I promised.

Saarnio's dark-blue CLS-series Mercedes waited at the back of the ice hall parking lot. Saarnio was standing outside of it, and when he saw me he waved. Because of its tinted windows, it was impossible to see inside, but I soon saw that out-looking visibility was impeccable. A ride like that would have been fantastic for stakeouts.

Saarnio opened the right rear door for me and then slid in next to me. The car wasn't running but still felt warm after being in the freezing ice arena. Saarnio shook my hand as if we were beginning a business negotiation, then asked, "How much do you follow politics?"

"Pretty actively."

"So you know that there are people in the country right now who are concerned about the direction we're going in. They believe that Finland will become marginalized if we don't take drastic action. Individual and business taxes have to be lowered significantly, it has to be easier to fire and hire, work needs to be more flexible, and the social support structures have to be dismantled. According to them, we simply don't have the resources to maintain the welfare state we have now."

I nodded. I'd heard these ideas before. Saarnio continued:

"In our foreign affairs, Finland has slid in the wrong direction. We have to join NATO immediately, and Finland's position in the EU has to be strengthened through alliances with the right powers. That's why we have to have a pro-NATO president come out of the next election."

Saarnio suddenly glanced at my lap.

"You aren't taping this, are you?"

"No."

"Good. The fact that I'm telling you what I know goes against everything I've believed my entire life. But maybe it's time to change my beliefs. So these people are looking for a presidential candidate. Paavo Lipponen would work for some of them, but he's been ruled out because he's from the same party as the current president. And they believe that, after twenty-four years of social democratic control, a Finland that focuses on the middle class needs a right-wing president. They want to keep Vanhanen as prime minister, and Aho isn't going to risk losing again. The National Coalition doesn't have anyone that can step into

President Niinistö's shoes, if he won't do it. In the case of Ahtisaari, advancing a candidate without any current political alignment worked perfectly, so now they want to try the same thing. But now they have someone in mind who is much more familiar to the common man . . ."

"Ilari Länsimies?" I said.

Saarnio nodded.

"Ilari has experience in politics and diplomacy. Lately *Surprise Guests* had been focusing on foreign policy questions and legislative issues—like the prostitution debate. What I hear is that the possibility was put forward half in jest during a sauna discussion about how to undermine the current president's popularity. Länsimies was positively inclined toward running, and gradually others have warmed to the idea. He performs well in public, and his wife also enjoys the spotlight. And there's another perspective too," Saarnio said, embarrassed. "The quote-unquote bitches have had their chance. There's been a woman as president and as prime minister, and we've seen where that led. Now it's time to return to a normal state of affairs."

Now I understood why Kaartamo had been so enthusiastic to proclaim Riitta Saarnio or the Russian mafia guilty. He must have friends in high places, and they knew about these plans for Länsimies.

"But Länsimies also has another side. He gets caught up in things. He believes he can do anything and takes on too much. Riitta called him a narcissist. She called me that too, actually." Saarnio grimaced. "Jaakko was worried that Länsimies was mixed up in Lulu Nightingale's death. Lulu must have had clients who were involved in this project."

Saarnio looked into my eyes, obviously expecting me to confirm his theory, but of course I did nothing of the sort.

"Jaakko told me this in private, and now I'm betraying that trust. They didn't consider me an appropriate member of their little cabal, because I arouse too much ire in the average voter. I think I'm a bit too high up in the competition for most hated man in Finland." Saarnio tried to smile, but it didn't work. His lips moved, but the expression of his eyes didn't change. "I've always thought I didn't care. Dogs bark, but the caravan moves on. But that isn't quite how it is."

Saarnio leaned back. Even the back seats of the Mercedes had headrests, and they were covered in the same dark-gray leather as the rest of the car's interior. Antti's and my combined yearly income probably wasn't enough to buy a car like this.

"But why would Länsimies have endangered this entire undertaking by knocking people off? If Lulu Nightingale was dangerous to him in some way, why kill her in a place that would connect the killing to him?" I said more to myself than to Arto Saarnio.

The overall picture was starting to take shape. Now the photoshopped picture of the president and Lulu we'd found made sense. Apparently Länsimies and his supporters had been preparing some truly dirty tricks. Had Lulu become difficult when she found out what her picture was being used for?

"Maybe he thought that the ends justified the means," Saarnio said. "There are psychological studies that claim the worst psychopaths aren't in the criminal underworld, they're in the upper echelons of society. I was called a psychopath after the Copperwood layoffs. People said I didn't know how to put myself in the shoes of those I was firing and that I only cared about the benefits to the shareholders. And maybe it looked that way, but I doubt my empathy would have been a help to anyone. Crying doesn't make streamlining a business any easier."

"Would Länsimies have any real chance of becoming president?"

"Popular opinion has changed before. Remember the last election? The previous fall, it looked like the president would be Riitta Uosukainen. People can be influenced if there's enough money and media connections at play."

I thought for a moment and then told Saarnio that I'd heard the same tip the day before. "Now I really believe it. Can you give me any more details?"

"What do you want to know?"

"As much as possible. I promise I won't reveal my sources. I'll be interviewing Länsimies today. Officer Honkanen and I will be meeting him at the airport. By the way, did you hire a private investigator to find Oksana?"

"No. It's probably pointless, since I think she's dead anyway. And my wife, the woman I loved for two-thirds of my life . . . I never stopped loving Riitta, even when she didn't want me anymore. That was the worst thing about it. But I loved Oksana too. Can you love two people at the same time?"

Saarnio looked straight into my eyes again. Saarnio hadn't really loved Oksana, he'd just been infatuated, but over the years I'd learned that there was no objective truth to be found in matters of the heart. There was no one right way to love. You just had to try to love, sometimes against all reason. I couldn't give him the answer he wanted to hear, so instead I said, "Thank you for your assistance, Arto."

Saarnio climbed out of the car, and he held the door open for me as I stepped out. We shook hands again, and Saarnio's grip was firm and steady.

I returned to the ice arena feeling agitated and wondering whether I should call Koivu. No, it was best to see Länsimies first. I'd told Ursula that I'd pick her up at 3:45. My unmarked Saab would be a better fit for a run to the airport.

Taneli looked small out on the ice, and I was amazed at how fast he already dared to skate. After practice, both kids were hungry, and back at home they wolfed down the pasta and meat sauce I prepared for them. Antti called his mother and was on the phone for quite a while. Marjatta would be happy about his decision, and I'd get the glory even though he'd made it himself.

After lunch a text message came from Puustjärvi: *Hi! There's a few seconds of tape showing a man in a black coat and hat. He enters the mall from the theater side door and leaves the same way. His face is covered. That's all I can do for now—I'm going home. Copies of the tape on your desk.*

Puustjärvi had used up his Saturday too, but fortunately he'd finally found what we were looking for. Maybe I'd stop by the office to review the tape on the way back from the airport. That would still leave Saturday evening to spend with the family. Maybe we could heat the sauna and play a game all together. I started dreaming about how, in our new house, we could have a real sauna instead of the cramped steam closet we had now. And a bathtub if possible. And a music room. Then I remembered that Söderholm's police punk band would be practicing next Friday. Before then I'd need to really shake the rust off my fingers.

I did some chores around the house, even though my thoughts were stuck on Länsimies. Was he really reckless enough to kill people to achieve his goal? I could sort of understand the reason for Lulu's murder, but what about the others? How could he have believed he wouldn't get caught?

I went to watch the last two groups of the women's long program on TV with Iida and Taneli. Iida waved her Finnish flag and almost burst with joy when Susanna Pöykiö got eighth place. After the competition ended, the television must have remained on, because when I was taking laundry into the kids' room, I saw a black man rapping on the screen. Black people made up a tiny minority in Finland, and the children were spellbound by the music video. Was I a racist for hating the pimp fashion of so many of the rappers? The man on the video seemed to be selling half-naked women. Maybe rappers were advocating for racial equality, but this song didn't seem to pay much attention to gender equality. I switched the TV off, despite the kids' cries of protest, and instead played Uno with them.

I arrived at Ursula's apartment ten minutes early, but fortunately she was ready to go. Like me she was dressed for business in a dark-blue pantsuit and pale-pink blouse. Her makeup was subdued. I wore my dark pinstripes. I'd always envied the simplicity of a man's suit and tie. Not that Antti ever wore that outfit—he hated suits and only wore one under extreme duress. The last time he'd done so was at his father's funeral.

"How did your date go?" I asked Ursula once we'd merged onto the Ring I beltway. As usual, we ran into traffic. I was grateful that we had extra time.

"According to plan." Ursula gave a wry smile. I didn't pump her for information, since it seemed as though she wanted to be mysterious about her private life.

"We had dinner at the Kämp Hotel," Ursula went on. "One-hundred-euro champagne . . . And so what, if he's buying? By the way, where are we going to take Länsimies for questioning? The airport concourse?"

"We can take him back to the police station if he doesn't want to talk in a public place." I'd thought of the same issue and was relying on the airport staff to provide us with assistance and a place to interrogate our suspect if necessary.

The flight from Kuopio was a little early, but we still managed to reserve the airport press room. We waited for Länsimies in the arrivals terminal. Before long he appeared, surrounded by men in dark suits, pulling a leather roller bag. Länsimies attracted stares, and one person even abandoned her luggage to rush after him and ask for an autograph. Länsimies gave the girl a broad smile as he scribbled his name in her notebook. He looked relaxed and happy and unaware of our presence, so I stepped in front of him.

"Hello, Mr. Länsimies. Officer Honkanen has been trying to reach you for quite some time. We have business to discuss with you."

Länsimies's expression turned sour. "What could be so serious that you had to come all the way to the airport?"

"I'm sure you know. Shall we talk here, or would you prefer to come to the police station?"

Länsimies's companions moved out of the way. Anyone who had read the newspaper knew what was going on.

"I have time right now," Länsimies said. On the collar of his camel-hair coat was a hair, which he brushed off. When he turned to follow Ursula, I bent down, ostensibly to retrieve the gloves I'd just dropped, but I also gently picked up the hair and placed it in a plastic bag.

An airport official unlocked the press room for us. Ursula fetched coffee for herself and Länsimies and a Diet Coke for me. Länsimies said he understood that we wanted to talk about Riitta Saarnio's death but, unfortunately, he didn't have anything more to tell us.

"As I said, Riitta stayed at the studio after I left. We arranged to talk Monday since Riitta knew I'd be in Kuopio at this seminar all day Friday."

"Was there anything out of the ordinary in her behavior?"

"She was extremely agitated. We all were. What happened last week affected everyone. Thankfully Nuppu was there this time so Riitta didn't have to fetch the guests from their dressing rooms. That would have been too much for her. I was very satisfied with our whole team, which was why I was so enthusiastic Friday morning when you called. I think we performed admirably during the broadcast, despite the nightmare of the previous week. But now . . . we'll have to rethink everything. Riitta's death is a terrible loss. Did she kill herself?"

"What makes you think that?"

Länsimies didn't immediately answer my question, instead taking a moment to think carefully. When he continued, he whispered as if telling a great secret.

"She's suffered from depression for a long time. During her good times she's an amazing colleague, but when things are bad her work just doesn't get done. But I've tried to be understanding, and I should have seen what was coming . . ."

I quickly drained my Coke, while the others' coffee cups were still almost full. The airport was calm. It felt like a space between two realities, a place where we shouldn't have been working, where we should have been waiting to fly off to a new life.

"I value experience, and Riitta had it, and at the same time she could also approach new things with an open mind. I knew the ire directed at Arto was hard on her, even though she didn't always approve of the hard line he often chose. A while back we talked about it, when we were debating whether we could invite him on the show for a discussion about changes in the labor market brought on by globalization. Riitta didn't want to, and I thought it would be unethical since Arto owns stock in West Man Productions—not because he was Riitta's husband. God, I need to call Arto too. Or at least send flowers. Riitta used to handle things like that."

Länsimies seemed to be gradually returning to the relaxed state he'd been in upon arrival. He leaned back in his chair and slowly sipped his coffee. His gaze shifted from me to Ursula, who smiled.

"Do you intend to continue with *Surprise Guests*?" Ursula asked. She and Länsimies hadn't met before, but I sensed a mutual curiosity. Ursula was attracted to men with power and money, and Länsimies, like most men, was drawn to beautiful blonds like Ursula. *Maybe,* I thought, *I should allow her to do some more questioning.*

"The guests for the next couple of shows are already booked. The network wants to keep it running. On our next show, we're going to have some sort of tribute to Riitta. Hopefully you'll have figured out who's behind all of this by then. You don't think Riitta's suicide has anything to do with the . . . rest of it, other than that it depressed her even more?"

"Why do you assume she committed suicide?" Ursula asked quickly. We hadn't yet released any information about Riitta Saarnio's suicide note or her cause of death to the press.

"Didn't she?" Länsimies responded. Gradually his expression began to change. If it was an act, Länsimies was a very good actor. "What are you trying to tell me?"

"We aren't trying to tell you anything." Then I decided to take a risk, even though the police didn't usually reveal their evidence. "Riitta Saarnio left behind a suicide note. We're examining its authenticity, since her death is connected to a series of unexplained homicides or attempted homicides. I don't believe that you or the other employees of West Man Productions are in any danger. That being said, a certain amount of street sense is in order. And I hope you'll stay available for any follow-up questions."

"I had to keep my phone off because the reporters have been hounding me," Länsimies said in his defense. "How is Lulu's bodyguard doing anyway?"

"His condition is unchanged. He'll probably live, but we don't have any idea if or when we'll be able to interview him." I watched Länsimies carefully: Did he react? If he was the criminal we were hunting, Sulonen's recovery would be extremely dangerous for him. We'd instructed the Jorvi Hospital staff to not allow anyone to be left alone with him, and that we'd need a list of all visitors. So far, the only visitor had been his friend Pate Mustajärvi.

"Unfortunately, I can't offer any more help," Länsimies said and swirled his spoon in his empty coffee cup. "Is there anything else? I haven't really had time to process Riitta's death. This seminar was booked solid. You know how they can be: even while drinking beer in the sauna we talked shop. Getting over losing Riitta isn't going to be easy. It's such a terrible tragedy. I should have seen that something was wrong."

"The worst thing about suicide is that everyone left behind blames themselves," Ursula said kindly, gazing empathetically into Länsimies's eyes. She received a heartsick smile in return.

"How am I supposed to go on? I know Riitta would have wanted me to keep the show alive. Maybe the topic for our final show this spring could be depression . . ." Länsimies seemed to be talking more to himself than to us, but it also seemed deliberate.

"What about last Thursday?" Ursula asked.

"I went home between the morning meeting and the taping."

"Anyone who could corroborate that?"

"I . . . I can't think of anyone off the top of my head. Riitta said she went somewhere too," he reported. "But no, she didn't say that she went to the Big Apple!" Länsimies shook his head. "I still can't believe . . . How could we not have seen it coming? I'm sorry, I need to be alone," Länsimies said, his voice cracking. "This is too much."

We left him there in the press room, his head buried in his hands. The domestic terminal was a beehive of activity, with people leaving early for Easter ski vacations in Lapland. I couldn't shake a feeling of doubt as we navigated the crowd.

"That guy would be a strong candidate for our murderer, if he had a motive," Ursula said once we were in the car. "He had access to the studio, and he chose the guests. Maybe it wasn't just a coincidence that so many of them had a connection to Lulu. Länsimies might have done that on purpose. But what the hell would have been the point? Did Lulu threaten to tell the whole country on live TV that Länsimies had a tiny dick and was terrible in bed?"

I wondered whether I could trust Ursula but decided to stay silent. I asked, "Do you want to come to the station to see the security footage Puustjärvi found? I could drop you off at home after. Two sets of eyes are always better than one."

"I'd be happy to come. But really, Maria, I'm serious. Think about it. Länsimies was the only one who had the opportunity to forge Riitta Saarnio's suicide note. Maybe he used Saarnio's signature from another document, or maybe Länsimies tricked her into writing her name . . ."

"Yes, and the cyanide in Lulu's car—we know that Länsimies met with Lulu outside of the studio. He could have hidden the bottle then, if he'd planned far enough ahead. Maybe the whole program was arranged just so Länsimies could get rid of Lulu."

"The picture!" Ursula exclaimed. "Lulu and the president. Lulu intended to reveal that it was a fake and that Länsimies was behind it. Lulu was probably blackmailing Länsimies. He doesn't show up in her client records, but this might be about something other than sex. OK, come on, Grandma," Ursula said with a sigh as I stopped the car at a crosswalk to let an elderly woman cross. A police officer was supposed to be polite.

Our unit's hallway was empty, and the conference room coffee pot was half-full and cold. I grabbed the tapes from my office and found that Puustjärvi had rewound them to the right spots. The figure in the black coat and wide-brimmed hat who stepped through the doors of the shopping center had attempted to conceal his face. A black scarf covered the area around his mouth, and his hat was pulled down low. He also wore sunglasses. All we could see was his nose. He was carrying a flat plastic bag, which could have contained the mask. I paused the tape to examine the image more closely: it was a regular K-Market plastic bag, and the contents did indeed seem relatively light.

"If that's our guy, then why didn't any of the witnesses say anything about a scarf covering his mouth?"

"Because he must have taken it off once inside. Maybe he thought it would attract too much attention. But wait. Next to the theater there's a restroom. Maybe he went in there to put on the mask. Of course, there aren't any cameras in the bathroom. Let's have a look at that other tape."

The man leaving the mall looked similar in terms of clothing, but now he didn't have the plastic bag in his hand. The sunglasses and scarf were there, but the scarf was down lower than in the first image, and the man's profile looked different.

"Now he's wearing the mask. But it's the same guy. He moves in the same way."

"Yes, he does. But one thing . . . even though cameras make people look heavier, this person is significantly larger than Länsimies."

We looked at each other in disappointment for a moment, but then Ursula spoke. "If he was thinner than Länsimies, then we'd be in trouble. Or if he was two inches taller. But you can look fatter just by adding a couple of layers of clothing and some padding. Länsimies works in TV, so he must know some tricks."

This observation was so obvious that I started to laugh. "OK, now we need to show these tapes to the people who saw the shooter. Let's see what they say. Then we'll compare this man's gait to Länsimies's. Coming up with a reason to request old tapes of his show from the network archives won't be hard."

"I already have the shows from the night of the murder and last night," Ursula said. "I thought they might be useful." She blushed a little. "I watched the prostitution episode purely out of professional curiosity, because of Oksana. Will we ever find out what happened to her?"

"Hopefully. But for now we'll have to go through the trash in that restroom to see if that K-Market bag turns up. I've got to go. You still want a ride?"

"No, I'm going to stick around and finish up a couple of things. I don't have a date tonight, so I might as well."

I was in a better mood than I'd been in a long time as I drove home, even though it was still sleeting. Tomorrow we were going to look at houses, the murder investigation was progressing, Antti wasn't in love with someone else, and I was getting along with Ursula. Now all I could do was wait for more information about Länsimies's possible motives, then it would be time to share my suspicions with my unit.

Back at home I prepared crepes for after our sauna. I couldn't wait until the kids went to sleep and Antti and I could be alone. My desire for him hadn't ever really left me, and it began to flow in the sauna when our hot, bare skin touched. But the kids were in the sauna too, so I had to wait. Of course, that only increased my eagerness.

Taneli was already asleep and Antti was reading to Iida when my phone rang. I saw that it was Ursula, so I answered. Ursula wasn't in the habit of calling without a good reason.

"Hi, Maria. I have Lulu and Sulonen's shared phone logs. The Dearlulu number."

"Yeah?"

"There are a bunch of calls here to Sulonen and a few to customers we already know about, but one is interesting. It's a call to Lulu's cell phone on Wednesday, March 9, the same day Oksana Petrenko disappeared from the hospital." Ursula paused. I bit my lip to avoid rushing her.

"When I looked up the caller's number, I found that it belonged to a woman named Mari Asikkala. Asikkala is a nurse at Jorvi Hospital, in the same department where Oksana was. I checked her schedule: she was on shift when Oksana disappeared. She told me that she'd stashed her phone in a drawer at the front desk—this is against protocol, but her son was sick and she was waiting to hear from the day care. When she finally got the call, Oksana came into the hall."

"So Oksana borrowed her phone?"

"Exactly! Oksana must have called Lulu, and Lulu must have called her back on her room phone when she was ready to pick her up. It just so happened that someone turned on Lulu's spare phone for a few seconds. It's somewhere in West Newland—Barösund, I think. I have the coordinates here."

Barösund was in Inkoo, and someone had just mentioned it . . . Pastor Pihlaja! She'd remembered that Lulu had been irritated at graduation, when her parents were talking up the summer cabin they'd bought in Barösund. What if Oksana was alive and staying at Lulu's parents' summer house?

"Ursula, call Lulu's parents! They should have a cabin in Barösund, near Inkoo. Get the address, then check to see if the coordinates for Lulu's phone match its location. If they do, we're going there. But don't tell Lulu's parents why we need to know!"

I put my phone on speaker and took off my robe and nightshirt. A few seconds later Antti entered the bedroom and looked at me in surprise.

"Are you going somewhere?"

"Inkoo. It might be an emergency." Had Oksana been in Inkoo for a week and a half, all alone? I'd just managed to get my jeans and sweater on when I heard Ursula's voice on the speaker.

"Maria, it matches."

"OK. Pick me up in ten minutes in your personal car. Let's go see what we can find in Barösund."

18

"The call isn't going through," I said in frustration once we were about halfway to Barösund. There wasn't any other traffic, so Ursula put the pedal to the metal. On this road speeding seemed to be the norm. "Hopefully it's not a bad signal. Of course, we should have called the Mäkinens to ask for a key, but let's not complicate things. I have a lock pick. We met in the hospital, so Oksana knows me. We should say upfront that we're police but that we aren't a threat to her. We don't have any reason to arrest her—we just want to know who cut her." Oksana may have been in the country illegally, but immigration enforcement wasn't our job.

We stopped at a gas station to buy some food, because we worried Oksana would be hungry. And maybe that'd give her a reason to open the door.

After the turnoff to the village of Siuntio there were no more streetlights. The little remaining snow didn't help to illuminate the landscape and the sky was clouded over, so we were now driving in almost perfect darkness. Now and then a truck passed, and the traffic signals at the intersections near Degerby and Inkoo flashed like beacons. I squinted hard at the map, trying to read it in the dark. I'd sailed the Barösund Channel several times, but I'd only set foot on land there once, so I didn't know the roads.

Fortunately, the Mäkinens' cabin was on the mainland, so we didn't have to wait for the ferry. I'd brought my Russian dictionary with me. Arto Saarnio had said that Oksana's English was wanting. How had customers explained what they wanted, or weren't words necessary in that kind of work? Maybe Oksana's service offerings weren't as extensive as Lulu Nightingale's.

The summer cabin sat a quarter of a mile from the seashore. There were a lot of other cabins in the area too, and according to the land register they all shared access to the water. There were no lights as far as I could see, not even in the Mäkinens' cabin. Had Oksana spent more than a week sitting in the dark, too afraid to turn on the lights?

Ursula parked the car one cabin away. I couldn't see a thing right after she cut the headlights, but gradually I began to make out the trees in the darkness. The Mäkinens' cabin was small, about four hundred square feet. It had two doors, one to the living area and another to the sauna. No smoke rose from the chimney. Farther off a shed loomed in the darkness, a tiny building likely used for storing the wood and as an outhouse.

Ursula got out of the car and grabbed the bag of food and a flashlight from the back seat. I'd also brought a flashlight. In its beam, I saw that Ursula was wearing a holster under her arm. Suddenly she buttoned her coat.

"You never know. Maybe someone's following us," she whispered.

"Like who?"

"I wasn't expecting those two guys who jumped me after I left the Mikado that night either," she replied. We walked through the yard of the neighboring cabin to the Mäkinens' lot. There were tracks in the snow, in the size and shape of a man's boots, that led to the shed. Instead of following them, we approached the front door and knocked, but no one answered. I turned the door handle—nothing. The windows that faced the road were covered on the inside with thick fabric, so we couldn't see in.

"Is anyone there?" I yelled in Finnish. "Police, open up!"

No answer. We circled to the other side of the cabin, where there was also a window. It had curtains as well. We walked to the outhouse and lifted the latch. The smell was unmistakable: it had been used recently. If it had gone unused all winter, the excrement would have frozen and wouldn't smell.

We walked back to the porch of the cabin and knocked again. I raised my eyebrows at Ursula and motioned for her to give talking a try.

"Hello, Oksana, open the door! My name is Ursula. I'm a friend. Lulu's friend. I've come to help you. I have food," Ursula shouted in English loud enough that it echoed all the way to the shore. Her hand was on her holster.

We listened hard. From inside we heard a faint rustling, as if someone was trying to tiptoe across the floor. I took off my winter gloves and traded them for latex. Then I took out my lock picks.

The lock was a simple Abloy model that took about five minutes to open. I wasn't any expert picklock, but I knew the basics. I reasoned that Oksana might be starving and maybe even in danger because of her infected wounds, which justified these illegal means. When the door finally opened, I let Ursula enter first. She shined her flashlight in, holding it in her left hand. Her right hand was on her holster. There was a rustling from the corner at the back of the room. We moved closer and saw someone huddled on the floor. I recognized Oksana Petrenko, although she looked even worse than she had in the hospital. Her hair was matted from not having been washed. The wound on her face was swollen and seeping. Instead of a fur coat, she wore a dark-green quilted coat and pants, which looked like they were from the 1970s. She cautiously crawled toward us. The flashlights dazzled her. She was shaking. In her trembling hand, she held a bread knife.

"Don't worry, Oksana. We are friends. Lulu's friends. We have food for you. Here." Ursula showed her the bag of food. Oksana stared as if she didn't believe her eyes. Her gaze was glossed over and feverish.

Ursula ordered Oksana to put the knife away, but she didn't comply. She did stand up slowly, though, leaning one arm on the table. The knife shook in her hand so violently that taking it would have been child's play. Ursula stepped closer and smiled.

I intentionally stayed in the shadows.

"Gde Lulu?" Oksana had difficulty speaking, as if her throat hurt. *"Lulu umer?"*

I knew Ursula didn't understand that Oksana was asking where Lulu was and whether she was dead. Instead of saying anything, Ursula nodded toward the oil lamp on the table, and when Oksana didn't object, she lit it. Oksana lowered the knife a little and stared at the bag of food. Then she noticed me. Her expression, which had relaxed a little, changed back to terror. Ursula noticed, dropped her flashlight on the table, and grabbed her wrist. Even though Oksana tried to resist, she was no match and the knife dropped to the floor, where I lunged to grab it.

"Sto eto? Ana milisiya . . ." Oksana tried to wrench free of Ursula's grip, but Ursula was stronger. She grabbed onto the same wrist with her other hand.

"There's no reason to get rough," I told Ursula. It was obvious the girl was exhausted. "The key is in the lock on the inside, so I'll lock us in. Let her go."

Ursula obeyed and made Oksana sit at the table. Sitting down obviously hurt, and Oksana's eyes welled up. I took care of the door. Then I took a few steps toward her.

"My tvoi druz'ya," I said gently. "Don't worry. We come as friends," I continued in my clumsy Russian. *Druz'ya*—every school child forced to watch the Finnish-Soviet propaganda film *Trust* in the 1970s knew that word.

The cabin was only about fifty degrees Fahrenheit and smelled of oil, though apparently the oil heater wasn't working. There was a fireplace, also cold. Of course, any smoke rising from the chimney would have revealed that someone was in the cabin. On another table was a radio and a small portable television set from a time before anyone ever dreamed of a digital receiver. Beyond that was a small kitchenette: two gas burners, a faucet that provided only cold water, and a sink. In an alcove was a three-tier bunk bed. All the bedding from them was piled on the foldout sofa. There weren't any paintings or books in the cabin, but woven rugs and embroidery covered the walls. On one wall was a lighter spot where Oksana had removed a hanging rug to cover the window facing the road. Curtains covered the windows that opened onto the forest.

"Yes, we are the police," I told Oksana. Ursula pulled out a lighter and lit the oil lamp, then started unloading the food onto the table. A baguette, cheese, apples, orange juice, meatballs, and tea bags. I noticed a pot next to the cooktop, filled it with water, and started looking for matches. I couldn't find any, just two empty boxes. Ursula noticed my attempts and threw me her lighter. Oksana hadn't made any move to take the food. In the kitchenette, I found a butter knife and a cheese plane, which I gave to Ursula so that she could make some sandwiches. In the cupboard there were heavy, brown ceramic coffee cups, which would have to do for drinking tea.

"Here you are," Ursula said and handed Oksana a sandwich. The girl hesitated for a moment before accepting it. Ursula passed me the bread knife for safekeeping, then opened the packet of meatballs and pushed it toward Oksana, who'd managed to wolf down the entire sandwich in that short amount of time. She now began scarfing the cold meatballs.

Maybe keeping her hungry would have made her more cooperative, but Oksana had already suffered enough. When the water boiled, I added three bags of tea. I looked for sugar in the cupboards but didn't find any. There were only the remnants of a tube of mustard and a quarter-full bag of ground hot cereal. Maybe Oksana hadn't known what it was. But upon closer inspection I noticed a tear in the packaging and some mouse droppings inside.

We sat down at the table with our tea, and I tried to question Oksana. At first, she wouldn't say anything. She clearly didn't trust us and just glared at Ursula angrily, avoiding my gaze entirely and struggling against the chills that repeatedly wracked her body.

"Oksana, who did this to you?" I moved my hand as if slicing my own flesh with a knife. My Russian vocabulary was lacking, but I understood Oksana's response. *"Ya."* Me.

"Why?"

"I didn't want . . . I wanted to get away . . ." Oksana's speech was husky, and understanding her was difficult. She sipped the tea, and a few tears dripped into her cup.

"I have a friend . . . Arto. He promised to help me get a visa and find a real job. An honorable job. He is a rich man and very nice. But he won't want me any more now that I look like this."

"Why didn't you call Arto Saarnio?"

"I didn't have his number," she said. "And my phone is back in Espoo."

"Who took you to the park where you were found?"

"The girls. Sveta and Ludmila. They were afraid I would die . . ." Oksana explained something so quickly that I didn't have any chance of understanding. I asked why Sveta and Ludmila had left Oksana out in the cold, that she could have frozen to death.

"They wanted me to go to the hospital. But I wouldn't go. We fought," Oksana replied. "It doesn't matter if I die."

"Who is your pimp?" Ursula asked in English. "Who are you afraid of?"

Oksana didn't answer because she was fighting back tears. I took her by the hand, which was alarmingly hot. We had to get her treatment. I took one of the blankets from the sofa bed and wrapped it around her, then poured her more tea. The cheap bagged tea was bitter but warming. Ursula and I had left our coats on, and the cabin seemed to grow colder by the minute. The wind had picked up outside, and tree branches angrily tapped on the metal roof.

"I not say," Oksana finally replied, now in English. "They kill me. In Finland, at home. They kill me wherever I go. Police cannot help."

"Why did you contact Lulu?" Ursula poured herself more tea. Oksana was quiet again for a long time and then began an explanation in Russian that I only understood in bits and pieces. Oksana and Lulu had met a while back in a restaurant, and Lulu had warned Oksana about an investigation that the National Bureau of Investigation was conducting. When Oksana decided to flee the hospital, she called Lulu. Lulu had come to pick her up and offered her sanctuary at the cabin. On Wednesday night Lulu drove Oksana to Barösund and promised to figure out how to smuggle her into Sweden. Oksana told Lulu about Arto Saarnio, and the women had planned to ask him for money.

"Lulu said she would be on TV on Thursday. She told me to watch the show because there would be a surprise. I watched even though I didn't understand what anyone said. The policeman was the one Lulu had warned me about. The one who wanted to drive me out of Finland. But then something strange happened, and Lulu didn't come on the show, and from what the people did, I knew there had been an accident. I didn't dare call her or answer the phone."

I had to struggle to keep up with Oksana's rapid, breathless words.

"We have to get you to a hospital for those cuts. You must be in pain," I said.

Oksana nodded. "Lulu gave me medicine, but it ran out. The pain is bad, but I've experienced worse. Abortions. Sometimes customers are bad and Yev—" Oksana cut herself off, but I completed it:

"Yevgeni Urmanov"—here I made a hitting motion because I didn't remember the Russian word—"you."

At the mention of this name, Oksana's expression turned fearful, though she tried to control her reaction. I continued to look at her, and she lowered her eyes to her tea. Her hands were small, with slender fingers, and her nail polish had almost entirely worn off, leaving only a few dark red stripes around the edges.

"Do you have cigarettes?" she asked.

"No. Mishin—is he your boss?"

Oksana didn't reply, but the look in her eyes said enough. Even though no one had committed a crime against Oksana, we could continue questioning her with an interpreter because she had seen Lulu the day before her death. This girl would also be a godsend for Nordström, and eventually we would have to tell our colleagues at the NBI about finding her. But I was determined to protect my witness, so I wasn't going to notify Nordström just yet. That meant that under no circumstances could Kaartamo learn about our finding her.

The lights of a passing car swept through the cabin, and for a brief moment I saw how dusty the room was.

"We need to get Oksana to medical care," I said to Ursula in Finnish.

Oksana, understanding this much, shook her head.

"They find me," she said in English. "I don't want to go! You will tell the newspapers that I am at the hospital again so that they will think you are good."

"We won't tell. We have a guard for you, to keep you safe," I said, trying to assure her. Oksana looked defeated, but she didn't have any other options. She must have been desperate after being trapped in this cold cabin without food for so long, without any idea of whom to turn to for help. Apparently, she had understood enough of the TV news to know that Lulu was dead.

I wiped our fingerprints from everything that Ursula and I might have touched. There was nothing I could do about Oksana's prints, though. Lulu Nightingale's parents didn't need to know that a fugitive, a woman in the same industry as their daughter, had been living in their cabin. The austerity of the cabin told the same story about Lulu's parents that Autio and Puustjärvi had told: they didn't have much extra money. I straightened a cross-stitch of a kitten that was frayed at one corner.

We found Oksana's fur coat under the blankets on the sofa bed. The fur was damp with a mixture of blood and water, evidence of Oksana's failed attempt to clean it. Her high-heeled boots turned up behind a chair, and in them Oksana slipped and slid her way to the car.

Ursula drove, and I sat with Oksana in the back, both because I wanted to keep an eye on her and because I wanted to win her over. I called Jorvi Hospital and announced that we were bringing in the patient who had disappeared a week and a half earlier. That would give them time to look up her records. Then I arranged a guard for Oksana. That meant one fewer patrol officer in the field, but there was no way to help it.

In the dark car, it was easy to smell her festering wounds. Leaning back with her eyes closed, she looked as if she'd given up. Still I tried to ask her about the surprise Lulu had been planning to unveil on the television show, but my language skills were insufficient and Oksana didn't have the energy to struggle with English. I was able to get out of her that Lulu had promised to come back on Friday the eleventh, right after *Surprise Guests*, and bring more food and money. But then she clammed up and shivers shook her frame.

Suddenly we found ourselves at the ferry landing. Ursula must have taken a wrong turn at an intersection, and I was too busy talking to Oksana to have noticed. We turned around, and I tried my best to read the map by flashlight. At the turnoff to the Inkoo harbor, Oksana began to retch.

"Ursula!" I shouted. "Stop the car!" We'd just barely pulled over to the side of the road when Oksana opened the car door, leaned out, and threw up. The ground was frozen solid, and some of the vomit splashed back on her clothing.

I was relieved to see the streetlights at the Siuntio crossroads. I wouldn't want to live in such darkness. It felt unsafe. After our mailbox was bombed at our rental house in Hentta, we'd moved into our current apartment building with a locked entry door, which had felt like a haven. This time around, Antti and I hadn't thought beyond looking at apartments and houses with good access to a train station and to my work.

I realized that it might be difficult to get a Russian interpreter on a Sunday, although someone would be on call. Could I leave Oksana's interrogation to Ursula? We wouldn't need two witnesses since it would be an unofficial interview. Antti would be terribly disappointed if our house hunting date fell through.

At the hospital, the same nurse I'd met when I tried to interview Oksana before was on duty. When she saw the girl's wounds, her expression turned grave. "This swelling is bad. Are you sure she doesn't have blood poisoning?"

"We aren't doctors," Ursula replied brusquely. We took a seat in the hallway to wait for the results of the doctor's examination. Officer Haikala was already there waiting too.

"Who will be paying for her hospital bill?" the nurse asked.

"I'll look into it," I said and left it at that. Of course, the girl didn't have a Finnish health insurance card, and her home country wasn't a member of the European Union. Maybe she'd be able to turn to Arto Saarnio.

When—if—Oksana was nursed back to health, she would be interviewed by immigration officials and the border police, and that would alert Nordström to her whereabouts. Why, if we were on the same side, did I want to keep Oksana out of Nordström's reach?

Officer Haikala asked whether he was supposed to protect Oksana from intruders or make sure she didn't run away again. I said both. After fifteen minutes, the nurse came into the hall looking grim, and the doctor that followed her was equally dour.

"The patient has blood poisoning in the wounds on her breasts and her genitals. One more day and she would have been too far gone. The wounds haven't been cleaned properly, and she's also dangerously dehydrated. We're going to move her to the intensive care unit for at least tonight," the doctor said. Then they moved on. Ursula and I stood in the hallway, neither able to leave.

"It looks like we saved at least one life," Ursula finally said.

"I'm glad you called immediately about that phone ping in Barösund."

"You were the one who thought of the cabin. And we were lucky that Oksana didn't resist. Maybe she realized how close to death she was. She isn't stupid." Ursula paused. "How do you think it felt?"

"What?

"To cut herself like that." Ursula touched her own beautiful face. "That cut on her face is going to be there for the rest of her life. How could someone do that to themselves?"

"Maybe the other options were worse," I responded quietly. I thought about the stories I'd heard at international training events, stories about women and children kidnapped and forced to be sex slaves or whose families had sold them for a few dollars or a new television. What if someone kidnapped Taneli or Iida . . . That thought prompted such anxiety that I quickly pushed it out of my mind. Oksana had been lured to Finland with promises of a job as a waitress, but she had ended up selling herself. I'd always thought that, when it comes to sex, as long as there was free choice and mutual consent then anything goes. But how did you define free choice? And even if you were making what appeared to be a free choice, did you always have to pay for sex one way or another? Was Mauri Hytönen right after all?

I elected to distract myself from these unanswerable questions by checking in on Tero Sulonen. Ursula decided to come with me, so together we marched through the quiet buzz of the hospital ICU, where Sulonen still lay unconscious. Officer Saari was guarding him.

"A man called today claiming to be Sulonen's father," the ICU nurse said. "He asked for information about his son's status. According to our information, the patient doesn't have any next of kin, and since the patient is here as the victim of a crime, we decided to notify the police. The media calls constantly, so maybe this supposed father was one of them."

"Maybe. Best to follow a policy of silence. The police will make any necessary public statements."

I remembered promising to tell Arto Saarnio if we found Oksana, but I decided to put it off. I'd need to get Oksana's permission first. I'd never expected to find Oksana alive, and dead people don't have opinions. Now the situation was different.

Outside, the wind buffeted Ursula's small Renault as it clambered along Ring III.

"Ursula, listen. It's best if Kaartamo doesn't hear about Oksana yet. You understand, don't you?"

"I don't understand," Ursula responded, "but have it your way. Anyway, Oksana may be a key witness. Lulu knew that Arto Saarnio was one of Oksana's clients. What if that was the bombshell Lulu intended to drop on live TV? And what if Riitta Saarnio found out about it somehow? What if Lulu dropped too many hints? Lulu liked power, so maybe she liked making Mrs. Saarnio sweat, especially since the woman so clearly demonstrated that she hated Lulu and everyone like her. What if Riitta Saarnio was guilty after all?" Ursula said as she turned off Ring III onto the Turku Highway.

I no longer felt like holding back what I knew. Ursula had sometimes accused me of high-handedness and bias, and she'd been right.

"No, Ursula, I think this is about something much bigger than that. Länsimies wants to be president, and he has some powerful backers. I don't know if he's anything more than a megalomaniac, but he's dangerous. We need to find some concrete evidence so we can lock him up before someone else becomes his next victim."

19

At nine on Sunday morning, I woke up to the smell of coffee and the rustling of the newspaper. Antti was reading the real estate listings and taking notes on the properties worth seeing. By the time I'd returned home the previous night, he'd been fast asleep. I'd succeeded in crawling into bed next to him without waking him up, even though I'd wanted a hug. Then exhaustion won out over the need for intimacy.

"Here's a duplex in North Tapiola . . . the showing is at three. And then there's a house in Suna. It's pretty close to downtown Espoo."

I filled my coffee cup and kissed Antti on the neck.

"I may have to go in this morning to handle one interview, if we can get a Russian interpreter. But it shouldn't last long," I lied, knowing that everything depended on the interpreter's schedule. Ursula had promised to handle the arrangements and then call me. When I turned my phone on, a message from her was already waiting.

"The interpreter will meet us at Jorvi at ten thirty. That's the only time that worked. You'll be up by then, right?"

I texted her to tell her that I'd be there. Open houses rarely started before noon, and seeing two or three this first day would be enough. We didn't intend to buy the first place we found. We weren't in any hurry—we'd have to sell our apartment to avoid being saddled with two mortgages. I got ready to go, and Antti promised to contact potential real estate agents while I was gone.

Officer Saari had taken over for Akkila, and we found him outside Oksana's room, reading a car magazine. He said no one had tried to see her, and the assistant charge nurse told us that Oksana had been incredibly lucky. Her wounds had been so infected that they'd immediately begun an aggressive course of antibiotics. It was likely they would have to operate on her genital area because the wounds there were so severe. "Oksana needs rest," the nurse said. "You have half an hour."

"I should have said yesterday that you don't have to worry about Kaartamo. I've got him on a leash," Ursula whispered as we walked into Oksana's room, where the interpreter was already waiting at the door.

"What do you mean?" I asked Ursula, but she didn't have time to answer before the interpreter, Johanna Klimkin, came to greet us. She was a cheerful woman in her sixties, and working with her was always easy. Her amiable manner usually worked well with the witnesses too. Johanna was like padding between the police and the interviewee, offering comfort and tempering difficult questions, even though, as far as I understood, she translated everything with precision. Johanna spent a lot of time with her husband's female Russian relatives and said that they were frequently taken for prostitutes in Finland even though they were professionals, from a medical physicist to a master of business administration. Just the language and a style of dress that differed from the Finnish norm was enough to mark them.

"Good morning, Oksana. I hope you're feeling better," I said with Johanna interpreting. Oksana nodded. Half of Oksana's face was covered in bandages, and she was obviously under the influence of painkillers. "We want to talk about Lulu."

Through Johanna, Oksana said, "I didn't know if the Finnish police would help me. I was afraid of going to prison, either here or in Ukraine. We Russians never get to meet regular Finns beyond our clients. Meeting Lulu at the Mikado was pure coincidence. She confirmed my fears about the Finnish police. Another time we met again in the hallway at the Hesperia Hotel. Both of us had just left clients and we got to talking. When you police came to see me in the hospital, I knew I had to get away. I borrowed one of the nurse's phones. She'd left it on the desk. Lulu came to get me and took me to that cabin. She promised to come back on Friday." Oksana pulled the covers tighter around her. The IV needle looked large in her slender arm resting on the white sheet.

"You said yesterday that Lulu encouraged you to watch *Surprise Guests* on TV because she was going to deliver a big surprise. What did Lulu say about that?"

Oksana shook her head. "Lulu talked a lot, but it was all English, which I don't understand very well. This morning I've been trying to think about what she was trying to say. Lulu was good to me, and I want to help catch her murderer. I won't be able to help much if I get locked up or deported. Am I going to be put in prison?" Oksana asked, her voice pleading. I wondered why she hadn't asked Arto Saarnio for more help. Or had he intentionally kept her in the dark to make her more dependent on him?

"Illegal immigration can result in deportation. And according to Finnish law, selling sex in a public place is a punishable offense, but the pimps are the real criminals, so you won't go to prison for it," I replied. Who would even testify against Oksana for that crime anyway? "You can help us convict them."

"Lesha said that he bribes the police so we don't get arrested, and that was why we had to give him almost all our money. I only got ten euros out of a hundred, but Lesha also brought us food. All my money got left in that apartment. Hundreds of euros. Will I be able to get it back?"

I thought of the empty apartment in downtown Espoo. Oksana would never see the money she'd earned. I didn't know what had been promised to her, but none of those promises meant anything. Hope for a better life was a good sales pitch, but most people lost out in the deal.

"Oksana, what did Lulu say about the TV show?" I repeated.

"Lulu said that they could buy her body but not her soul and that no one could use her for something she didn't believe in. And something about the president or some wannabe president," Johanna Klimkin translated.

"Do you remember what this wannabe's name was?" Ursula asked before I could.

"No . . . some man. For some reason, I thought it was the man who asked the questions on the TV, on that program where Lulu was, but I really didn't understand everything. I didn't dare call Lulu on the phone she gave me after the TV show went so strangely, and later I understood that Lulu was dead . . . And I just . . . I was afraid."

"Why didn't you call Arto?"

"I didn't want him to see me like this, so . . . ugly. And I've had time to think. Men will say anything when they want a woman. But in the end, all their promises are empty. Arto claimed I was the only other woman besides his wife, and I was stupid enough to believe him. I thought I was something more than a whore to him. He even gave me this ring." Oksana pointed at her finger where a line of garnets sparkled. That seemed like the only glint of light in the young woman's being.

Oksana told us that she'd only dared to go to the outhouse in the dark. She borrowed Lulu's father's boots so she wouldn't leave her own tracks in the snow. In the end, she accepted that she would probably never leave the Mäkinens' cabin.

"It was my prison," she said.

I let Oksana talk for a while, because I could tell that she was enjoying talking to someone who understood Russian after so long being isolated and alone. Our time was running out, however, so eventually Ursula changed the subject.

"I looked for you last Saturday at the Mikado. Two guys came after me when I left. One was big and bald, with bushy black eyebrows and a broken tooth. His coat had a fur collar. The other one was big too and had red hair, and a big nose that looked like it'd been broken at least once. They beat me and another girl who works at the railway station."

Oksana listened to Johanna's translation with wide eyes.

"The big bald one with the fur collar is named Urmanov. I don't know the other one's name, but they're from the same gang. They work for Mishin. Urmanov is very bad. He's the one I'm most afraid of finding me here. Once he . . ." Oksana pulled down her collar so we could see a knife scar. "Even though they usually don't want to leave marks on us. So we won't scare off customers. Now I'm not fit for anyone, not even a good man . . ." Oksana began to cry. I walked to Oksana's bed and took her by the hand.

"Everything you remember is extremely important. We might need you to testify in court later. We only have a couple minutes left, so I need to ask you: Was Lulu afraid to go on the television show?" I asked, even as the nurse appeared at the door.

"No. She was happy," Oksana replied and continued before Johanna had finished interpreting. "A photo. She had a photo she was in. She was angry about it and angry at that man."

Bingo, I thought to myself. The evidence against Länsimies was starting to stack up. It was about time to bring him in for questioning.

"Your client Arto's full name is Arto Saarnio," I said, and Johanna Klimkin drew a sharp breath. "He's a big boss. He himself came to the police and told us who you were. He was very worried about you. His wife is dead now. Can I notify him that you're safe here in the hospital?"

Oksana burst into tears, and I understood without any translation that she thought she was too mutilated to see him. But then the knowledge that his wife was dead sunk in, and a new spark kindled in her eye.

"Please. Maybe poor Arto needs someone to comfort him."

"Thank you, Oksana. We'll talk again later." Ursula and I shook Oksana's hand and thanked the interpreter, who now shared the knowledge of these dangerous names, Mishin and Urmanov. And Arto Saarnio. But Johanna Klimkin knew the risks of her job.

We didn't say a word until we were in the car. Then Ursula blurted out, "So it must be Länsimies. Why didn't we arrest that asshole yesterday?"

"We didn't have enough evidence." My cell phone beeped. Even though I knew it was dangerous while driving, I looked at the text message. It was from the officer coordinating the emptying of the trash bins at the Big Apple. They had actually found the K-Market bag I was looking for, in the trash at the movie theater.

"Ha! Now we might have some hard evidence! Let's see what this plastic bag can tell us. Ursula, this is a dance without any room for false steps. Länsimies's backers have been preparing a *kompromat* smear campaign against the president. They were using Lulu, but she didn't want to be a part of it. OK, let's think about this. How would Länsimies know that Lulu had decided to be difficult? He would have had to hide the cyanide in Lulu's car when he was in it, before the show. Because of the show Länsimies had a plausible opportunity to meet Lulu and leave fingerprints and DNA in her car and in her dressing room. So none of that will work as evidence."

"Sometimes risk-takers overestimate their abilities. Pamela may be able to help ID Länsimies. All we have to do is get him for shooting Sulonen. Why would he have done that unless he killed Lulu Nightingale first?" Ursula said. Because she wasn't arguing against my theory connecting the crime to Länsimies's run for the presidency, I was starting to believe it more.

"I'm going to stop by the station. Antti and I have our open house at two, but I'd like to handle a couple of things first. How do you think Ilari Länsimies might react if he heard that Tero Sulonen was regaining consciousness? Would he try to silence him again?"

"Maybe."

Cyanide worked fast, but wouldn't Länsimies realize that Sulonen was under guard? The papers hadn't mentioned it, but still. Should the guard hide rather than sit in the hall per the usual protocol? No, that would be too risky. And besides, entrapment was illegal. But you could always give people rope to hang themselves with. Arto Saarnio could be my puppet. It would be perfectly natural for him to call his wife's business partner and hint that he'd heard Sulonen was coming to. Saarnio could claim the police were hoping Sulonen would tell them why Riitta had shot him.

I was starting to believe that Länsimies had killed Riitta Saarnio and tried to frame her for Lulu's murder and the attempt on Sulonen's life, because Sulonen had called Riitta's phone in his attempt to reach Länsimies. We had evidence of that, even though we didn't know what they had discussed. Länsimies certainly had the cool head and the ambition necessary to attempt such a scheme. What had Arto Saarnio said about psychopaths at the top of the social ladder? Sometimes people's calling every criminal a psychopath amused me, although I knew from experience that there were plenty of violent repeat offenders who lacked any sense of empathy. But was Länsimies a psychopath? Judging that wasn't my job.

"What did you mean when you said I didn't have to worry about Kaartamo?" I asked Ursula as I pulled over at the bus stop to drop her off.

"I meant about the Mikado thing. If he turns me in, Mrs. Kaartamo will receive a very interesting phone call," she said with a giggle.

"What on earth do you mean?"

"I mean that he's made it quite clear that he's in the market for a fling." Ursula looked at herself in the mirror, took out a compact, and dabbed some powder on her flawless skin. "I intend to toy with him for a little while longer and then end the game. He's disgusting. How could he think I'd be interested in a sixty-year-old geezer like him?" She laughed.

"There are a lot of women who are interested in money and power."

"Oh, I definitely am, but not in a package like that. Arto Saarnio might be another story, though. He doesn't come across as sixty at all. Do you consider me immoral?"

"No, but you're taking some pretty big risks. Kaartamo isn't the kind of person I'd play games with."

Ursula climbed out of the car, taking care to keep the hem of her bright-blue winter coat from touching the muddy ground. "See you tomorrow," she said. I saw in the rearview mirror how her blond hair shone above the blue hood of her coat like a halo.

Driving toward the station, I picked up my phone and called Arto Saarnio. A long time passed before he picked up.

"Hi, this is Maria Kallio."

"Hello." Saarnio's voice was raspy.

"We found Oksana Petrenko. She's alive."

"What? Wait just a second. My son's and daughter's families are here . . ." I heard a rustling of clothing and a cat's meow. "Yes, Miisi, you can come out too," I heard Saarnio murmur. Then a door banged, and I heard footsteps. "OK, I'm in the front yard. Where did you find her?"

"In a cabin where she's been hiding since her disappearance. She's at Jorvi Hospital now, but she can't have visitors yet." I heard a long sigh, which ended in a cough.

"Will she recover?"

"Yes. And she's been a big help to our investigation of Lulu Nightingale's murder and, indirectly, your wife's murder too. That's why I'd like to ask your help. I need you to call Ilari Länsimies and hint that Tero Sulonen is waking up."

"So you're sure that Ilari . . . I could strangle him with my bare hands!" It took a while for Saarnio to calm down. He didn't ask any more questions, just promised to contact Länsimies and then hung up. I knew that my trap wouldn't stand up to the brightest light of day, but I decided to take the risk and accept responsibility for whatever happened.

At the police station I wrote an arrest warrant and then ordered a patrol car to be sent to Ilari Länsimies's home. Before leaving, I watched some tape of *Surprise Guests* and reviewed the material from the mall security cameras. Despite being larger, the shooter's movements were very similar to Länsimies's.

"No sign of him," Liisa Rasilainen said, reporting from outside Länsimies's home. "Only his wife is here. Should we hang around?"

"Yes, please. Did you tell the wife why you're there?"

"We just said we had some routine questions. We'll park around the corner so he doesn't see us immediately. According to his wife, he's in a meeting about the future of his show. On a Sunday. Apparently network executives don't have it any easier than cops," Rasilainen said.

Since there wasn't anything else I could do, I decided to head home. Länsimies would have a much harder time fleeing than a normal criminal would, because three-fourths of the country knew him. He'd need that Putin mask again.

Antti had lunch ready, and after we ate we went to look at houses. We'd done plenty of apartment hunting a few years earlier, but with houses there were different things you had to consider. The house in Suna had three stories, which would be impractical for a family with children. The duplex in North Tapiola would have needed a lot more than the splash of paint the listing mentioned to get it in decent shape.

At least Iida was excited about both houses. She thought it would be amazing to live on the top floor of the three-story house, in particular because of the balcony and an aquarium. I reminded her that the aquarium wouldn't be part of the sale. At the duplex, we had to restrain Taneli to keep him away from the current residents' Lego collection.

Afterward, we went to Tapiola for ice cream. We were just leaving the ice cream shop when I received a text from Saarnio, saying that he had reached Länsimies, who had seemed extremely interested in the improvement in Tero Sulonen's condition. I walked outside the restaurant for a moment and notified Officer Haikala, who was guarding Sulonen, and told him that he should stay sharp. He said he was in civilian clothes in the ICU.

"Call Oksana Petrenko's guard to help you if Ilari Länsimies shows up. I've issued a warrant already. Yes, I'm talking about the guy from TV. I'm glad you'll recognize him."

The spring afternoon was warm, and soon it would be time to trade our winter clothes for lighter ones. Iida thought the melting ground smelled bad.

"That's the dog poop," Taneli said. To me the stench held the promise of future scents: spring rains, sprouting birch leaves, grass. It also gave me hope of change, of escaping the White Cube for somewhere that felt like a home rather than just a place to live. Back at home Antti and I went through the real estate listings again. The market was cooling off, so many of these places would still be for sale the next week.

At seven I headed out for a run. Earlier in the evening, it had started sleeting, so hardly anyone was out. My muscles felt stiff. As I turned onto the shortcut behind the parking garage next to our building, I heard footsteps behind me quickly approaching. I didn't have time to realize what was happening before someone was tackling me and trying to twist my arm behind my back. He clearly knew what he was doing. I fought with all my might, but I was at a disadvantage. I smelled aftershave, and as my hands struggled to counter his hold, I felt that my attacker was definitely a man. When he grabbed my hair and wrenched my head back, I saw who he was: Ilari Länsimies. He had a syringe in his hand, which he pressed against my carotid artery. Guessing what it was, I stopped struggling.

"Take it easy, Kallio. You don't want a dose of this, do you? You know what happened to Lulu and Riitta. Cyanide kills quickly. If you want to live, you're going to do exactly as I say. Now, don't make a sound!"

I felt nausea welling in my throat. Länsimies had hit me in the kidneys, and my internal organs felt like they'd been tied in a knot. I looked at the syringe, unable to decide whether I really smelled bitter almond or if I was imagining it. Fear made me break out in a sweat, and my legs suddenly lost all their strength.

Länsimies dragged me into the small stand of trees behind the parking garage. He held the syringe at my neck the whole time, so I didn't dare do anything but obey. How quickly would cyanide injected directly into the bloodstream take effect? Would death be instantaneous?

"You cops are such idiots! Trying to get me to go after Sulonen. What, do you have a camera in his room or something? I'm not going to fall for anything that basic. And besides, my wife told me that you were looking for me. Did you really think I'd walk right into your trap? Get down on your knees! Do you have a weapon?" Länsimies groped me, and to spare myself more unpleasantness I answered truthfully: "No."

"Phone?" Länsimies saw it in its belt holster. "Give it to me."

I handed the phone to him, and he threw it against the wall of the parking garage, shattering it and sending parts flying. My breathing was rapid, but I still felt like I couldn't get any oxygen.

"Undo my pants!" Länsimies ordered, stepping in front of me. From this position, his groin was at the height of my face, and I could see that he had an erection.

"Do it, you fucking whore!"

The forest along the wall of the parking garage had been left as a dense thicket but still I prayed that all the noise he was making would attract someone passing on the other side of the building. If only a dog walker would happen by. Or anyone . . . I unbuttoned Länsimies's trousers, and his penis thrust out eagerly. He shoved it in my mouth.

"On top of two murders and one attempted murder, rape is a minor issue. I'll get the maximum sentence anyway. But before that happens I'm going to teach you bitches a lesson. Lulu thought she could stop me too. At our last meeting she said she wouldn't let anyone think that picture of her and the president was real. She said she was going to expose my plot, that I could choose whether it happened on live TV or some other time. The cunt got what she deserved!"

I couldn't help retching, but I tried to listen as Länsimies spoke faster and faster. Every word would be important later—if I could just live to repeat it.

"And you're always going to be the cop who took it in the mouth from a murderer. Every client you deal with will remember that. I can't wait to talk about it in court. I'll describe every detail: how your lips felt, how you moved your tongue, even how you're gagging now. Don't bother biting. Remember it doesn't matter anymore how many people I kill—I'll get the same sentence. But I don't want to kill you. I want you to remember this for the rest of your life."

Länsimies's arousal seemed to increase from his own words, and his penis protruded deeper into my mouth, touching the back of my throat and making me feel like I was going to vomit. I'd instinctively closed my eyes because I didn't want to see Länsimies's thighs or the color of his pubic hair or the skin beneath his navel. Now I forced myself to open them, even though they were full of tears caused by choking. I felt like I was suffocating. Länsimies's left hand ripped at the hair on the back of my head, and his right held the syringe at my throat.

It wouldn't matter if anyone found us. Länsimies wouldn't interrupt his act, and having eyewitnesses would just mean more spectators for my humiliation. I groaned involuntarily. The snow under my knees was hard and wet, and it was difficult to keep my balance.

"And in prison I'm going to tell everyone what this was like. You could use your tongue a bit more . . ." I stopped listening and concentrated on his reactions: When would he be close enough to orgasm to be distracted enough for me to strike? When his breathing intensified and his testicles began to jerk, I grabbed his right wrist with my left hand as hard as I could. The syringe moved away from my throat.

Fast as lightning, I bit down.

20

I tore myself away from Länsimies and ran back to our yard, where I stopped a neighbor, who could tell without my saying so that I needed his help. I knew that I hadn't caused irreparable damage to Länsimies's genitals, but I had temporarily incapacitated him. Using the neighbor's phone to call for a patrol car, I led him to the forest, where Länsimies lay on the ground moaning. I searched for the cyanide syringe that had fallen from his hand and tucked it away for Patrol to collect. Everything moved in slow motion, and I felt as if I were watching myself in the third person: there goes Detective Kallio, who was just raped but is alive.

The patrol car arrived in under ten minutes. Officers Liskomäki and Himanen were new to the department, and I didn't know them well. As they arrived on the scene, Länsimies had recovered enough to crawl on his knees in a futile attempt to flee. Himanen took him down with an efficient soccer-style tackle, then slapped cuffs on him.

"I've been assaulted. Fuck you. Take me to a doctor," Länsimies demanded. "Let me go, you idiots. I'm not saying a word until my lawyer is present."

Liskomäki looked at me and asked if they should take him to the hospital. I left the decision to them. Mira Saastamoinen reported later that Länsimies had arrived at the hospital with some new and inexplicable bruises and scrapes. But that knowledge wouldn't provide me any comfort.

Liskomäki called me a taxi.

"Can you let my husband know that I've been assaulted but I'm okay, and that I'm going to see a doctor but there's nothing to worry about?" I asked him. He nodded. I couldn't bear to have Antti or, worse yet, the kids see me in this state.

I went to a private health center in Tapiola I knew had their lab open on Sunday evenings. Throughout the taxi ride I desperately wanted to drink water, to clean my mouth out and get rid of the taste of Länsimies, but I knew that I had wait. At the health center, the technicians swabbed my mouth for a DNA sample, and I held on the entire time, the police officer in me overpowering the part of me that wanted to flee. But once all the samples were taken, I collapsed. For a while, I just rocked back and forth in my chair, unable to speak.

It wasn't your fault. How many times had I said those words to a victim of rape or abuse? *The perpetrator is responsible for his crime.* This time, however, I just didn't believe it. Why had I set such a clumsy trap? Why had I gone out running instead of going to work and waiting to hear of his arrest? Why hadn't I stayed with Antti and the children?

I was incapable of completing the investigation, and a lieutenant on loan from the NBI took over for me. I was given six weeks of sick leave, sedatives, and crisis counseling. The sick leave saved me from the enormous onslaught of media attention following Länsimies's arrest. When the Call Girl Murders, which was what the news called the series of crimes, turned out to be part of political machinations, the columnists and commentators had a field day.

"Länsimies seems to have overestimated himself," said Koivu one day when he stopped by for coffee. "For some reason, his supporters have all disappeared now. I questioned Jaakko Aarnivuori, and according to him Länsimies was completely serious and believed he would be the next president. Aarnivuori was on board too until he heard from

Lulu about the forged pictures." Länsimies had claimed that unpopular foreign policy wouldn't be enough to topple the current president, and that they had to find something that would make even her faithful women voters change allegiances. In the end, it wouldn't matter whether people actually believed the picture was genuine—damage would have already been done.

The snow had finally melted, and the asphalt of the apartment building parking lot glistened. The birch trees looked pregnant, their buds close to bursting. The skylarks had already arrived. I tracked the changes in nature more avidly than the news about the case, but of course I followed that too. Länsimies's lawyer tried to challenge the confession he had made to me—only the two of us had been there—but the other evidence was less malleable. A golf buddy reported being on the trip to Italy when Länsimies bought the illegal hunting slingshot. A search of his house didn't turn up the slingshot, and Länsimies claimed he disposed of it after realizing it was illegal. But Forensics found skin flakes in the grooves of the handle from the earlier times Länsimies had played with the weapon without gloves. The DNA matched his.

"Both Pamela Lahtela and some of the Big Apple eyewitnesses have identified Länsimies from his picture," Koivu continued. "And as luck would have it, Länsimies's black coat and hat turned up in a flea market in Kuopio, where a colleague's secretary had taken them while they were traveling. She wondered why he wanted to get rid of such expensive clothing that was still in perfect condition. And the K-Market bag we chased down at the mall had Mrs. Kaarina Länsimies's fingerprints. We got her prints during the search of their house. So yeah, the prosecutor has plenty of material," Koivu said, satisfied. "How are you holding up?"

"One day at a time." I stirred more milk into my coffee and offered Koivu the plate of pulla. Baking was a good distraction—the aromas and the supple firmness of the rising dough calmed my mind.

Apparently Länsimies had spent his whole life searching for a way to reach the upper echelons of politics, and the presidency had been his goal even though the president of Finland no longer had the same authority as that office once held. While most ambitious young men had turned east, toward the Kremlin, to get ahead in politics, Länsimies had aligned himself with the United States.

Public and official statements from Länsimies's friends and partners said it all. Even his closest confidants were only too happy to describe his negative attributes: his belief in his own omnipotence, his complete lack of empathy. One college friend reported that Länsimies used to collect butterflies, so the cyanide might have been left over from those days. And if not, he'd surely know how to get his hands on some. A neighbor related that Länsimies's well-stocked bar always included Fernet Branca, which was also the neighbor's wife's favorite drink. Some enterprising reporter discovered that the police had been canvassing Alko outlets for records of Fernet Branca sales and connected the dots. Mrs. Kaarina Länsimies refused to comment on anything related to her husband, and she no longer showed her face at the shoe boutique. The television psychologists argued over the point at which Länsimies's narcissism had gone beyond normal ambition to dangerous. A well-liked TV personality had become a monster, an easy target to take a shot at. However, some of Länsimies's supporters stood by their presidential candidate's political views about the obsolescence of the welfare state and the possibility of Finland becoming a geopolitical and economic backwater while the Baltic states rose to prominence. Mauri Hytönen was one person who publicly defended Länsimies. The proud john seemed to have achieved permanent B-list status from his appearance on *Surprise Guests*, and he launched a campaign for the 2007 parliamentary elections and assembled his own slate of candidates in the Northern Savo election district. They called themselves the Real Men for Finland Party and pitched themselves as an antifeminist counterbalance to the feminist political party, Feminist Initiative, gaining traction in Sweden. In other circumstances, I would have followed the political discussion with interest, but now it reminded me of the shame I had to learn to live with.

I'd been a victim of a violent crime before. But none of those incidences had left me feeling like this. I had nightmares about men trying to take me by force. In my dreams, I was dressed in my own police uniform or in the nurse's costume I'd found at the Blue Nightingale, and the men who wanted me to fulfill their wishes had no faces. I didn't dream about Ilari Länsimies. Awake I thought that I might have some idea how Oksana and those like her felt.

Länsimies was charged with two counts of murder, one attempted murder, and one rape, just as he'd predicted. I hadn't been on duty at the time of the crime, but the fact that I was investigating a crime for which Länsimies was a suspect would serve as an aggravating factor in his sentencing.

Lasse Nordström called one afternoon after Easter. Taneli was playing with friends and Antti had taken Iida to ballet practice.

"Hi, it's Lasse. I'm running an errand near your place and wondered if I might drop in for a cup of coffee. I can catch you up on Operation Good Friday."

I didn't even think to ask how Nordström knew my address, which I only gave to those I trusted most. "Come on over. I'll make it double strength." Then I gave Nordström the downstairs door code.

He was outside my door within a few minutes. Through the peephole I saw that he had an unwrapped bouquet of white lilies in his hand, and I was flummoxed when he offered them to me.

"I hope you're recovering," he said, and for a moment it looked like he wanted to hug me. In the end, he just shook my hand. I escorted him into the living room, where I'd cleaned up the worst piles of toys, set some packaged oatmeal cookies on the table, and poured the coffee.

Nordström spent a while looking around before he began.

"You probably heard on the news that the operation was carried out according to plan on the night before Good Friday. It was a success, and we caught Mishin. We've been tied up with interrogations ever since. Mishin is silent as the grave, but a few of the girls—I mean women—have already broken. Some of them really are just girls. The youngest are fifteen. The bastards."

Nordström sipped his coffee. I'd filled mine half-full of milk, and still it tasted strong.

"This is good. You've always liked a strong drink. Do you remember those whiskey shindigs in college? You drank Kristian and me under the table. We should get everybody together again sometime and reminisce."

I didn't answer. Why was Nordström here?

"Yevgeni Urmanov got away. But Ursula was able to ID him from his picture. So we solved that case too."

"Did Ursula report the assault?"

"Yes. Apparently, she went to the Mikado to sniff around and someone took it the wrong way. She's a pretty hot chick after all. Still, it's better for her that they beat her as a call girl rather than as a cop." Nordström picked up the pitcher and poured himself more coffee.

"We can breathe for a while now, at least until the market gets divvied up again. Because there will always be a market. Don't think that doesn't piss me off. Just so you know, not everyone considers women to be commodities, even if there are a surprising number of men who do. I've decided recently that I think buying sex should be illegal. The world is a buyer's market, and it isn't easy fighting against the power of money."

I looked at Nordström's slender fingers, which fiddled with the long tail of Taneli's stuffed dog. Golden hair grew on the backs of his hands.

"You probably think I only do this job for the glory and to get my name in the papers. You're wrong, Kallio. I'm a do-gooder just like you, and that's why Anne left me. She said I cared more about the welfare of whores than my own wife. But when you see the reality . . ." Nordström shook his head. "That's why I despised Lulu Nightingale. She was trying to make something that's mostly just slavery and rape seem glamourous.

And as long as buying sex is legal, that slavery will continue, and the situation will only get worse as income inequality grows. But people aren't just pieces of meat, and they won't be treated as such if I'm around to do something about it."

Nordström stood up and walked to the balcony door. I wondered why he'd chosen me as the audience for this sermon. Maybe he thought I would understand.

"What do you think about Kaartamo?" he asked, not looking at me.

"I'm not a member of his fan club," I said carefully. I still didn't entirely trust this man.

"Well, I'm not either! He's exactly the kind of guardian of law and order who's causing everything to go to shit like it is. Guys like him think there are different rules for different people. Real men have needs that must be met despite the costs, tax evasion is just a national sport . . . What do you think a normal cop can do about men like that?"

I didn't know how to answer him. Nordström returned to the couch and drank another half cup of coffee. He ignored the cookies. His stubble had grown since I'd last seen him.

"The girls will be deported, and the Finnish justice system will wash its hands of the whole affair. Next week they'll be in Switzerland or Poland, caught in the same situation," said Nordström.

"The operation was a success, but you're left with a moral hangover?"

"I guess. I'd prefer a physical one. Let's go out for whiskey sometime, and if you don't want to see Kristian, we'll go just the two of us. I don't have anything against you, Maria, I just wasn't completely sure which side you were on."

"Law and order, of course," I said, trying to smirk. It wasn't easy.

Nordström held forth for the time it took to drink another cup of coffee and then disappeared as suddenly as he had come. We agreed to revisit the whiskey-drinking idea, just as soon as the pub terraces opened.

I asked Ursula about the crime report one night when we were having a girls' night at Liisa Rasilainen's place. I'd accepted the invitation because I thought it would cheer me up, even though seeing coworkers reminded me of work.

"I thought I'd do it just to tease Kaartamo," Ursula claimed. "The guy who asked me my price wasn't exactly going to show up at the station. You were taking the whole thing way too seriously."

"I guess I was," I admitted, all the while thinking that unfortunately I thought the same things as Nordström about some of my colleagues. You never knew who was on what side.

"I'm no feminist," Ursula proclaimed, as she had many times before, "but how do these guys think they're going to get anything done if the educated women stay home? They're afraid is what it is. We're so much smarter than they are, and they're such slaves to their drives. In twenty years we'll be running circles around them. There are a lot of women in my generation who would rather have a career than children. That's why the men are massing their forces now, but they're still going to lose the battle of the sexes."

I was amused: before, Ursula had under no circumstances wanted to join forces with other women, but now her attitude had changed. I didn't have a clue as to the reason why, but I guessed it had something to do with Kaartamo. Ursula had completely avoided our lady cops' soccer team, but now she sat on Liisa's couch declaring war between the sexes as vehemently as anyone else. Myself, I was tired of declarations of war. I wanted to build a peace in which neither sex would feel like they'd lost.

"I'm still surprised Länsimies took the idea of running for president so seriously," Katri Reponen said.

"A lot of other people did too, based on how widely the rumors circulated," I said, trying not to cringe at the sound of his name. Länsimies and his lawyer were still trying to pin everything on Riitta Saarnio, but it wasn't going to work. The DNA evidence, samples of Riitta Saarnio's writing, and the images from the Big Apple's security cameras had been sent abroad for analysis, and even though that slowed down the investigation, it was worth it. A decisive factor would be that Länsimies didn't have an alibi for the time of the attack on Sulonen. His fingerprints were found in Riitta Saarnio's car, and as his bad luck would have it, the car had been detailed a couple of days earlier. Therefore the prints must have been from when he borrowed Riitta's car to drive it to the mall. Riitta Saarnio just wasn't around anymore to tell what the pretense had been for borrowing it.

On the last day of March, Sauli Niinistö announced his candidacy for the presidency. So Länsimies's dreams of ruling the realm would have collapsed in the face of a true political heavyweight anyway. Prime Minister Vanhanen announced his own intentions somewhat later, and his divorce set off frenzied rumors. The presidential race would be dirty enough without Länsimies.

On the twenty-third of April, the doctors decided to allow Tero Sulonen to wake up from the medically induced coma they'd kept him in. Sulonen's memory returned slowly, but he was absolutely sure of one thing: Ilari Länsimies had agreed to meet him in the men's restroom at the Big Apple movie theater. Perhaps Länsimies had decided to try a more imaginative method. But the slingshot hadn't been up to the job, and now he would pay for his audacity.

Sulonen wanted to take revenge for Lulu's death himself, which was why he'd taken the risk of meeting Länsimies, Koivu reported to me over the phone a couple of days before May Day. "Aarnivuori had bragged to Lulu about personally choosing the next president, and he also orchestrated the manipulation of the pictures of Lulu and the president. At first Lulu didn't realize what was going on, and when she heard, she started making trouble. Länsimies must have panicked. One whore wasn't going to stand in the way of his great plan."

Even though I was hopeful as I tracked the progress of the investigation, recovering from the rape was slow. I was surprised by the panic I felt when Antti tried to undress me for the first time. I was incapable of making love to him and had to retreat. He tried to be understanding, but my fear still wounded him.

"Antti, give me time! My brain knows that what Länsimies did has nothing to do with you. My emotions and my body just don't understand it yet. They'll learn, though. I still want you."

There were tears in Antti's eyes, and that made me burst out crying. Thank God the kids were already asleep. They didn't know much—all I'd told them was that a bad man had hurt Mommy but that I'd get better soon. Taneli was confused because I didn't have any visible wounds, but Iida understood.

"Sometimes the hurt can be inside a person and you can't see it. Like Tuulia's dad's ulcer."

Playing music helped, so I strummed my bass almost every day, and during that last week of April I even made it to a band practice. Beforehand I'd listened to the Flatfeet's demo tape. I got along surprisingly well at the practice. The band didn't have any gigs booked at the moment, so I had time to learn the songs. Luckily for me, "police punk" turned out to be pretty basic three- or four-chord rock 'n' roll, so I didn't have to try to be any Pekka Pohjola or Geddy Lee.

On May Day Eve, Finnish workers everywhere were given another reason to rejoice when it was announced that Arto "Hatchetman" Saarnio was resigning from all professional duties effective immediately. Saarnio had made the decision soon after his wife's passing but waited to make it official until his replacement at Copperwood had been found. In the meantime, Länsimies's confederates had leaked Saarnio and Oksana's relationship in an attempt to cast suspicion on Riitta Saarnio. That had hurt the already bad reputation he had as one of the least popular swine in the country, but it had also increased some men's admiration for him. Oksana was deported from Finland, and in his final interview Saarnio said that after he stepped down, his first order of business would be to go on vacation in Ukraine.

"From here on out, I'm a private person, with no need to share my personal business with the public," he said at the end of the interview. I suspected it would still take a few years before the death threats against him would end.

After May Day, I decided that it was time for me to work up the courage to jog by myself again. Until then I'd only gone on walks with the family or jogging with Anu Wang-Koivu or Leena. I knew I'd feel safer in more populated areas, so I ran up Olari Street to Central Park. Buds still gave the brownish forest a sense of renewal, and green forced its way from under the dried brown grass. A Nordic walker had stopped to look at the wood anemones growing along the path. At first, I didn't pay any attention to her, but I stopped when she said my name.

It turned out that the walker with the poles was Pastor Terhi Pihlaja. She looked at me with a serious expression. "How are you doing? I'm glad to see you out exercising."

"This is actually the first time I've gone by myself since . . . well, you know. They say you have to get back in the saddle as soon as your wounds have healed from the fall. I guess that's what I'm trying to do."

Pastor Pihlaja nodded. "It's good to see that you're on the mend. And I'm glad that I ran into you. I thought you might like to know that I went to Lilli's funeral. I believe her parents were comforted to know she had tried to help that other girl, that she wasn't just looking out for herself. And it was a great relief to all of us to hear that her murder was solved before she was laid to rest. The horrible truth is better than uncertainty. Poor Lilli. It's strange to remember how I hated her during school! I begged God to take away my anger, but gradually I realized that was my own task."

I had given myself permission to hate Ilari Länsimies, and that hate hadn't yet worn away. I knew that the memory of what Länsimies had done would follow me, just like he'd wanted. In a way that was worse than the rape itself: Länsimies had wanted to break me.

"I've been praying for you. I hope that doesn't offend you." Pastor Pihlaja's expression was serious. I smiled.

"No, it doesn't offend me. But I have to admit that I am a little afraid of priests."

"Why on earth is that?"

"For the same reason some people fear the police. I imagine you can see my innermost thoughts and my most shameful deeds." My own words surprised me, and I laughed in embarrassment. "So . . . would you like to go out walking sometime and help me get over my clergy phobia?"

Now Pastor Pihlaja laughed, and we arranged to go out together the following Thursday, assuming nothing unexpected came up. We'd have to do it sooner rather than later—my sick leave was quickly running out.

We said our good-byes, and then I continued with my run. I jogged along the river, past the community garden with its cottages. People tinkered about in their yards, planting and turning the soil, helping new life to grow. The previous Sunday, after a long break, Antti and I had resumed our house hunting. One house in Saunalahti had tolerable access to the Kauklahti station and downtown Espoo, where there was a bus connection to the airport. The yard had berry bushes and apple trees, and the house itself was the same homey postwar wood model as the one we'd lived in before the White Cube. We decided to make an offer on it if the preinspection report came back clean. The house would need remodeling, but Antti would have time over the summer. Maybe next spring I would be puttering in my own garden.

On my last day of sick leave, Leena came to visit. I imagined she sensed I was afraid to go to work. Friends pick up on things like that. Sitting over a mug of tea, she was clearly working up to saying something, but I couldn't guess what it was.

"Aunt Allu left me three hundred thousand euros," she finally revealed.

"Wow! Now you can take that sabbatical you've always wanted!"

Leena smiled. "I intend to quit my job and start a new life. I've been asking myself what Allu would want me to do, and yesterday I found the answer: I'm going to start my own law firm that serves the underprivileged. For people who wouldn't otherwise have the money to hire a good attorney."

I looked into Leena's dark eyes and saw the flash of enthusiasm there. We'd become friends during college when we were both hopeless do-gooders. Kristian had mocked us incessantly. According to him, people only chose to go into law for the money.

"I don't want to do it alone," Leena continued. "I need a partner. You."

"But I'm not licensed!"

"Not yet, but you have the education and there will be plenty of legal advisory work for you to do. Maria, I've been worried about you for a long time, and then all this happened . . . You need a change before you burn yourself out completely. I think it would be amazing to work with you. Aunt Allu's capital will mean we can choose our cases and our pace."

"An idealistic feminist law firm?" I couldn't help smiling. This was what we'd dreamed about in law school, but Leena had ended up as legal aid counsel and then as a criminal lawyer, and I'd returned to my career in policing.

"Exactly. We could call ourselves Allu's Angels."

"Are we talking more Drew Barrymore or Jaclyn Smith?" I asked. "I'll have to think about it and talk to Antti. How long do I have to decide?"

"As long as you need."

The next afternoon I stood in the parking lot outside the Espoo Police Station. My first day of work was behind me, and I'd managed as well as could be expected. My stand-in had praised my unit, and my subordinates said they'd missed me. Kaartamo took me out for coffee and told me about all the kudos we'd received "from the very top" for handling such a complex and sensitive criminal investigation so quickly. Rumors were already circulating in the building about Kaartamo's successor, and most were placing their money on Taskinen once he returned to Finland. That would mean the directorship of the Criminal Division would open up, and Kaartamo hinted that the chief of police had said he wouldn't mind seeing me in the position. I didn't feel much of a calling to that, however, since it would be entirely administrative. I got along better with people than with papers.

The sun shone, and the grass was gradually turning green and covering a landscape tormented by winter. No one would ever call the Espoo Police Station beautiful, but over the years I'd become used to it. I thought of Pertti Ström, my deceased coworker, whose downward spiral had started when I was named head of our unit instead of him. Nearly eight years had passed since then. While his loss was infinitely greater, gaining this position had placed me on a hamster wheel of constant stress. A hamster wheel that only I could free myself from.

I tried to call Leena, but her phone was off. So I sent her a text message: *Let's meet ASAP and start planning Allu's Angels. We only live once.*

I decided to leave my work car in the garage and walk. If I got tired, I could hop on a bus. If I left the Espoo Police, I would miss my colleagues, especially Koivu and Puupponen, and the lovely women of the Patrol Division, but I could handle that. If we were real friends, we'd keep in touch.

I walked through the tunnel under the Turku Highway along with a small white dog. It was like a miniature Samoyed, but I didn't know the name of its breed. The dog's nose quivered ecstatically as it investigated the scents of spring and left its marks along the side of the path. It rushed back and forth, then suddenly sprang toward me and sniffed my shoes. Smelling Venjamin, it harrumphed and continued on. I laughed at the dog, whose collar said "Luna." It wasn't on a leash, so its owner was breaking the law. I couldn't have cared less.

For the first time in a long time, I felt free.

ABOUT THE AUTHOR

Photo © 2011 Tomas Whitehouse

Leena Lehtolainen was born in Vesanto, Finland, to parents who taught language and literature. A keen reader, she made up stories in her head before she could even write. At the age of ten, she began her first book—a young adult novel—and published it two years later. She released her second book at the age of seventeen. She has received numerous awards for her writing, including the 1997 Vuoden Johtolanka (Clue) Award for the best Finnish crime novel and the Great Finnish Book Club prize in 2000. Her work has been published in twenty-nine languages.

Besides writing, Leena enjoys classical singing, her beloved cats, and—her greatest passion—figure skating. Her nonfiction book about the sport, *Taitoluistelun lumo* (*The Enchantment of Figure Skating*), was chosen as the Sport Book of the Year 2011 in Finland. Leena lives in Finland with her husband and two sons.

ABOUT THE TRANSLATOR

Photo © 2015 Aaron Turley

Owen F. Witesman is a professional literary translator with a master's in Finnish and Estonian-area studies and a PhD in public affairs from Indiana University. He has translated dozens of Finnish books into English, including novels, children's books, poetry, plays, graphic novels, and nonfiction. His recent translations include the first nine novels in the Maria Kallio series, the dark family drama *Norma* by Sofi Oksanen, and *Oneiron* by Laura Lindstedt, 2015 winner of the Finlandia Prize for Literature. He currently resides in Springville, Utah, with his wife, three daughters, one son, two dogs, a cat, five chickens, and twenty-nine fruit trees.